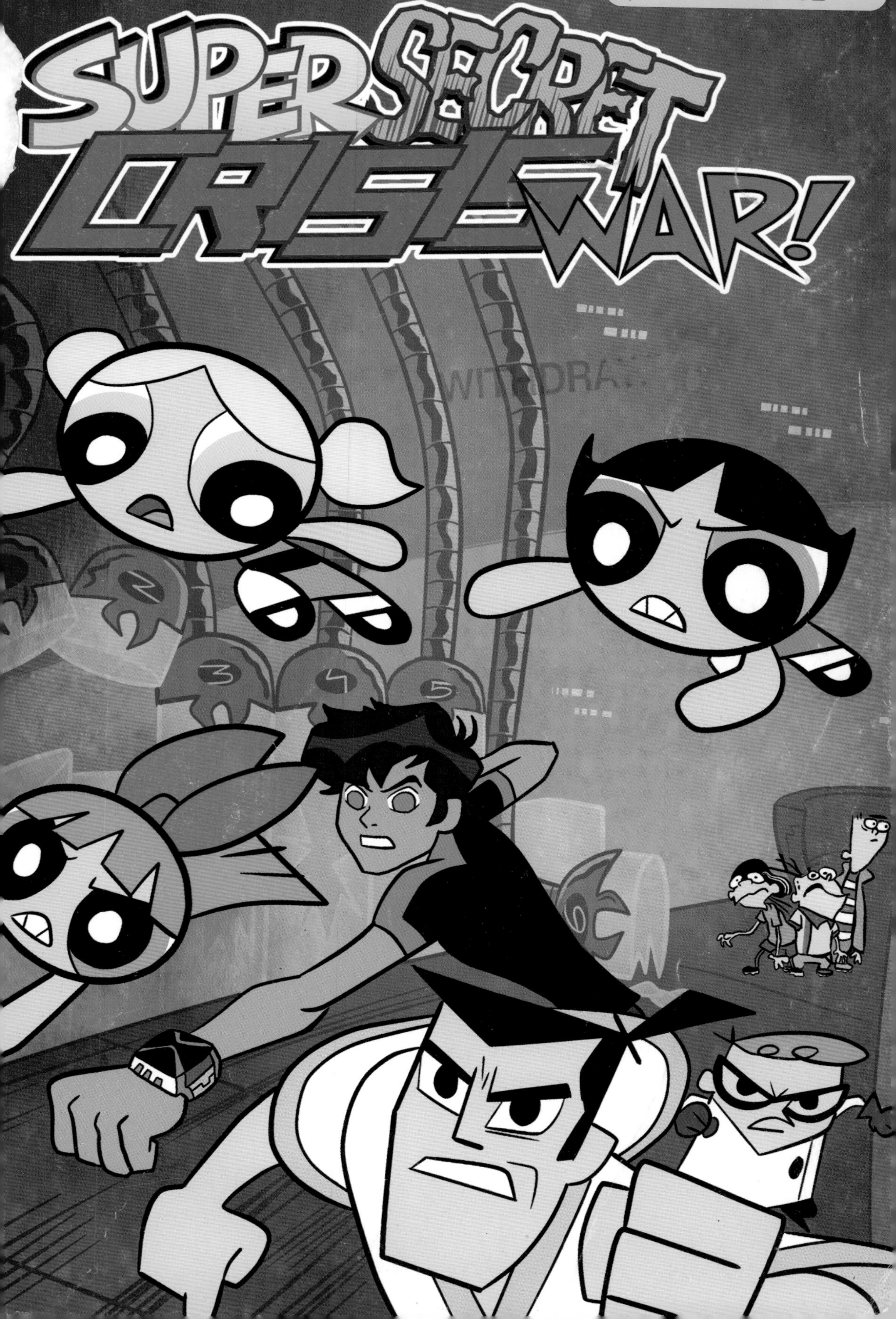
SUPER SECRET CRISIS WAR!

Written by
Louise Simonson

Art by
Derek Charm

Letters by
Tom B. Long

Series Edits by
Sarah Gaydos and Carlos Guzman

Cover by
Derek Charm

Collection Edits by
Justin Eisinger and Alonzo Simon

Collection Design by
Claudia Chong

Samurai Jack created by Genndy Tartakovsky, Ben 10 created by Man of Action Studios,
Dexter's Laboratory created by Genndy Tartakovsky, The Powerpuff Girls created by Craig McCracken.
and Ed, Edd, N' Eddy created by Danny Antonucci.

Special thanks to Laurie Halal-Ono, Rick Blanco, Jeff Parker, and Marisa Marionakis of Cartoon Network.

ISBN: 978-1-63140-207-4   18 17 16 15   1 2 3 4

IDW ® **CN** CARTOON NETWORK.

www.IDWPUBLISHING.com
IDW founded by Ted Adams, Alex Garner, Kris Oprisko, and Robbie Robbins.

Ted Adams, CEO & Publisher
Greg Goldstein, President & COO
Robbie Robbins, EVP/Sr. Graphic Artist
Chris Ryall, Chief Creative Officer/Editor-in-Chief
Matthew Ruzicka, CPA, Chief Financial Officer
Alan Payne, VP of Sales
Dirk Wood, VP of Marketing
Lorelei Bunjes, VP of Digital Services
Jeff Webber, VP of Digital Publishing & Business Development

Facebook: facebook.com/idwpublishing
Twitter: @idwpublishing
YouTube: youtube.com/idwpublishing
Instagram: instagram.com/idwpublishing
deviantART: idwpublishing.deviantart.com
Pinterest: pinterest.com/idwpublishing/idw-staff-faves

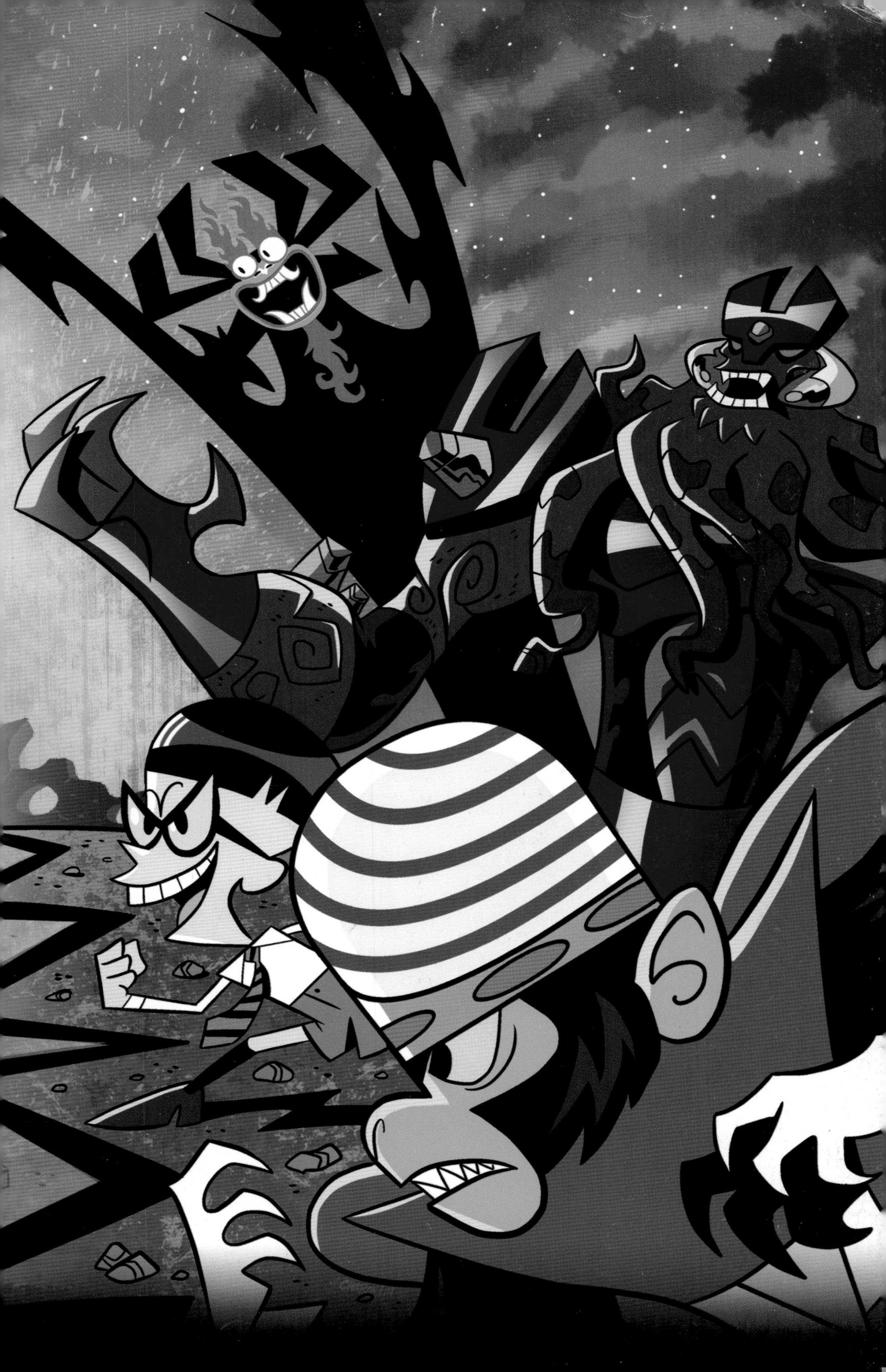

Chapter 1

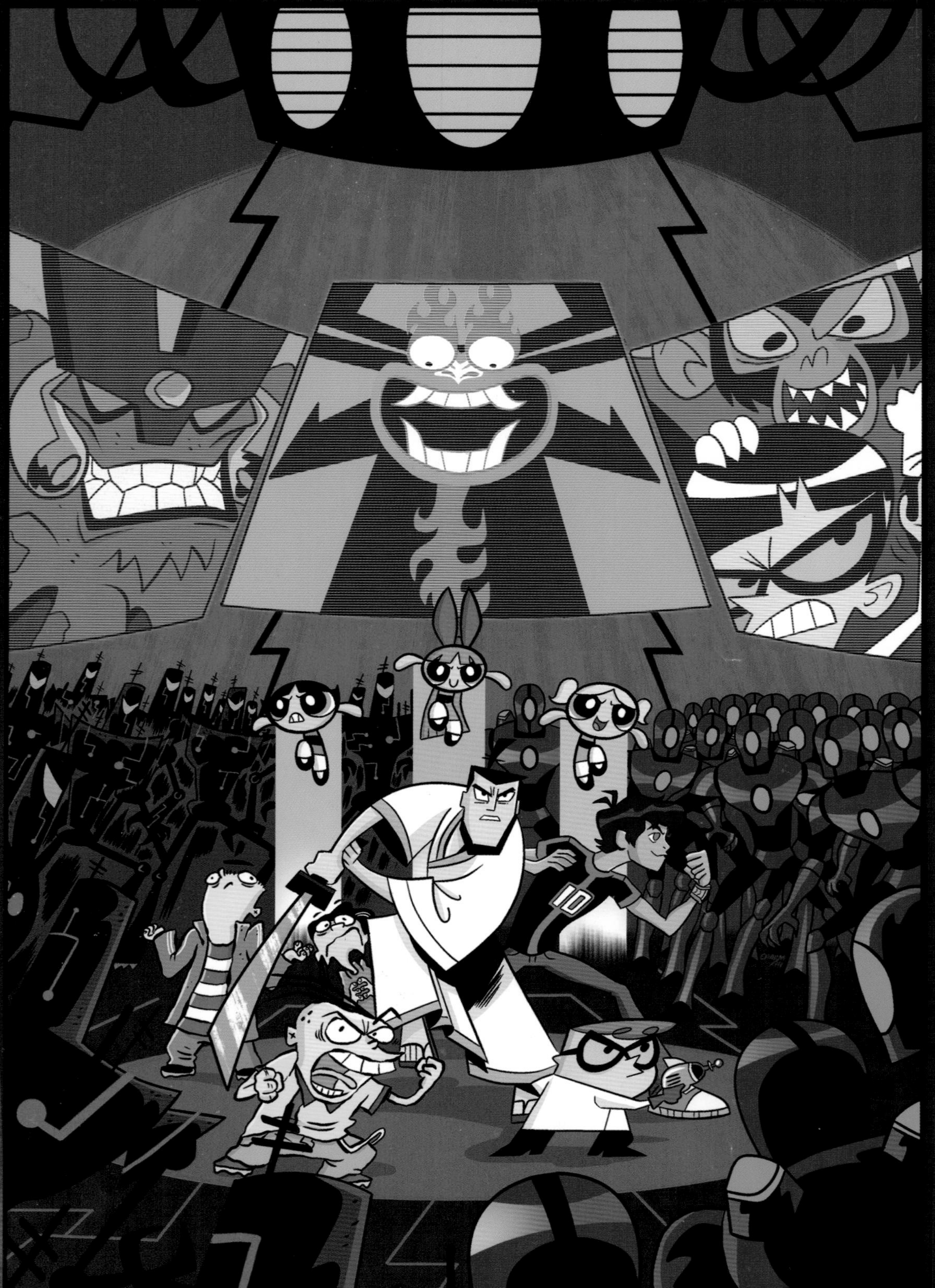

Cover Art by Derek Charm

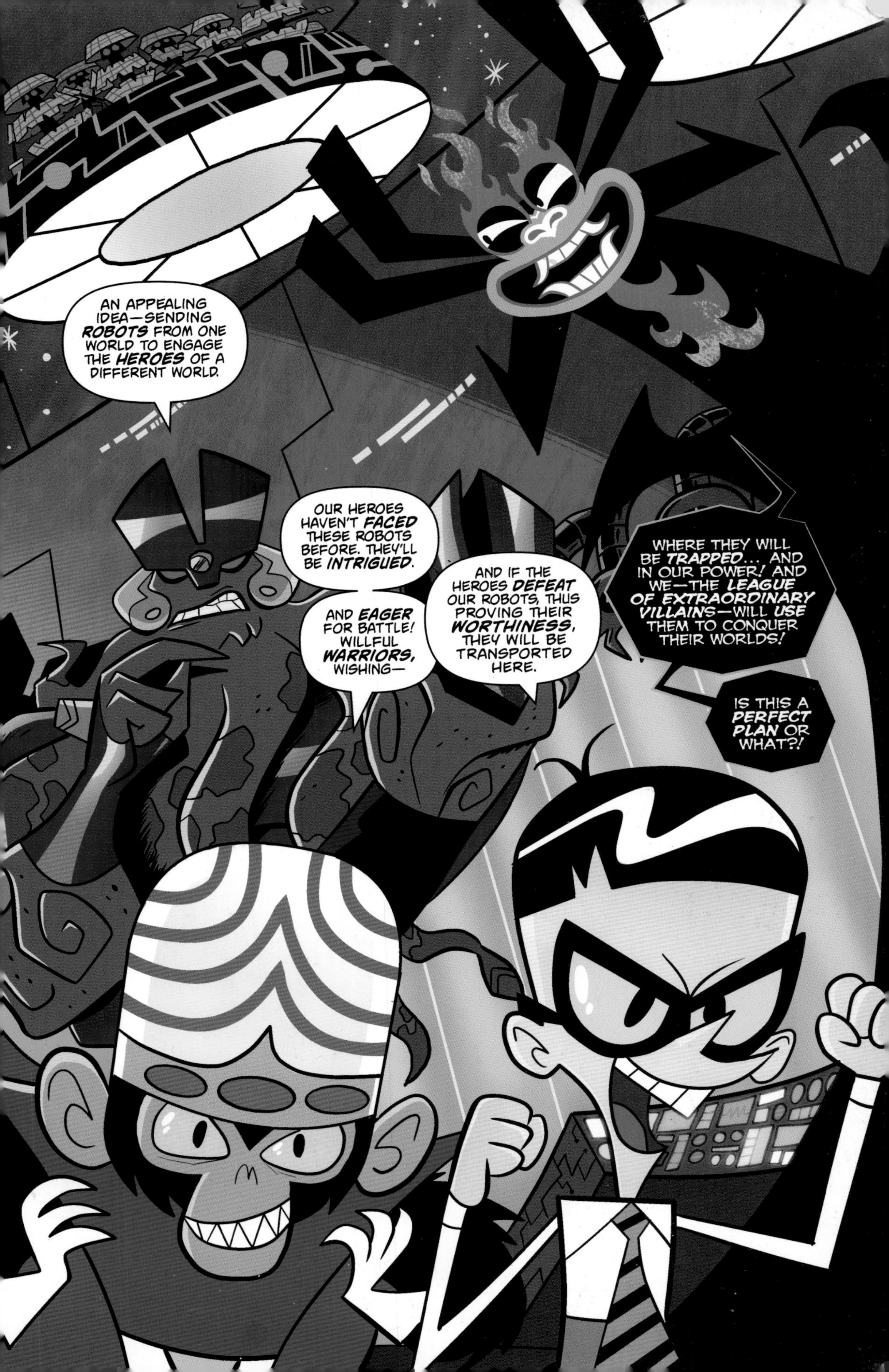
AN APPEALING IDEA—SENDING ROBOTS FROM ONE WORLD TO ENGAGE THE HEROES OF A DIFFERENT WORLD.
OUR HEROES HAVEN'T FACED THESE ROBOTS BEFORE. THEY'LL BE INTRIGUED.
AND EAGER FOR BATTLE! WILLFUL WARRIORS, WISHING—
AND IF THE HEROES DEFEAT OUR ROBOTS, THUS PROVING THEIR WORTHINESS, THEY WILL BE TRANSPORTED HERE.
WHERE THEY WILL BE TRAPPED... AND IN OUR POWER! AND WE—THE LEAGUE OF EXTRAORDINARY VILLAINS—WILL USE THEM TO CONQUER THEIR WORLDS!
IS THIS A PERFECT PLAN OR WHAT?!

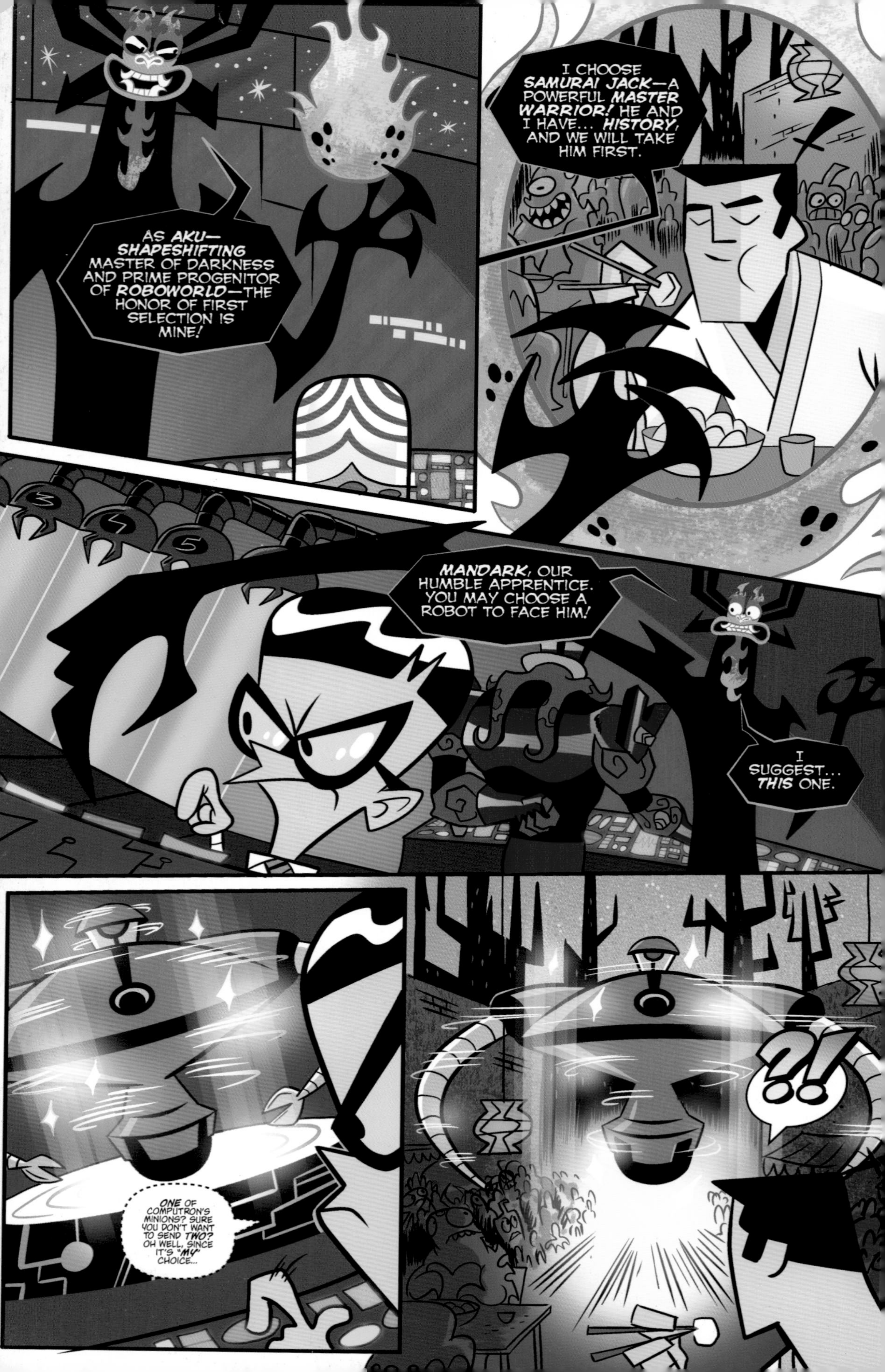
AS AKU—SHAPESHIFTING MASTER OF DARKNESS AND PRIME PROGENITOR OF ROBOWORLD—THE HONOR OF FIRST SELECTION IS MINE!
I CHOOSE SAMURAI JACK—A POWERFUL MASTER WARRIOR! HE AND I HAVE... HISTORY, AND WE WILL TAKE HIM FIRST.
MANDARK, OUR HUMBLE APPRENTICE. YOU MAY CHOOSE A ROBOT TO FACE HIM!
I SUGGEST... THIS ONE.
ONE OF COMPUTRON'S MINIONS? SURE YOU DON'T WANT TO SEND TWO? OH WELL, SINCE IT'S "MY" CHOICE...
?!

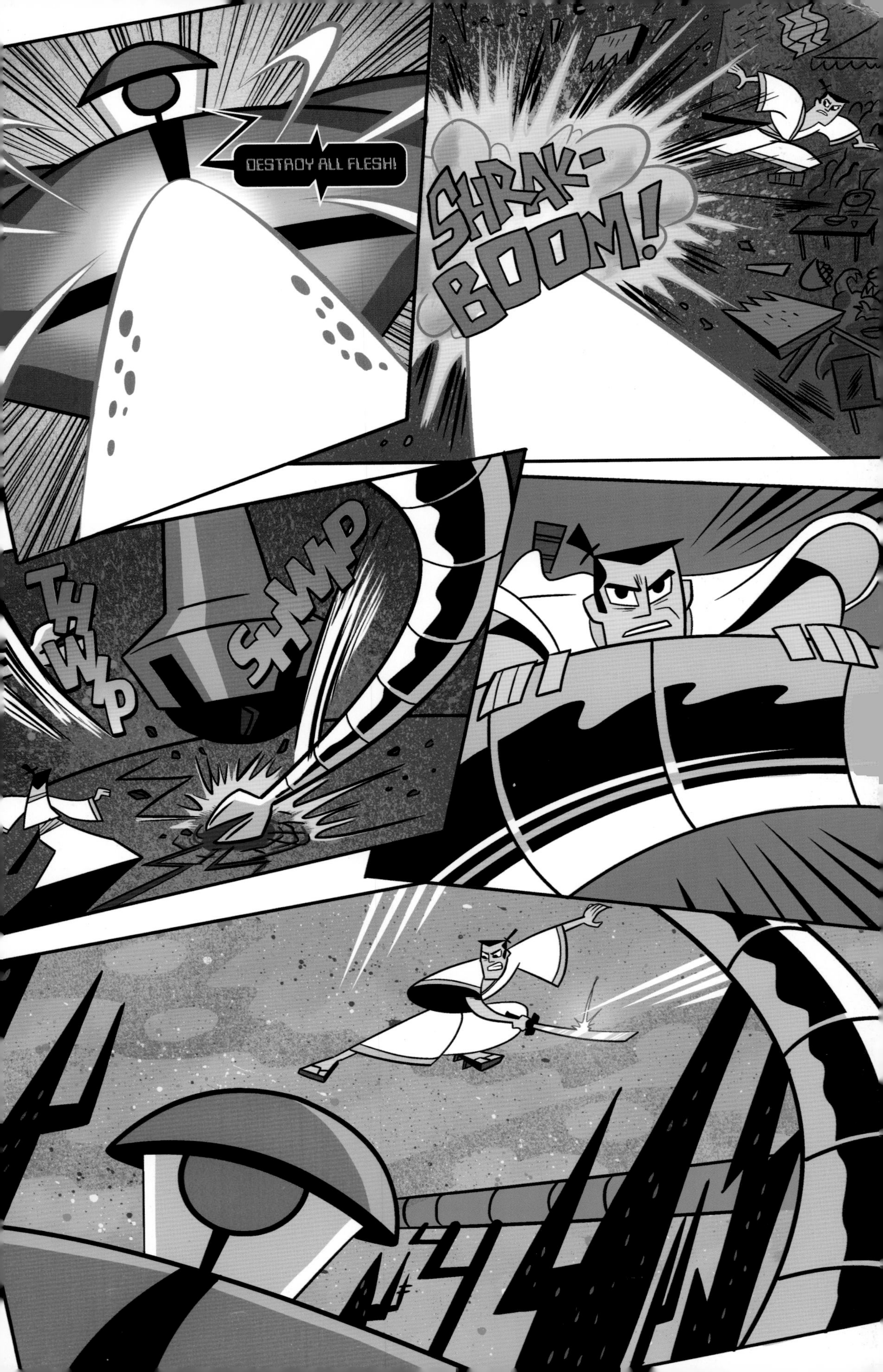
DESTROY ALL FLESH!
SHRAK-BOOM!
THWIP
SHWIP

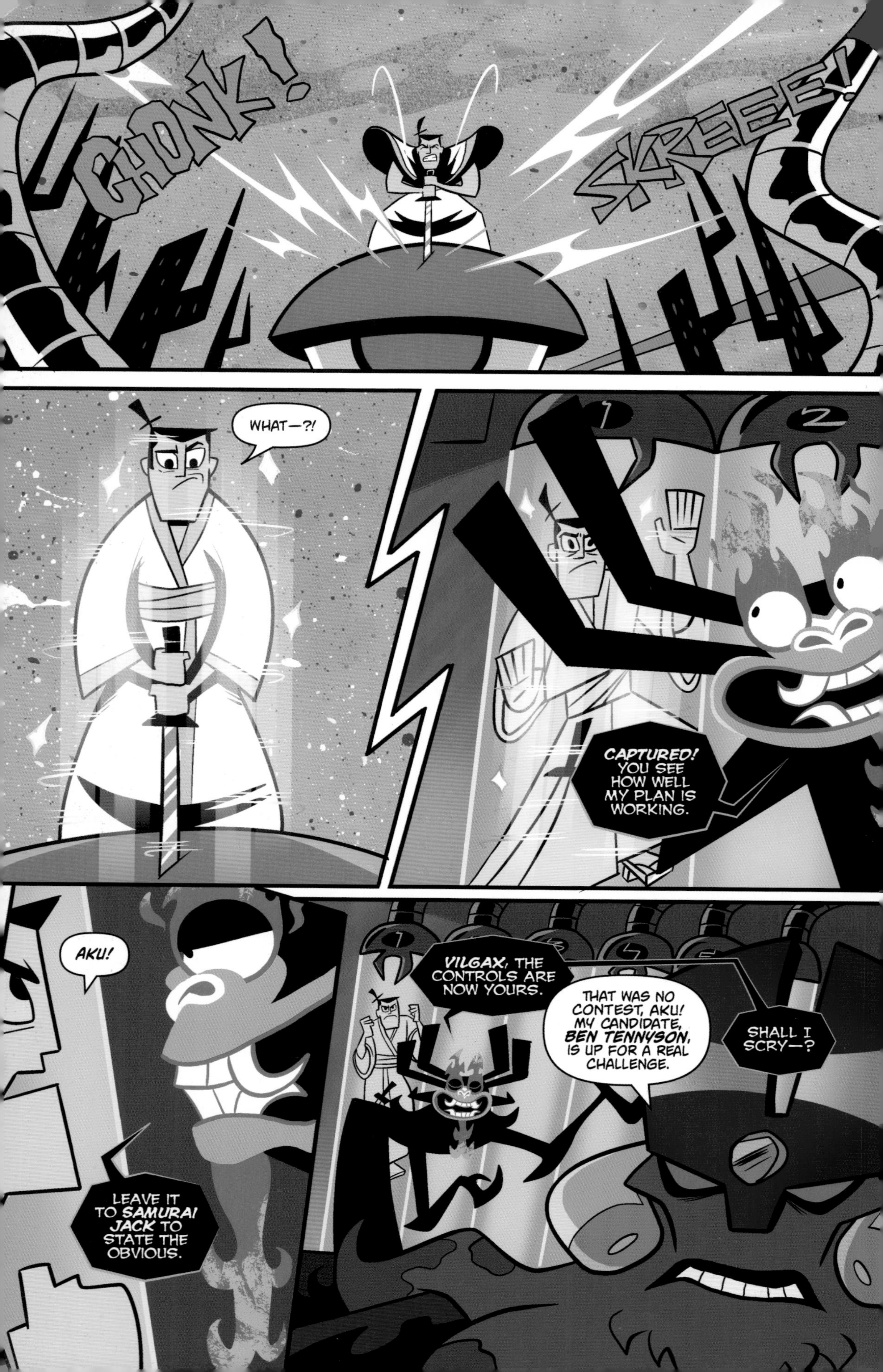
CHONK!
SKREEE!
WHAT—?!
CAPTURED! YOU SEE HOW WELL MY PLAN IS WORKING.
AKU!
LEAVE IT TO SAMURAI JACK TO STATE THE OBVIOUS.
VILGAX, THE CONTROLS ARE NOW YOURS.
THAT WAS NO CONTEST, AKU! MY CANDIDATE, BEN TENNYSON, IS UP FOR A REAL CHALLENGE.
SHALL I SCRY—?

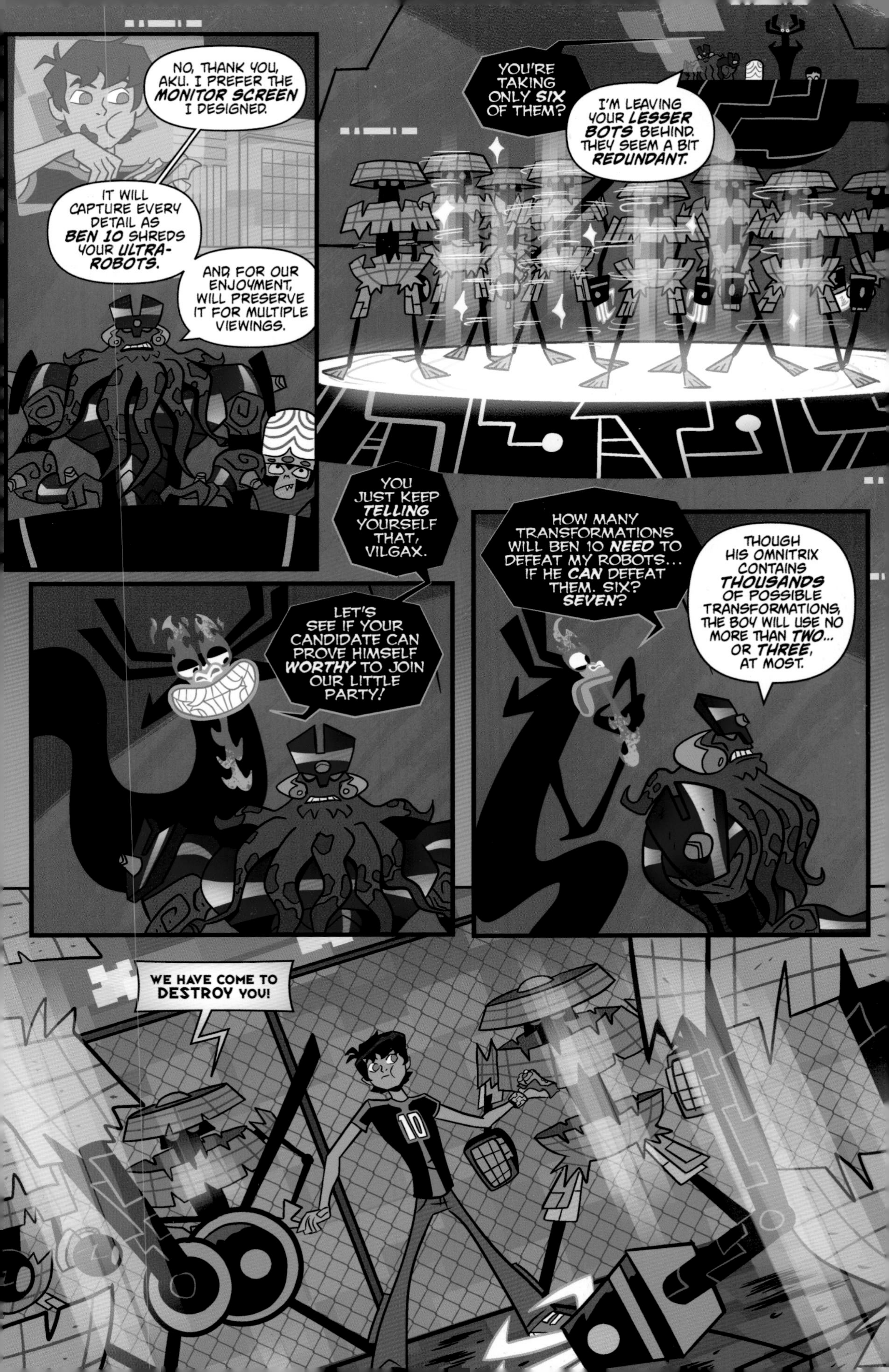

NO, THANK YOU, AKU. I PREFER THE MONITOR SCREEN I DESIGNED.
IT WILL CAPTURE EVERY DETAIL AS BEN 10 SHREDS YOUR ULTRA-ROBOTS.
AND, FOR OUR ENJOYMENT, WILL PRESERVE IT FOR MULTIPLE VIEWINGS.
YOU'RE TAKING ONLY SIX OF THEM?
I'M LEAVING YOUR LESSER BOTS BEHIND. THEY SEEM A BIT REDUNDANT.
YOU JUST KEEP TELLING YOURSELF THAT, VILGAX.
LET'S SEE IF YOUR CANDIDATE CAN PROVE HIMSELF WORTHY TO JOIN OUR LITTLE PARTY!
HOW MANY TRANSFORMATIONS WILL BEN 10 NEED TO DEFEAT MY ROBOTS... IF HE CAN DEFEAT THEM. SIX? SEVEN?
THOUGH HIS OMNITRIX CONTAINS THOUSANDS OF POSSIBLE TRANSFORMATIONS, THE BOY WILL USE NO MORE THAN TWO... OR THREE, AT MOST.
WE HAVE COME TO DESTROY YOU!

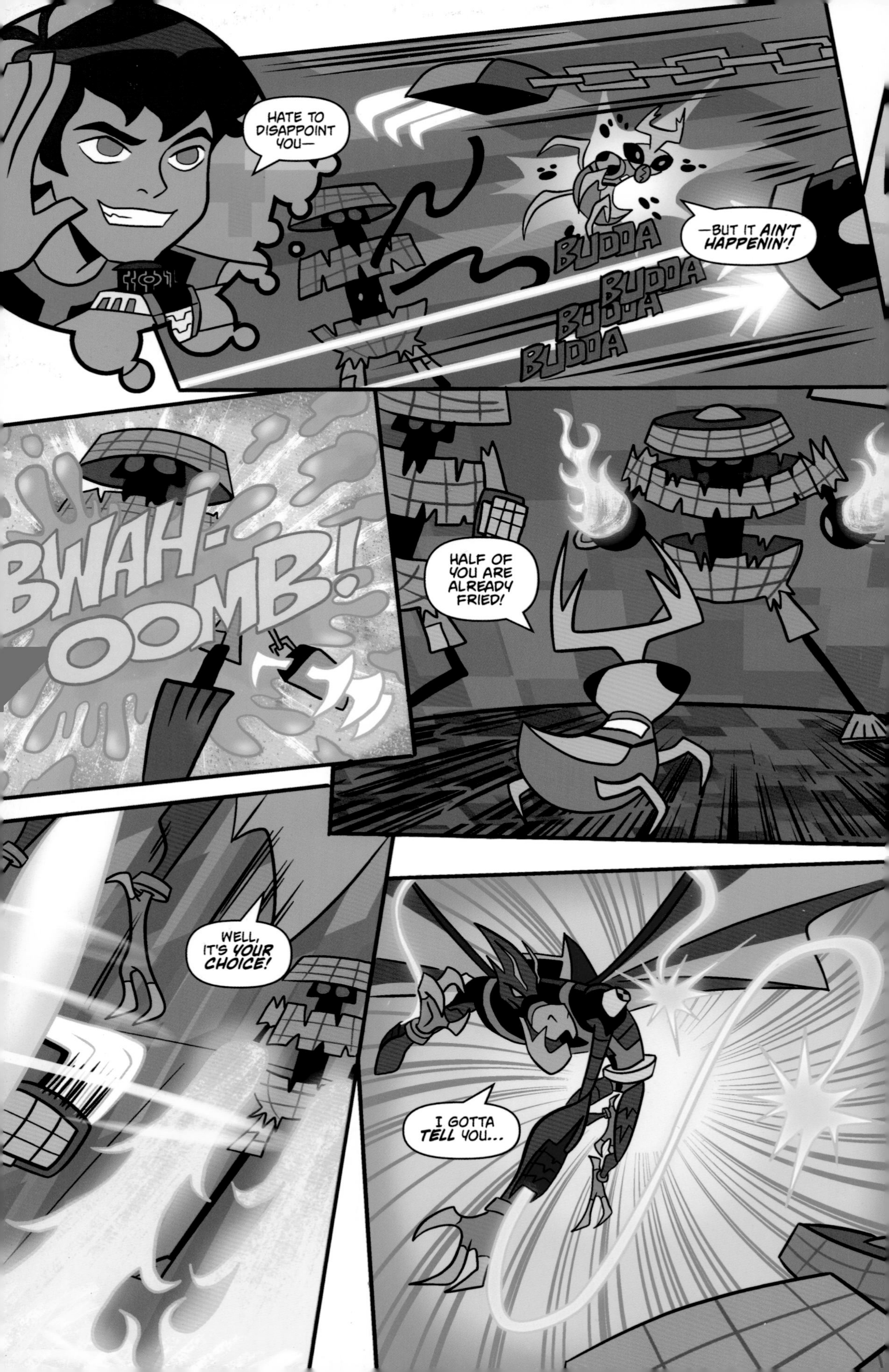
HATE TO DISAPPOINT YOU—
BUDDA
BUDDA
BUDDA
BUDDA
—BUT IT AIN'T HAPPENIN'!
BWAH-OOMB!
HALF OF YOU ARE ALREADY FRIED!
WELL, IT'S YOUR CHOICE!
I GOTTA TELL YOU...

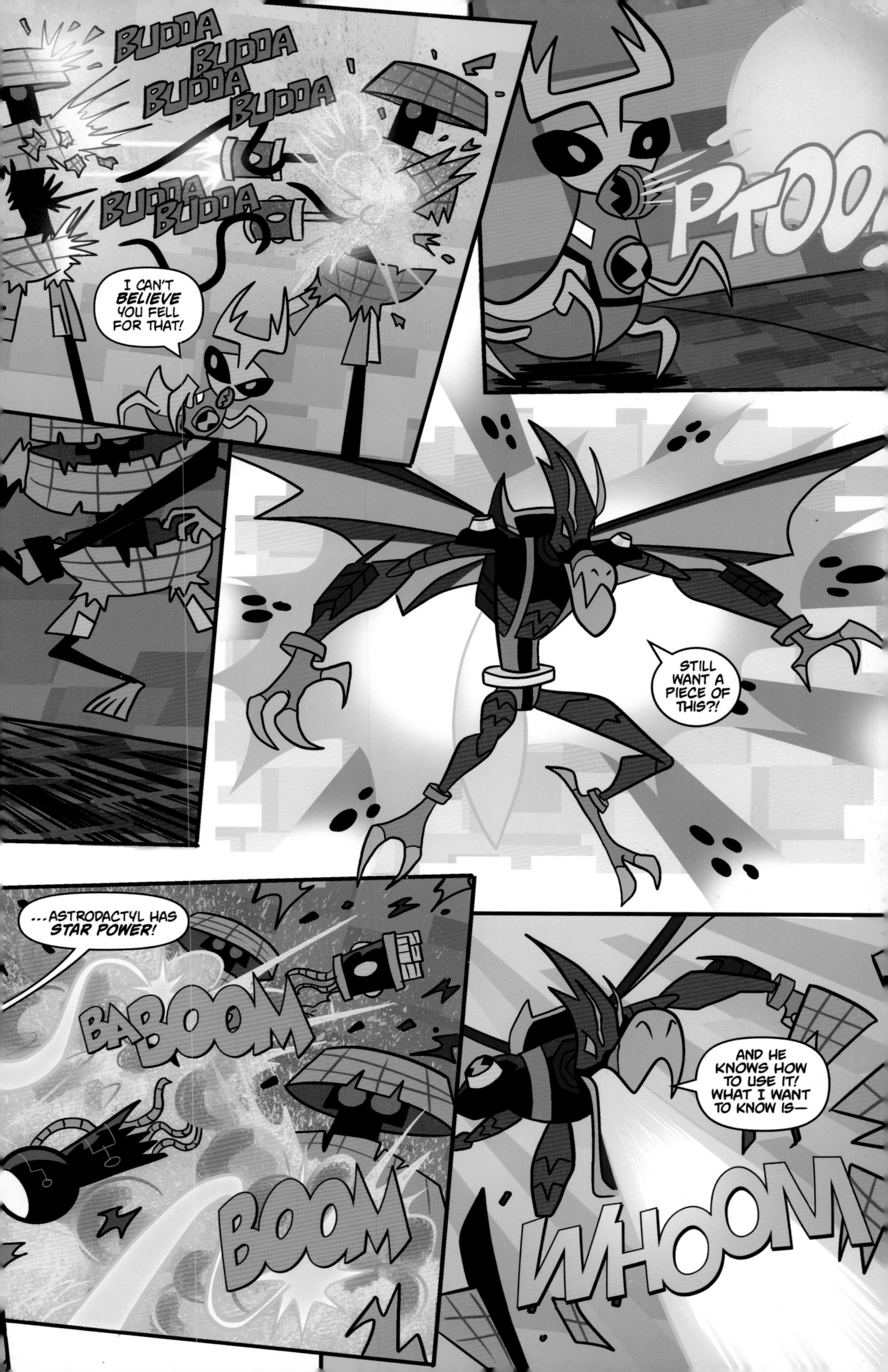
BUDDA BUDDA BUDDA BUDDA
BUDDA BUDDA
I CAN'T BELIEVE YOU FELL FOR THAT!
PTOO!
STILL WANT A PIECE OF THIS?!
...ASTRODACTYL HAS STAR POWER!
BABOOM
BOOM
AND HE KNOWS HOW TO USE IT! WHAT I WANT TO KNOW IS—
WHOOM

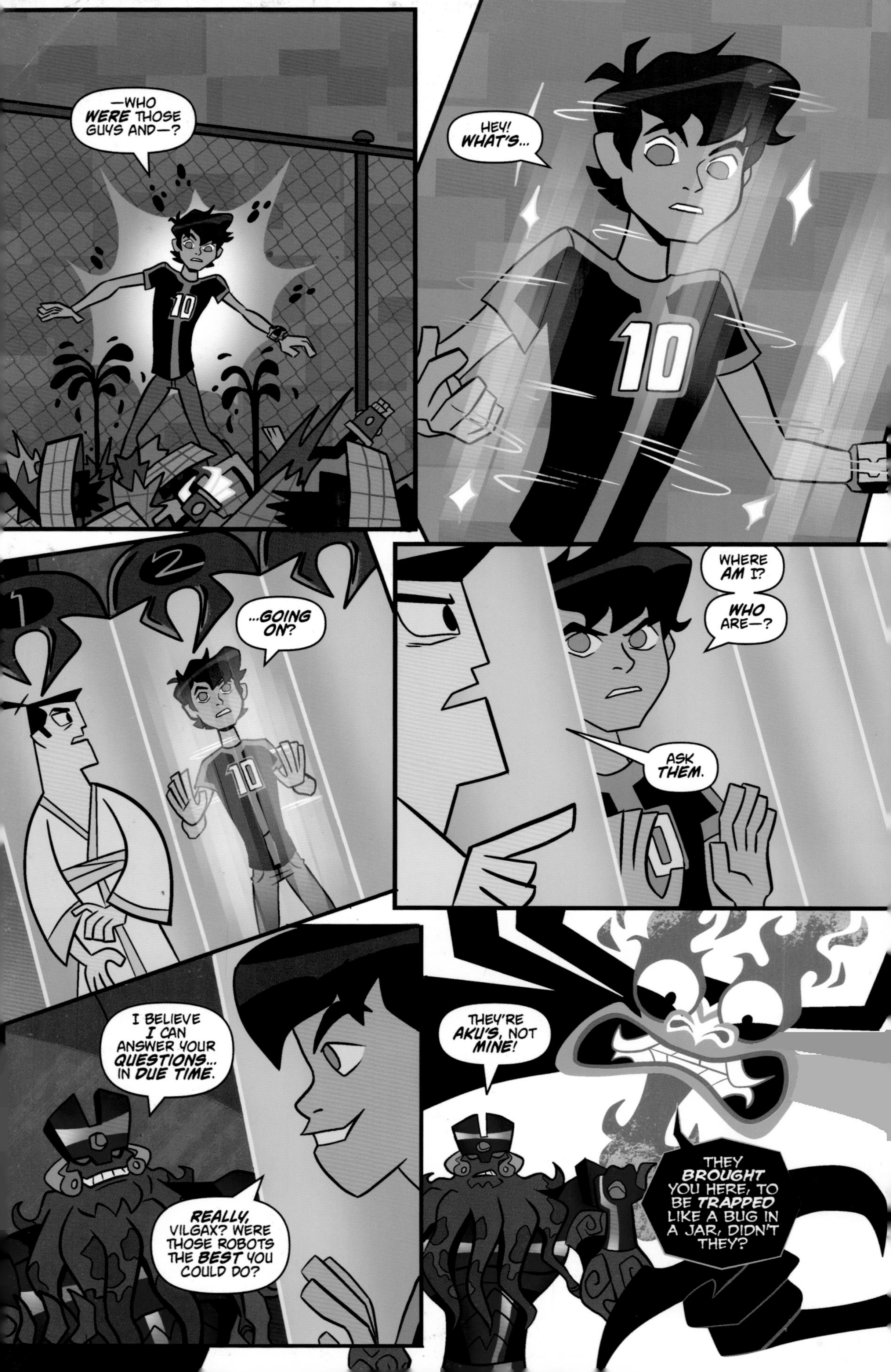
—WHO WERE THOSE GUYS AND—?
HEY! WHAT'S...
...GOING ON?
WHERE AM I?
WHO ARE—?
ASK THEM.
I BELIEVE I CAN ANSWER YOUR QUESTIONS... IN DUE TIME.
REALLY, VILGAX? WERE THOSE ROBOTS THE BEST YOU COULD DO?
THEY'RE AKU'S, NOT MINE!
THEY BROUGHT YOU HERE, TO BE TRAPPED LIKE A BUG IN A JAR, DIDN'T THEY?

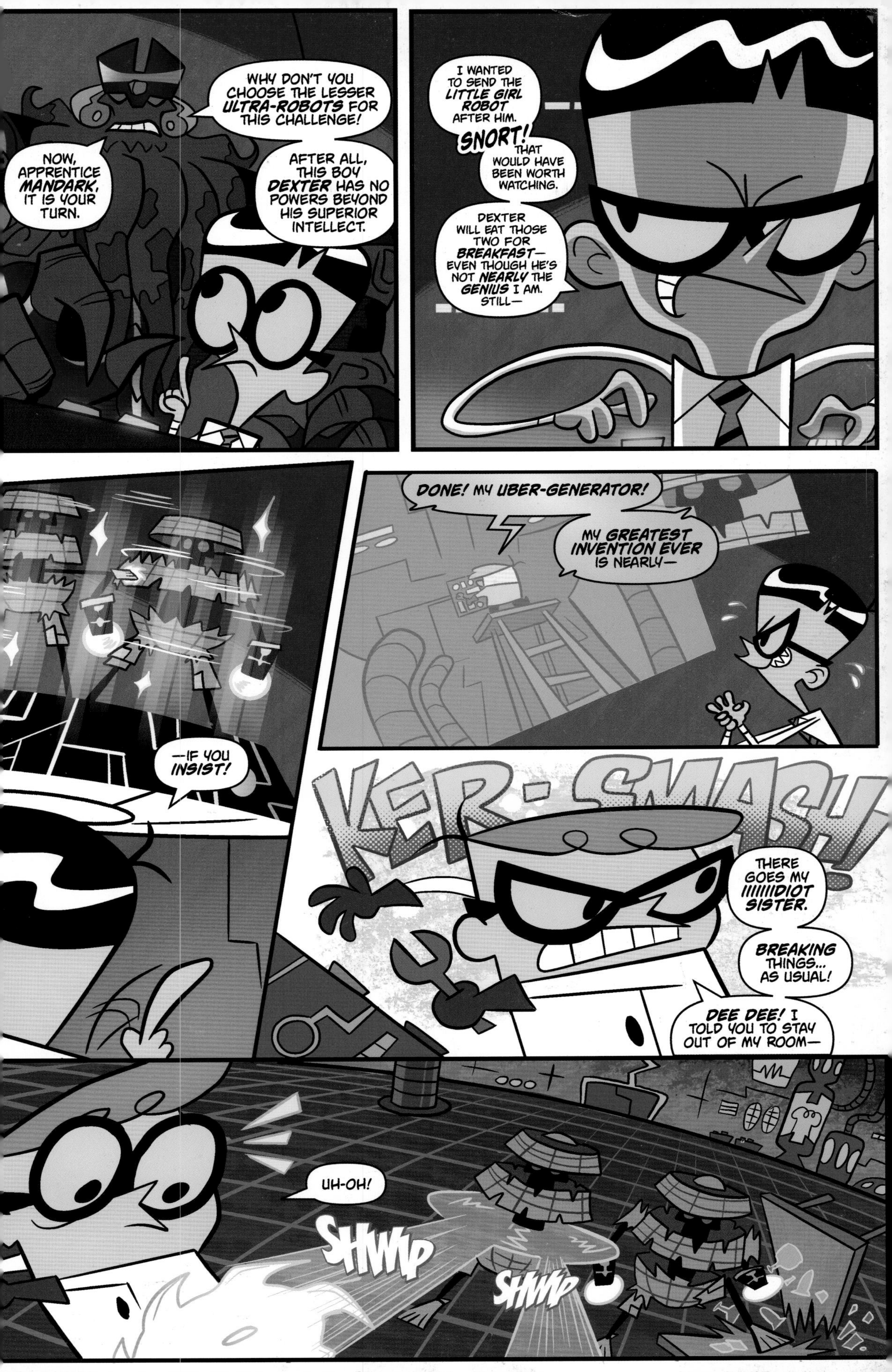
NOW, APPRENTICE MANDARK, IT IS YOUR TURN.
WHY DON'T YOU CHOOSE THE LESSER ULTRA-ROBOTS FOR THIS CHALLENGE!
AFTER ALL, THIS BOY DEXTER HAS NO POWERS BEYOND HIS SUPERIOR INTELLECT.
I WANTED TO SEND THE LITTLE GIRL ROBOT AFTER HIM.
SNORT!
THAT WOULD HAVE BEEN WORTH WATCHING.
DEXTER WILL EAT THOSE TWO FOR BREAKFAST— EVEN THOUGH HE'S NOT NEARLY THE GENIUS I AM. STILL—
—IF YOU INSIST!
DONE! MY UBER-GENERATOR!
MY GREATEST INVENTION EVER IS NEARLY—
KER-SMASH!
THERE GOES MY IIIIIIIDIOT SISTER.
BREAKING THINGS... AS USUAL!
DEE DEE! I TOLD YOU TO STAY OUT OF MY ROOM—
UH-OH!
SHWMP
SHWMP

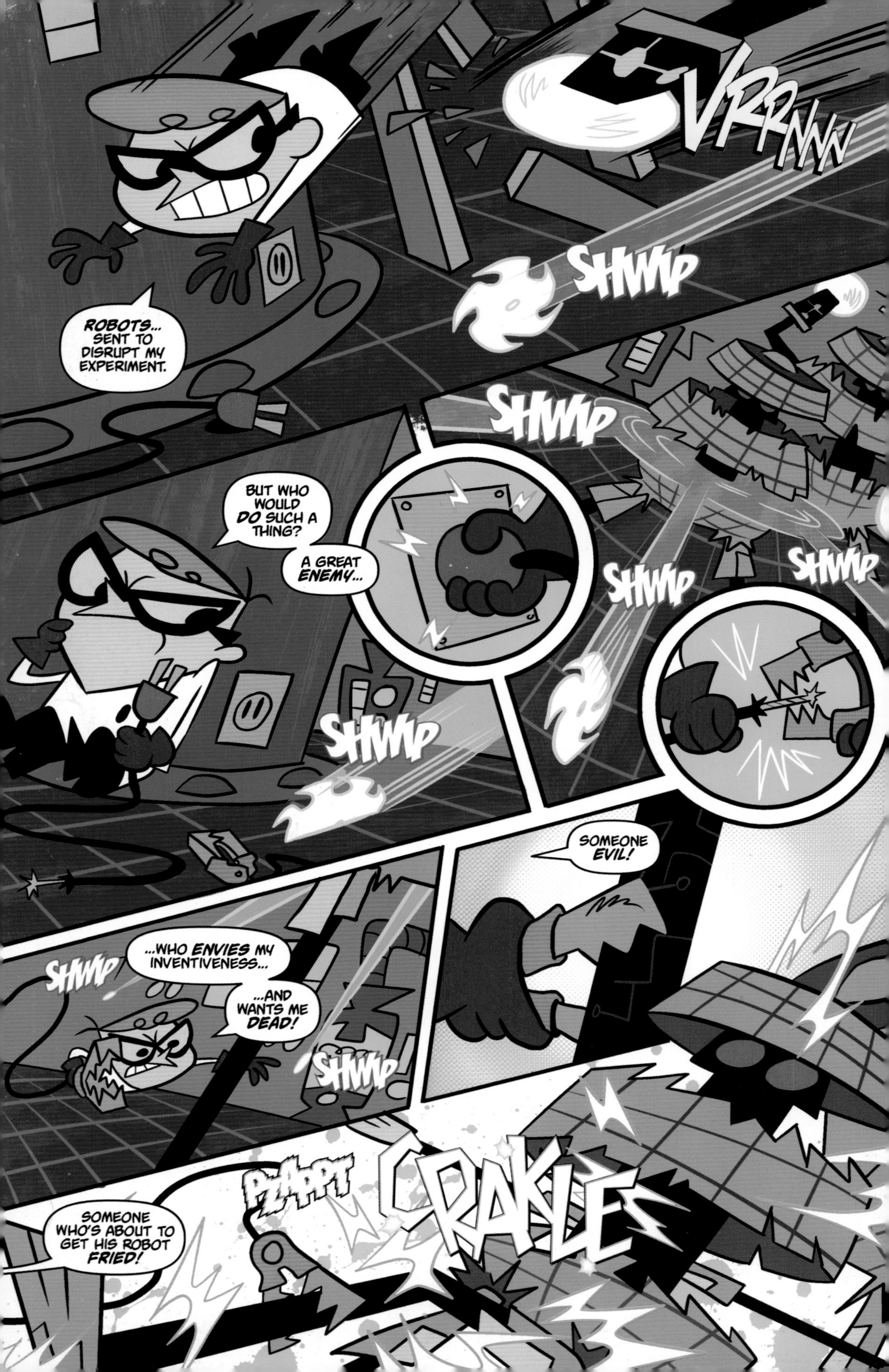
VRRNNN
SHWIP
ROBOTS... SENT TO DISRUPT MY EXPERIMENT.
SHWIP
BUT WHO WOULD DO SUCH A THING?
A GREAT ENEMY...
SHWIP
SHWIP
SHWIP
SOMEONE EVIL!
SHWIP
...WHO ENVIES MY INVENTIVENESS...
...AND WANTS ME DEAD!
SHWIP
PZAPPT
CRAKLE
SOMEONE WHO'S ABOUT TO GET HIS ROBOT FRIED!

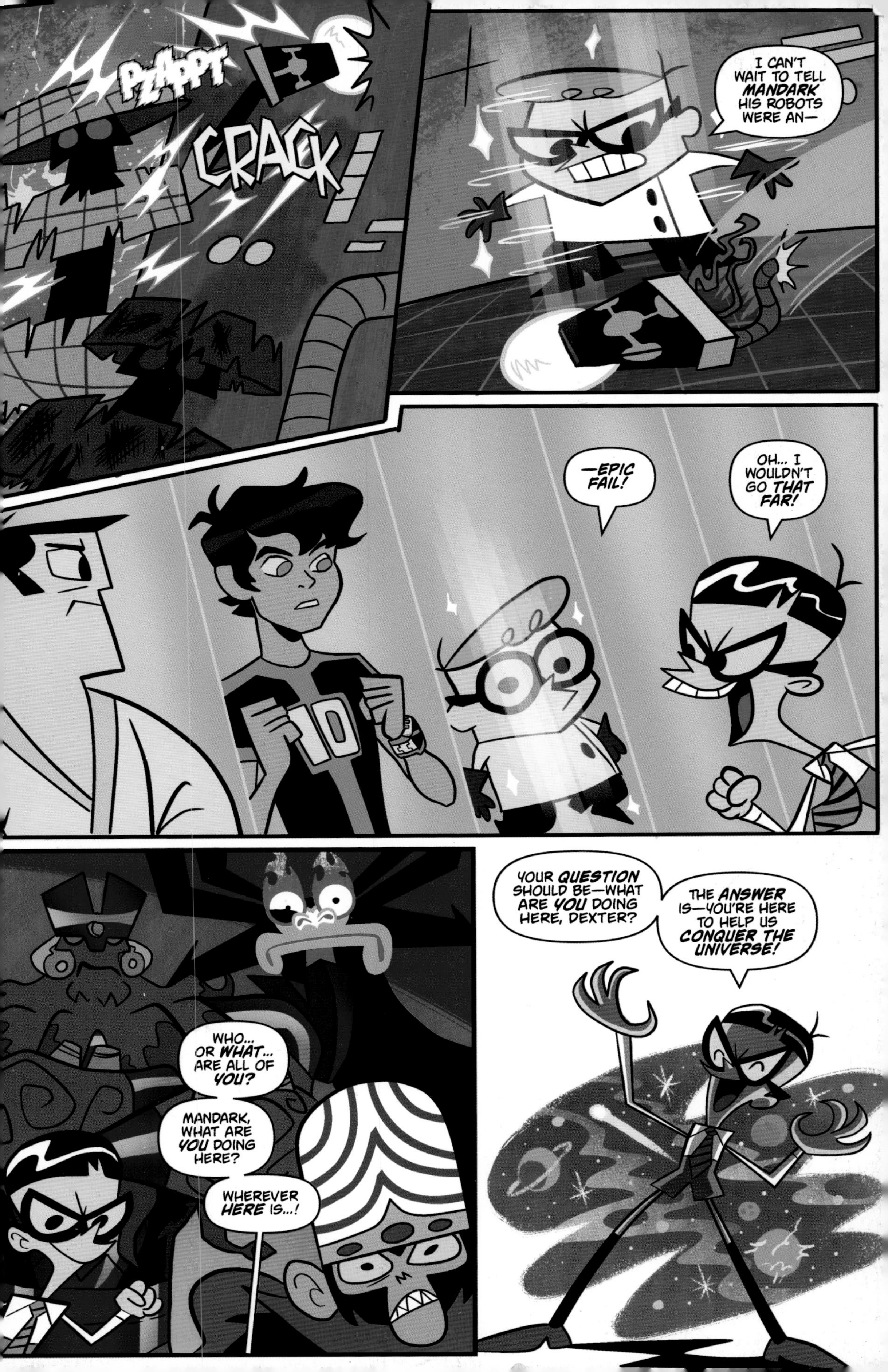
PZAPPT
CRACK
I CAN'T WAIT TO TELL MANDARK HIS ROBOTS WERE AN—
—EPIC FAIL!
OH... I WOULDN'T GO THAT FAR!
WHO... OR WHAT... ARE ALL OF YOU?
MANDARK, WHAT ARE YOU DOING HERE?
WHEREVER HERE IS...!
YOUR QUESTION SHOULD BE—WHAT ARE YOU DOING HERE, DEXTER?
THE ANSWER IS—YOU'RE HERE TO HELP US CONQUER THE UNIVERSE!

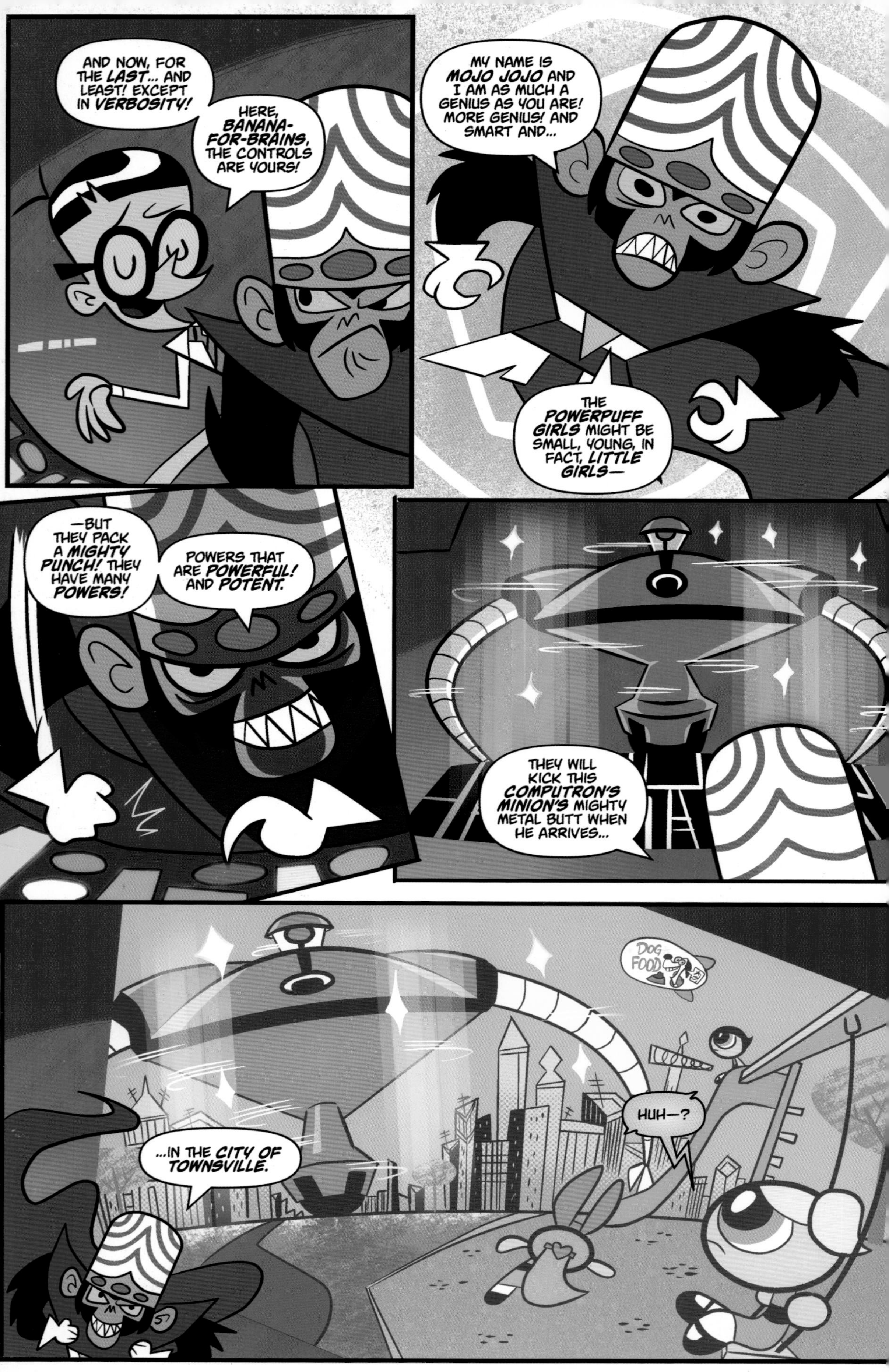
AND NOW, FOR THE LAST... AND LEAST! EXCEPT IN VERBOSITY!
HERE, BANANA-FOR-BRAINS, THE CONTROLS ARE YOURS!
MY NAME IS MOJO JOJO AND I AM AS MUCH A GENIUS AS YOU ARE! MORE GENIUS! AND SMART AND...
THE POWERPUFF GIRLS MIGHT BE SMALL, YOUNG, IN FACT, LITTLE GIRLS—
—BUT THEY PACK A MIGHTY PUNCH! THEY HAVE MANY POWERS!
POWERS THAT ARE POWERFUL! AND POTENT.
THEY WILL KICK THIS COMPUTRON'S MINION'S MIGHTY METAL BUTT WHEN HE ARRIVES...
DOG FOOD
...IN THE CITY OF TOWNSVILLE.
HUH—?

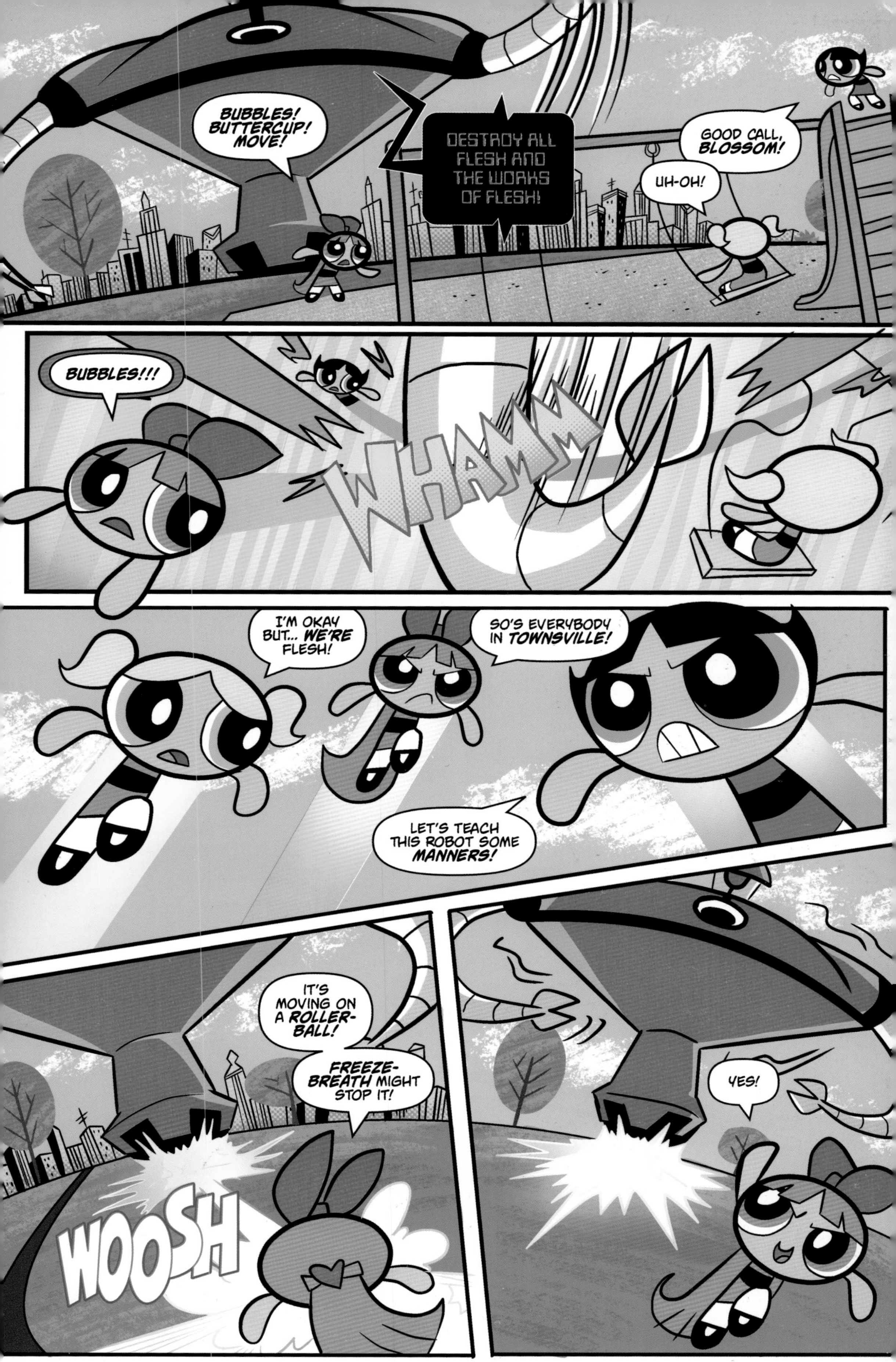
BUBBLES! BUTTERCUP! MOVE!
DESTROY ALL FLESH AND THE WORKS OF FLESH!
GOOD CALL, BLOSSOM!
UH-OH!
BUBBLES!!!
WHAMM
I'M OKAY BUT... WE'RE FLESH!
SO'S EVERYBODY IN TOWNSVILLE!
LET'S TEACH THIS ROBOT SOME MANNERS!
IT'S MOVING ON A ROLLER-BALL!
FREEZE-BREATH MIGHT STOP IT!
WOOSH
YES!

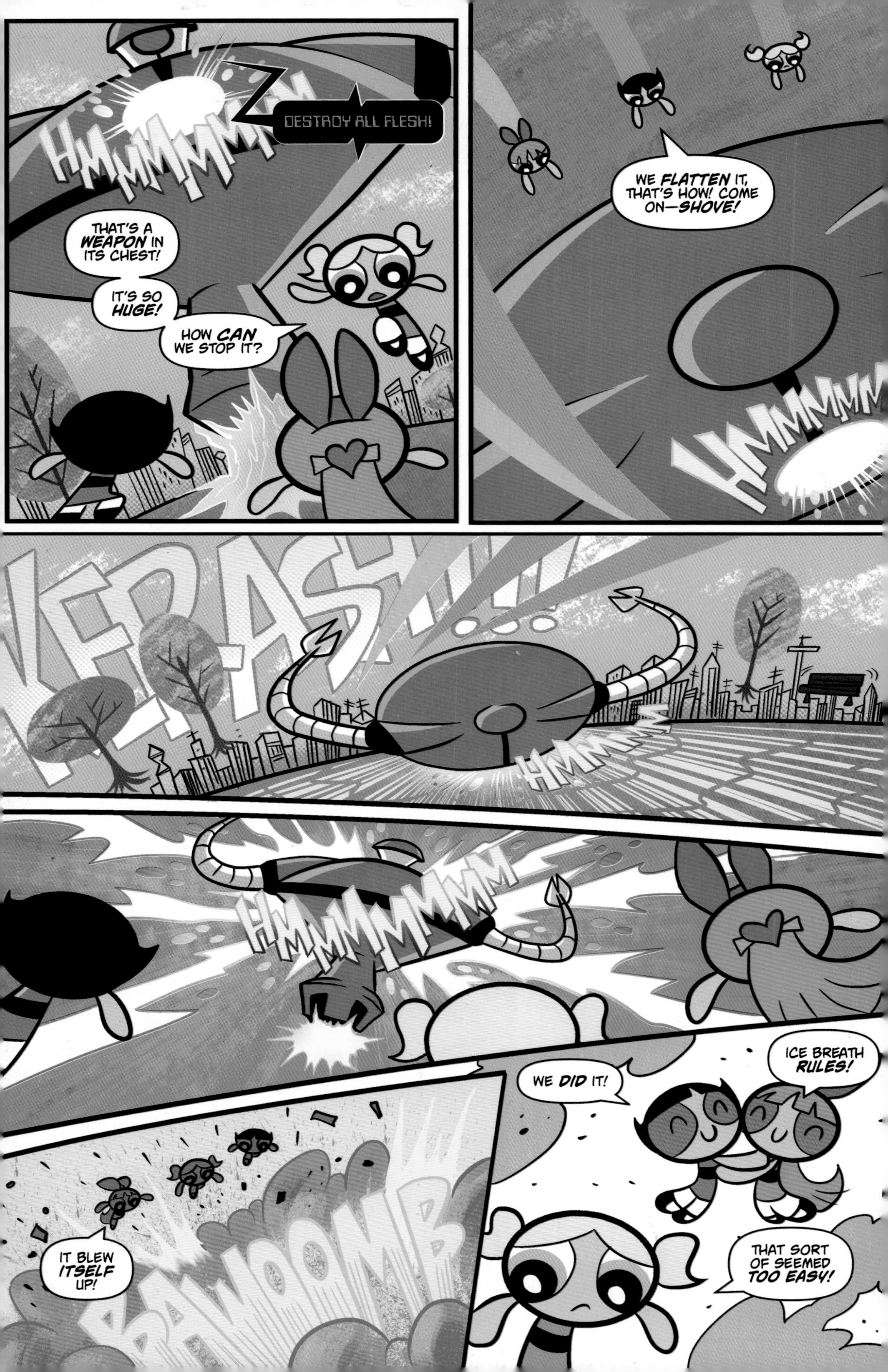
HMMMMMMM
DESTROY ALL FLESH!
THAT'S A WEAPON IN ITS CHEST!
IT'S SO HUGE!
HOW CAN WE STOP IT?
WE FLATTEN IT, THAT'S HOW! COME ON—SHOVE!
HMMMMMM
KRASH
HMMMM
HMMMMMMM
IT BLEW ITSELF UP!
BAWOOMB
WE DID IT!
ICE BREATH RULES!
THAT SORT OF SEEMED TOO EASY!

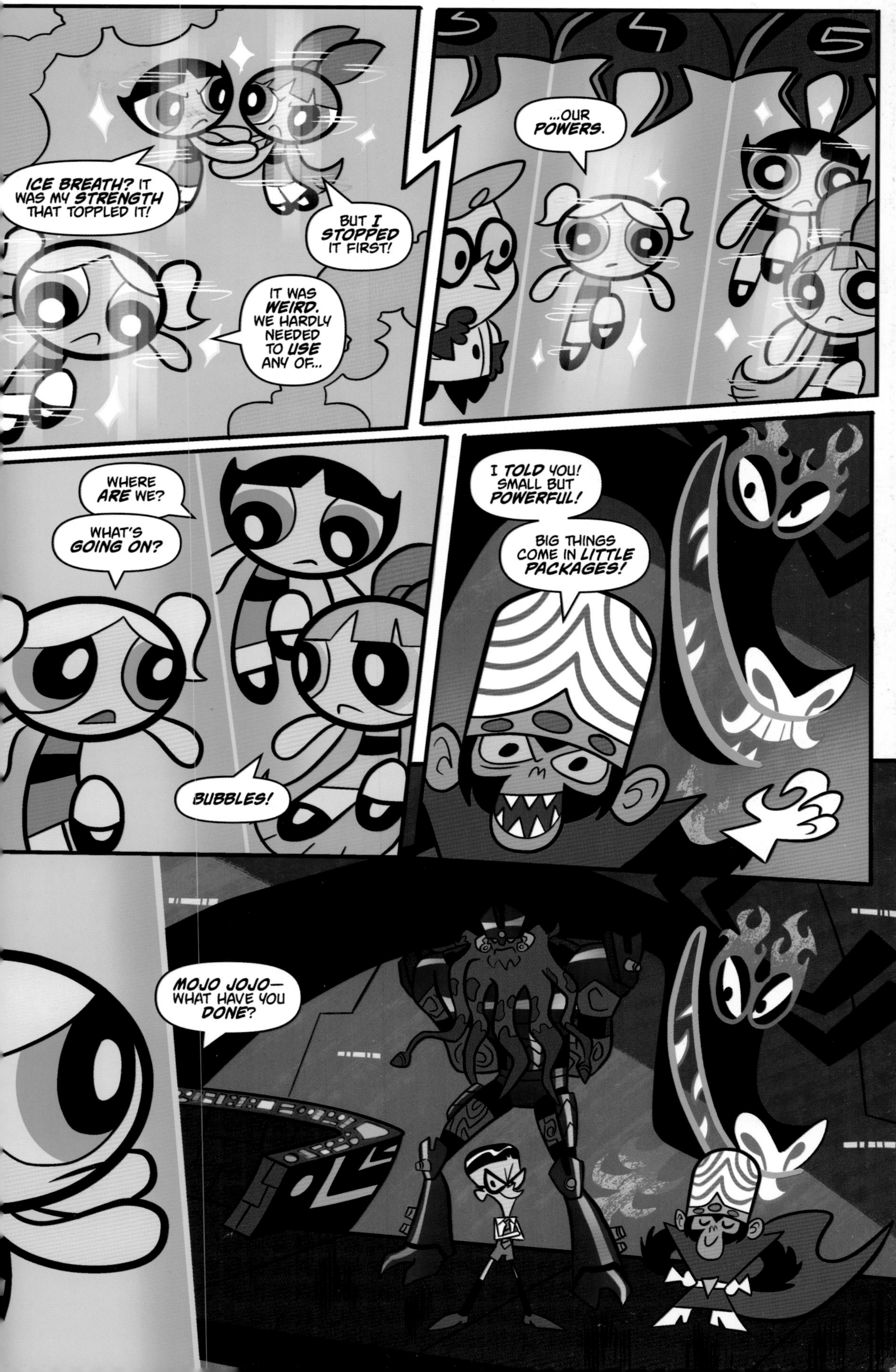
ICE BREATH? IT WAS MY STRENGTH THAT TOPPLED IT!
BUT I STOPPED IT FIRST!
IT WAS WEIRD. WE HARDLY NEEDED TO USE ANY OF...
...OUR POWERS.
WHERE ARE WE?
WHAT'S GOING ON?
BUBBLES!
I TOLD YOU! SMALL BUT POWERFUL!
BIG THINGS COME IN LITTLE PACKAGES!
MOJO JOJO— WHAT HAVE YOU DONE?

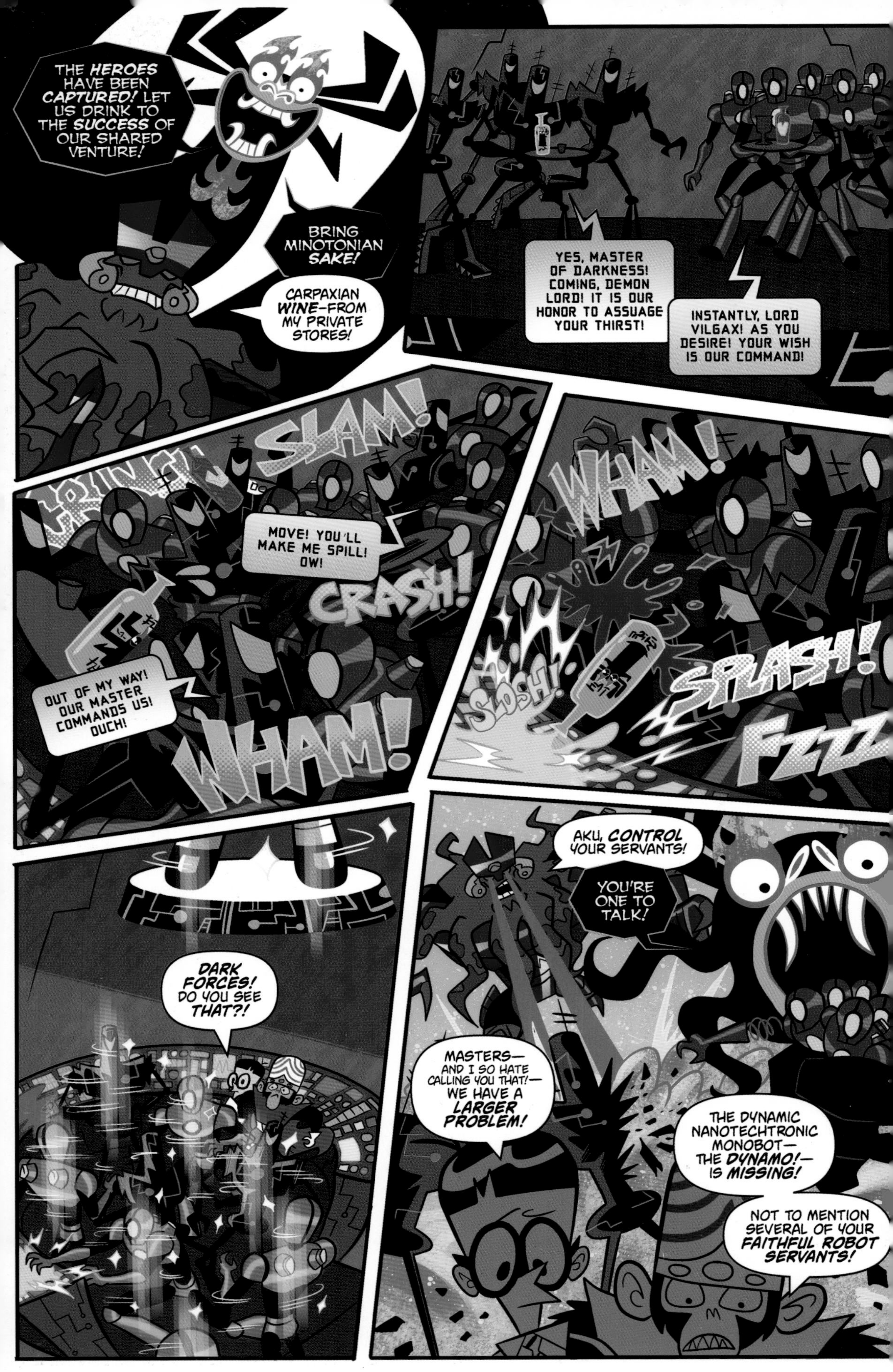
THE HEROES HAVE BEEN CAPTURED! LET US DRINK TO THE SUCCESS OF OUR SHARED VENTURE!
BRING MINOTONIAN SAKE!
CARPAXIAN WINE—FROM MY PRIVATE STORES!
YES, MASTER OF DARKNESS! COMING, DEMON LORD! IT IS OUR HONOR TO ASSUAGE YOUR THIRST!
INSTANTLY, LORD VILGAX! AS YOU DESIRE! YOUR WISH IS OUR COMMAND!
SLAM!
MOVE! YOU'LL MAKE ME SPILL! OW!
CRASH!
OUT OF MY WAY! OUR MASTER COMMANDS US! OUCH!
WHAM!
WHAM!
SLOSH!
SPLASH!
FZZZ
DARK FORCES! DO YOU SEE THAT?!
AKU, CONTROL YOUR SERVANTS!
YOU'RE ONE TO TALK!
MASTERS— AND I SO HATE CALLING YOU THAT!— WE HAVE A LARGER PROBLEM!
THE DYNAMIC NANOTECHTRONIC MONOBOT— THE DYNAMO!— IS MISSING!
NOT TO MENTION SEVERAL OF YOUR FAITHFUL ROBOT SERVANTS!

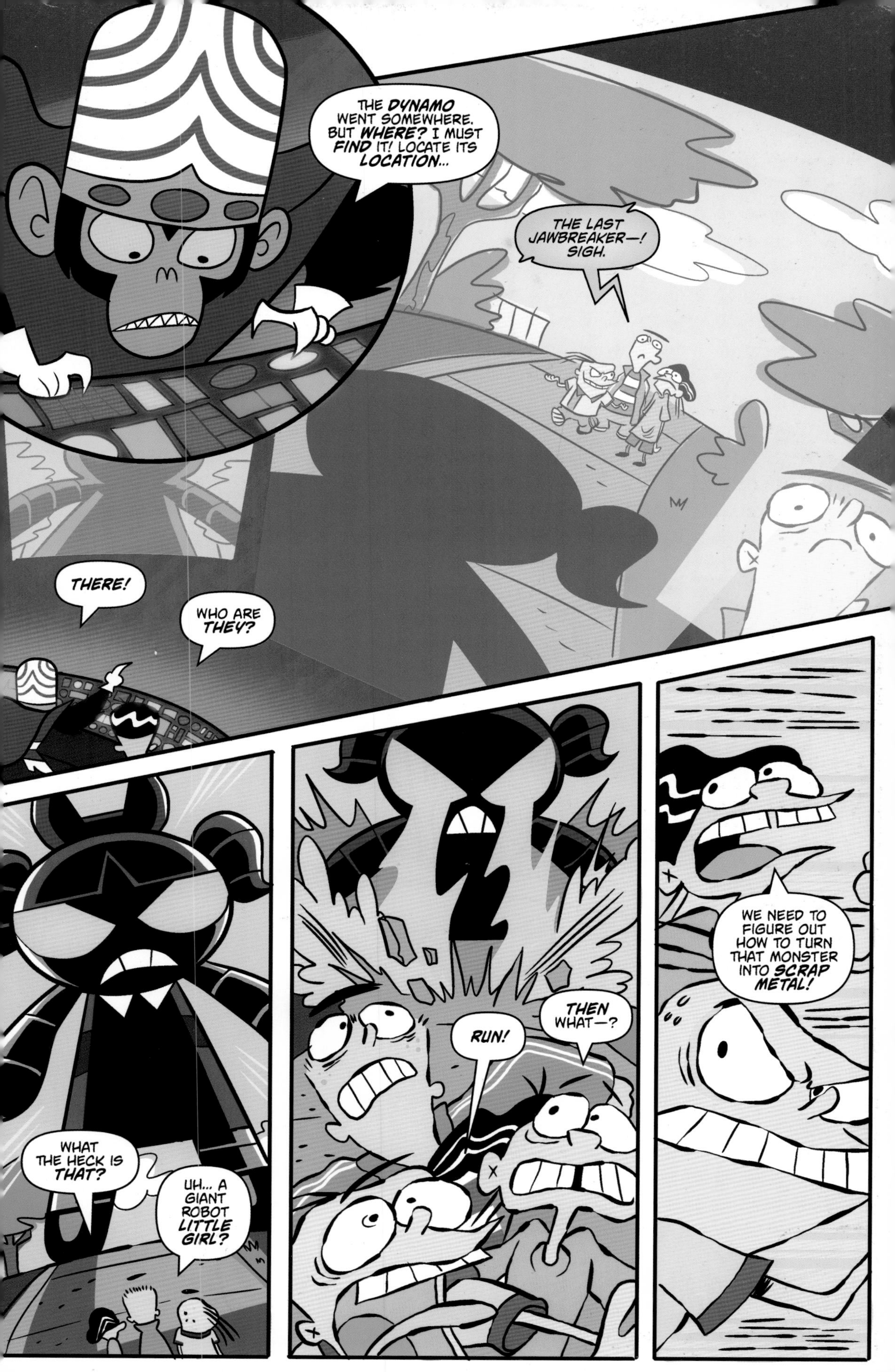
THE DYNAMO WENT SOMEWHERE. BUT WHERE? I MUST FIND IT! LOCATE ITS LOCATION...
THE LAST JAWBREAKER—! SIGH.
THERE!
WHO ARE THEY?
WHAT THE HECK IS THAT?
UH... A GIANT ROBOT LITTLE GIRL?
THEN WHAT—?
RUN!
WE NEED TO FIGURE OUT HOW TO TURN THAT MONSTER INTO SCRAP METAL!

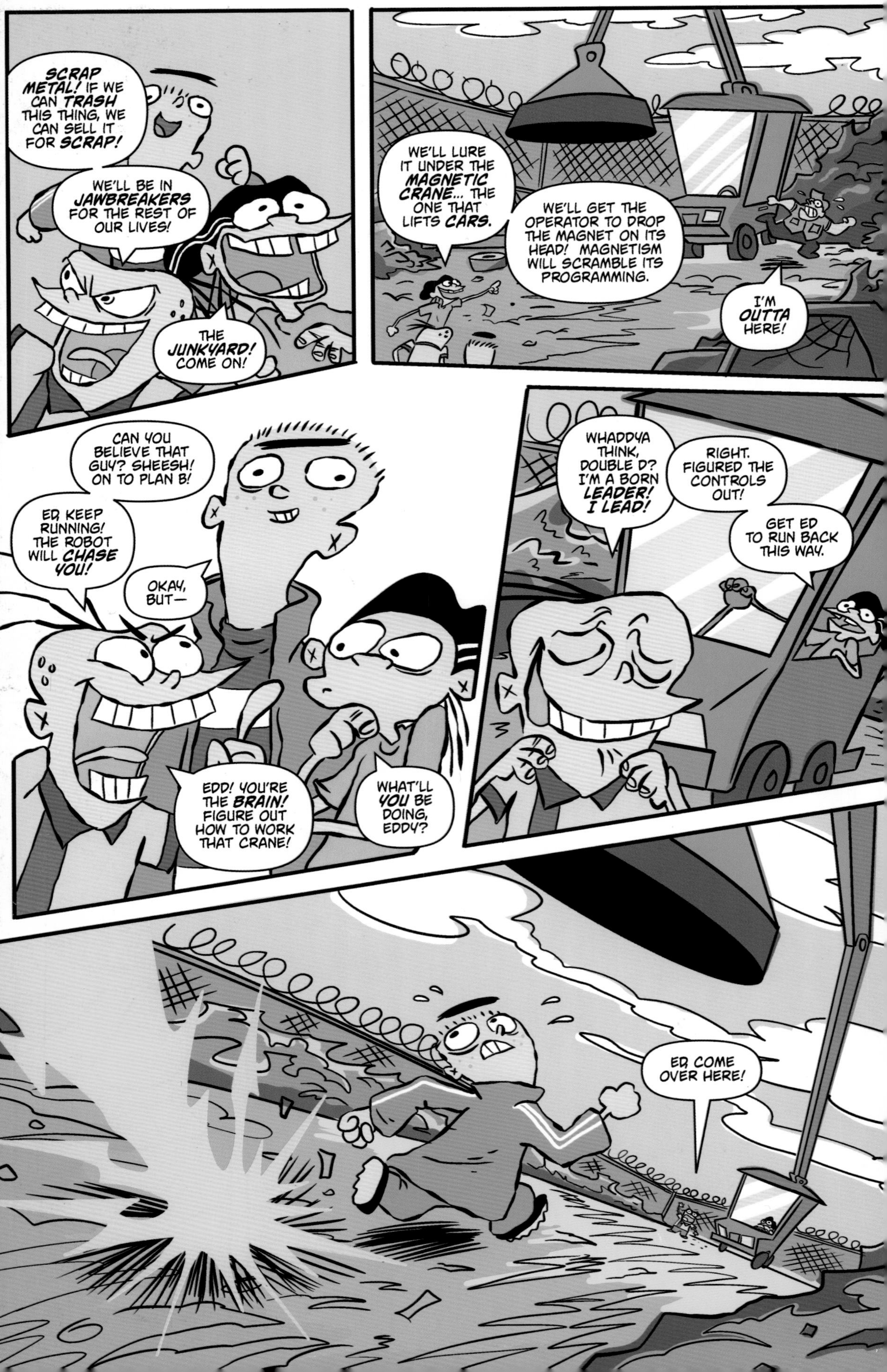
SCRAP METAL! IF WE CAN TRASH THIS THING, WE CAN SELL IT FOR SCRAP!
WE'LL BE IN JAWBREAKERS FOR THE REST OF OUR LIVES!
THE JUNKYARD! COME ON!
WE'LL LURE IT UNDER THE MAGNETIC CRANE... THE ONE THAT LIFTS CARS.
WE'LL GET THE OPERATOR TO DROP THE MAGNET ON ITS HEAD! MAGNETISM WILL SCRAMBLE ITS PROGRAMMING.
I'M OUTTA HERE!
CAN YOU BELIEVE THAT GUY? SHEESH! ON TO PLAN B!
ED, KEEP RUNNING! THE ROBOT WILL CHASE YOU!
OKAY, BUT—
EDD! YOU'RE THE BRAIN! FIGURE OUT HOW TO WORK THAT CRANE!
WHAT'LL YOU BE DOING, EDDY?
WHADDYA THINK, DOUBLE D? I'M A BORN LEADER! I LEAD!
RIGHT. FIGURED THE CONTROLS OUT!
GET ED TO RUN BACK THIS WAY.
ED, COME OVER HERE!

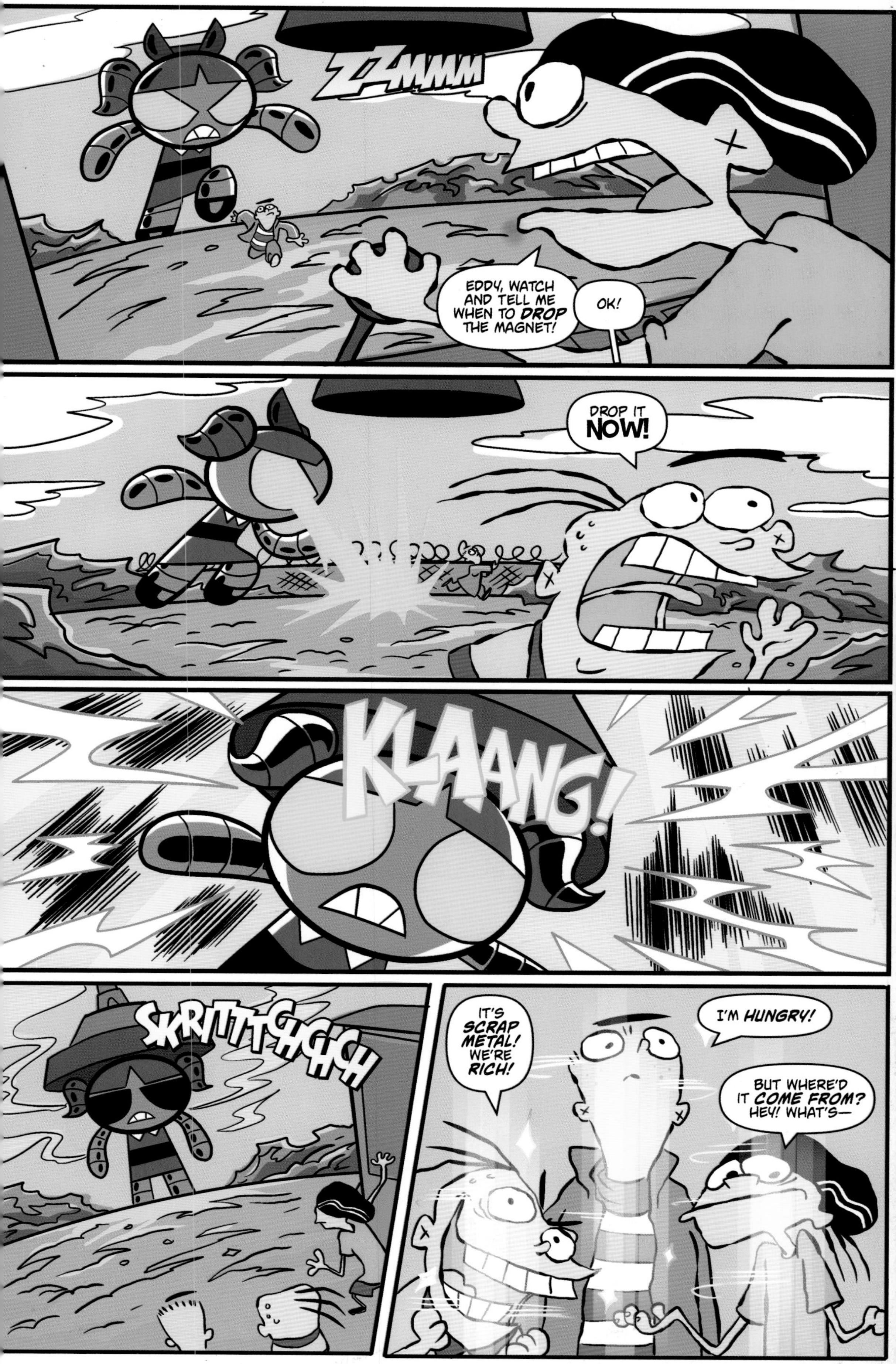
ZZMMMM
EDDY, WATCH AND TELL ME WHEN TO DROP THE MAGNET!
OK!
DROP IT NOW!
KLAANG!
SKRITTTCHCHCH
IT'S SCRAP METAL! WE'RE RICH!
I'M HUNGRY!
BUT WHERE'D IT COME FROM? HEY! WHAT'S—

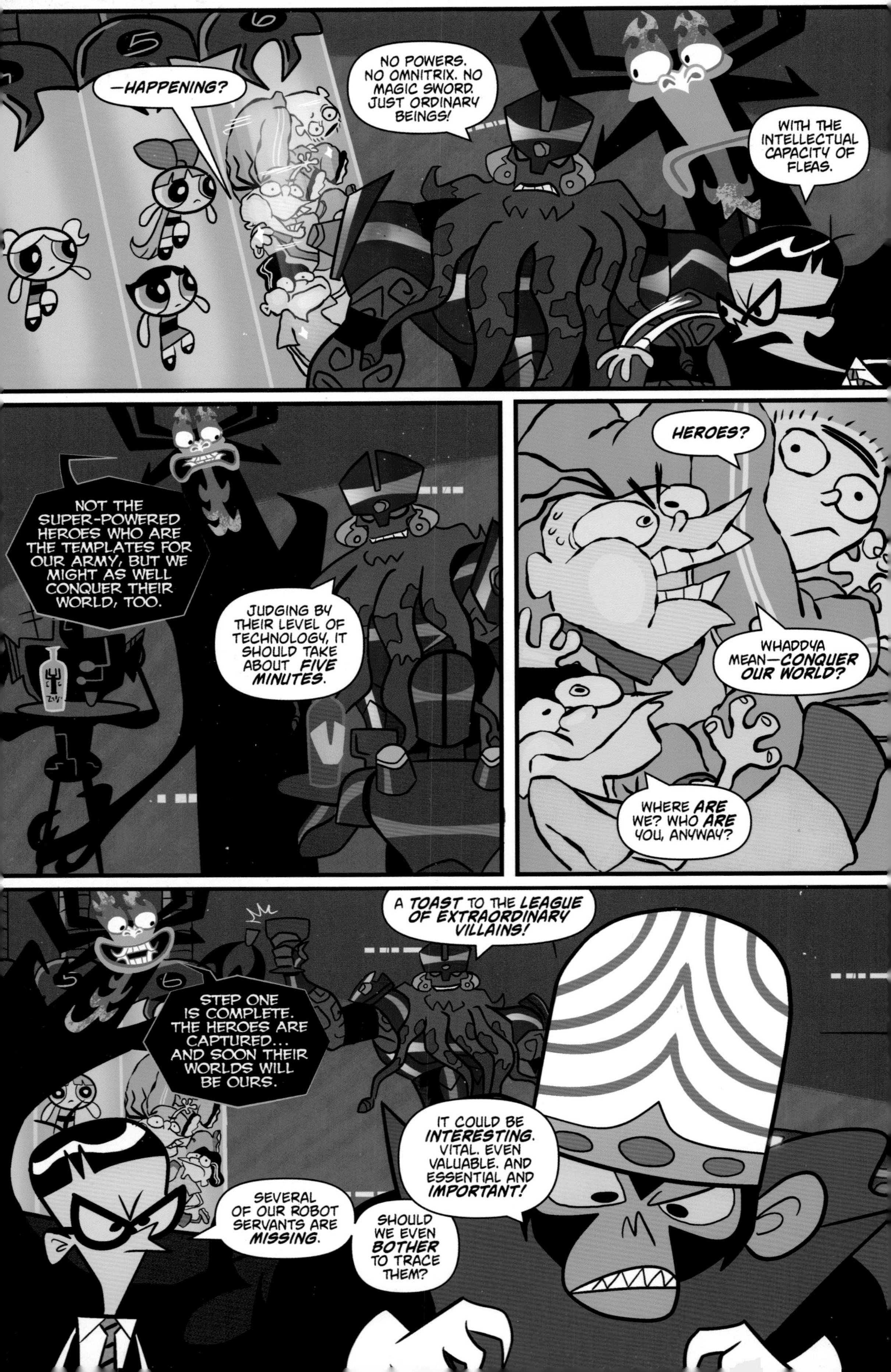

—HAPPENING?
NO POWERS. NO OMNITRIX. NO MAGIC SWORD. JUST ORDINARY BEINGS!
WITH THE INTELLECTUAL CAPACITY OF FLEAS.
NOT THE SUPER-POWERED HEROES WHO ARE THE TEMPLATES FOR OUR ARMY, BUT WE MIGHT AS WELL CONQUER THEIR WORLD, TOO.
JUDGING BY THEIR LEVEL OF TECHNOLOGY, IT SHOULD TAKE ABOUT FIVE MINUTES.
HEROES?
WHADDYA MEAN—CONQUER OUR WORLD?
WHERE ARE WE? WHO ARE YOU, ANYWAY?
A TOAST TO THE LEAGUE OF EXTRAORDINARY VILLAINS!
STEP ONE IS COMPLETE. THE HEROES ARE CAPTURED... AND SOON THEIR WORLDS WILL BE OURS.
IT COULD BE INTERESTING. VITAL. EVEN VALUABLE. AND ESSENTIAL AND IMPORTANT!
SEVERAL OF OUR ROBOT SERVANTS ARE MISSING.
SHOULD WE EVEN BOTHER TO TRACE THEM?

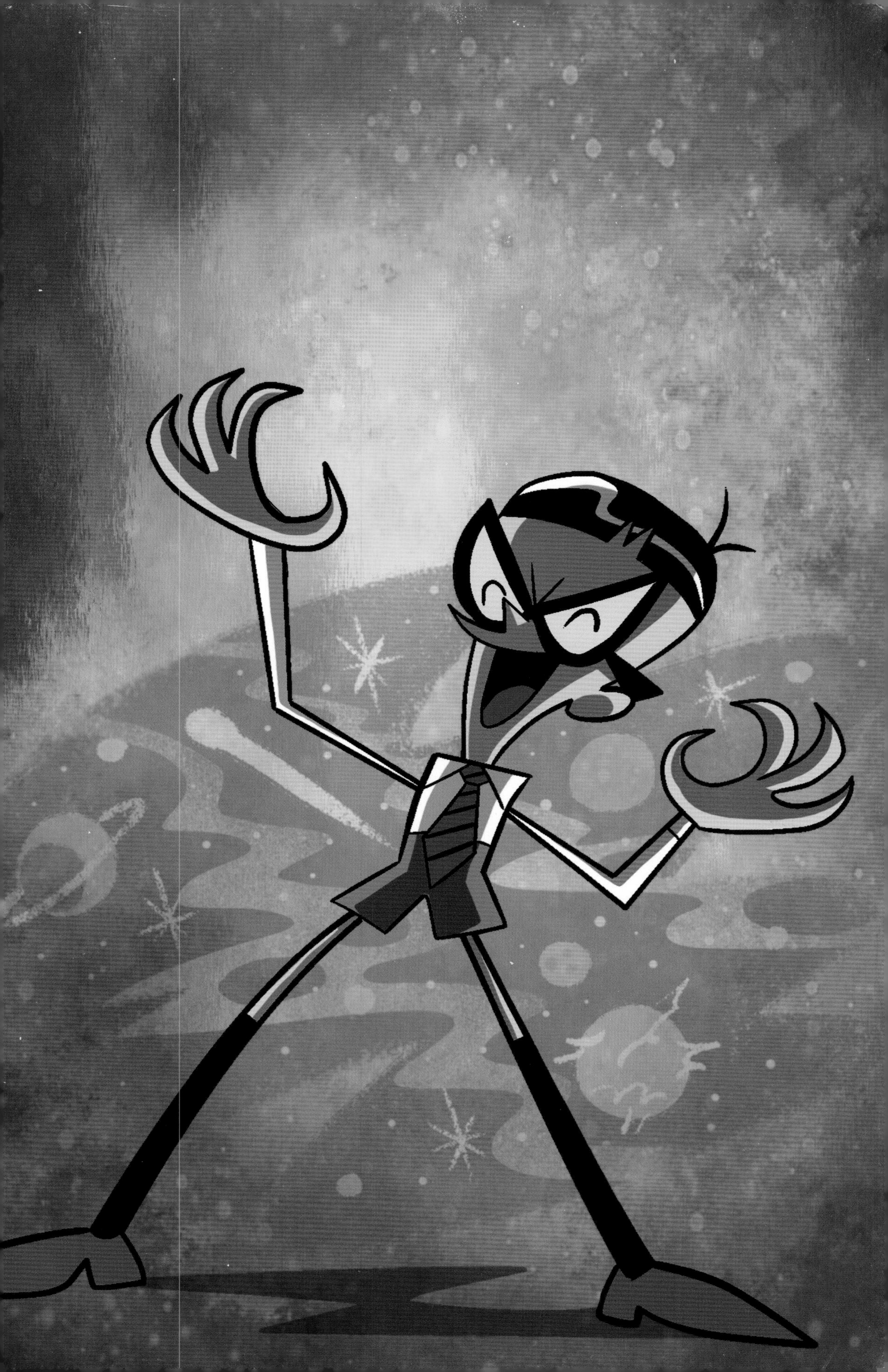

Chapter 2

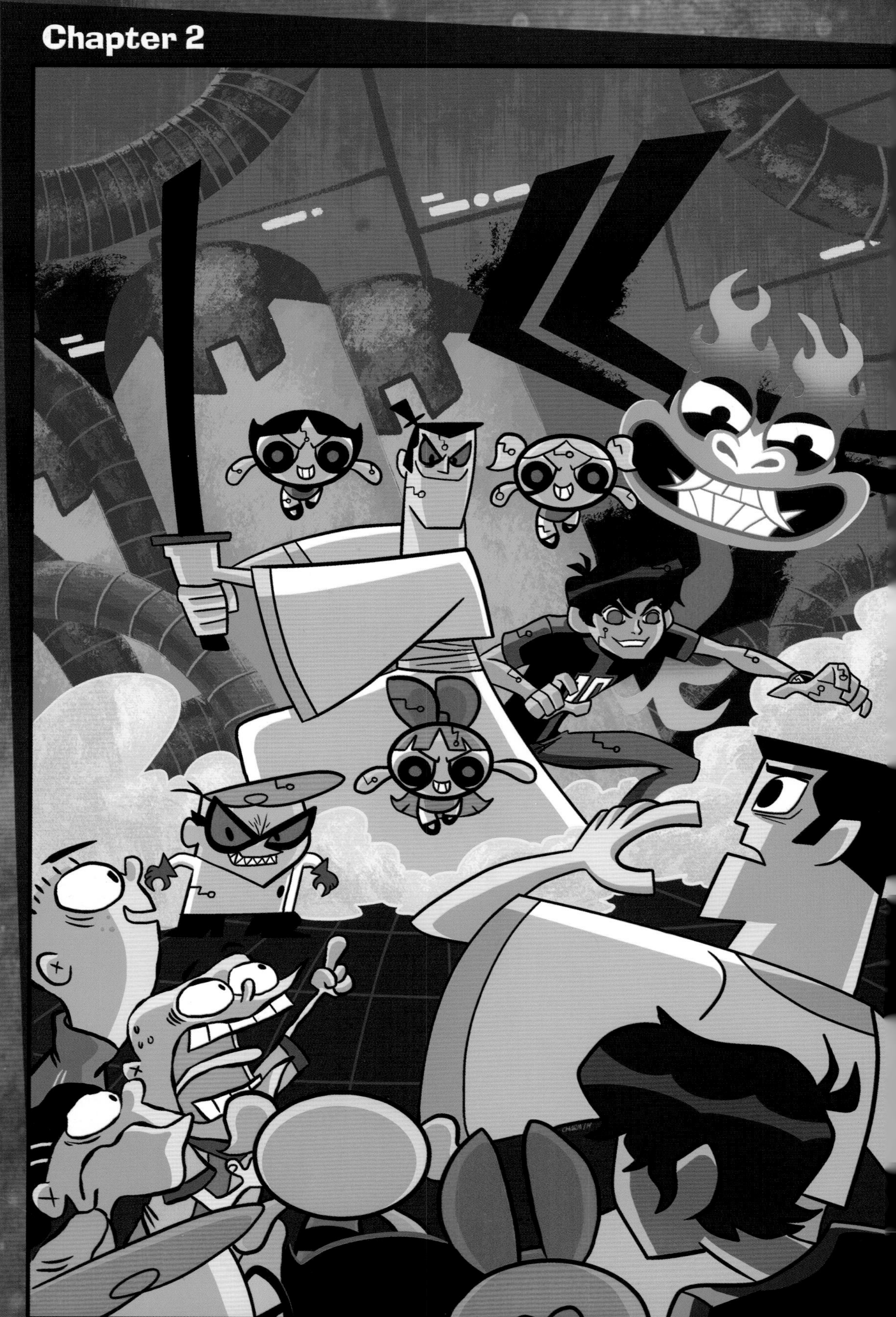

Cover Art by Derek Charm

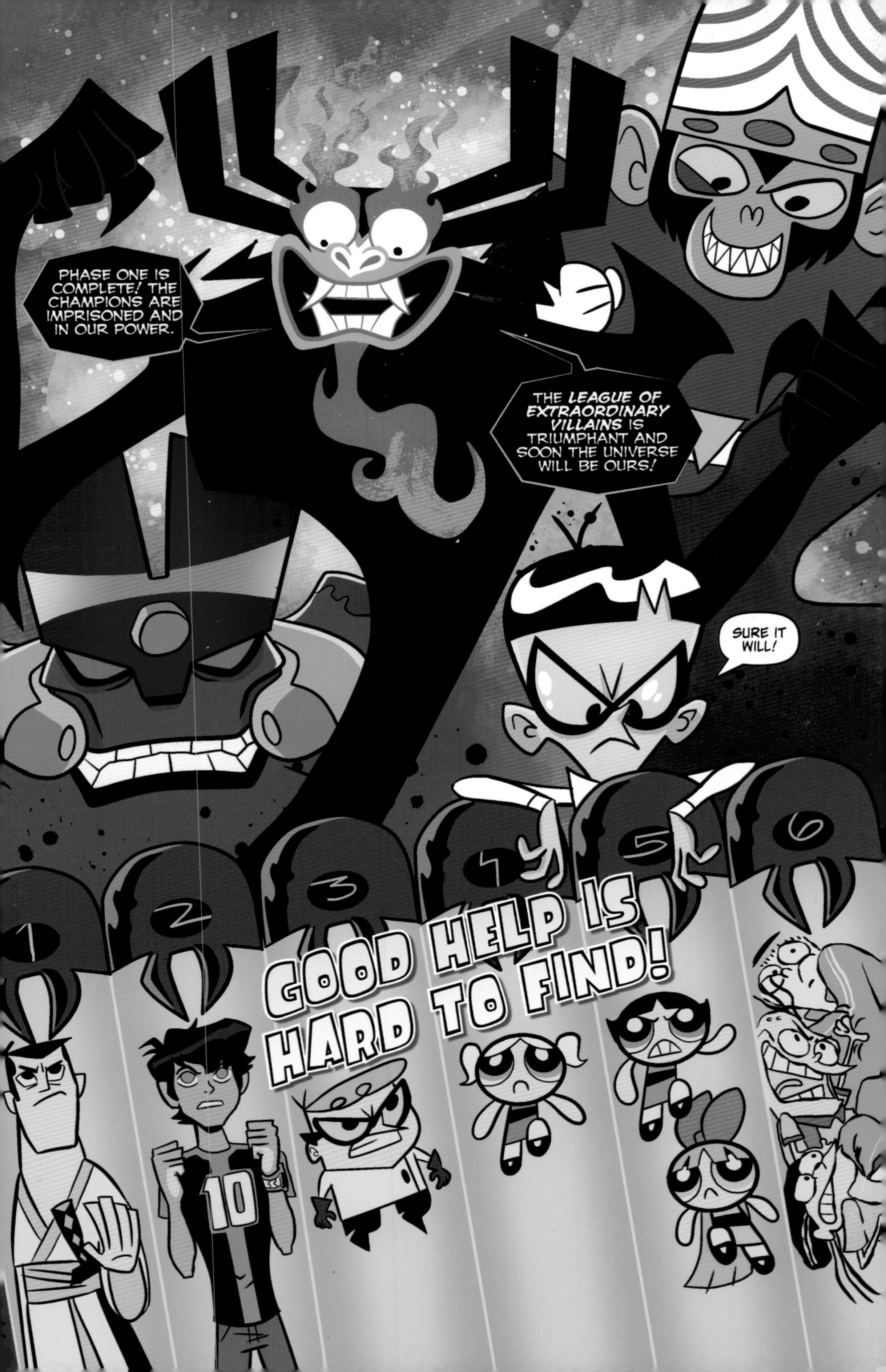
PHASE ONE IS COMPLETE! THE CHAMPIONS ARE IMPRISONED AND IN OUR POWER.
THE LEAGUE OF EXTRAORDINARY VILLAINS IS TRIUMPHANT AND SOON THE UNIVERSE WILL BE OURS!
SURE IT WILL!
1
2
3
4
5
6
GOOD HELP IS HARD TO FIND!
10

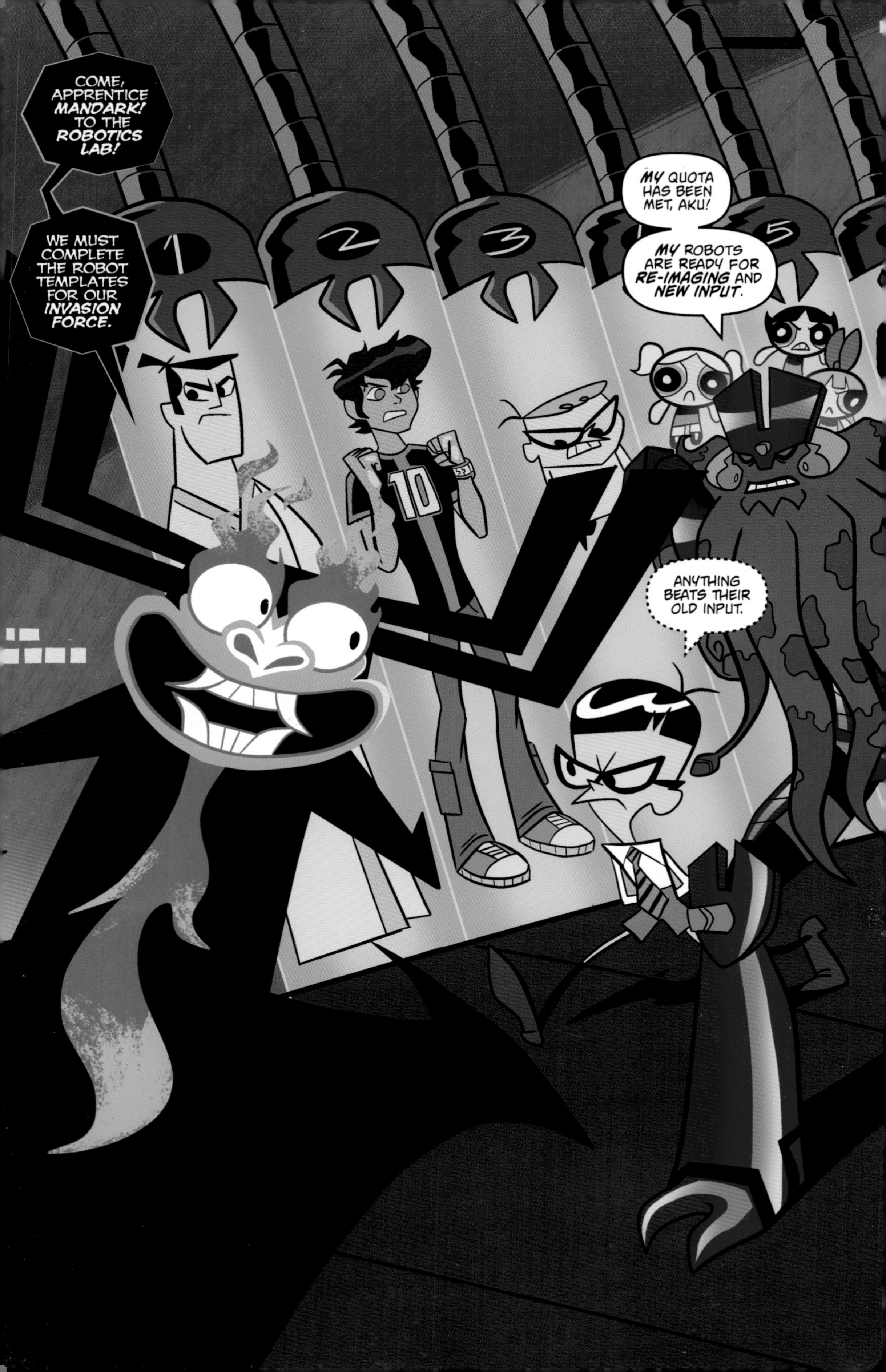
COME, APPRENTICE MANDARK! TO THE ROBOTICS LAB!
WE MUST COMPLETE THE ROBOT TEMPLATES FOR OUR INVASION FORCE.
MY QUOTA HAS BEEN MET, AKU!
MY ROBOTS ARE READY FOR RE-IMAGING AND NEW INPUT.
ANYTHING BEATS THEIR OLD INPUT.

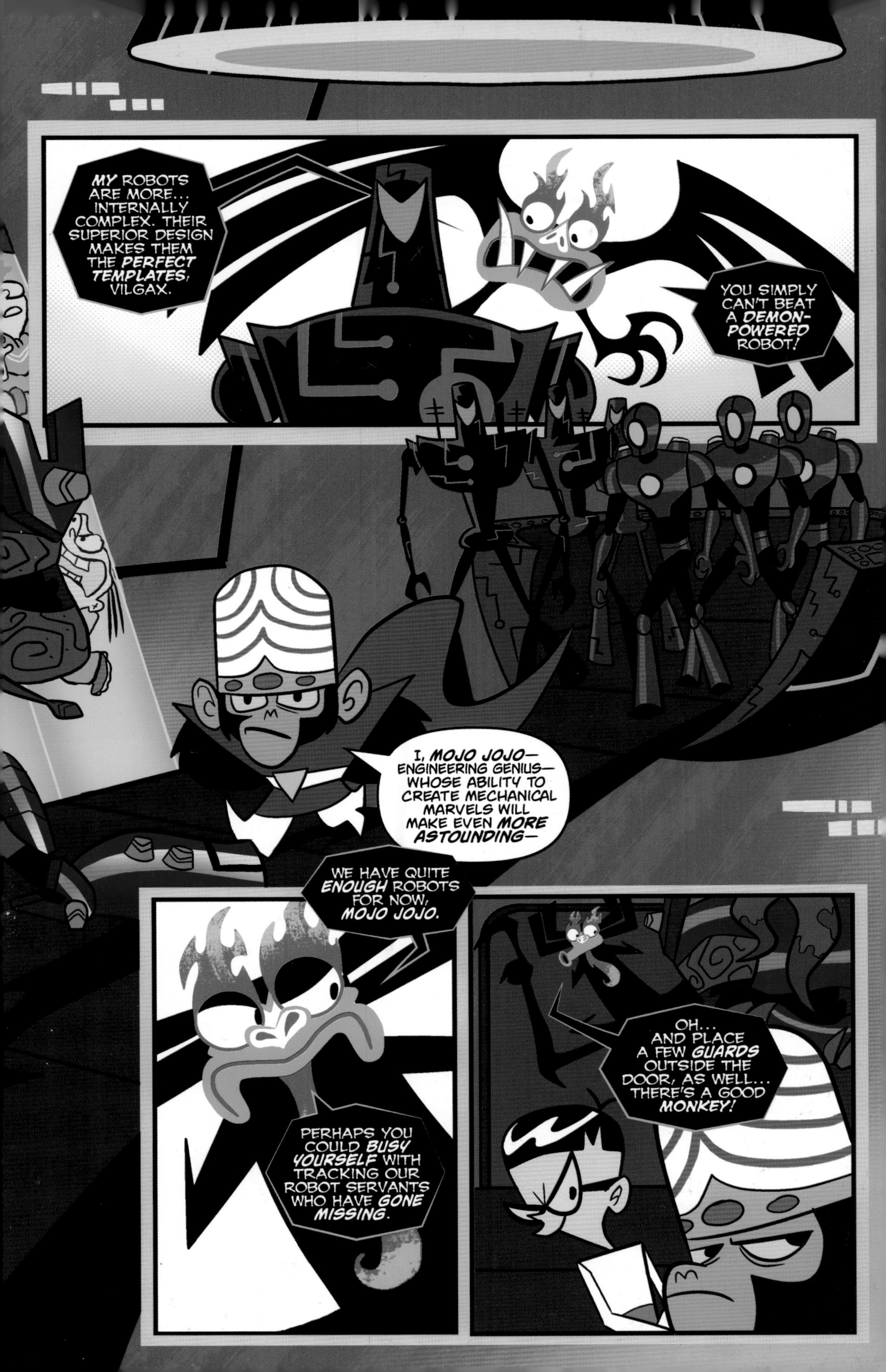
MY ROBOTS ARE MORE... INTERNALLY COMPLEX. THEIR SUPERIOR DESIGN MAKES THEM THE PERFECT TEMPLATES, VILGAX.
YOU SIMPLY CAN'T BEAT A DEMON-POWERED ROBOT!
I, MOJO JOJO— ENGINEERING GENIUS— WHOSE ABILITY TO CREATE MECHANICAL MARVELS WILL MAKE EVEN MORE ASTOUNDING—
WE HAVE QUITE ENOUGH ROBOTS FOR NOW, MOJO JOJO.
PERHAPS YOU COULD BUSY YOURSELF WITH TRACKING OUR ROBOT SERVANTS WHO HAVE GONE MISSING.
OH... AND PLACE A FEW GUARDS OUTSIDE THE DOOR, AS WELL... THERE'S A GOOD MONKEY!

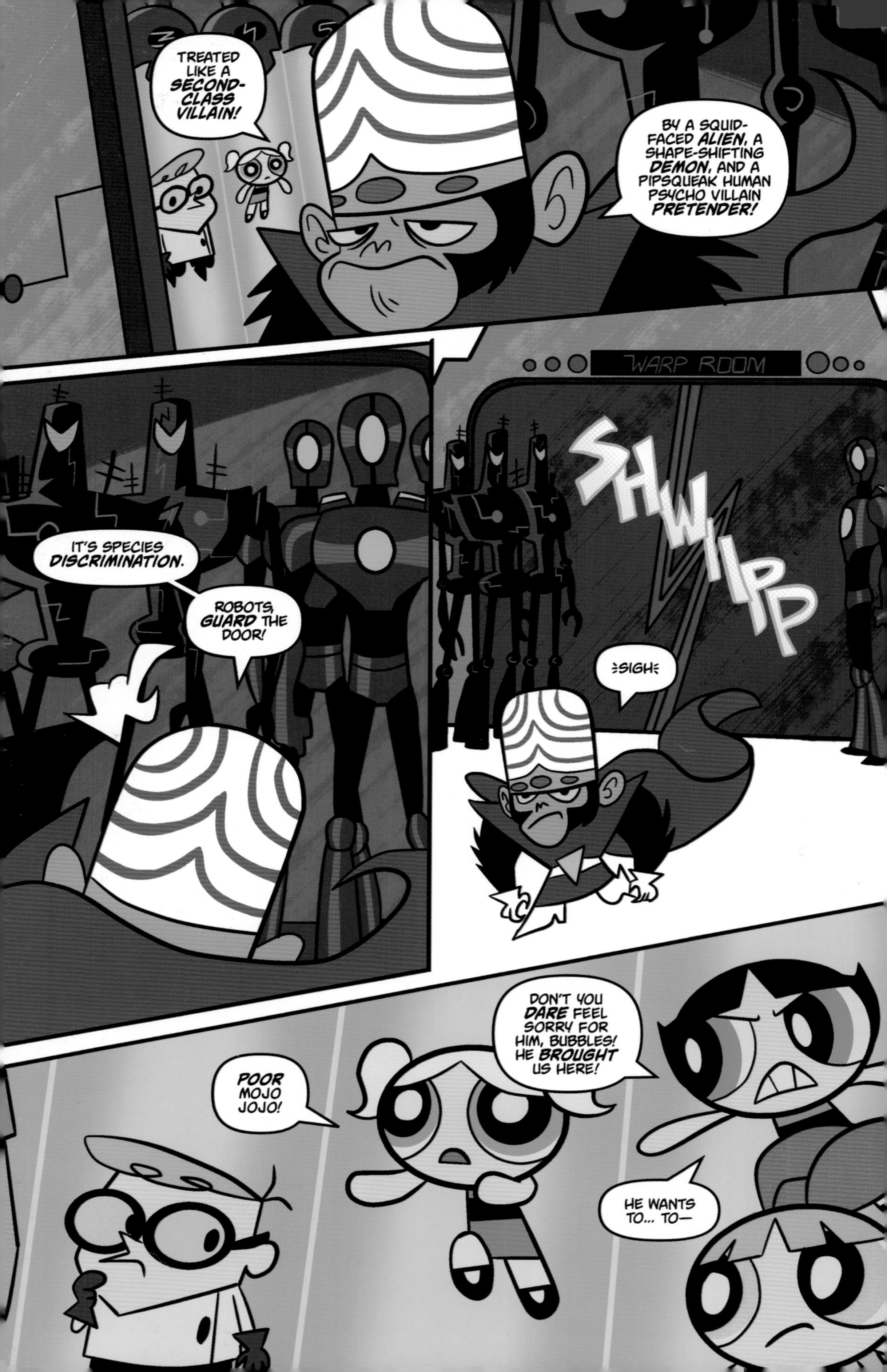
TREATED LIKE A SECOND-CLASS VILLAIN!
BY A SQUID-FACED ALIEN, A SHAPE-SHIFTING DEMON, AND A PIPSQUEAK HUMAN PSYCHO VILLAIN PRETENDER!
IT'S SPECIES DISCRIMINATION.
ROBOTS, GUARD THE DOOR!
WARP ROOM
SHWIIPP
SIGH
DON'T YOU DARE FEEL SORRY FOR HIM, BUBBLES! HE BROUGHT US HERE!
POOR MOJO JOJO!
HE WANTS TO... TO—

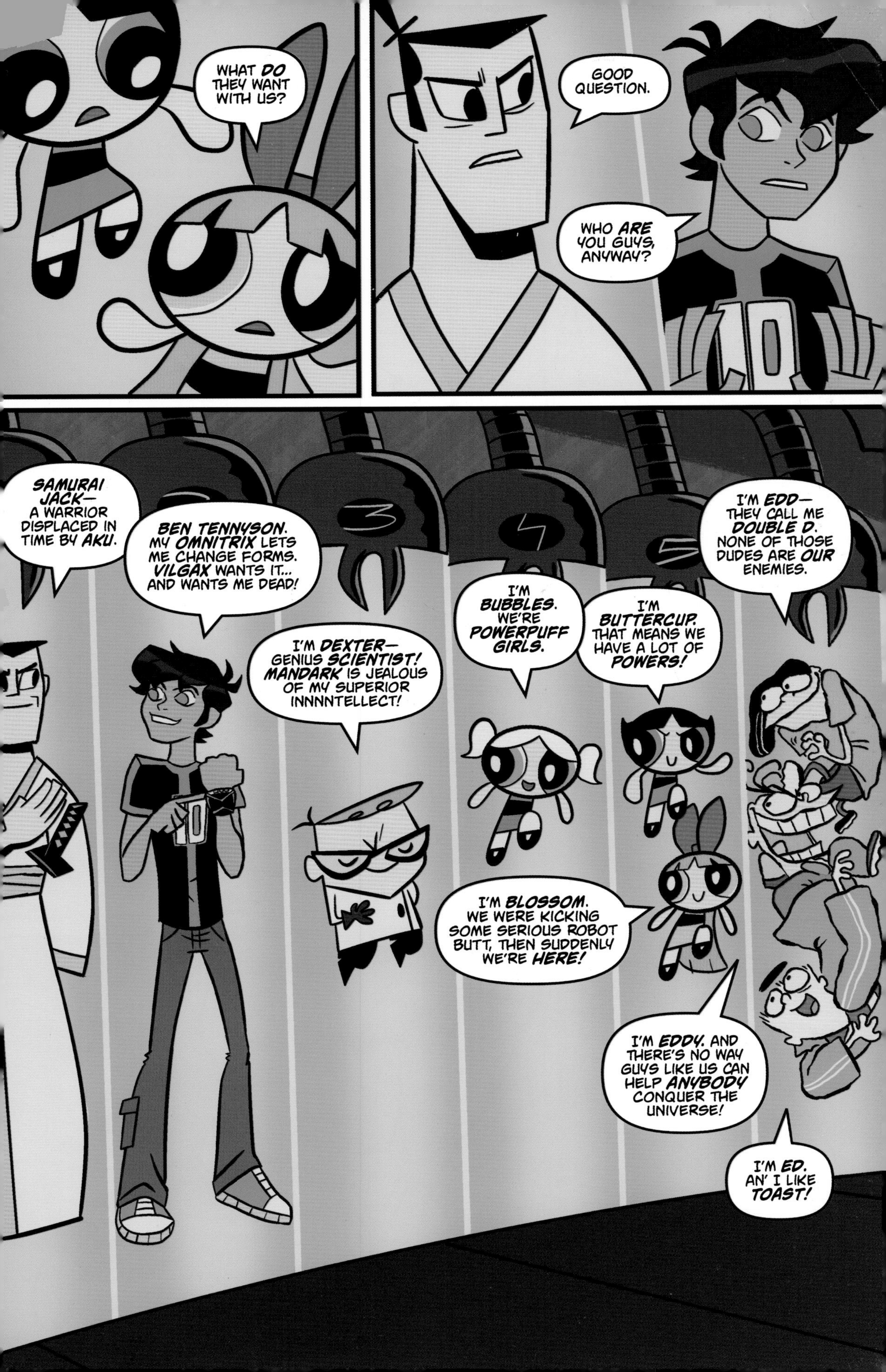
WHAT DO THEY WANT WITH US?
GOOD QUESTION.
WHO ARE YOU GUYS, ANYWAY?
SAMURAI JACK— A WARRIOR DISPLACED IN TIME BY AKU.
BEN TENNYSON. MY OMNITRIX LETS ME CHANGE FORMS. VILGAX WANTS IT... AND WANTS ME DEAD!
I'M DEXTER— GENIUS SCIENTIST! MANDARK IS JEALOUS OF MY SUPERIOR INNNNTELLECT!
I'M BUBBLES. WE'RE POWERPUFF GIRLS.
I'M BUTTERCUP. THAT MEANS WE HAVE A LOT OF POWERS!
I'M EDD— THEY CALL ME DOUBLE D. NONE OF THOSE DUDES ARE OUR ENEMIES.
I'M BLOSSOM. WE WERE KICKING SOME SERIOUS ROBOT BUTT, THEN SUDDENLY WE'RE HERE!
I'M EDDY. AND THERE'S NO WAY GUYS LIKE US CAN HELP ANYBODY CONQUER THE UNIVERSE!
I'M ED. AN' I LIKE TOAST!

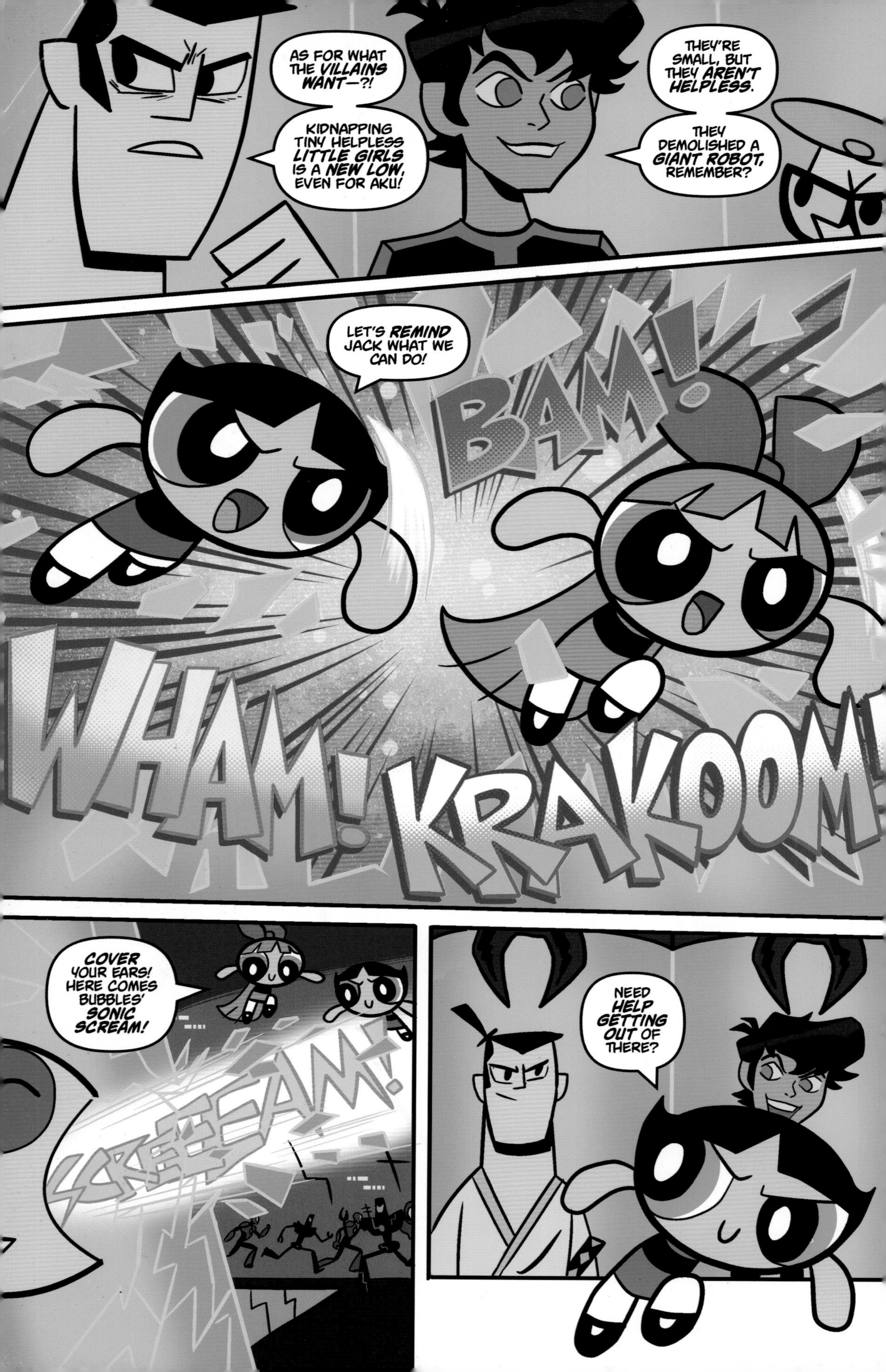

AS FOR WHAT THE VILLAINS WANT—?!
KIDNAPPING TINY HELPLESS LITTLE GIRLS IS A NEW LOW, EVEN FOR AKU!
THEY'RE SMALL, BUT THEY AREN'T HELPLESS.
THEY DEMOLISHED A GIANT ROBOT, REMEMBER?
LET'S REMIND JACK WHAT WE CAN DO!
BAM!
WHAM!
KRAKOOM!
COVER YOUR EARS! HERE COMES BUBBLES' SONIC SCREAM!
SCREEEAM!
NEED HELP GETTING OUT OF THERE?

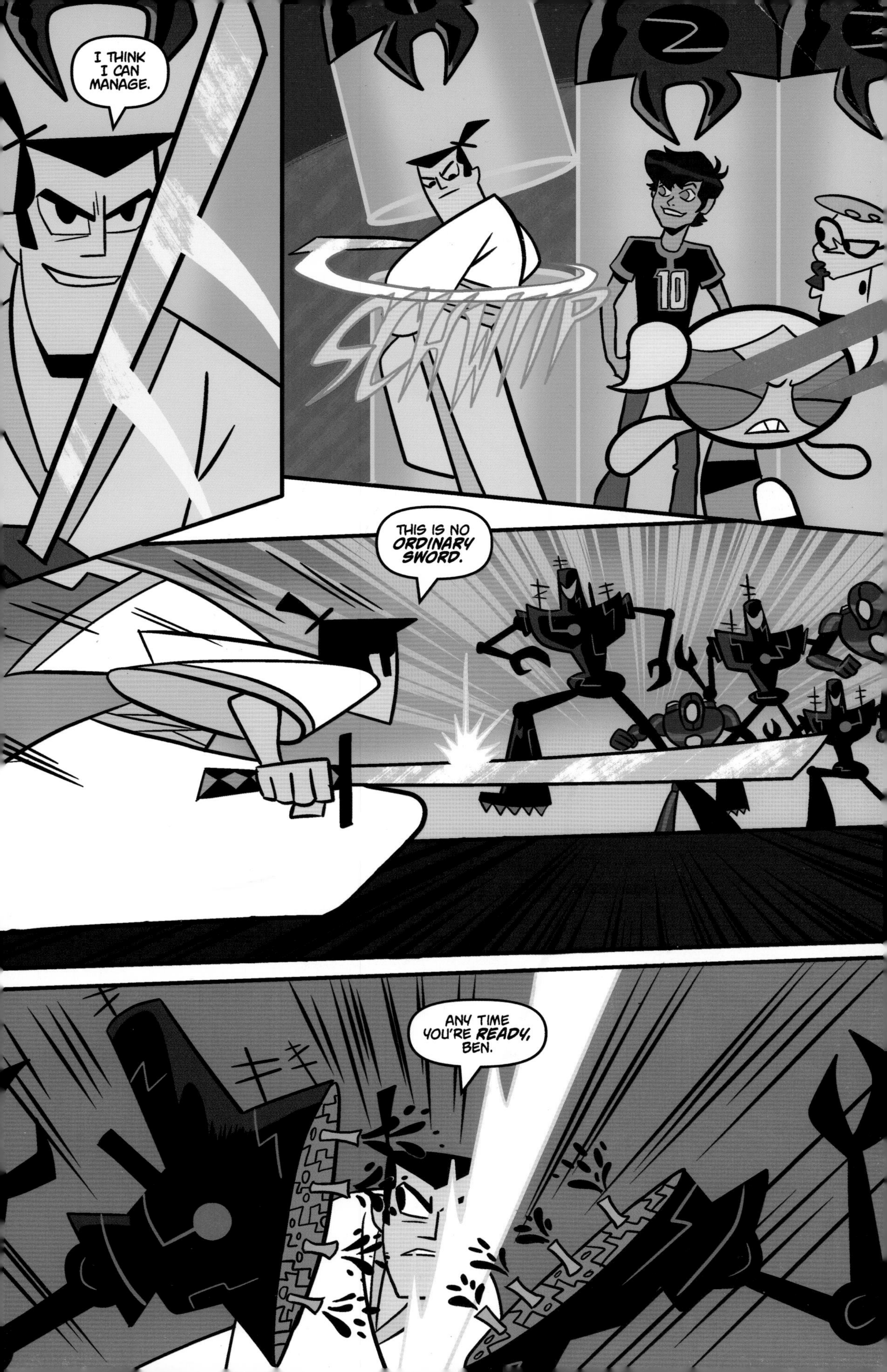
I THINK I CAN MANAGE.
SCHWIIP
10
THIS IS NO ORDINARY SWORD.
ANY TIME YOU'RE READY, BEN.

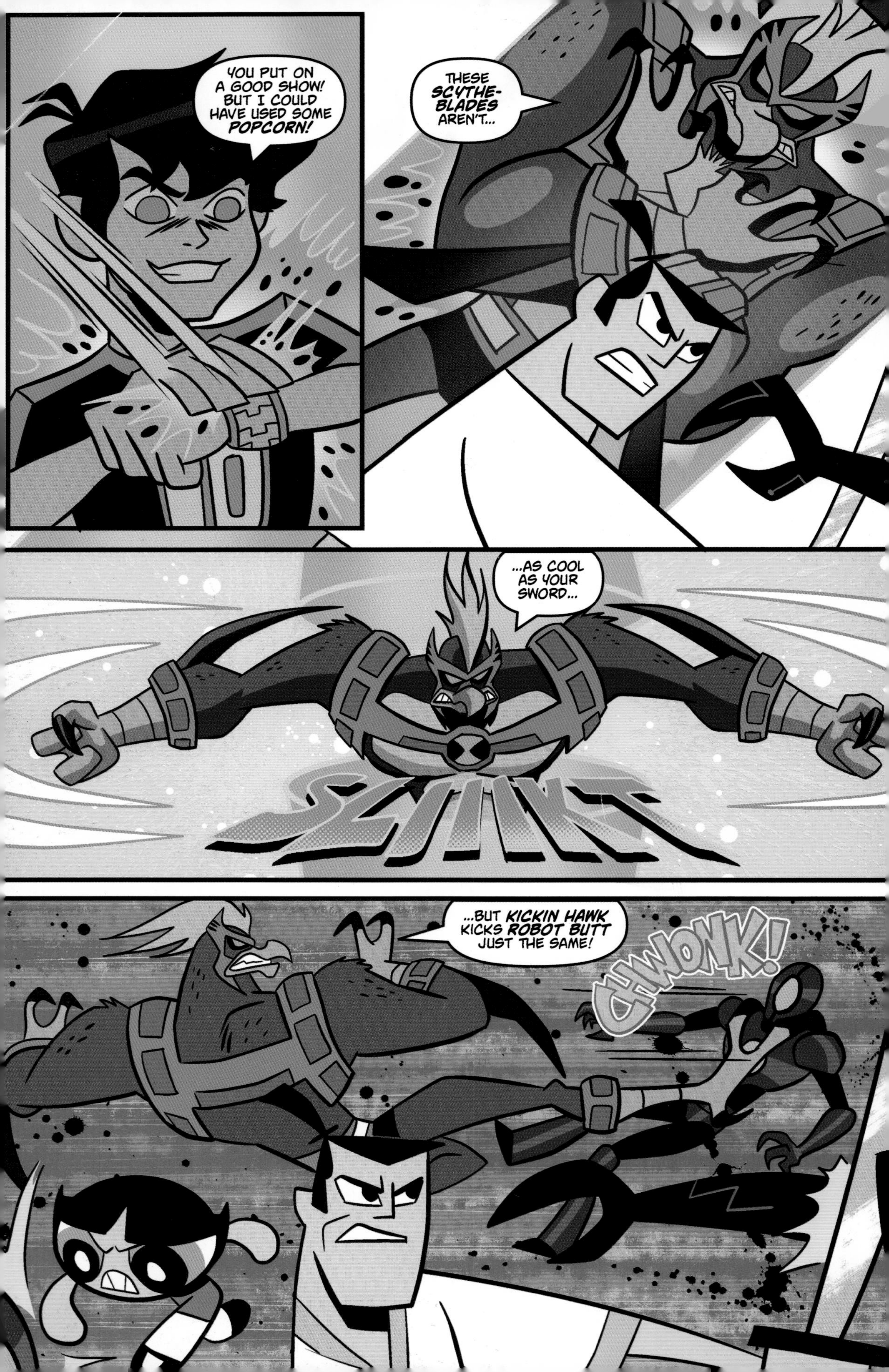
YOU PUT ON A GOOD SHOW! BUT I COULD HAVE USED SOME POPCORN!
THESE SCYTHE-BLADES AREN'T...
...AS COOL AS YOUR SWORD...
SLIIIKT
...BUT KICKIN HAWK KICKS ROBOT BUTT JUST THE SAME!
CHWONK!

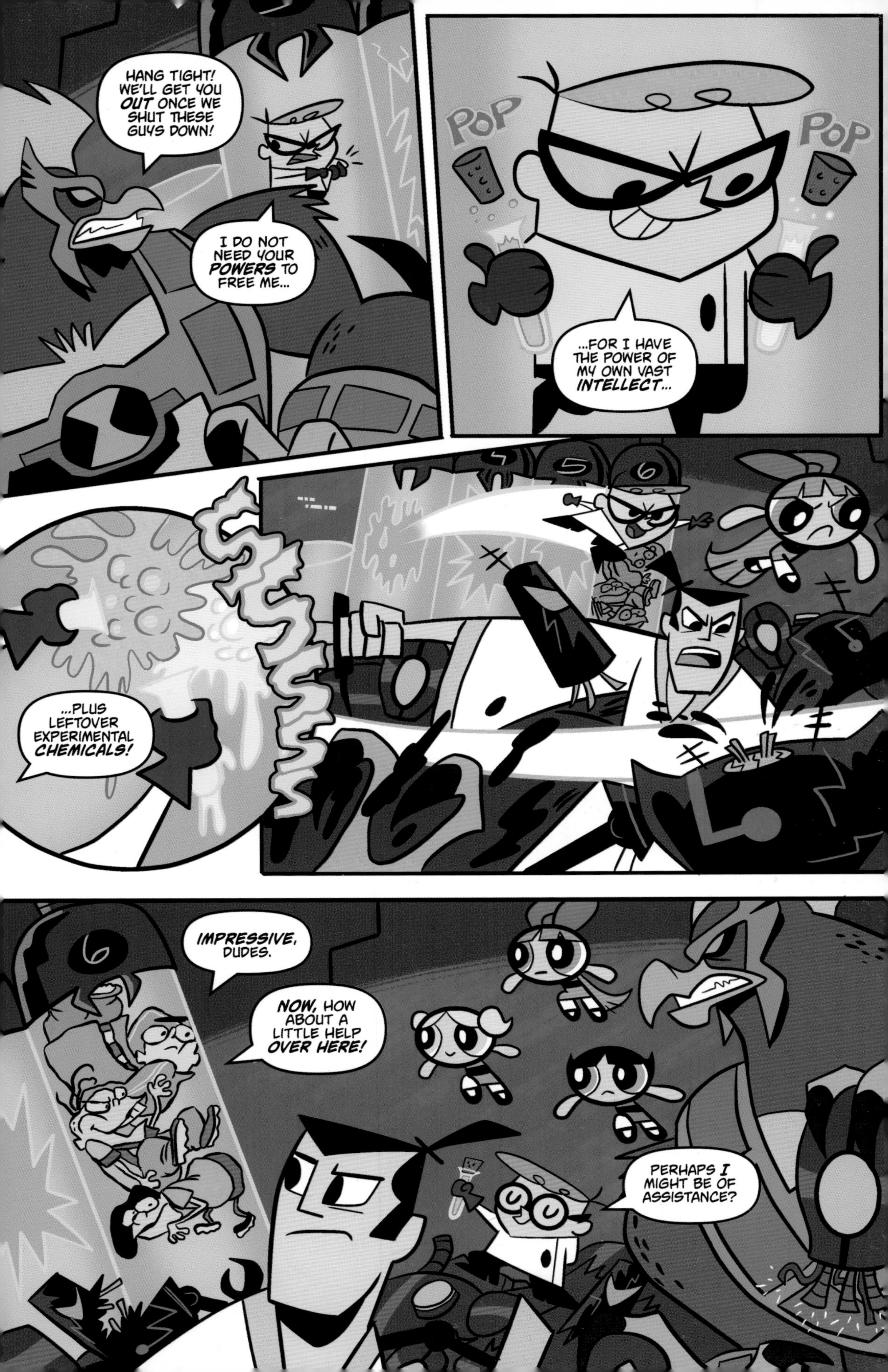
HANG TIGHT! WE'LL GET YOU OUT ONCE WE SHUT THESE GUYS DOWN!
I DO NOT NEED YOUR POWERS TO FREE ME...
POP
POP
...FOR I HAVE THE POWER OF MY OWN VAST INTELLECT...
...PLUS LEFTOVER EXPERIMENTAL CHEMICALS!
IMPRESSIVE, DUDES.
NOW, HOW ABOUT A LITTLE HELP OVER HERE!
PERHAPS I MIGHT BE OF ASSISTANCE?

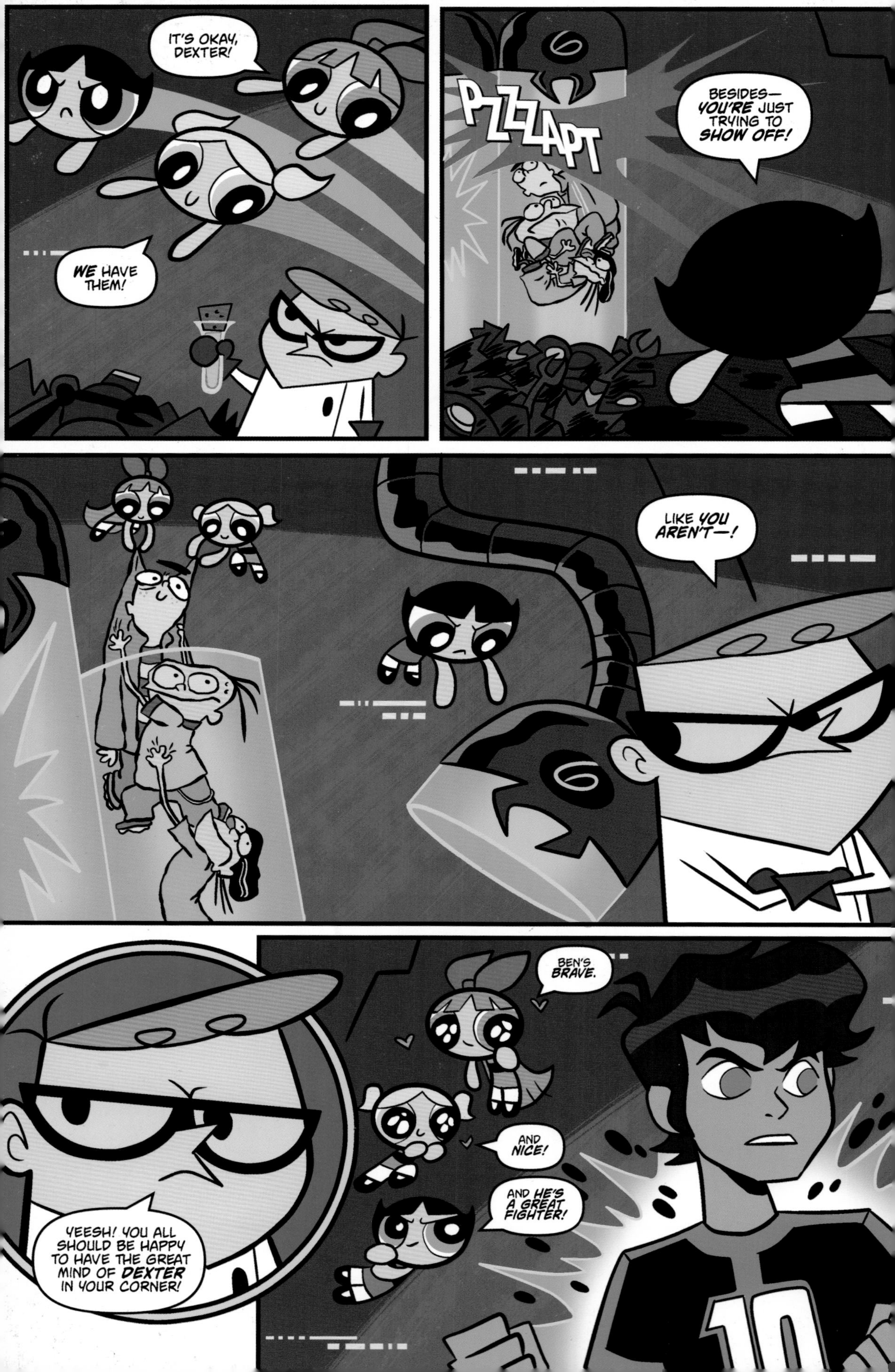
IT'S OKAY, DEXTER!
WE HAVE THEM!
PZZZAPT
BESIDES— YOU'RE JUST TRYING TO SHOW OFF!
LIKE YOU AREN'T—!
BEN'S BRAVE.
AND NICE!
AND HE'S A GREAT FIGHTER!
YEESH! YOU ALL SHOULD BE HAPPY TO HAVE THE GREAT MIND OF DEXTER IN YOUR CORNER!
10

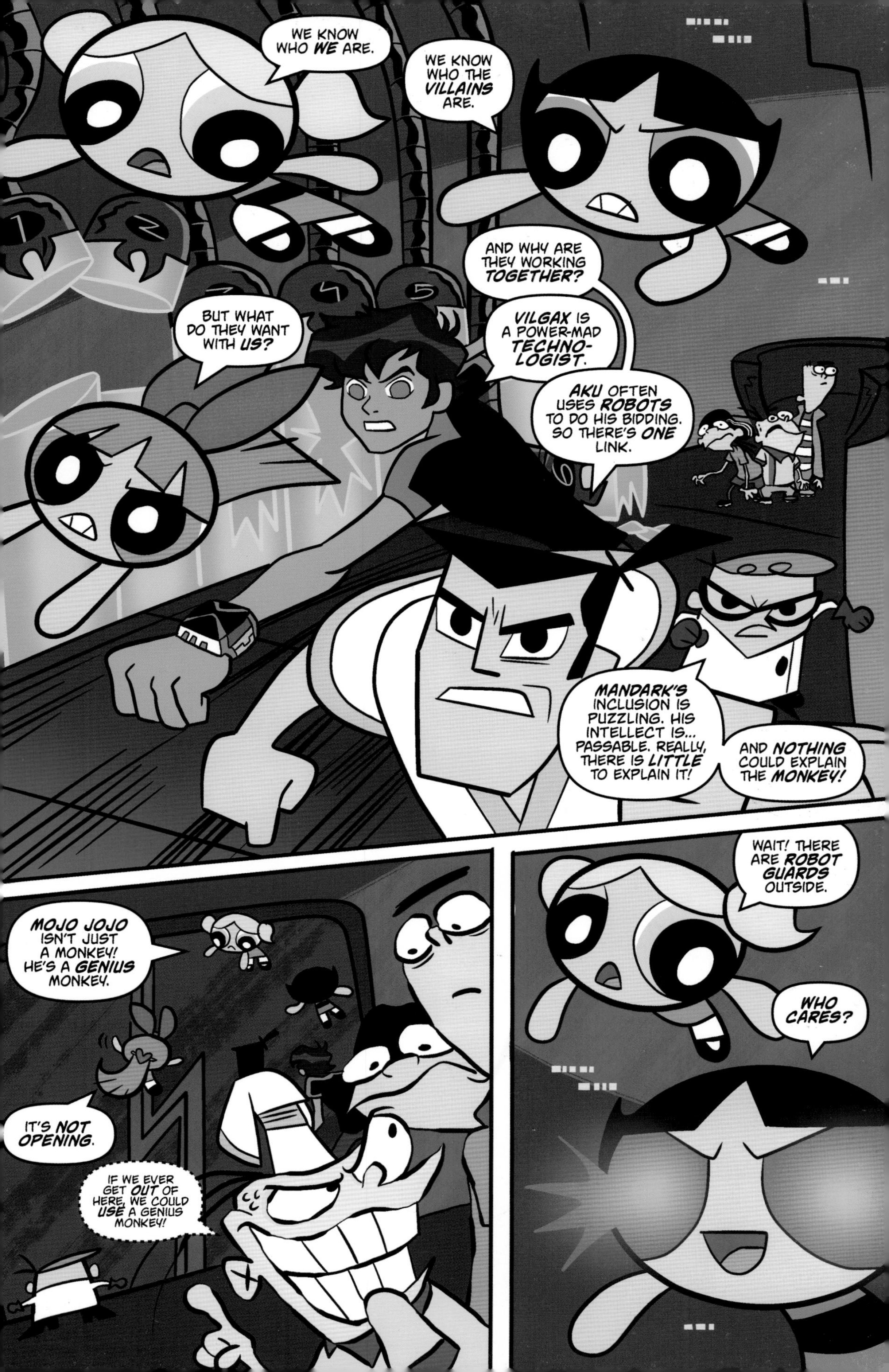
WE KNOW WHO WE ARE.
WE KNOW WHO THE VILLAINS ARE.
AND WHY ARE THEY WORKING TOGETHER?
BUT WHAT DO THEY WANT WITH US?
VILGAX IS A POWER-MAD TECHNO-LOGIST.
AKU OFTEN USES ROBOTS TO DO HIS BIDDING. SO THERE'S ONE LINK.
MANDARK'S INCLUSION IS PUZZLING. HIS INTELLECT IS... PASSABLE. REALLY, THERE IS LITTLE TO EXPLAIN IT!
AND NOTHING COULD EXPLAIN THE MONKEY!
MOJO JOJO ISN'T JUST A MONKEY! HE'S A GENIUS MONKEY.
IT'S NOT OPENING.
IF WE EVER GET OUT OF HERE, WE COULD USE A GENIUS MONKEY!
WAIT! THERE ARE ROBOT GUARDS OUTSIDE.
WHO CARES?

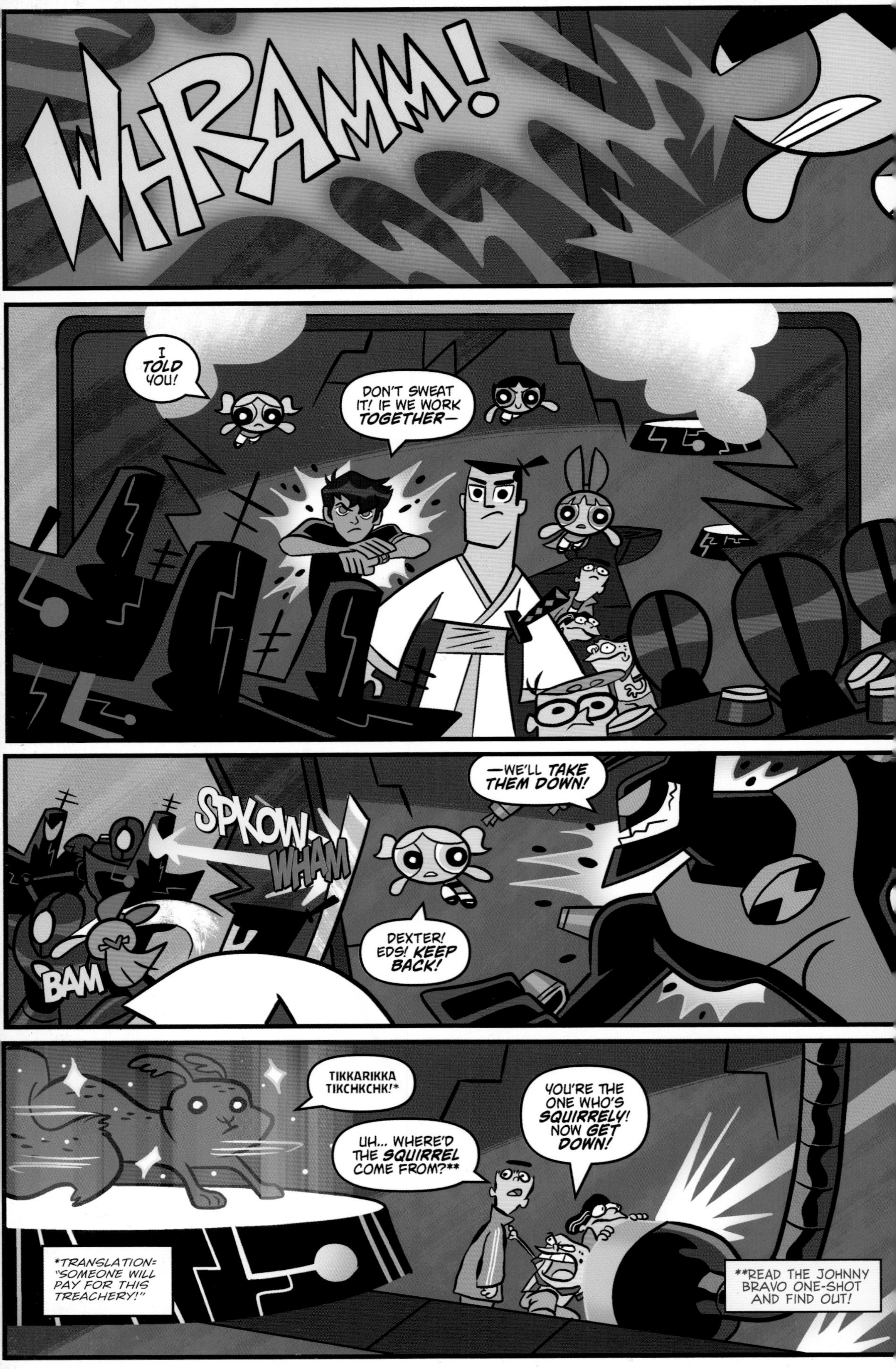
WHRAMM!
I TOLD YOU!
DON'T SWEAT IT! IF WE WORK TOGETHER—
SPKOW
WHAM
—WE'LL TAKE THEM DOWN!
BAM
DEXTER! EDS! KEEP BACK!
TIKKARIKKA TIKCHKCHK!*
UH... WHERE'D THE SQUIRREL COME FROM?**
YOU'RE THE ONE WHO'S SQUIRRELY! NOW GET DOWN!
*TRANSLATION= "SOMEONE WILL PAY FOR THIS TREACHERY!"
**READ THE JOHNNY BRAVO ONE-SHOT AND FIND OUT!

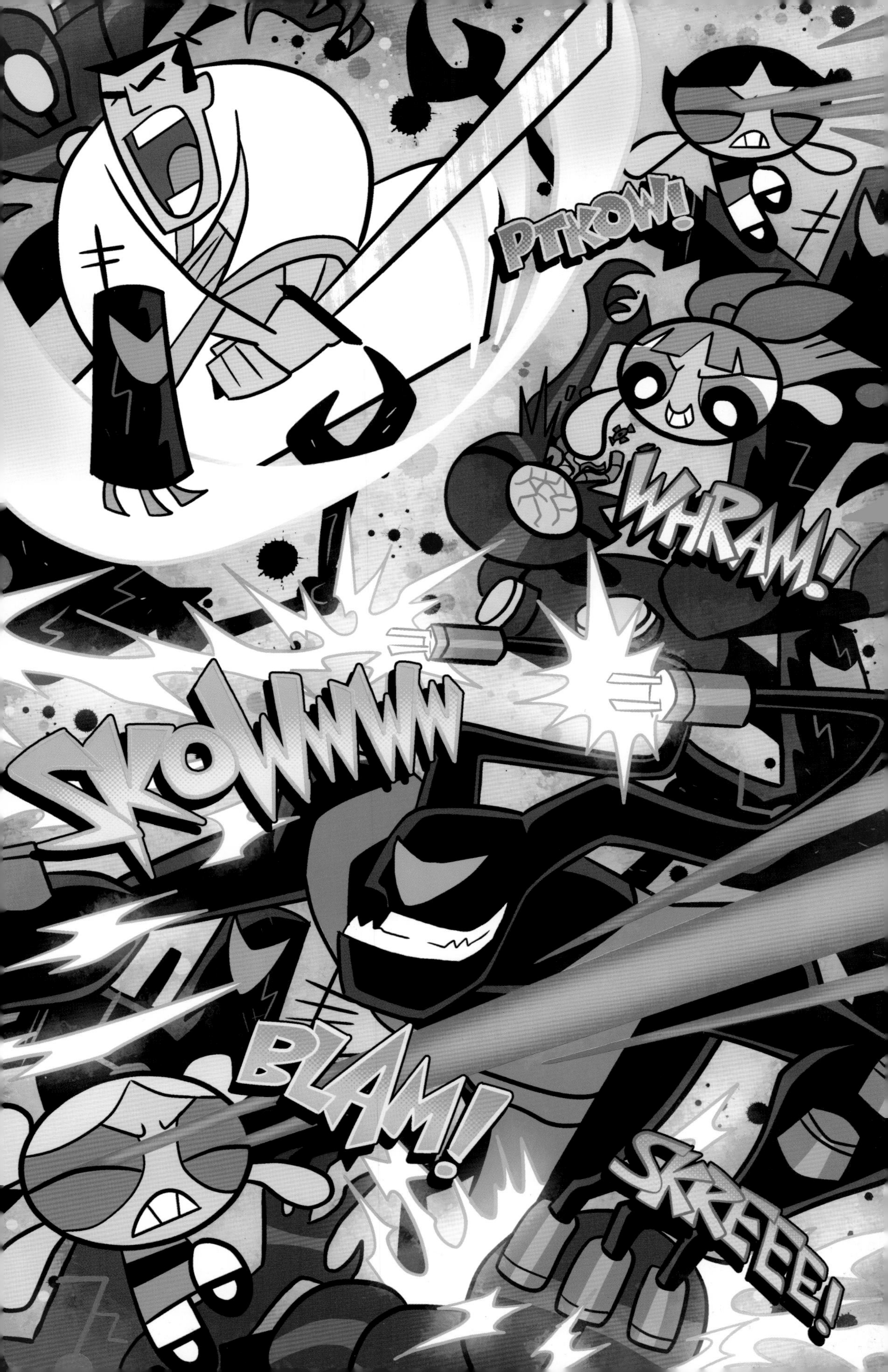
PTKOW!
WHRAM!
SKOWWWW
BLAM!
SKREEE!!

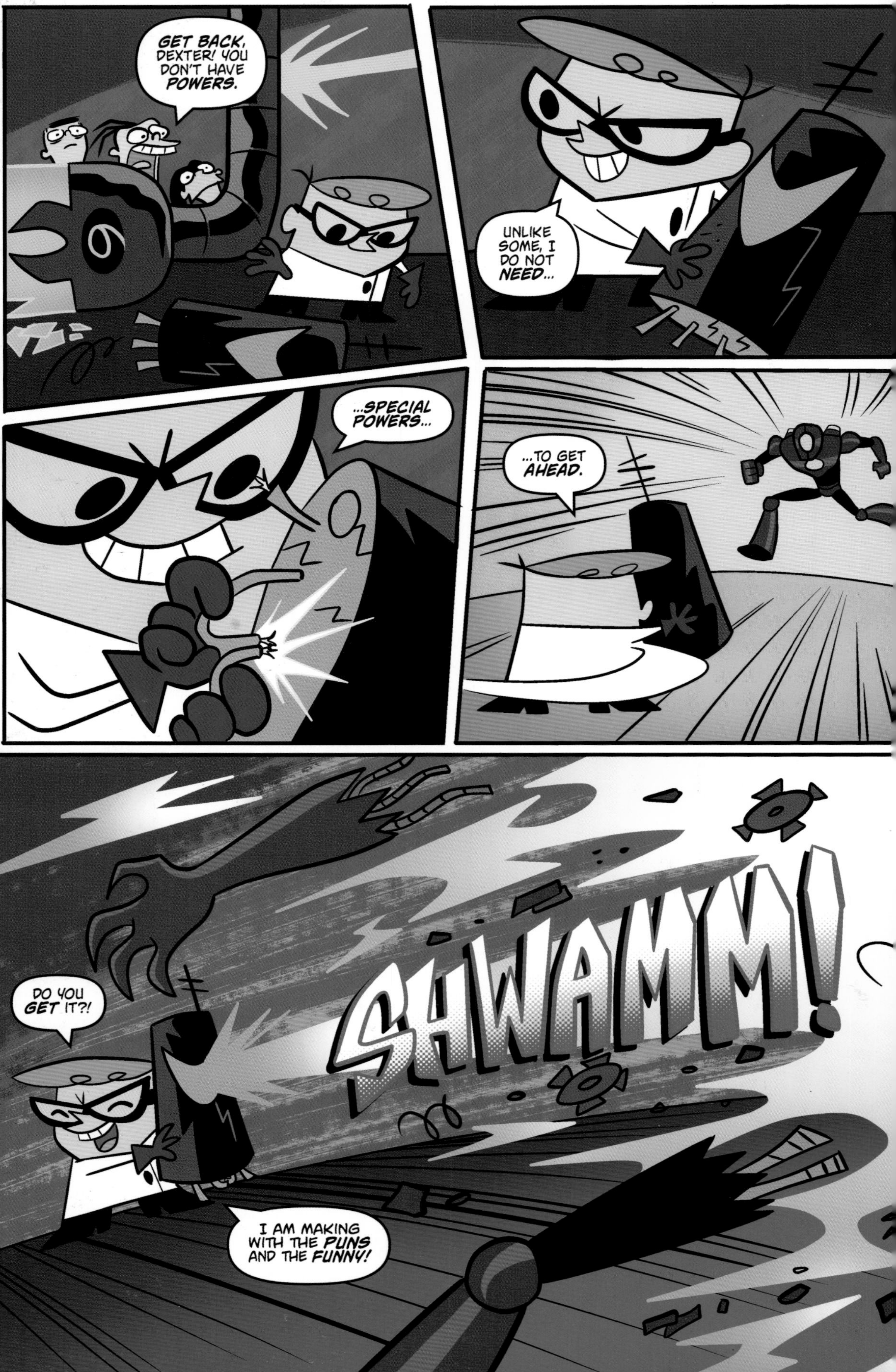

GET BACK, DEXTER! YOU DON'T HAVE POWERS.
UNLIKE SOME, I DO NOT NEED...
...SPECIAL POWERS...
...TO GET AHEAD.
SHWAMM!
DO YOU GET IT?!
I AM MAKING WITH THE PUNS AND THE FUNNY!

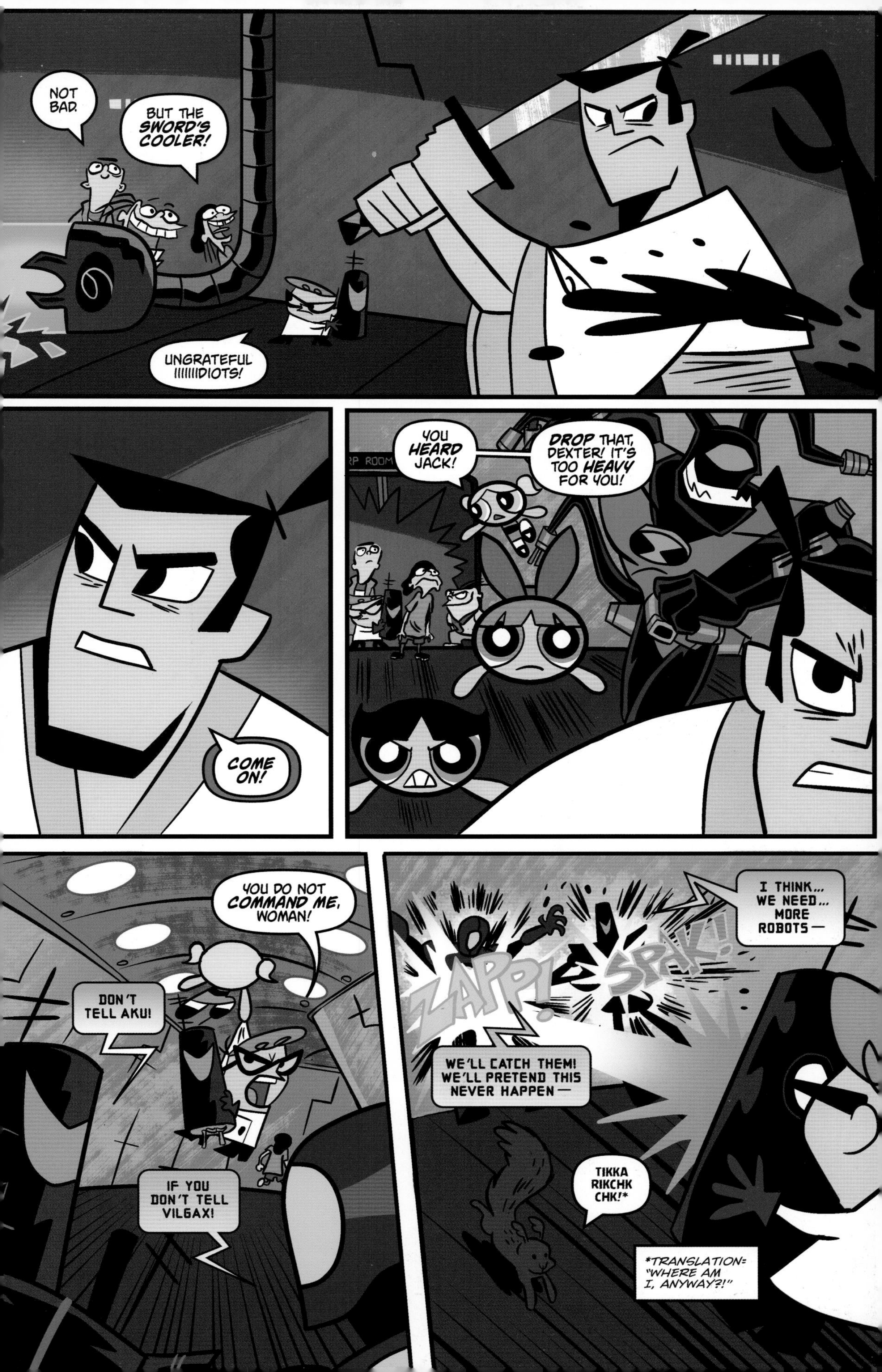
NOT BAD.
BUT THE SWORD'S COOLER!
UNGRATEFUL IIIIIIIDIOTS!
COME ON!
YOU HEARD JACK!
DROP THAT, DEXTER! IT'S TOO HEAVY FOR YOU!
YOU DO NOT COMMAND ME, WOMAN!
DON'T TELL AKU!
IF YOU DON'T TELL VILGAX!
ZAPP!
SPAK!
I THINK... WE NEED... MORE ROBOTS —
WE'LL CATCH THEM! WE'LL PRETEND THIS NEVER HAPPEN —
TIKKA RIKCHK CHK!*
*TRANSLATION= "WHERE AM I, ANYWAY?!"

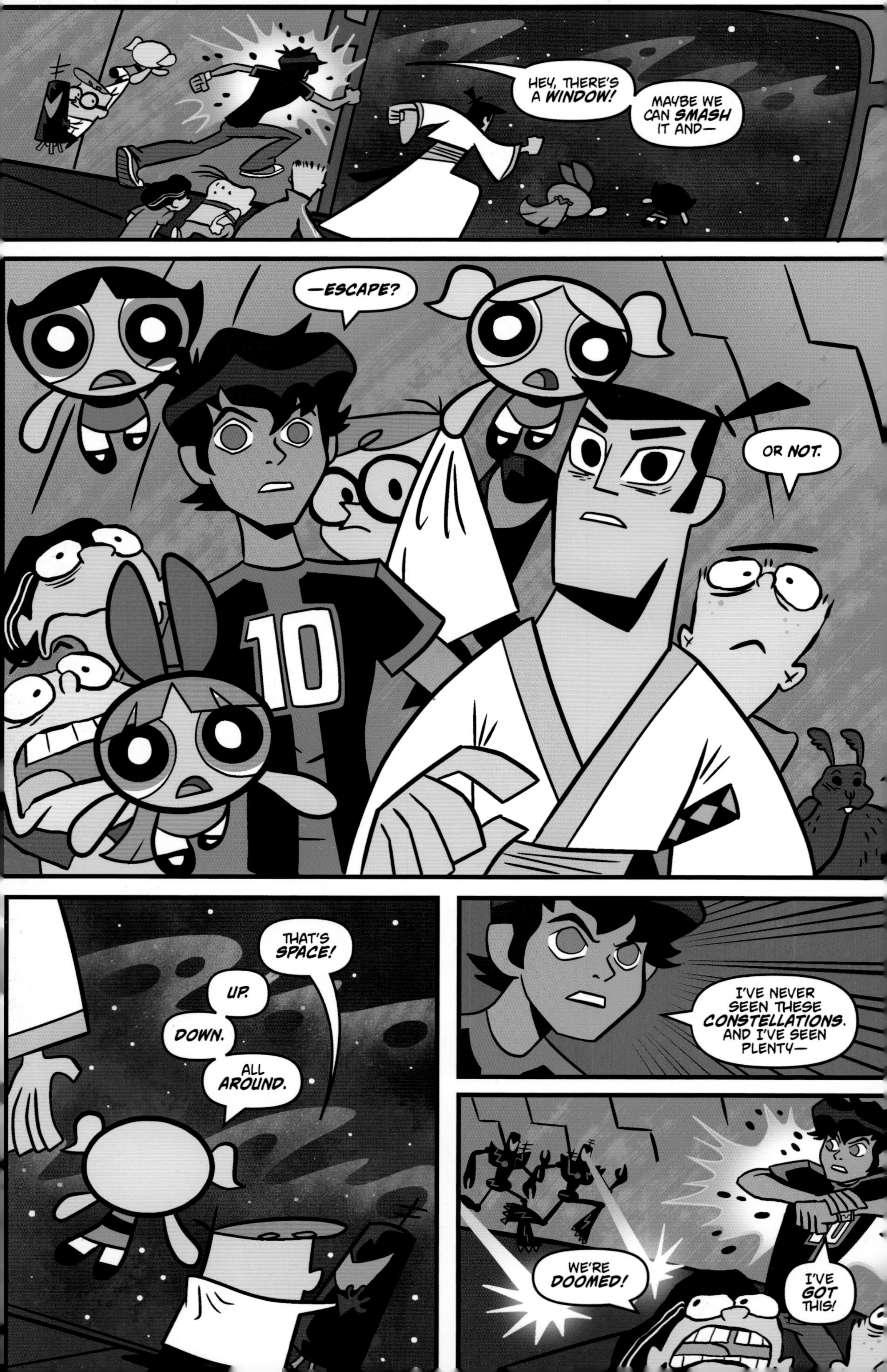
HEY, THERE'S A WINDOW!
MAYBE WE CAN SMASH IT AND—
—ESCAPE?
OR NOT.
THAT'S SPACE!
UP.
DOWN.
ALL AROUND.
I'VE NEVER SEEN THESE CONSTELLATIONS. AND I'VE SEEN PLENTY—
WE'RE DOOMED!
I'VE GOT THIS!

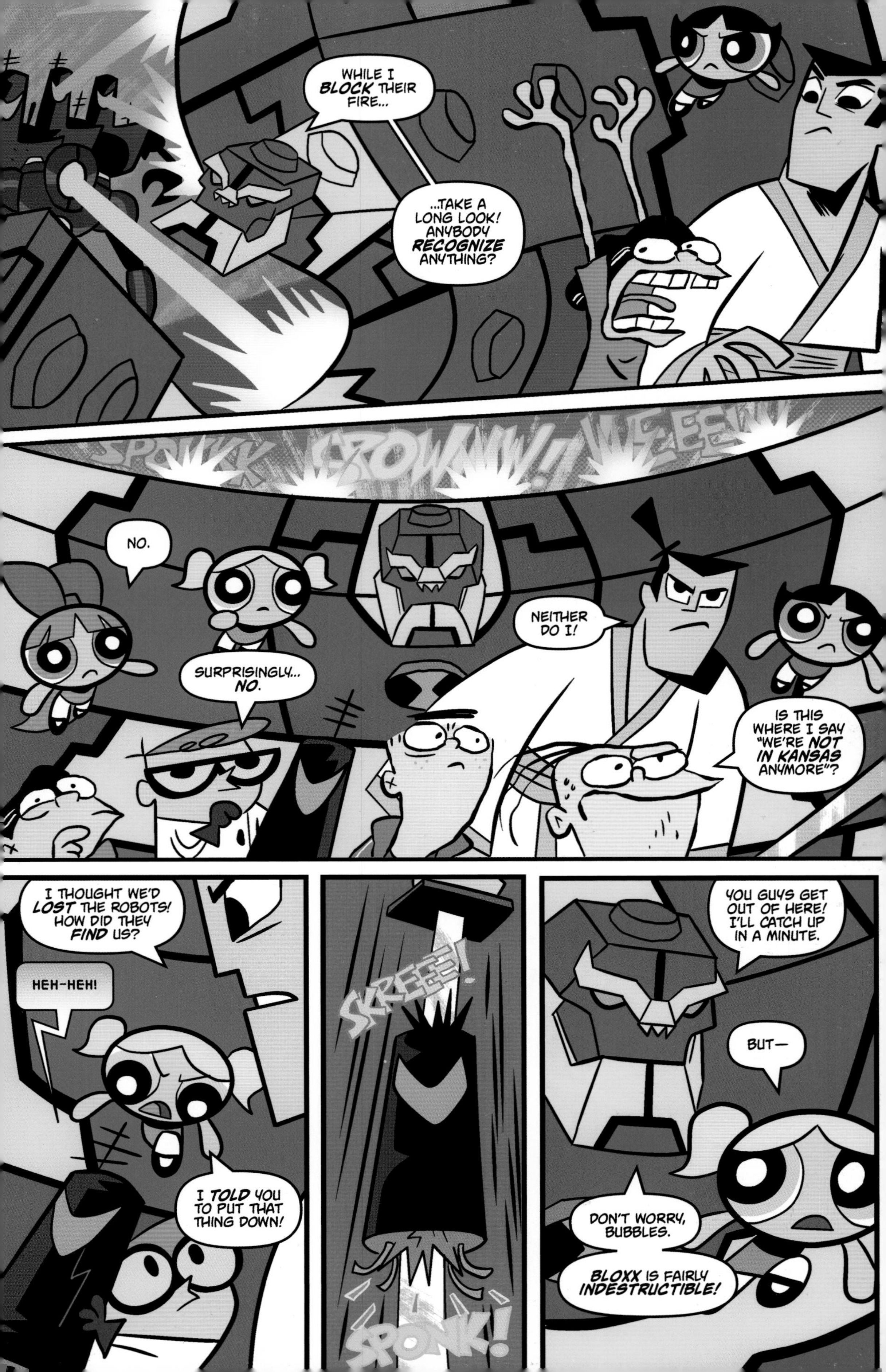
WHILE I BLOCK THEIR FIRE...
...TAKE A LONG LOOK! ANYBODY RECOGNIZE ANYTHING?
SPONKK
CROWWW!
WZEEW
NO.
SURPRISINGLY... NO.
NEITHER DO I!
IS THIS WHERE I SAY "WE'RE NOT IN KANSAS ANYMORE"?
I THOUGHT WE'D LOST THE ROBOTS! HOW DID THEY FIND US?
HEH-HEH!
I TOLD YOU TO PUT THAT THING DOWN!
SKREEE!
SPONK!
YOU GUYS GET OUT OF HERE! I'LL CATCH UP IN A MINUTE.
BUT—
DON'T WORRY, BUBBLES.
BLOXX IS FAIRLY INDESTRUCTIBLE!

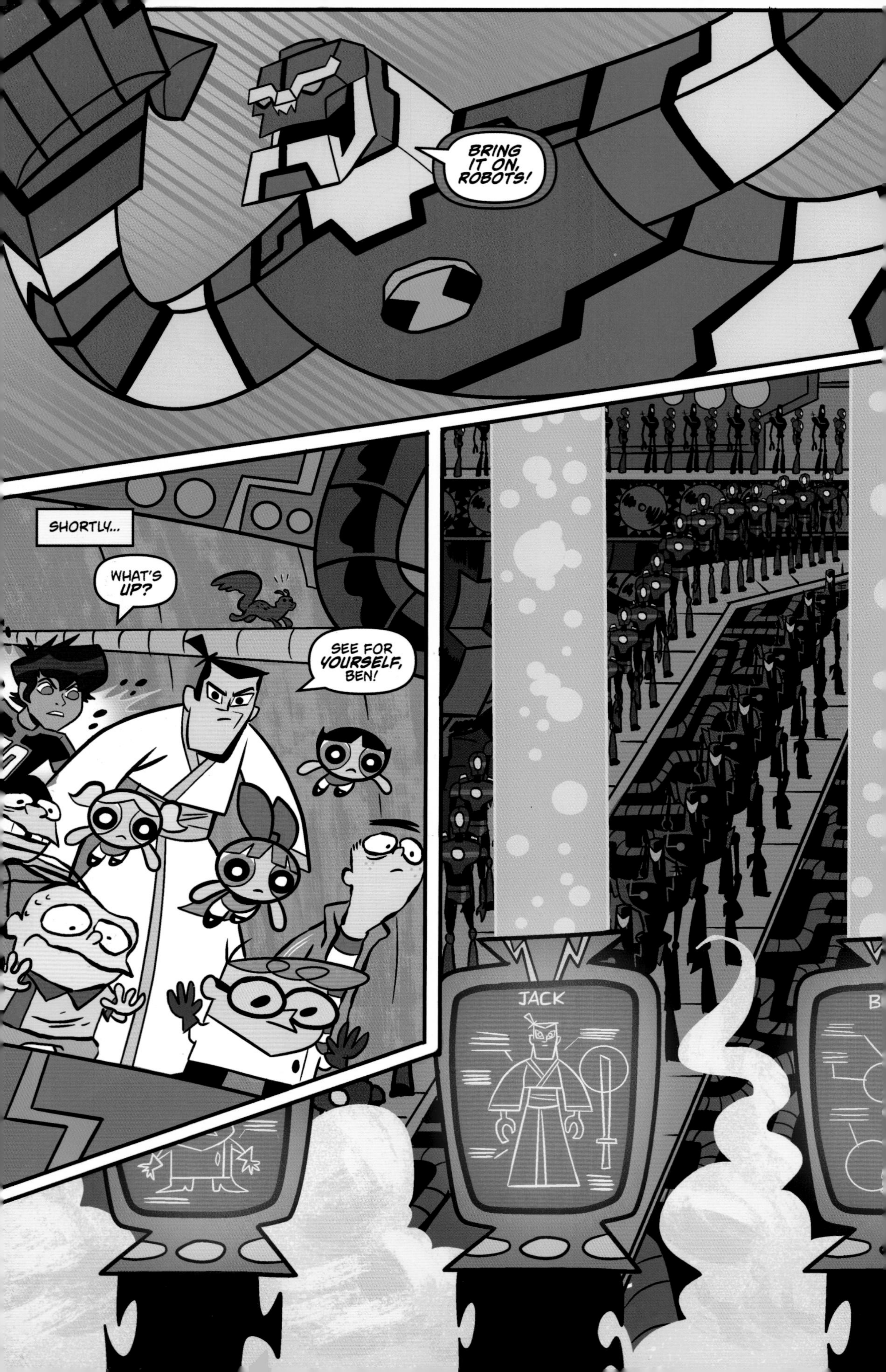
BRING IT ON, ROBOTS!
SHORTLY...
WHAT'S UP?
SEE FOR YOURSELF, BEN!
JACK
JACK

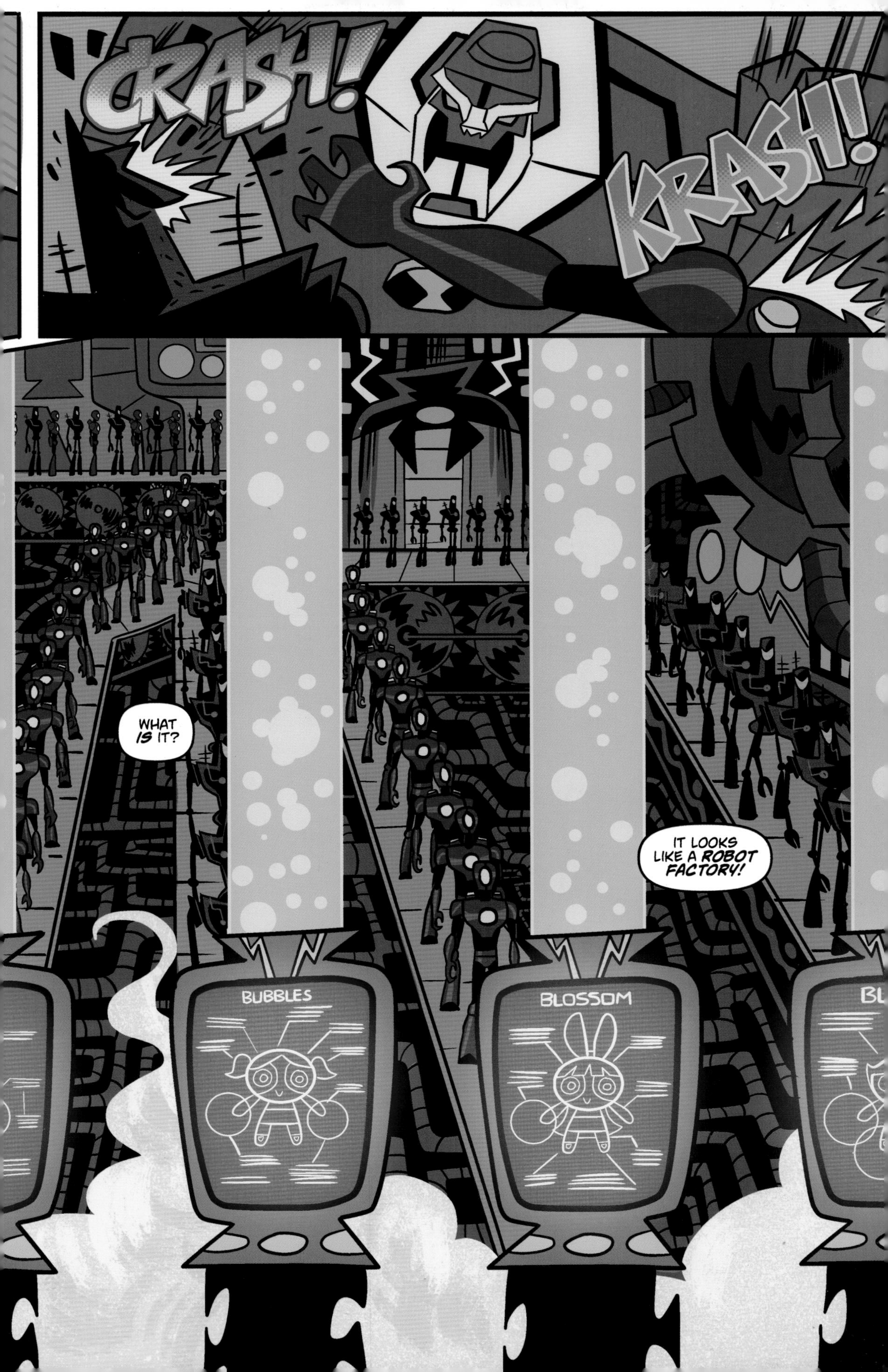
CRASH!
KRASH!
WHAT IS IT?
IT LOOKS LIKE A ROBOT FACTORY!
BUBBLES
BLOSSOM

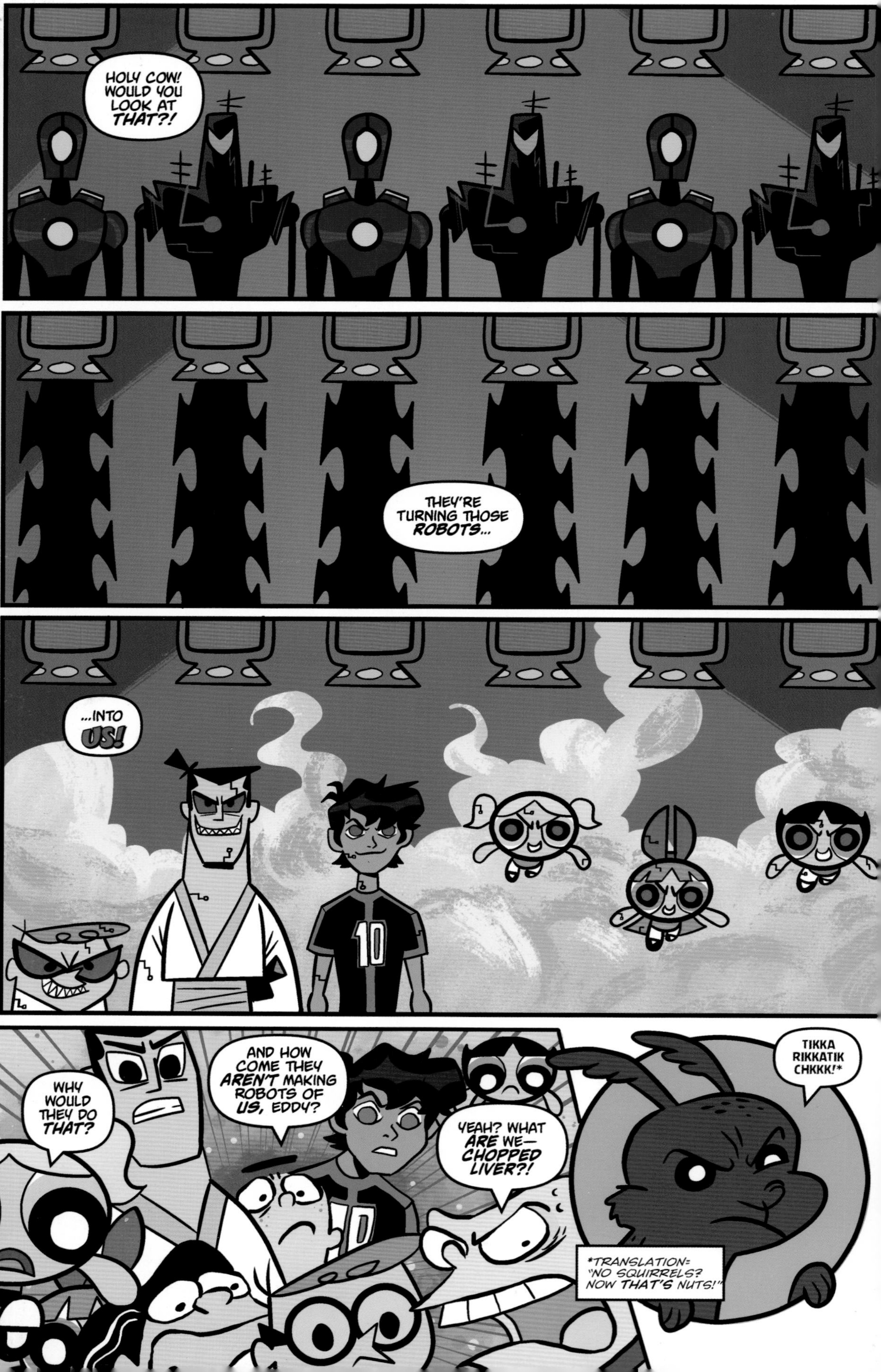
HOLY COW! WOULD YOU LOOK AT THAT?!
THEY'RE TURNING THOSE ROBOTS...
...INTO US!
WHY WOULD THEY DO THAT?
AND HOW COME THEY AREN'T MAKING ROBOTS OF US, EDDY?
YEAH? WHAT ARE WE— CHOPPED LIVER?!
TIKKA RIKKATIK CHKKK!*
*TRANSLATION: "NO SQUIRRELS? NOW THAT'S NUTS!"

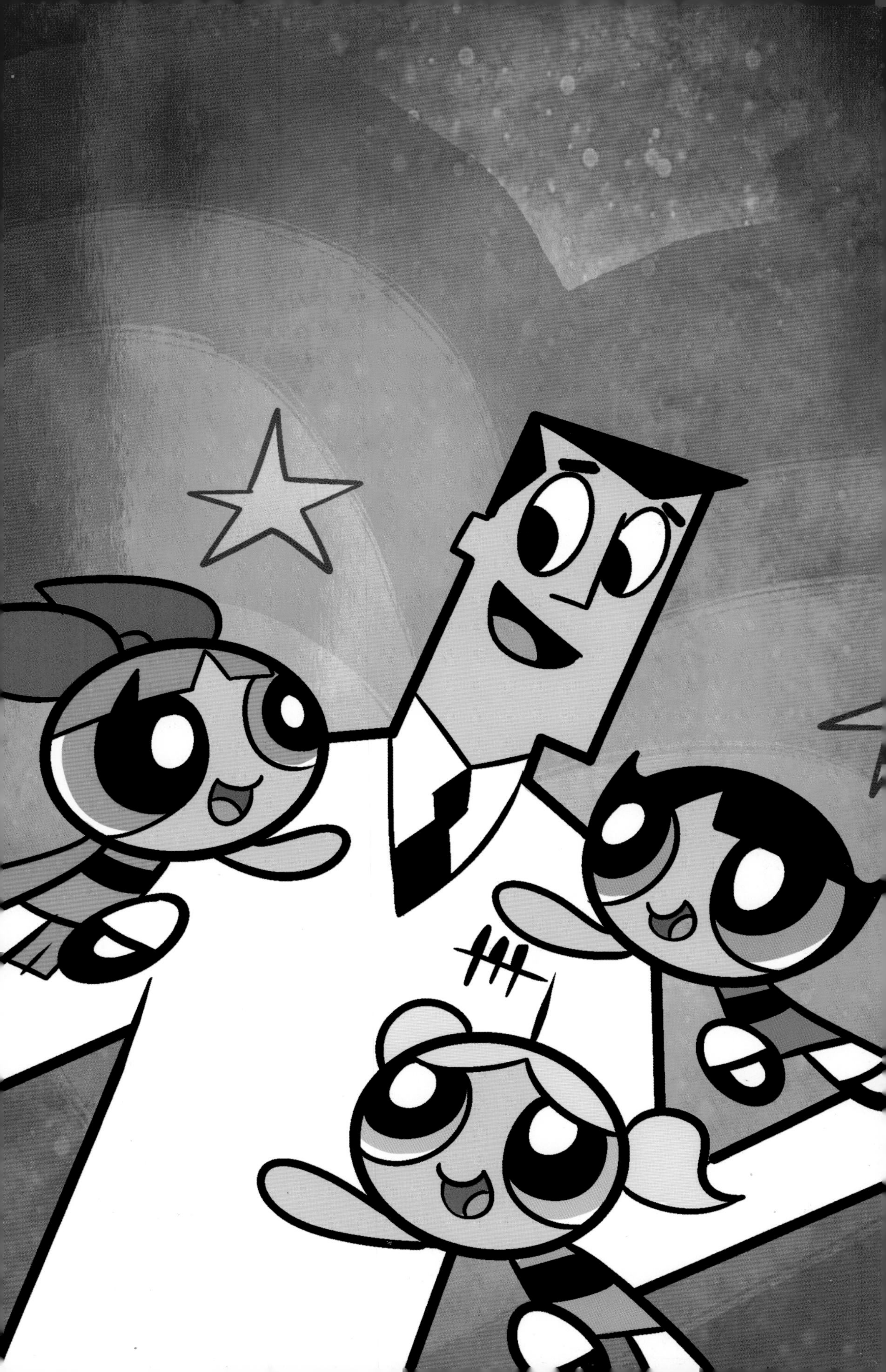

Chapter 3

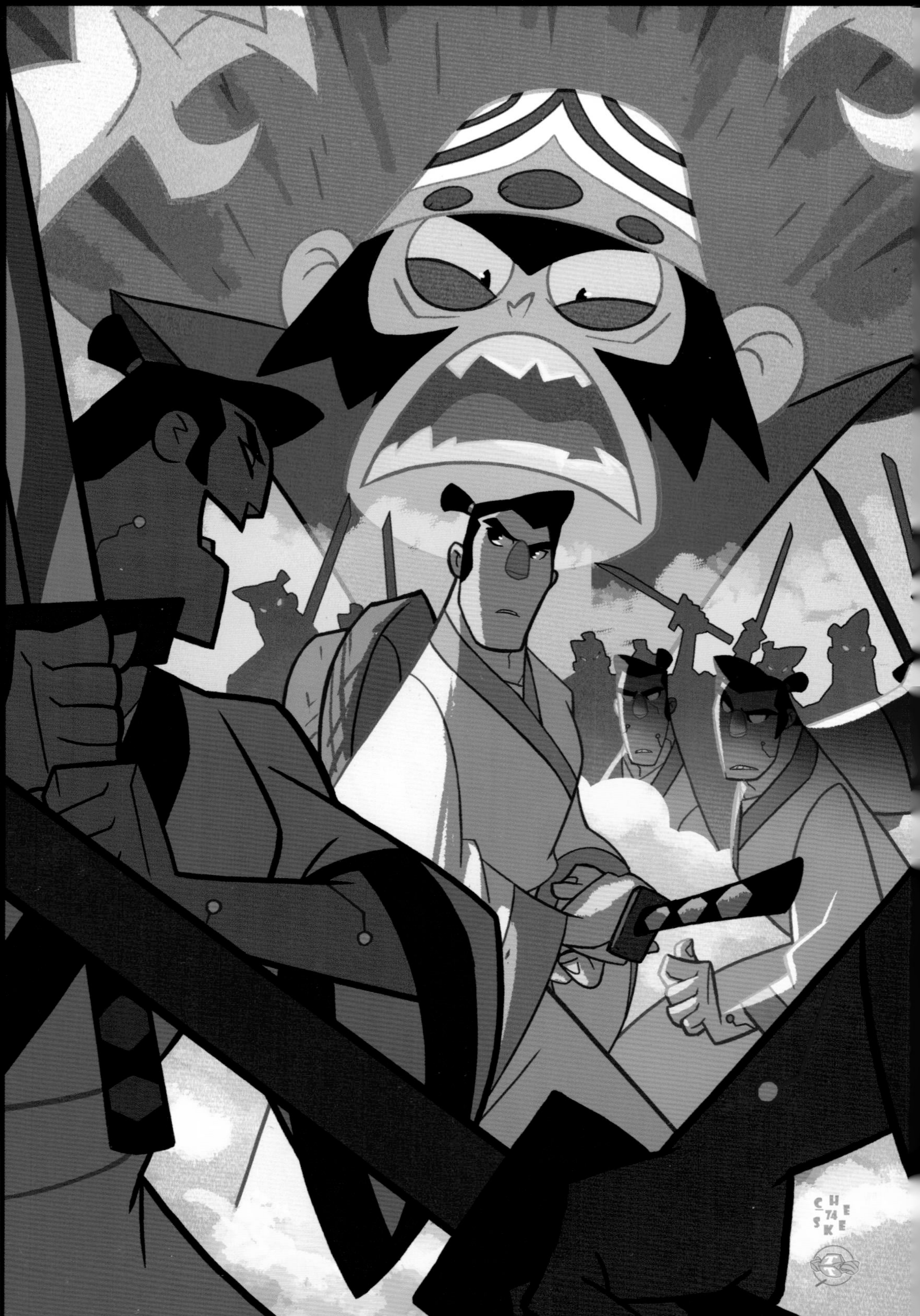
CHEESKE 74

Cover Art by Sean "Cheeks" Galloway

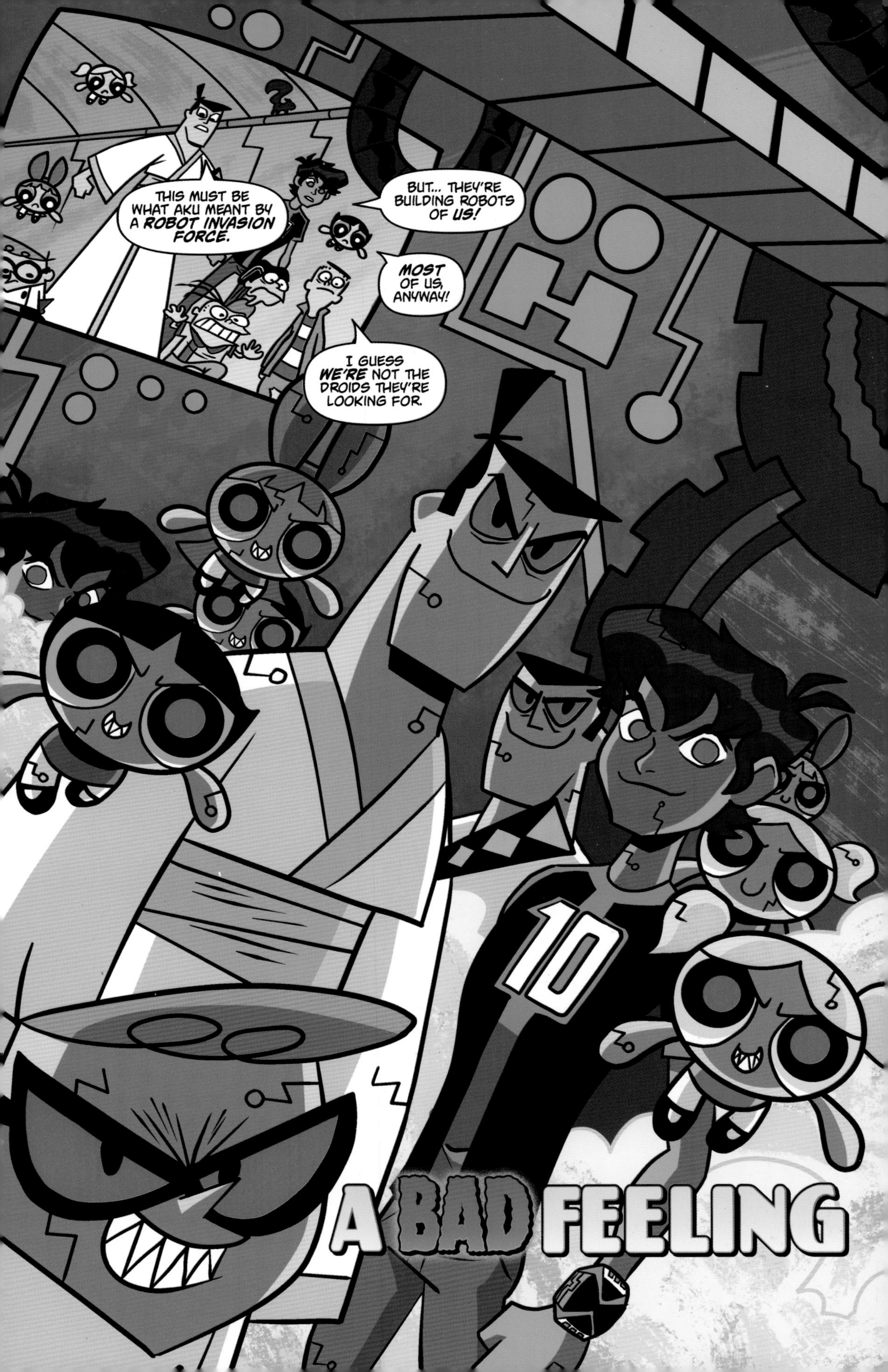
THIS MUST BE WHAT AKU MEANT BY A ROBOT INVASION FORCE.
BUT... THEY'RE BUILDING ROBOTS OF US!
MOST OF US, ANYWAY!
I GUESS WE'RE NOT THE DROIDS THEY'RE LOOKING FOR.
A BAD FEELING
10

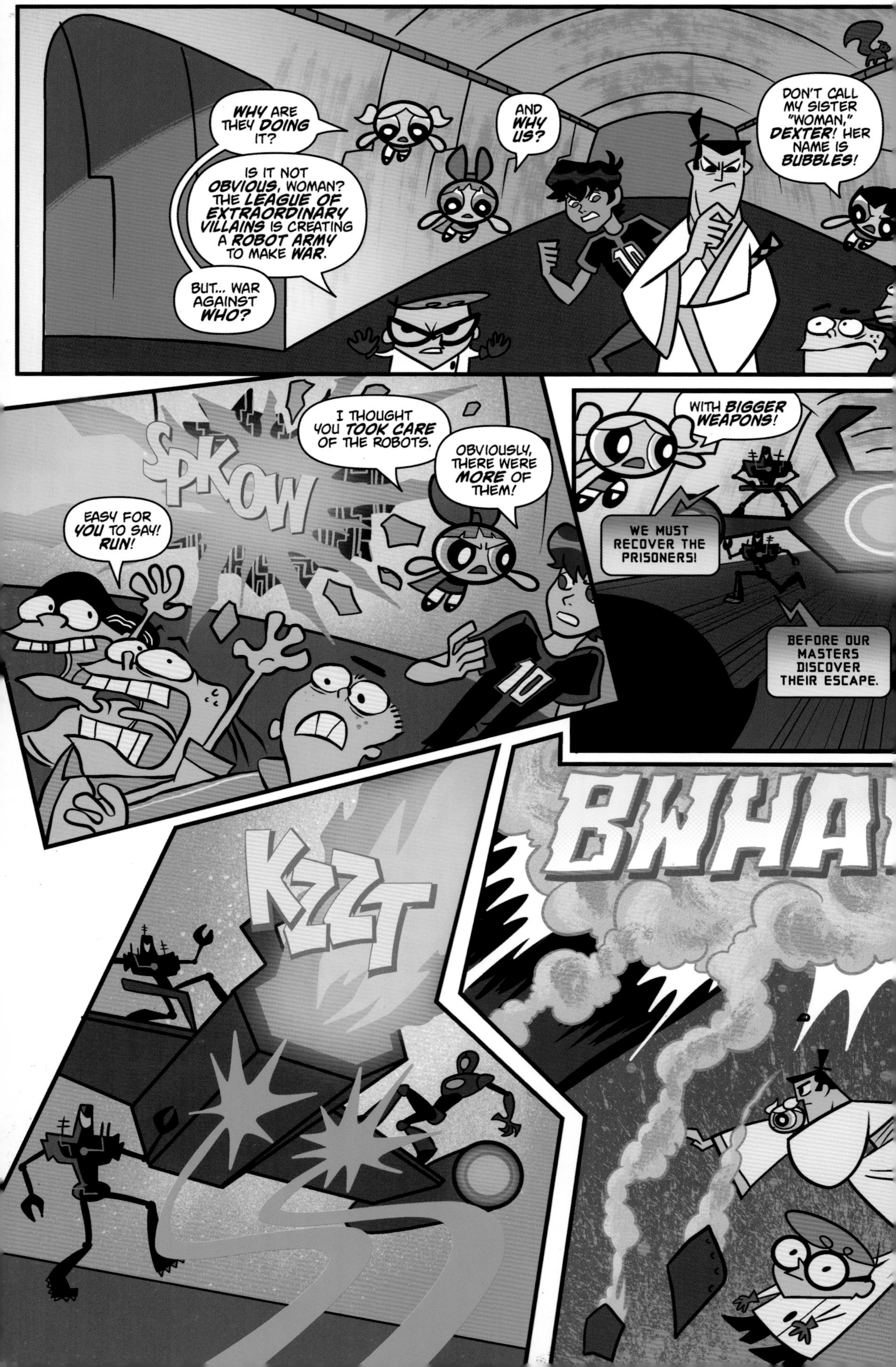

WHY ARE THEY DOING IT?
IS IT NOT OBVIOUS, WOMAN? THE LEAGUE OF EXTRAORDINARY VILLAINS IS CREATING A ROBOT ARMY TO MAKE WAR.
BUT... WAR AGAINST WHO?
AND WHY US?
DON'T CALL MY SISTER "WOMAN," DEXTER! HER NAME IS BUBBLES!
SPKOW
I THOUGHT YOU TOOK CARE OF THE ROBOTS.
OBVIOUSLY, THERE WERE MORE OF THEM!
EASY FOR YOU TO SAY! RUN!
WITH BIGGER WEAPONS!
WE MUST RECOVER THE PRISONERS!
BEFORE OUR MASTERS DISCOVER THEIR ESCAPE.
KZZT

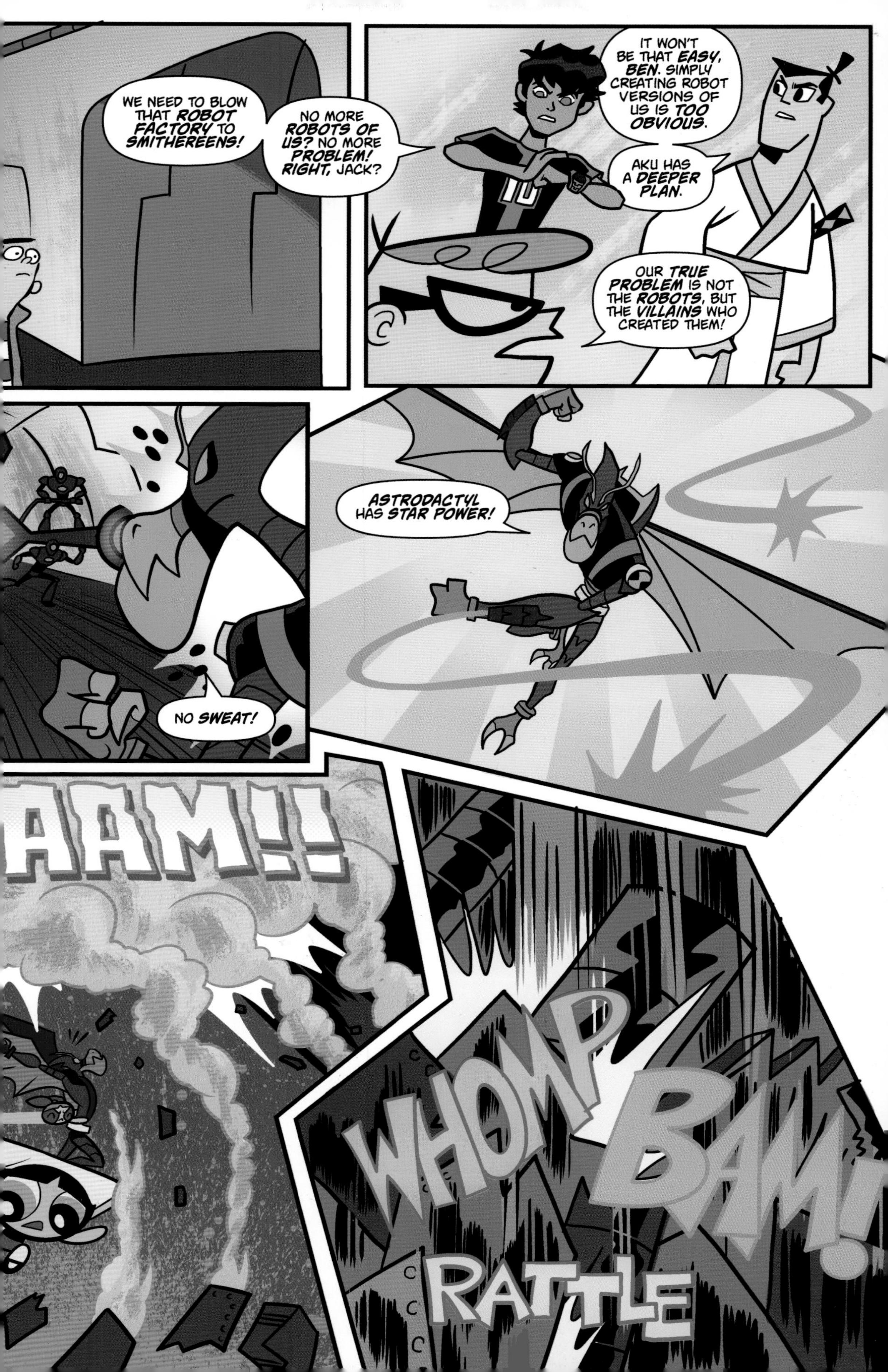
WE NEED TO BLOW THAT ROBOT FACTORY TO SMITHEREENS!
NO MORE ROBOTS OF US? NO MORE PROBLEM! RIGHT, JACK?
IT WON'T BE THAT EASY, BEN. SIMPLY CREATING ROBOT VERSIONS OF US IS TOO OBVIOUS.
AKU HAS A DEEPER PLAN.
OUR TRUE PROBLEM IS NOT THE ROBOTS, BUT THE VILLAINS WHO CREATED THEM!
NO SWEAT!
ASTRODACTYL HAS STAR POWER!
AAM!!
WHOMP
BAM!
RATTLE

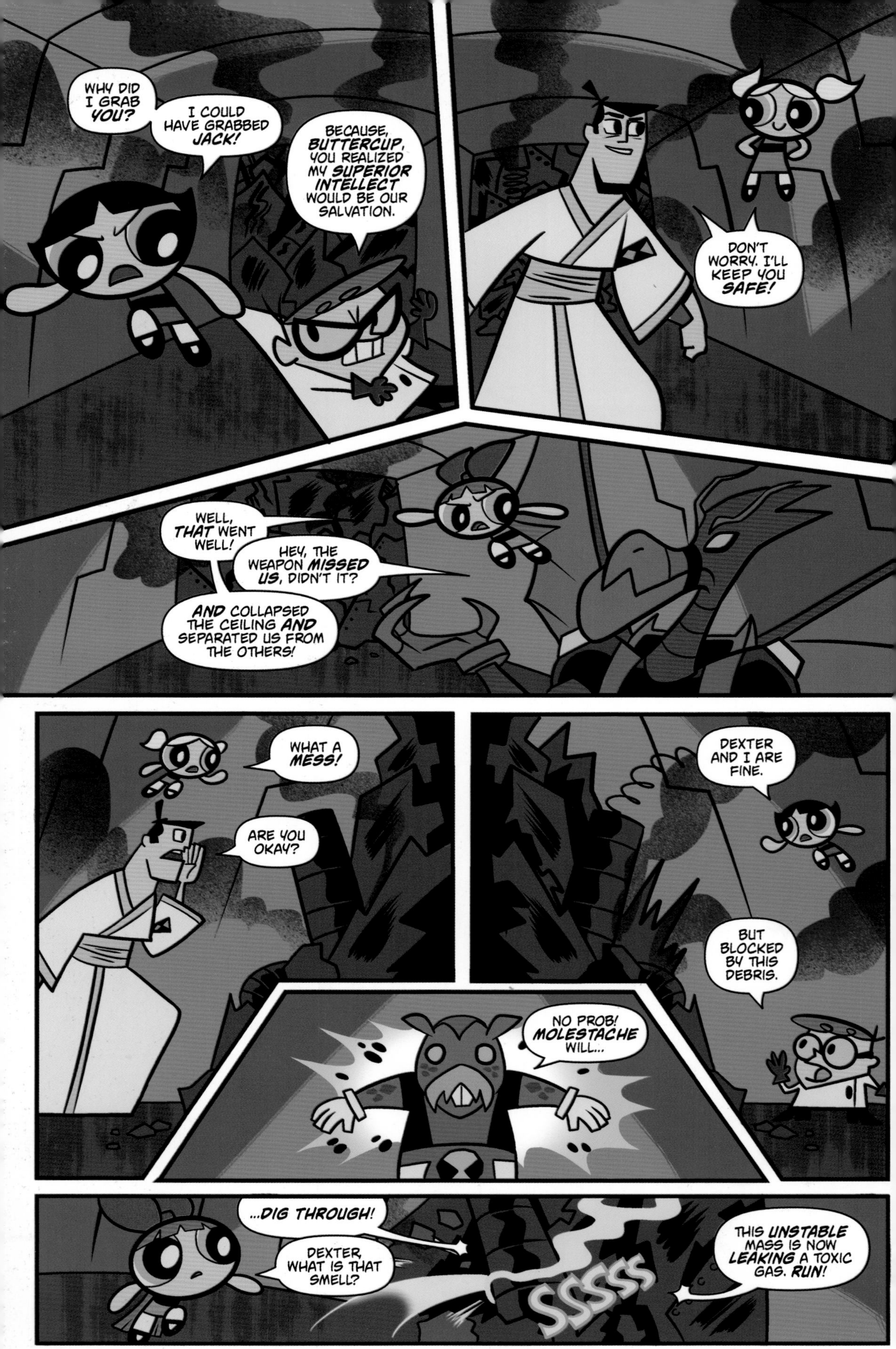
WHY DID I GRAB YOU?
I COULD HAVE GRABBED JACK!
BECAUSE, BUTTERCUP, YOU REALIZED MY SUPERIOR INTELLECT WOULD BE OUR SALVATION.
DON'T WORRY. I'LL KEEP YOU SAFE!
WELL, THAT WENT WELL!
HEY, THE WEAPON MISSED US, DIDN'T IT?
AND COLLAPSED THE CEILING AND SEPARATED US FROM THE OTHERS!
WHAT A MESS!
ARE YOU OKAY?
DEXTER AND I ARE FINE.
BUT BLOCKED BY THIS DEBRIS.
NO PROB! MOLESTACHE WILL...
...DIG THROUGH!
DEXTER, WHAT IS THAT SMELL?
SSSSS
THIS UNSTABLE MASS IS NOW LEAKING A TOXIC GAS. RUN!

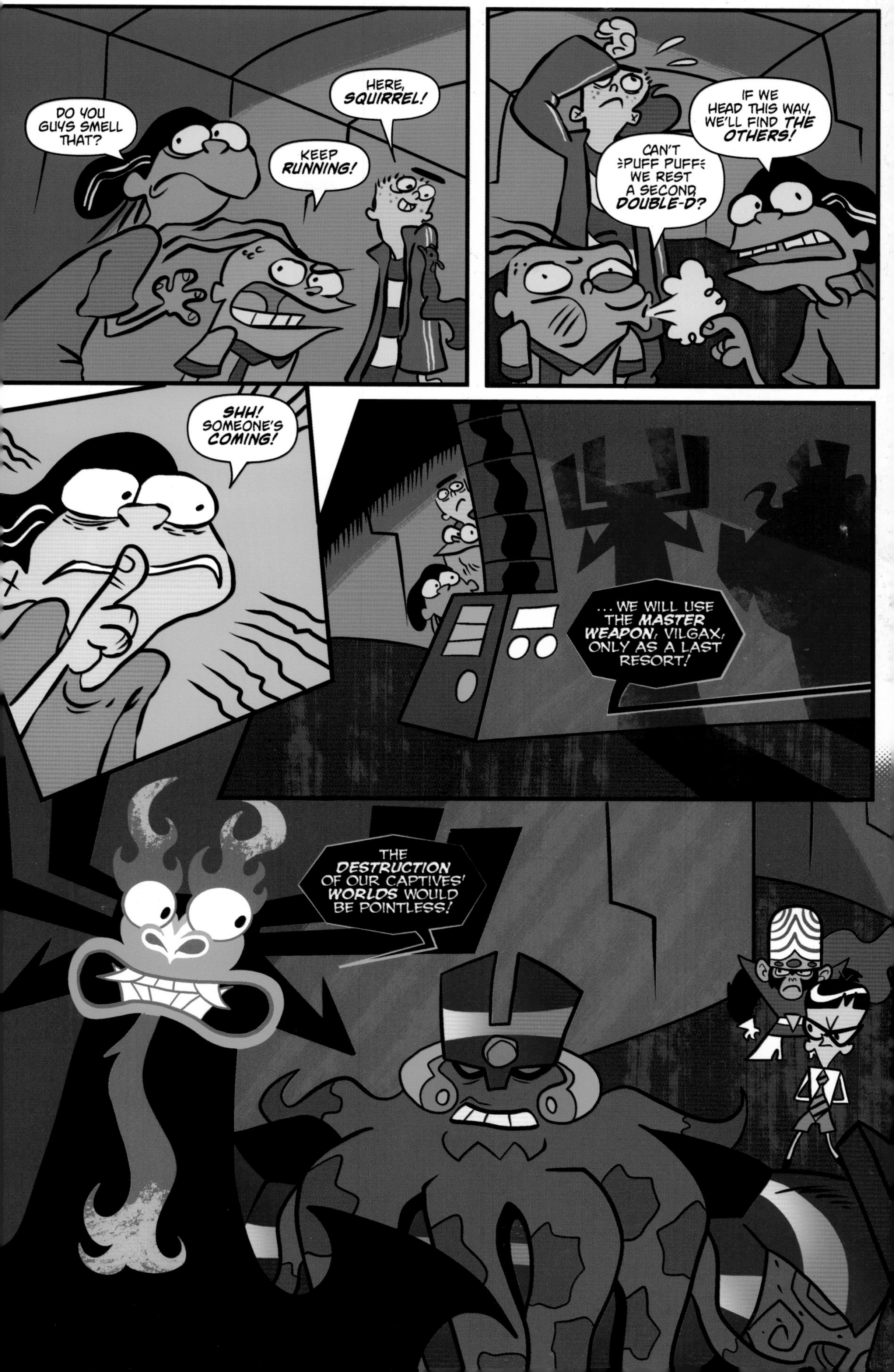
DO YOU GUYS SMELL THAT?
HERE, SQUIRREL!
KEEP RUNNING!
IF WE HEAD THIS WAY, WE'LL FIND THE OTHERS!
CAN'T *PUFF PUFF* WE REST A SECOND, DOUBLE-D?
SHH! SOMEONE'S COMING!
...WE WILL USE THE MASTER WEAPON, VILGAX, ONLY AS A LAST RESORT!
THE DESTRUCTION OF OUR CAPTIVES' WORLDS WOULD BE POINTLESS!

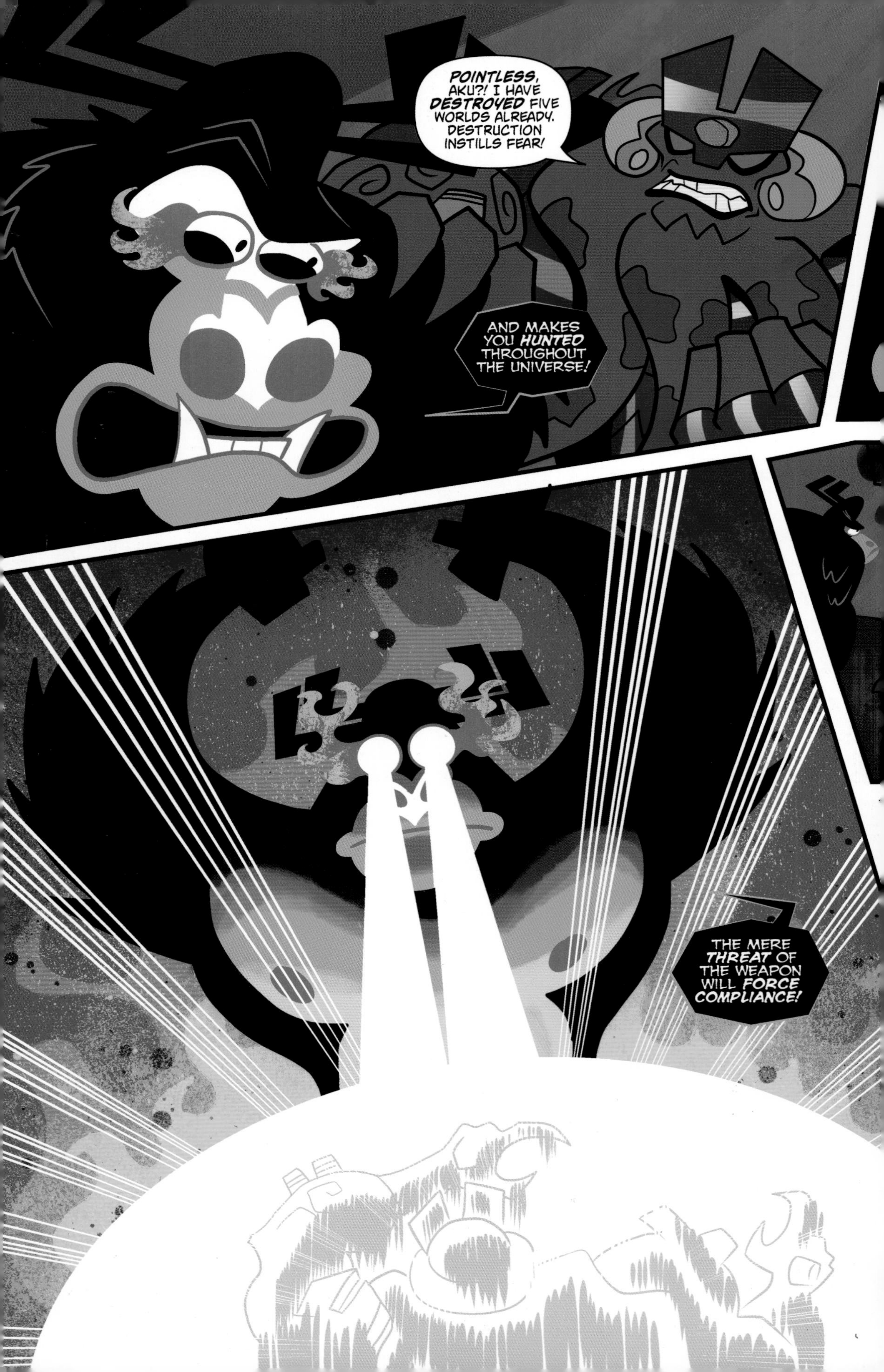
POINTLESS, AKU?! I HAVE DESTROYED FIVE WORLDS ALREADY. DESTRUCTION INSTILLS FEAR!
AND MAKES YOU HUNTED THROUGHOUT THE UNIVERSE!
THE MERE THREAT OF THE WEAPON WILL FORCE COMPLIANCE!

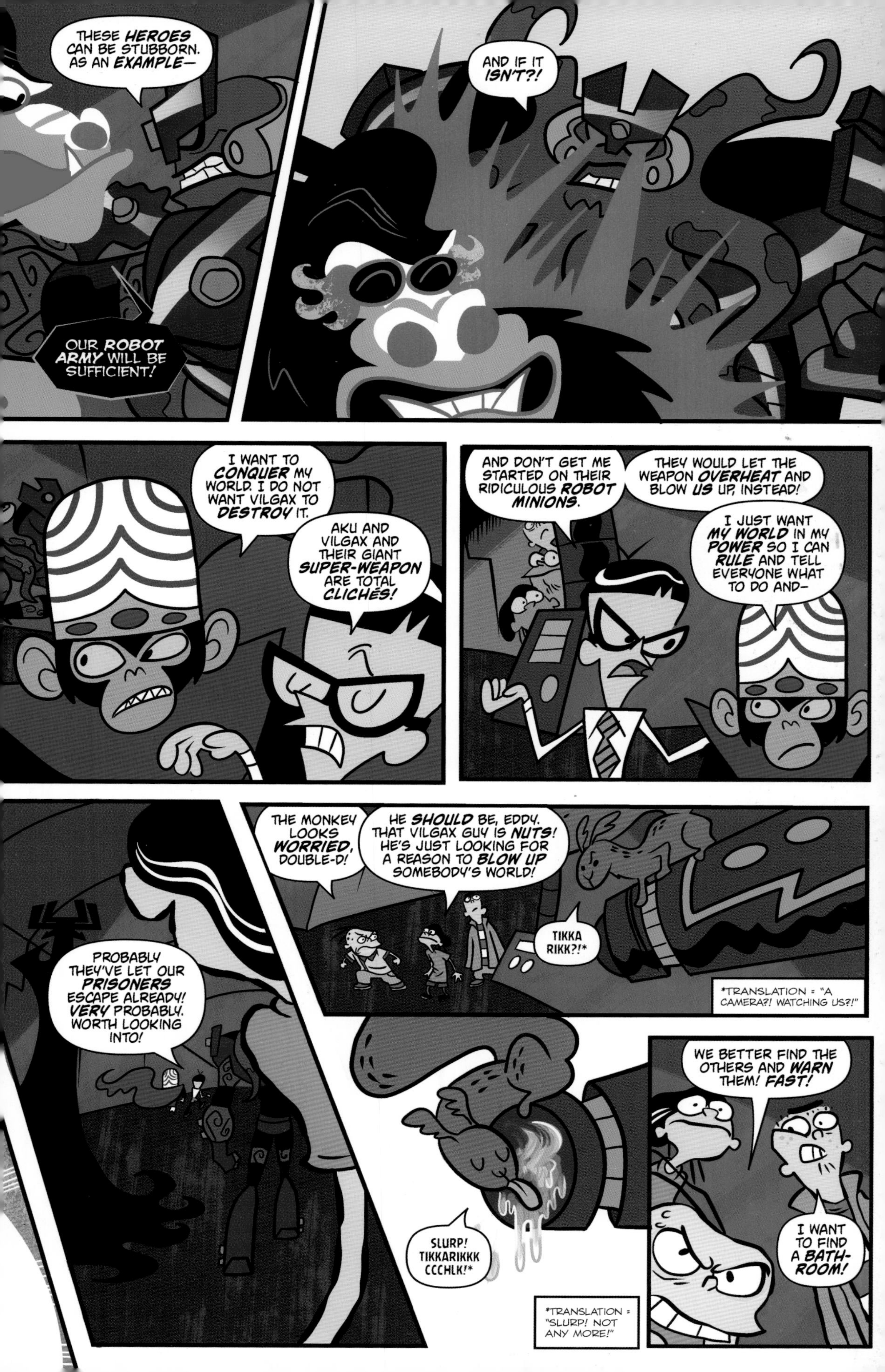
THESE HEROES CAN BE STUBBORN. AS AN EXAMPLE—
OUR ROBOT ARMY WILL BE SUFFICIENT!
AND IF IT ISN'T?!
I WANT TO CONQUER MY WORLD. I DO NOT WANT VILGAX TO DESTROY IT.
AKU AND VILGAX AND THEIR GIANT SUPER-WEAPON ARE TOTAL CLICHÉS!
AND DON'T GET ME STARTED ON THEIR RIDICULOUS ROBOT MINIONS.
THEY WOULD LET THE WEAPON OVERHEAT AND BLOW US UP, INSTEAD!
I JUST WANT MY WORLD IN MY POWER SO I CAN RULE AND TELL EVERYONE WHAT TO DO AND—
PROBABLY THEY'VE LET OUR PRISONERS ESCAPE ALREADY! VERY PROBABLY. WORTH LOOKING INTO!
THE MONKEY LOOKS WORRIED, DOUBLE-D!
HE SHOULD BE, EDDY. THAT VILGAX GUY IS NUTS! HE'S JUST LOOKING FOR A REASON TO BLOW UP SOMEBODY'S WORLD!
TIKKA RIKK?!*
*TRANSLATION = "A CAMERA?! WATCHING US?!"
SLURP! TIKKARIKKK CCCHLK!*
*TRANSLATION = "SLURP! NOT ANY MORE!"
WE BETTER FIND THE OTHERS AND WARN THEM! FAST!
I WANT TO FIND A BATH-ROOM!

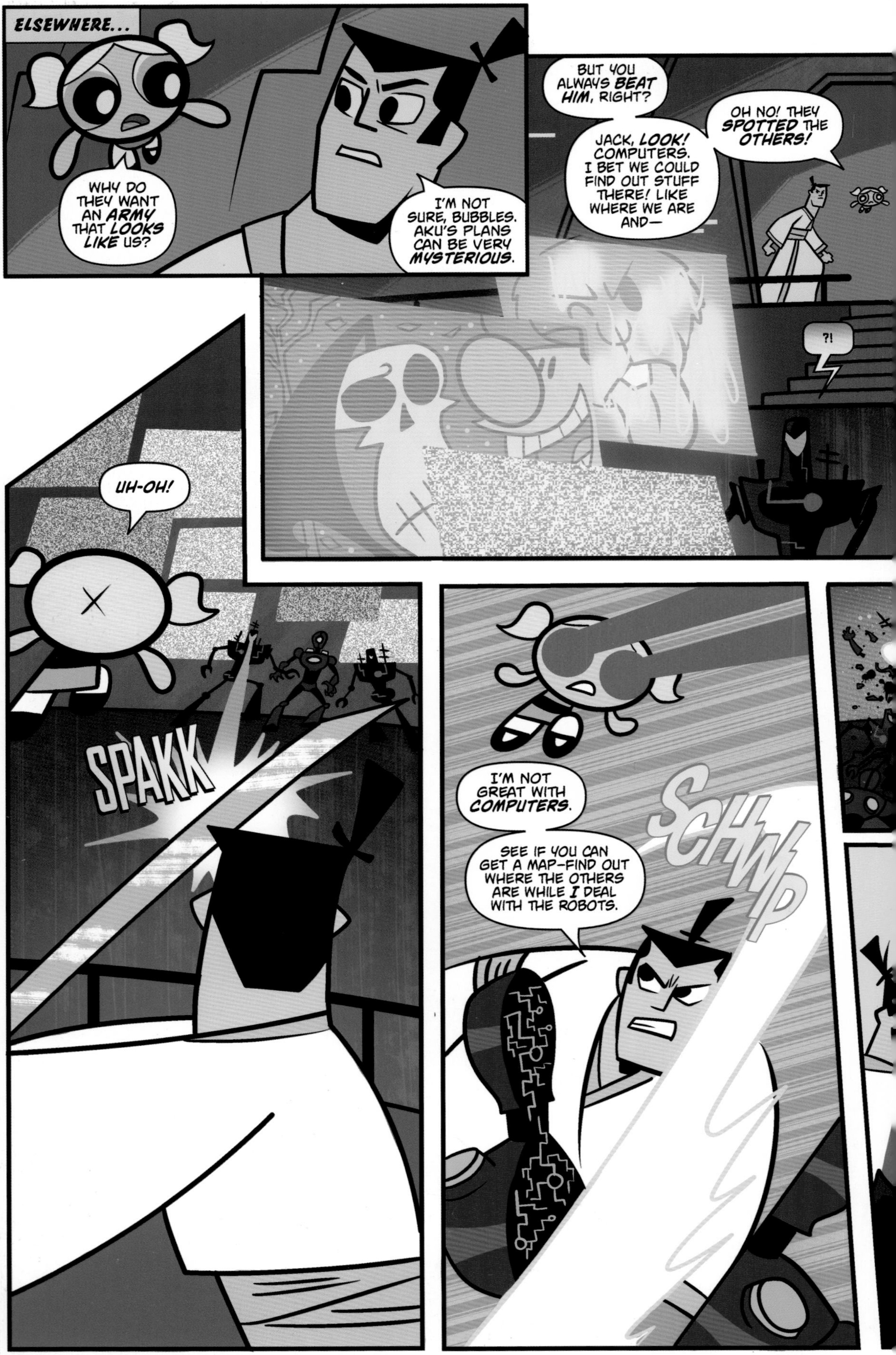
ELSEWHERE...
WHY DO THEY WANT AN ARMY THAT LOOKS LIKE US?
I'M NOT SURE, BUBBLES. AKU'S PLANS CAN BE VERY MYSTERIOUS.
BUT YOU ALWAYS BEAT HIM, RIGHT?
JACK, LOOK! COMPUTERS. I BET WE COULD FIND OUT STUFF THERE! LIKE WHERE WE ARE AND—
OH NO! THEY SPOTTED THE OTHERS!
?!
UH-OH!
SPAKK
I'M NOT GREAT WITH COMPUTERS.
SEE IF YOU CAN GET A MAP—FIND OUT WHERE THE OTHERS ARE WHILE I DEAL WITH THE ROBOTS.
SCHWP

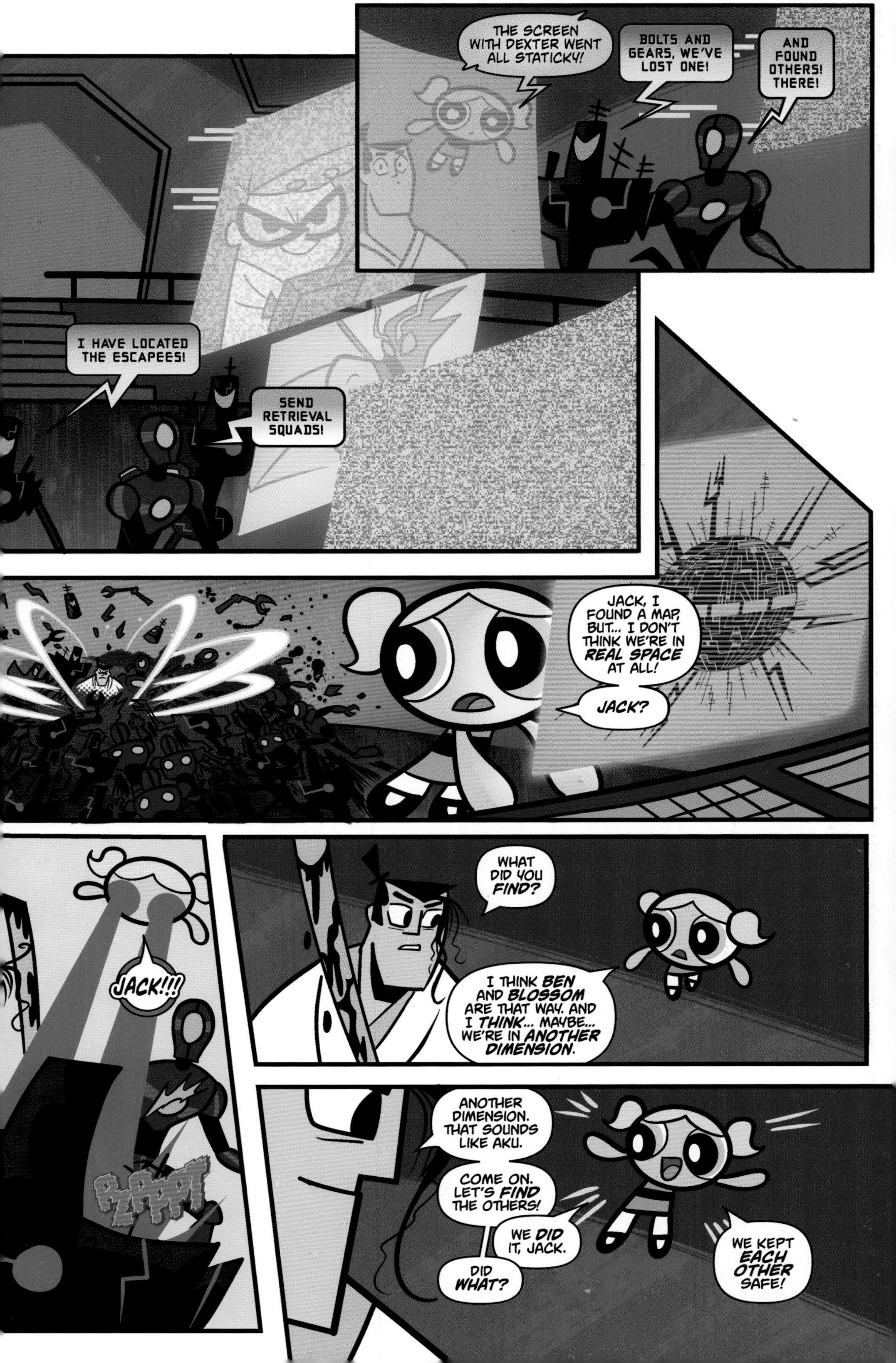
THE SCREEN WITH DEXTER WENT ALL STATICKY!
BOLTS AND GEARS, WE'VE LOST ONE!
AND FOUND OTHERS! THERE!
I HAVE LOCATED THE ESCAPEES!
SEND RETRIEVAL SQUADS!
JACK, I FOUND A MAP, BUT... I DON'T THINK WE'RE IN REAL SPACE AT ALL!
JACK?
JACK!!!
PZZZT
WHAT DID YOU FIND?
I THINK BEN AND BLOSSOM ARE THAT WAY. AND I THINK... MAYBE... WE'RE IN ANOTHER DIMENSION.
ANOTHER DIMENSION. THAT SOUNDS LIKE AKU.
COME ON. LET'S FIND THE OTHERS!
WE DID IT, JACK.
DID WHAT?
WE KEPT EACH OTHER SAFE!

VILGAX WILL LOOK FOR A REASON TO DESTROY MY WORLD.

BUT I WILL FIND A WAY TO STOP HIM.

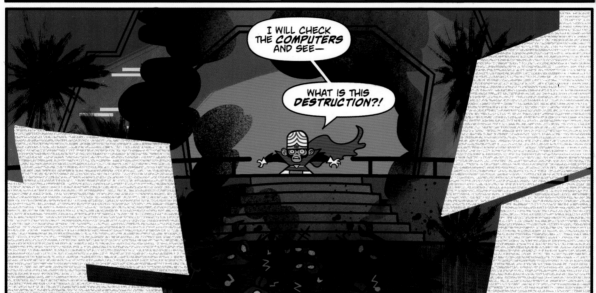

I WILL CHECK THE *COMPUTERS* AND SEE—

WHAT IS THIS *DESTRUCTION?!*

A *POWERPUFF GIRL* HAS BEEN HERE! USING *HEAT VISION!*

AND THOSE *ROBOTS*— SLICED TO RIBBONS!

BY SAMURAI JACK'S *SWORD!*

MANDARK WAS *RIGHT.* YOU *DID* LET THE PRISONERS ESCAPE!

DON'T TELL MASTER AKU!

VILGAX WILL MELT US INTO SLAG!

IF I *CAPTURE* THEM, MAYBE AKU AND VILGAX WILL *LISTEN* TO ME AND NOT *BLOW UP* MY WORLD AND—

THERE! THAT MONITOR IS SMEARY BUT I SEE *HUMAN FIGURES...*

...JUST A FEW CORRIDORS OVER! IT IS TIME TO *RETAKE* THE PRISONERS!

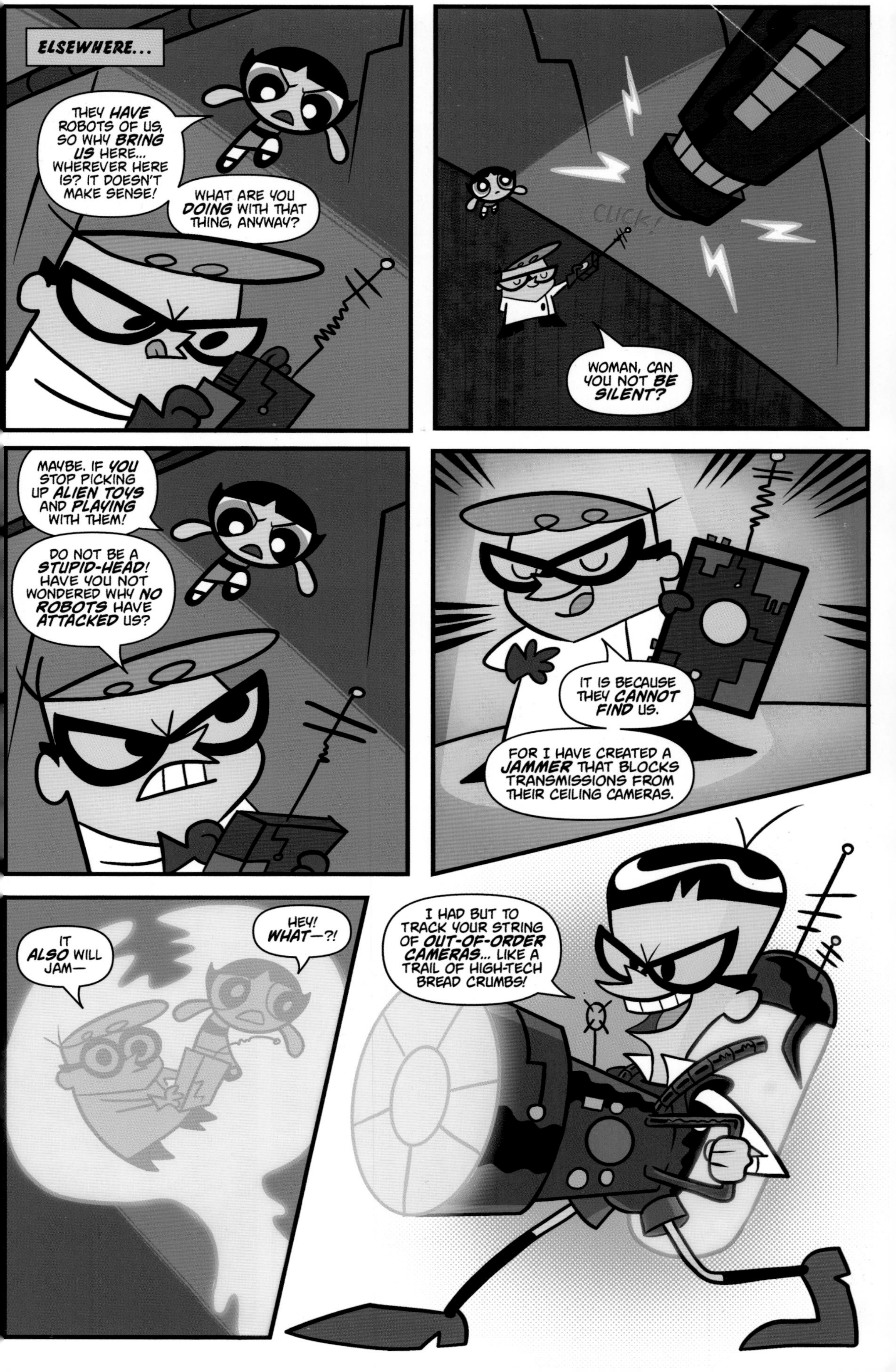
ELSEWHERE...
THEY HAVE ROBOTS OF US, SO WHY BRING US HERE... WHEREVER HERE IS? IT DOESN'T MAKE SENSE!
WHAT ARE YOU DOING WITH THAT THING, ANYWAY?
CLICK!
WOMAN, CAN YOU NOT BE SILENT?
MAYBE. IF YOU STOP PICKING UP ALIEN TOYS AND PLAYING WITH THEM!
DO NOT BE A STUPID-HEAD! HAVE YOU NOT WONDERED WHY NO ROBOTS HAVE ATTACKED US?
IT IS BECAUSE THEY CANNOT FIND US.
FOR I HAVE CREATED A JAMMER THAT BLOCKS TRANSMISSIONS FROM THEIR CEILING CAMERAS.
IT ALSO WILL JAM—
HEY! WHAT—?!
I HAD BUT TO TRACK YOUR STRING OF OUT-OF-ORDER CAMERAS... LIKE A TRAIL OF HIGH-TECH BREAD CRUMBS!

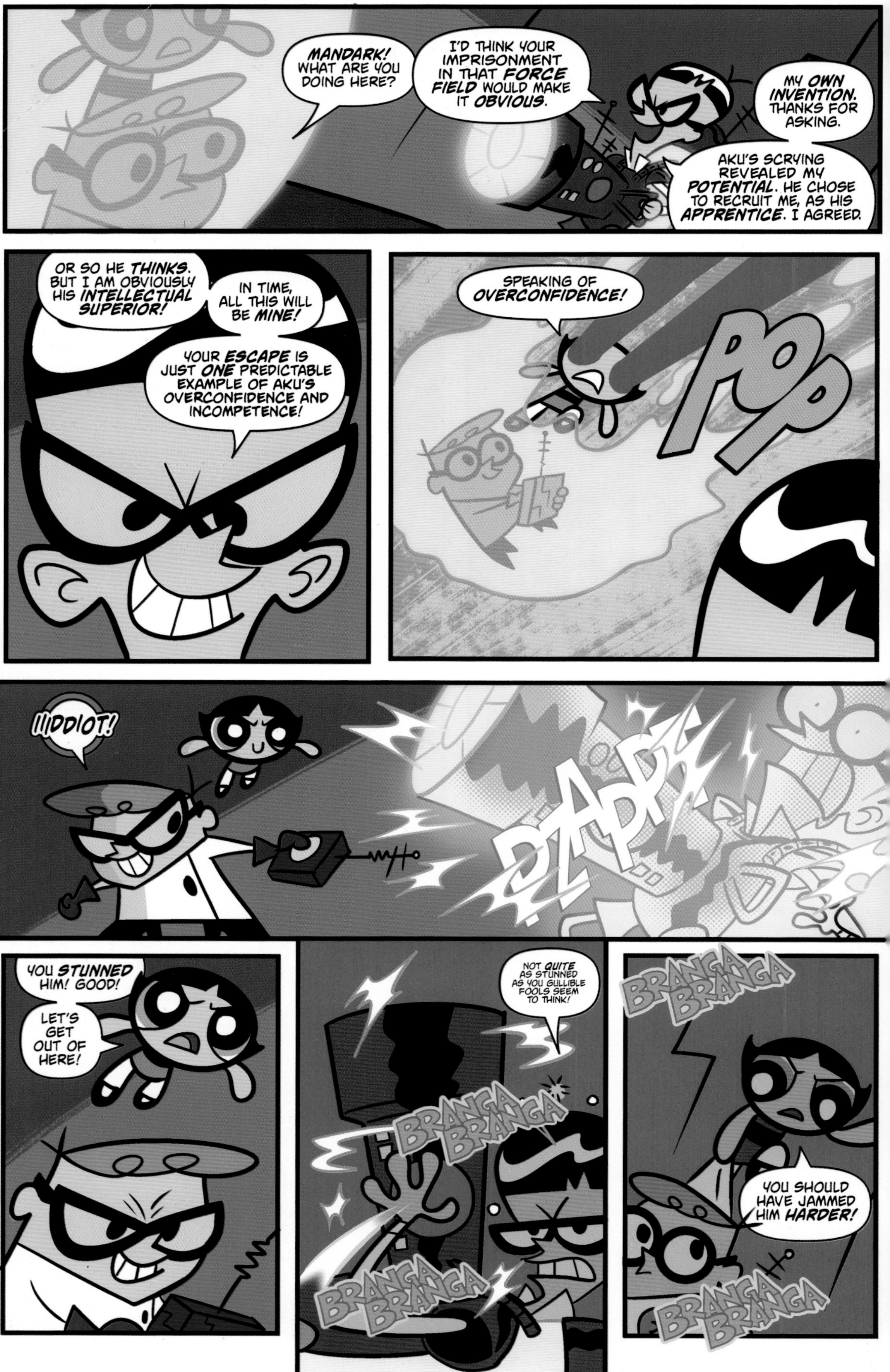
MANDARK! WHAT ARE YOU DOING HERE?
I'D THINK YOUR IMPRISONMENT IN THAT FORCE FIELD WOULD MAKE IT OBVIOUS.
MY OWN INVENTION. THANKS FOR ASKING.
AKU'S SCRYING REVEALED MY POTENTIAL. HE CHOSE TO RECRUIT ME, AS HIS APPRENTICE. I AGREED.
OR SO HE THINKS. BUT I AM OBVIOUSLY HIS INTELLECTUAL SUPERIOR!
IN TIME, ALL THIS WILL BE MINE!
YOUR ESCAPE IS JUST ONE PREDICTABLE EXAMPLE OF AKU'S OVERCONFIDENCE AND INCOMPETENCE!
SPEAKING OF OVERCONFIDENCE!
POP
IIIDDIOT!
DZAPPZ
YOU STUNNED HIM! GOOD!
LET'S GET OUT OF HERE!
NOT QUITE AS STUNNED AS YOU GULLIBLE FOOLS SEEM TO THINK!
BRANGA BRANGA
BRANGA BRANGA
BRANGA BRANGA
YOU SHOULD HAVE JAMMED HIM HARDER!
BRANGA BRANGA

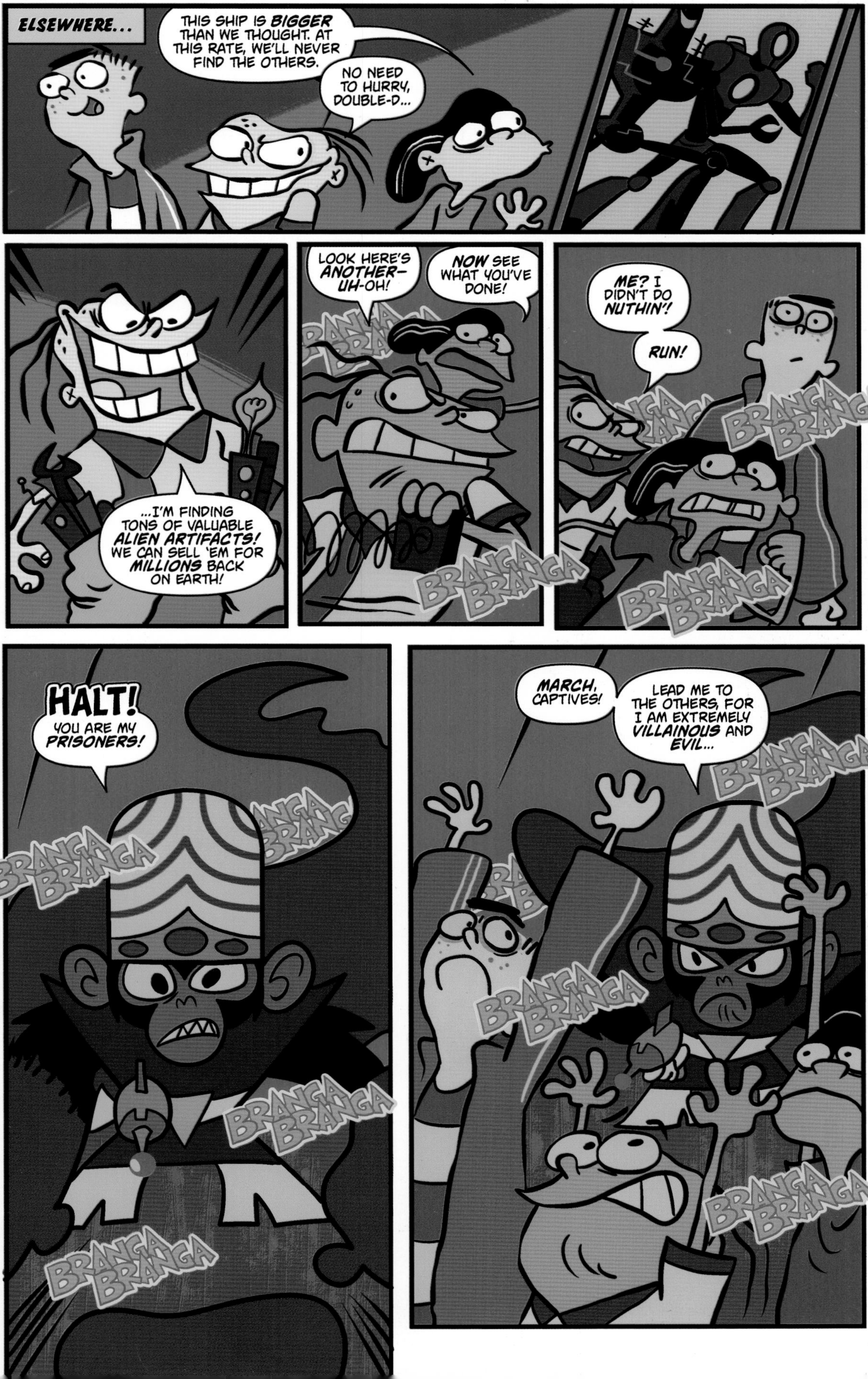
ELSEWHERE...
THIS SHIP IS BIGGER THAN WE THOUGHT. AT THIS RATE, WE'LL NEVER FIND THE OTHERS.
NO NEED TO HURRY, DOUBLE-D...
...I'M FINDING TONS OF VALUABLE ALIEN ARTIFACTS! WE CAN SELL 'EM FOR MILLIONS BACK ON EARTH!
LOOK HERE'S ANOTHER-UH-OH!
NOW SEE WHAT YOU'VE DONE!
BRANGA BRANGA
ME? I DIDN'T DO NUTHIN'!
RUN!
BRANGA BRANGA
HALT! YOU ARE MY PRISONERS!
BRANGA BRANGA
MARCH, CAPTIVES!
LEAD ME TO THE OTHERS, FOR I AM EXTREMELY VILLAINOUS AND EVIL...
BRANGA BRANGA

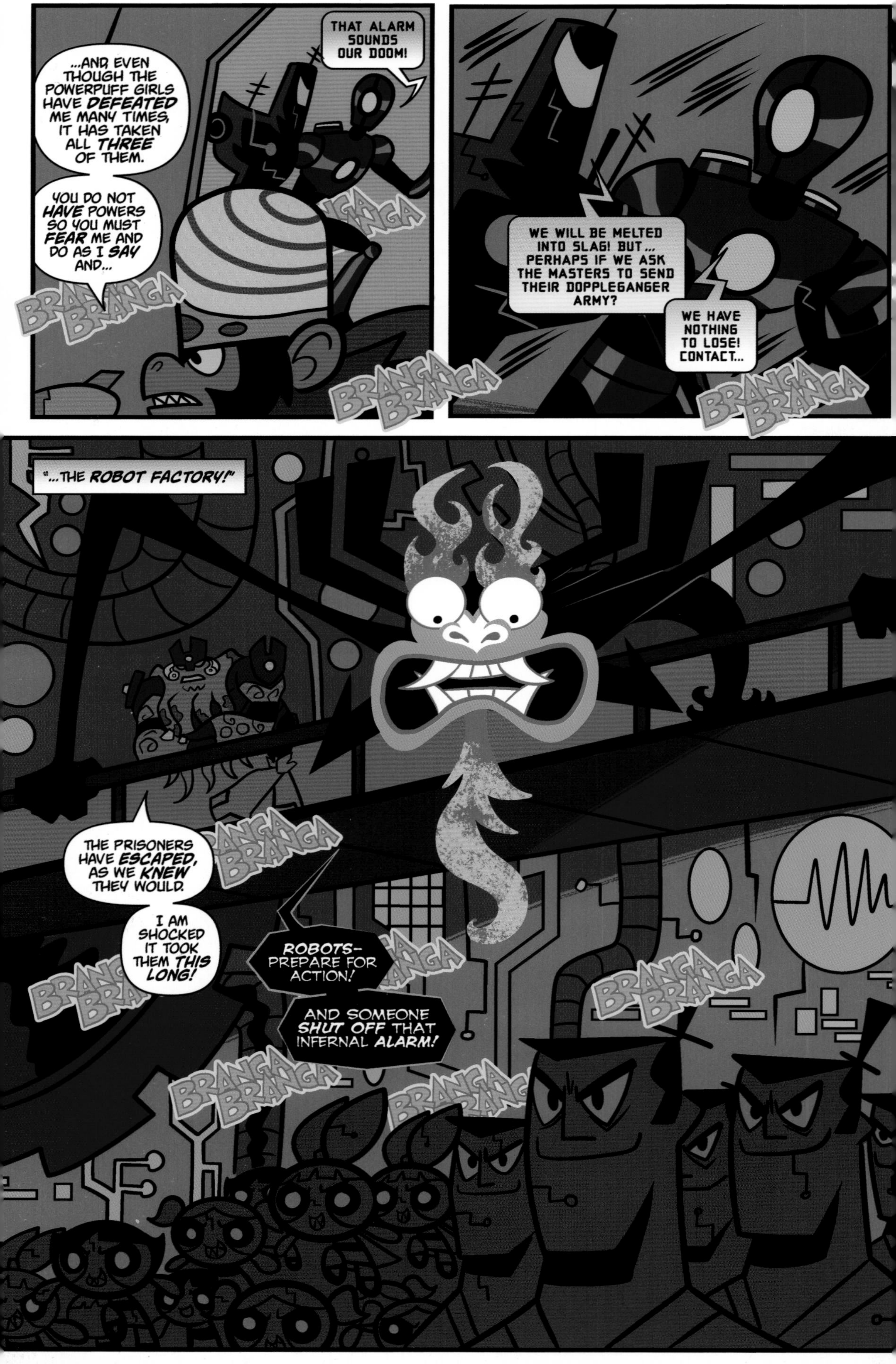
...AND, EVEN THOUGH THE POWERPUFF GIRLS HAVE DEFEATED ME MANY TIMES, IT HAS TAKEN ALL THREE OF THEM.
THAT ALARM SOUNDS OUR DOOM!
YOU DO NOT HAVE POWERS SO YOU MUST FEAR ME AND DO AS I SAY AND...
BRANGA BRANGA
BRANGA BRANGA
WE WILL BE MELTED INTO SLAG! BUT... PERHAPS IF WE ASK THE MASTERS TO SEND THEIR DOPPLEGANGER ARMY?
WE HAVE NOTHING TO LOSE! CONTACT...
BRANGA BRANGA
"...THE ROBOT FACTORY!"
THE PRISONERS HAVE ESCAPED, AS WE KNEW THEY WOULD.
I AM SHOCKED IT TOOK THEM THIS LONG!
ROBOTS- PREPARE FOR ACTION!
AND SOMEONE SHUT OFF THAT INFERNAL ALARM!
BRANGA BRANGA

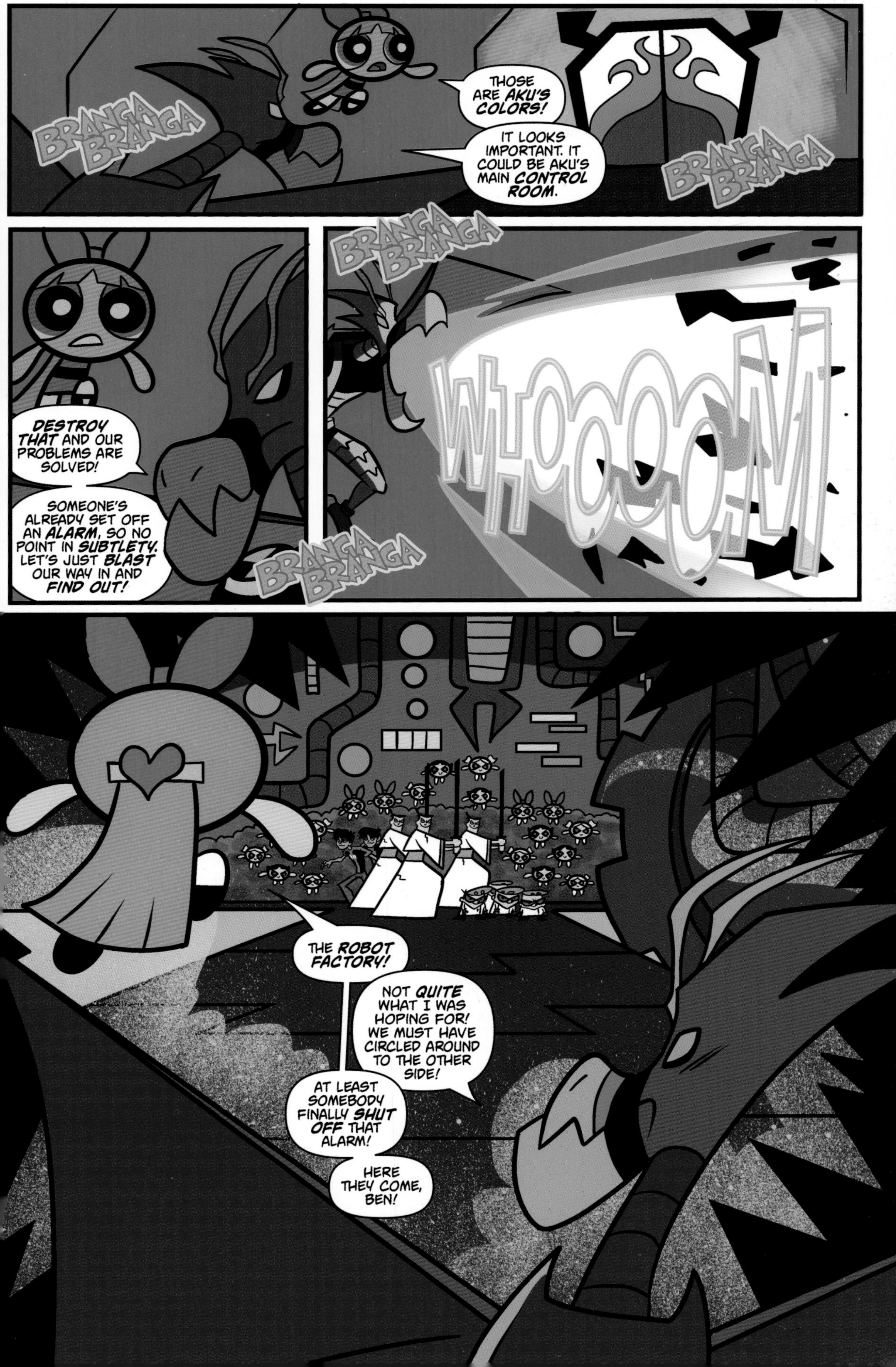
BRANGA BRANGA
THOSE ARE AKU'S COLORS!
IT LOOKS IMPORTANT. IT COULD BE AKU'S MAIN CONTROL ROOM.
BRANGA BRANGA
DESTROY THAT AND OUR PROBLEMS ARE SOLVED!
SOMEONE'S ALREADY SET OFF AN ALARM, SO NO POINT IN SUBTLETY. LET'S JUST BLAST OUR WAY IN AND FIND OUT!
BRANGA BRANGA
BRANGA BRANGA
WHOOOOOM!
THE ROBOT FACTORY!
NOT QUITE WHAT I WAS HOPING FOR! WE MUST HAVE CIRCLED AROUND TO THE OTHER SIDE!
AT LEAST SOMEBODY FINALLY SHUT OFF THAT ALARM!
HERE THEY COME, BEN!

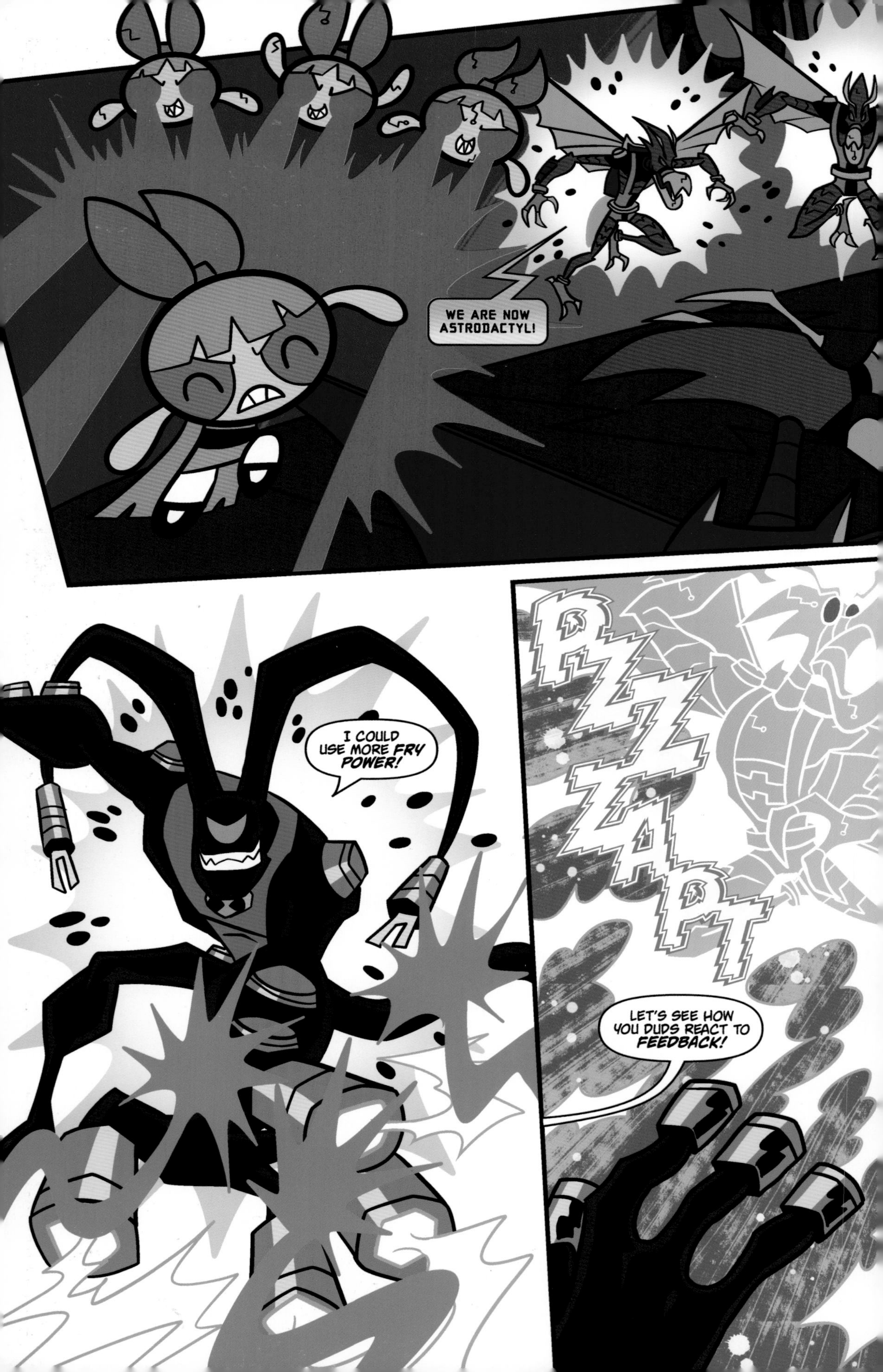
WE ARE NOW ASTRODACTYL!
I COULD USE MORE FRY POWER!
PZZZAPT
LET'S SEE HOW YOU DUDS REACT TO FEEDBACK!

SHEESH! IF THEIR ROBOTS CAN EVEN *MIMIC* OUR *POWERS*, WHY BOTHER TO CAPTURE US?

I WAS JUST *THINKING* THAT!

NO MATTER HOW MANY WE *DESTROY*, OTHERS KEEP COMING!

WE'LL *NEVER* STOP THEM ALL!

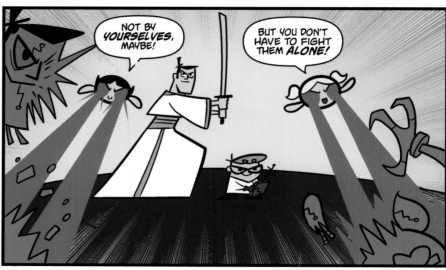

NOT BY *YOURSELVES*, MAYBE!

BUT YOU DON'T HAVE TO FIGHT THEM *ALONE*!

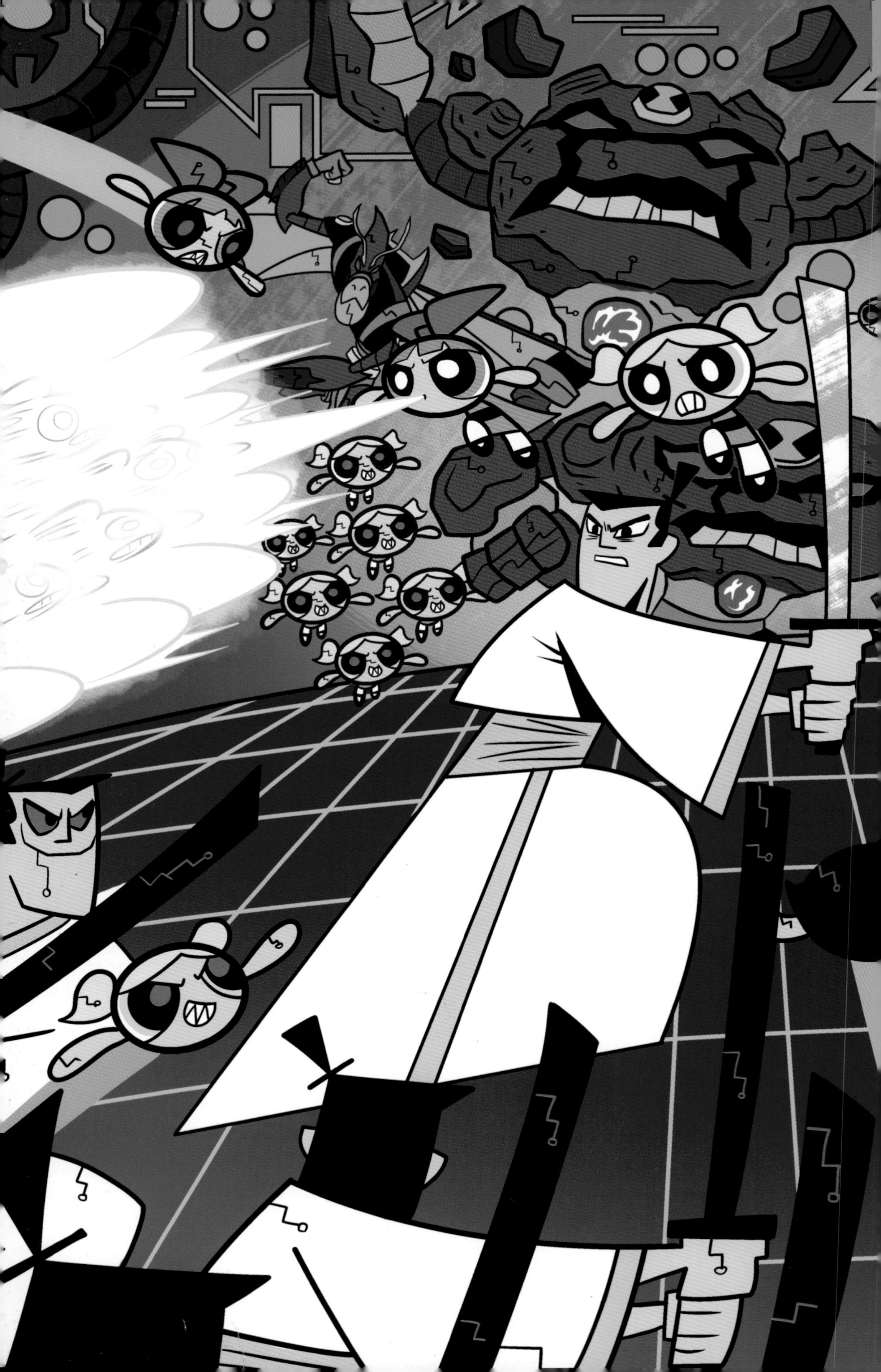

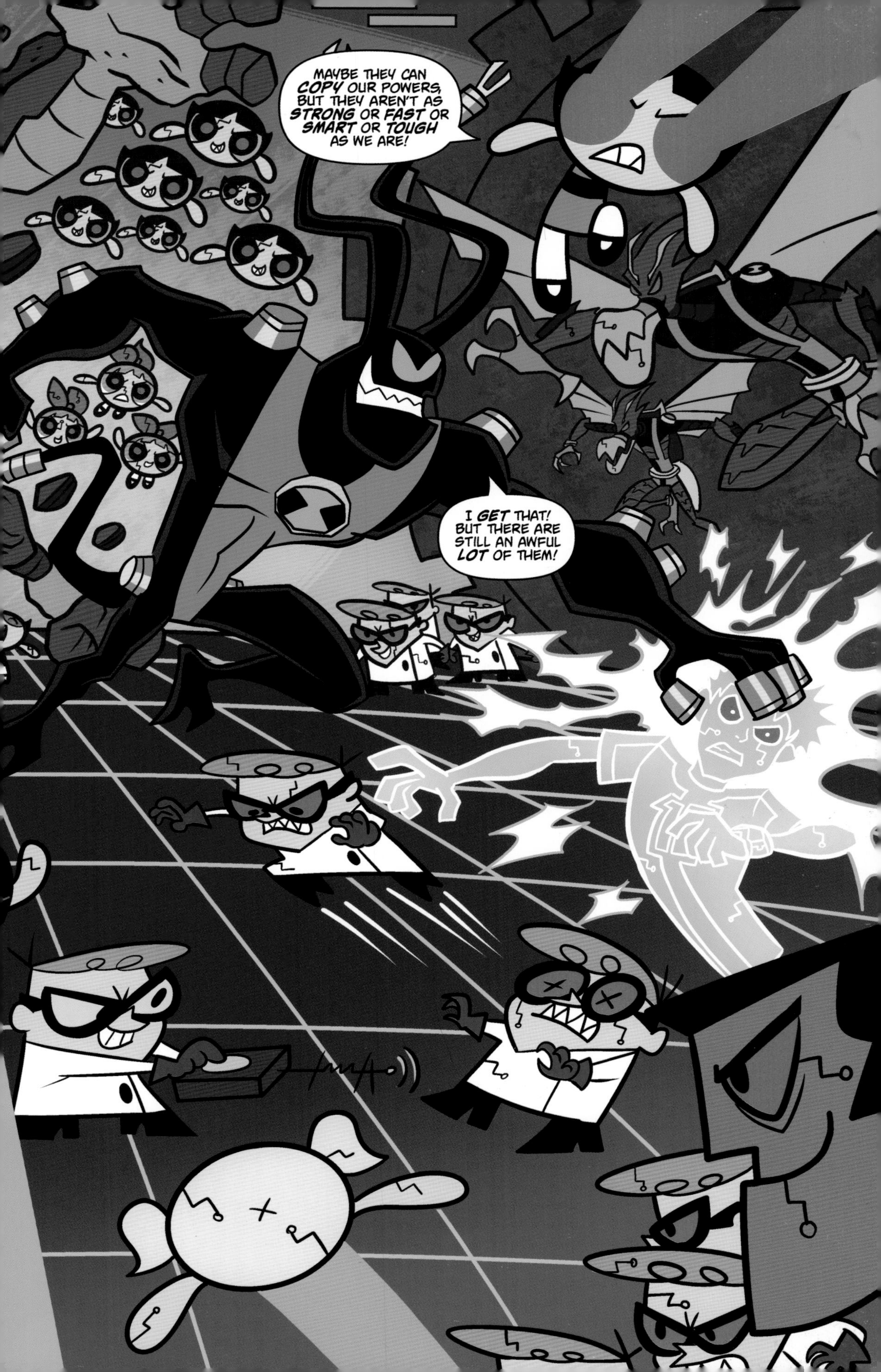
MAYBE THEY CAN COPY OUR POWERS, BUT THEY AREN'T AS STRONG OR FAST OR SMART OR TOUGH AS WE ARE!
I GET THAT! BUT THERE ARE STILL AN AWFUL LOT OF THEM!

AT LAST! OUR CHANCE TO TEST THE READINESS OF OUR ROBOT ARMY!
THE PRISONERS ESCAPED!
OF COURSE THEY DID, MY BOY! IT WAS UNDERSTOOD THAT THEY WOULD.
LET ME GUESS! YOU SET OFF THE ALARM? GOOD FOR YOU, BUT, AS YOU SEE, WE HAVE THINGS UNDER CONTROL.
UNDER CONTROL? THE HEROES ARE GOING TO WIN!
YES, THAT IS THE LIKELY OUTCOME OF THIS LITTLE SKIRMISH!
IN THE UNLIKELY EVENT THAT OUR ROBOTS ACTUALLY ARE VICTORIOUS, WE WON'T NEED TO TRANSFER THE CONSCIOUSNESSES OF OUR HEROES INTO THE ROBOTS' BODIES.
NOT THAT THERE WOULD BE ANY CONSCIOUSNESSES LEFT TO TRANSFER, ANYWAY.
BUT, IF AND WHEN THE HEROES WIN, WE HAVE ANOTHER WAY TO FORCE THEIR COMPLIANCE!
BEHOLD, THE DEATHSTARE! WITH THIS WEAPON, NO MATTER WHAT HAPPENS, VILGAX, THE LEAGUE OF EXTRAORDINARY VILLAINS WILL BE THE TRUE VICTORS!
JUST THIS ONCE, I PERSONALLY AM ROOTING FOR THE HEROES.

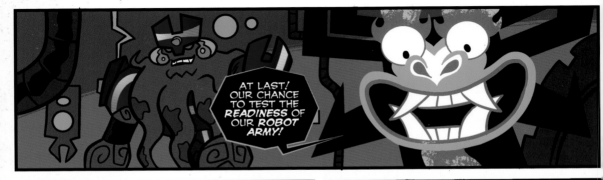

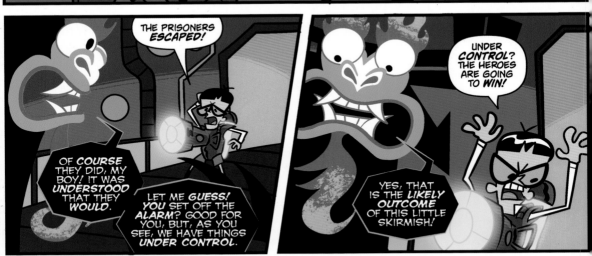

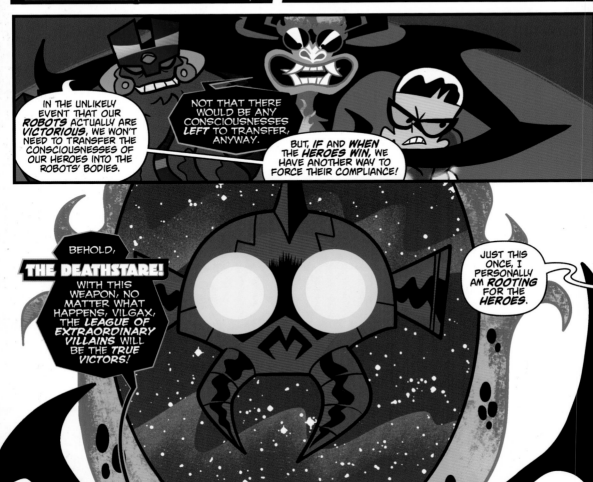

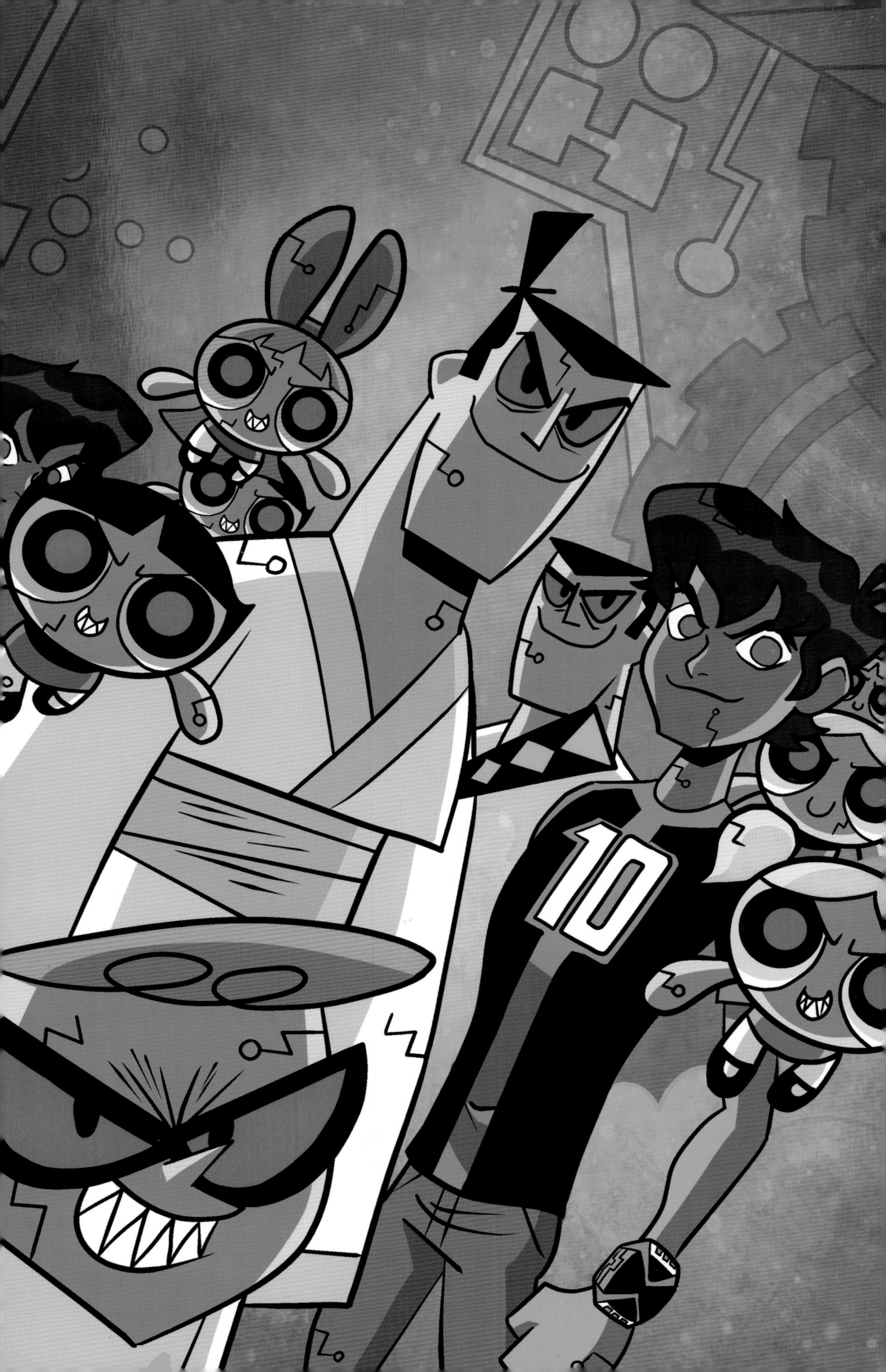
10

Chapter 4

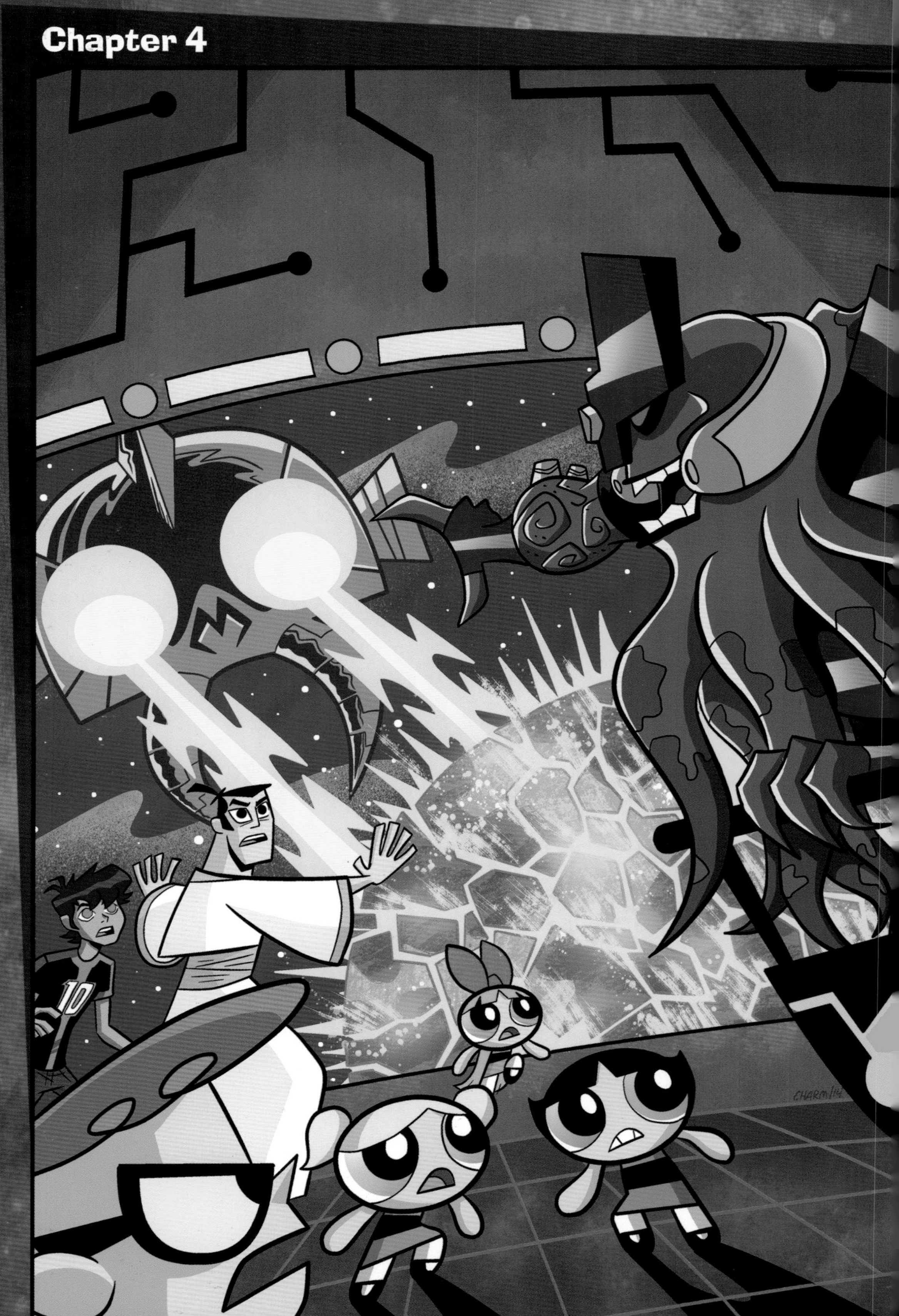
CHARM/14

Cover Art by Derek Charm

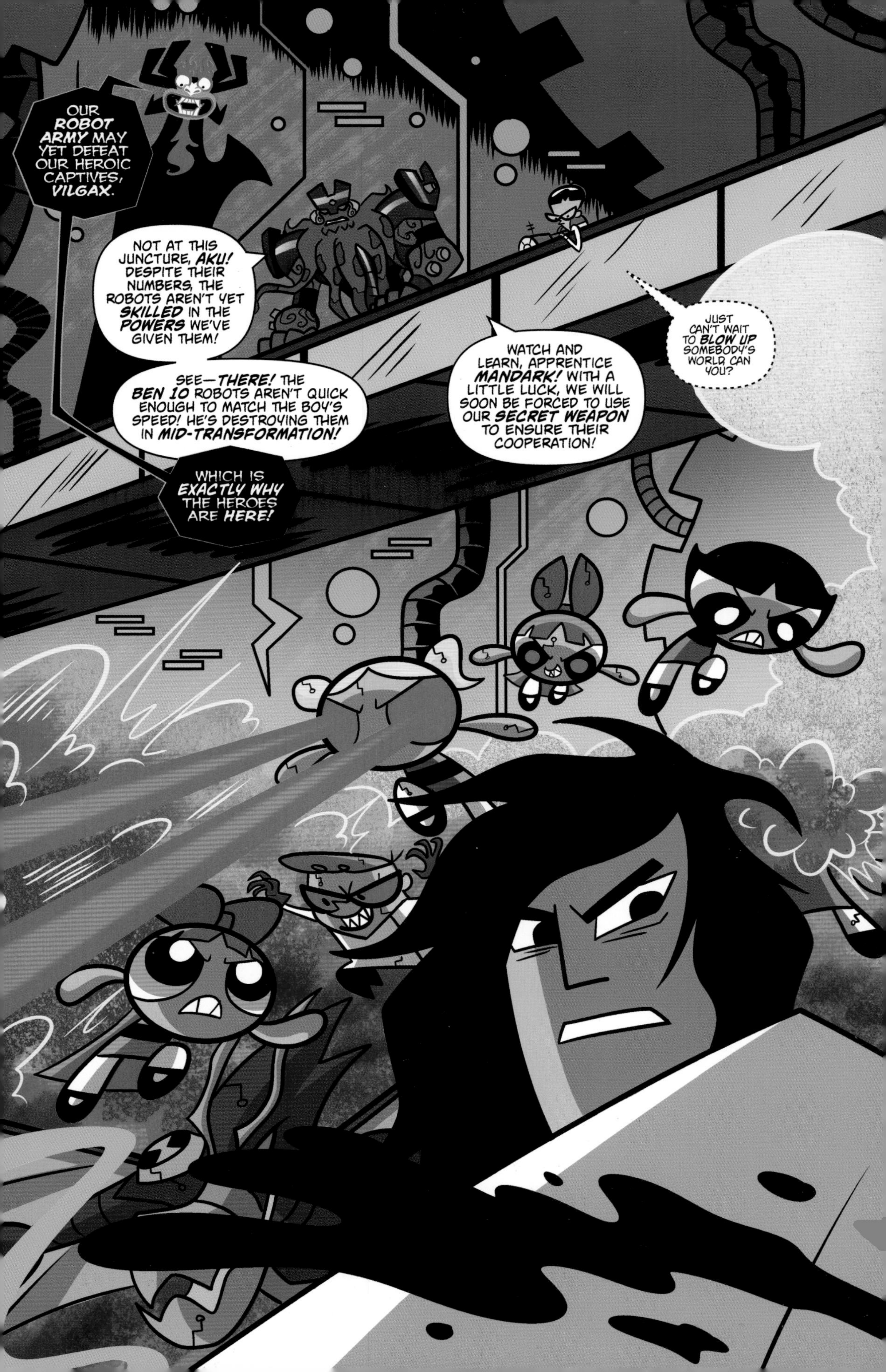
OUR ROBOT ARMY MAY YET DEFEAT OUR HEROIC CAPTIVES, VILGAX.
NOT AT THIS JUNCTURE, AKU! DESPITE THEIR NUMBERS, THE ROBOTS AREN'T YET SKILLED IN THE POWERS WE'VE GIVEN THEM!
SEE—THERE! THE BEN 10 ROBOTS AREN'T QUICK ENOUGH TO MATCH THE BOY'S SPEED! HE'S DESTROYING THEM IN MID-TRANSFORMATION!
WHICH IS EXACTLY WHY THE HEROES ARE HERE!
WATCH AND LEARN, APPRENTICE MANDARK! WITH A LITTLE LUCK, WE WILL SOON BE FORCED TO USE OUR SECRET WEAPON TO ENSURE THEIR COOPERATION!
JUST CAN'T WAIT TO BLOW UP SOMEBODY'S WORLD, CAN YOU?

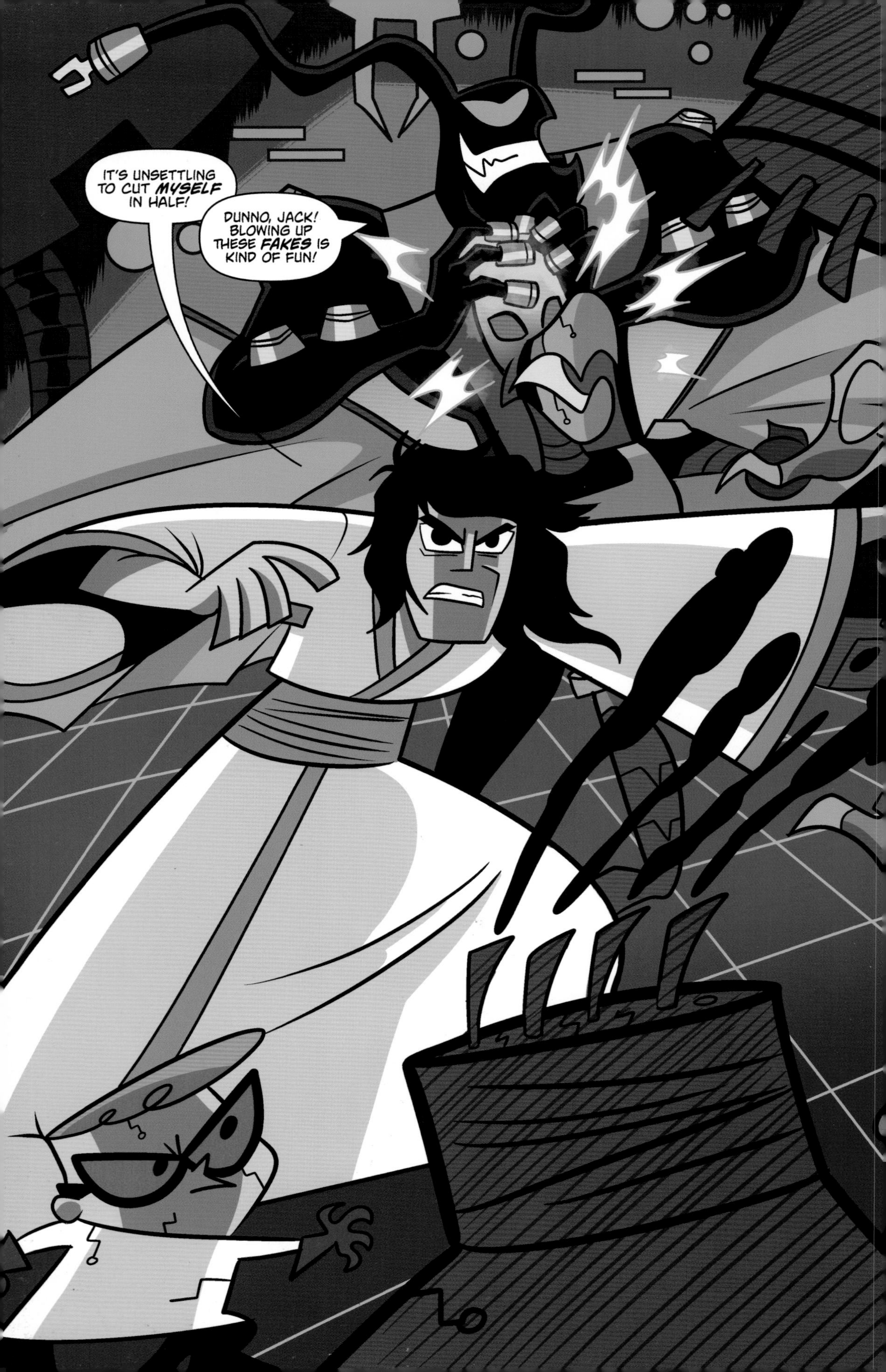
IT'S UNSETTLING TO CUT MYSELF IN HALF!
DUNNO, JACK! BLOWING UP THESE FAKES IS KIND OF FUN!

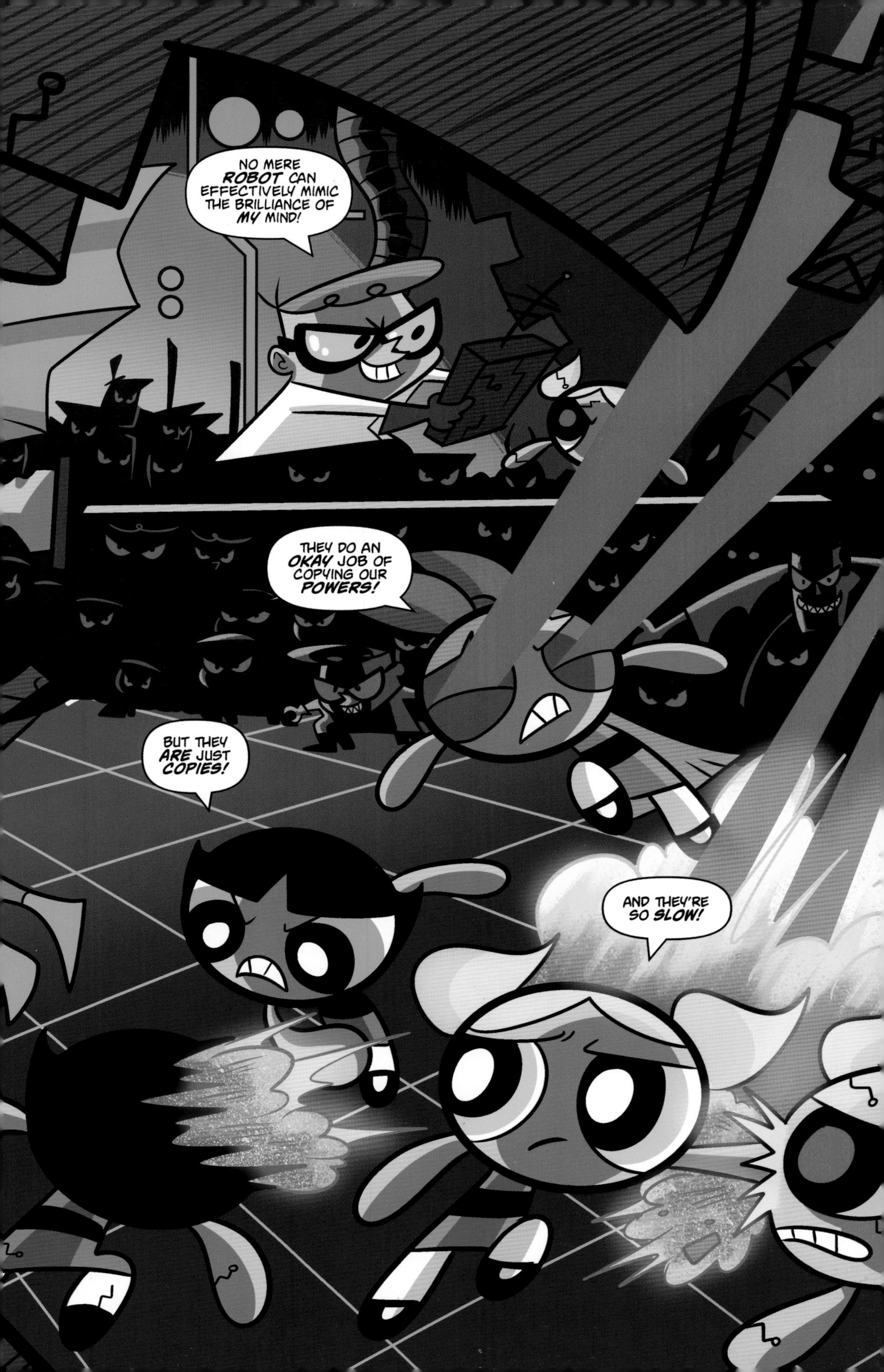
NO MERE ROBOT CAN EFFECTIVELY MIMIC THE BRILLIANCE OF MY MIND!
THEY DO AN OKAY JOB OF COPYING OUR POWERS!
BUT THEY ARE JUST COPIES!
AND THEY'RE SO SLOW!

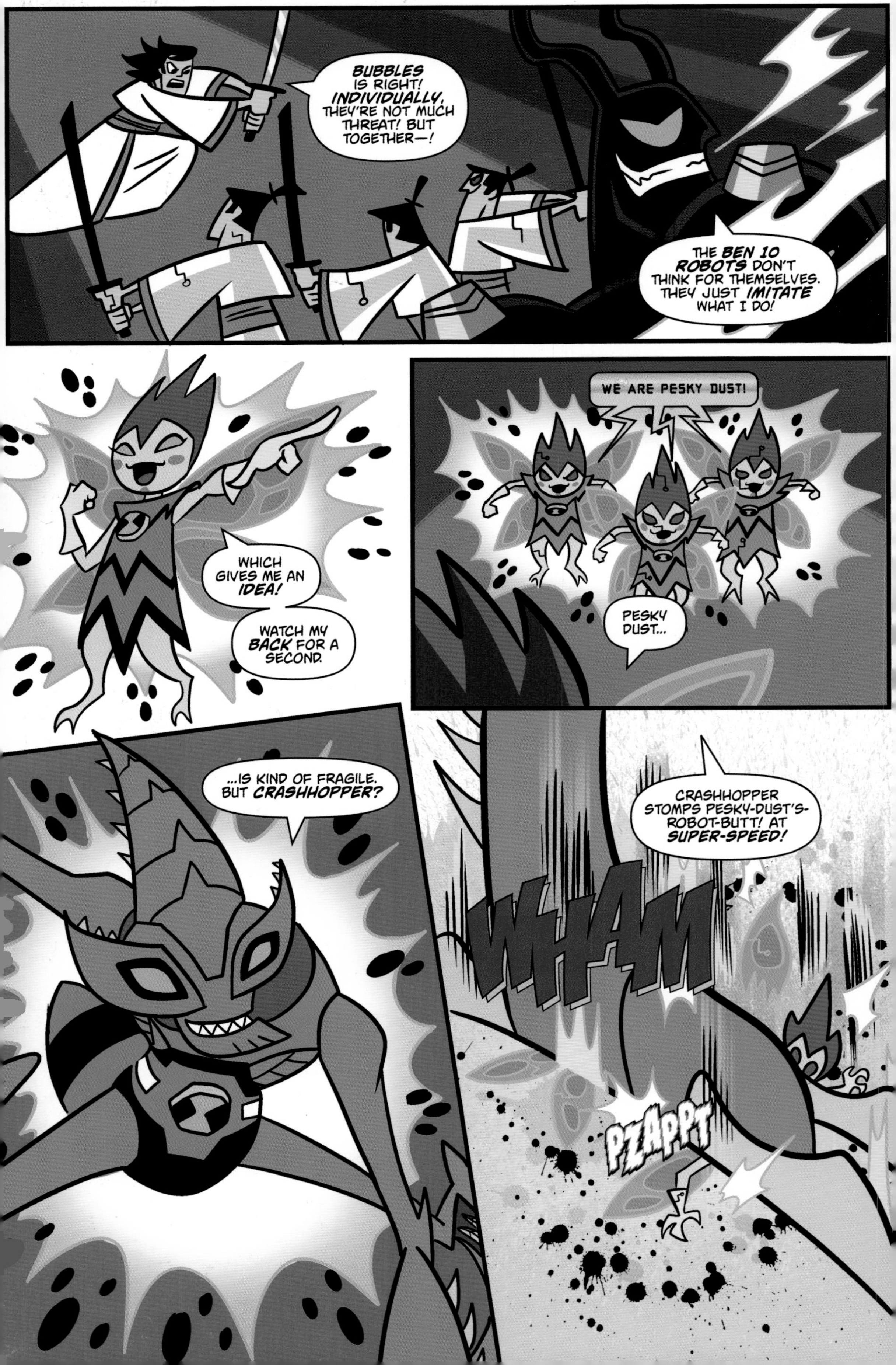
BUBBLES IS RIGHT! INDIVIDUALLY, THEY'RE NOT MUCH THREAT! BUT TOGETHER—!
THE BEN 10 ROBOTS DON'T THINK FOR THEMSELVES. THEY JUST IMITATE WHAT I DO!
WHICH GIVES ME AN IDEA!
WATCH MY BACK FOR A SECOND.
WE ARE PESKY DUST!
PESKY DUST...
...IS KIND OF FRAGILE. BUT CRASHHOPPER?
CRASHHOPPER STOMPS PESKY-DUST'S-ROBOT-BUTT! AT SUPER-SPEED!
WHAM
PZAPPT

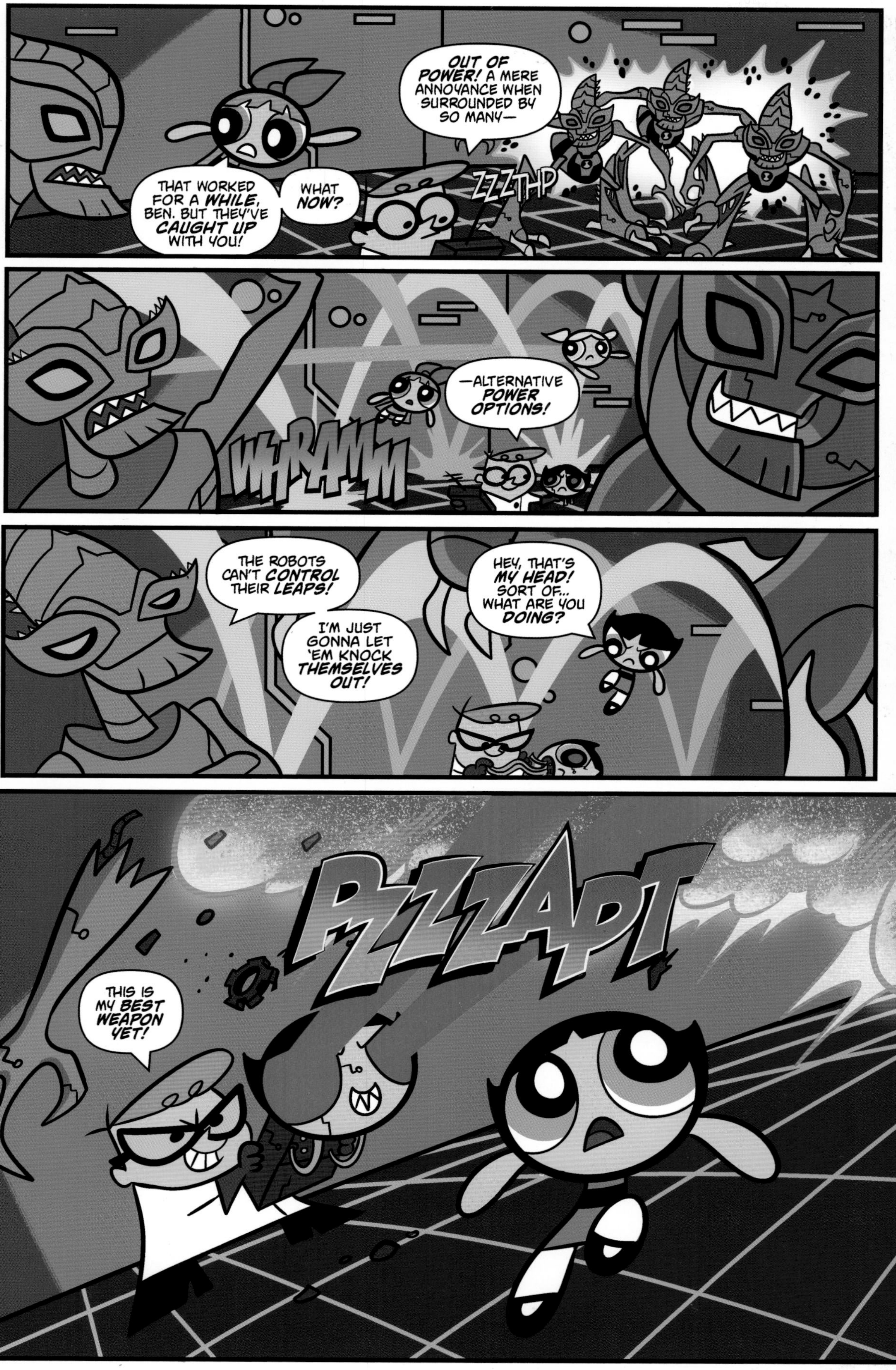
OUT OF POWER! A MERE ANNOYANCE WHEN SURROUNDED BY SO MANY—
THAT WORKED FOR A WHILE, BEN. BUT THEY'VE CAUGHT UP WITH YOU!
WHAT NOW?
ZZZTHP
—ALTERNATIVE POWER OPTIONS!
WHRAMM
THE ROBOTS CAN'T CONTROL THEIR LEAPS!
I'M JUST GONNA LET 'EM KNOCK THEMSELVES OUT!
HEY, THAT'S MY HEAD! SORT OF... WHAT ARE YOU DOING?
PZZZAPT
THIS IS MY BEST WEAPON YET!

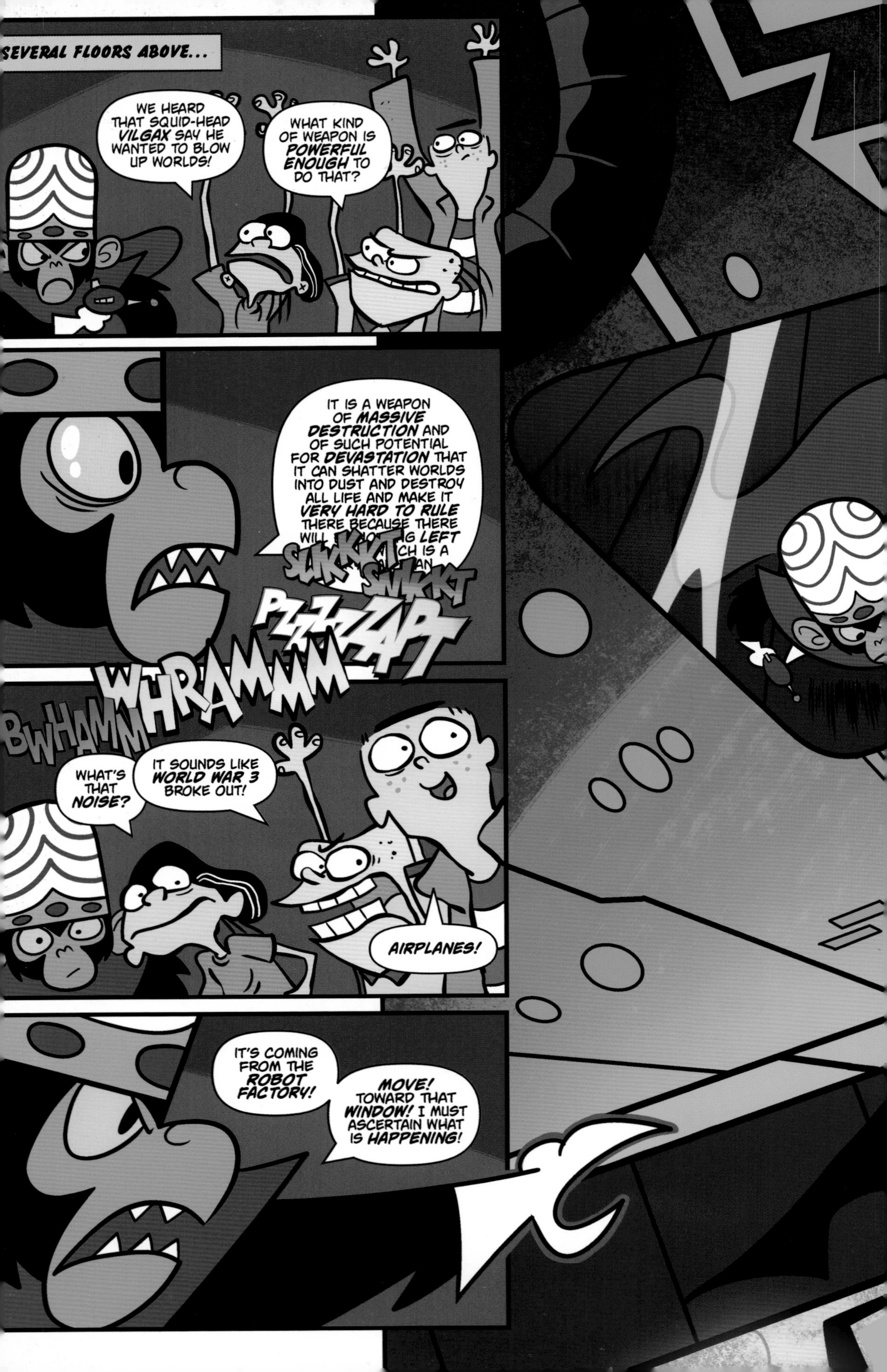
SEVERAL FLOORS ABOVE...
WE HEARD THAT SQUID-HEAD VILGAX SAY HE WANTED TO BLOW UP WORLDS!
WHAT KIND OF WEAPON IS POWERFUL ENOUGH TO DO THAT?
IT IS A WEAPON OF MASSIVE DESTRUCTION AND OF SUCH POTENTIAL FOR DEVASTATION THAT IT CAN SHATTER WORLDS INTO DUST AND DESTROY ALL LIFE AND MAKE IT VERY HARD TO RULE THERE BECAUSE THERE
SLIKKKT
SWIKKKT
PZZZZAPT
WHRAMMM
BWHAMM
WHAT'S THAT NOISE?
IT SOUNDS LIKE WORLD WAR 3 BROKE OUT!
AIRPLANES!
IT'S COMING FROM THE ROBOT FACTORY!
MOVE! TOWARD THAT WINDOW! I MUST ASCERTAIN WHAT IS HAPPENING!

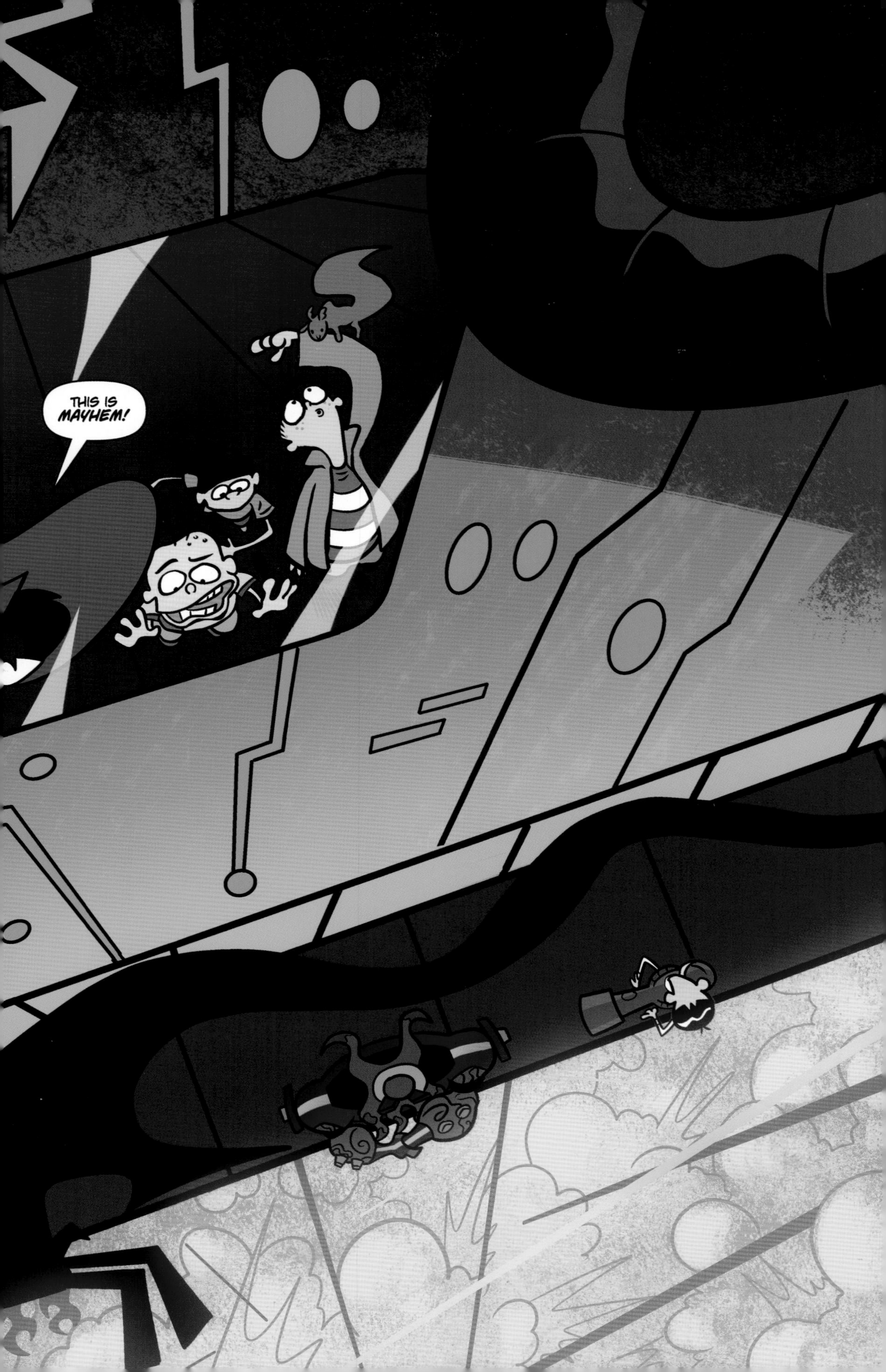
THIS IS MAYHEM!

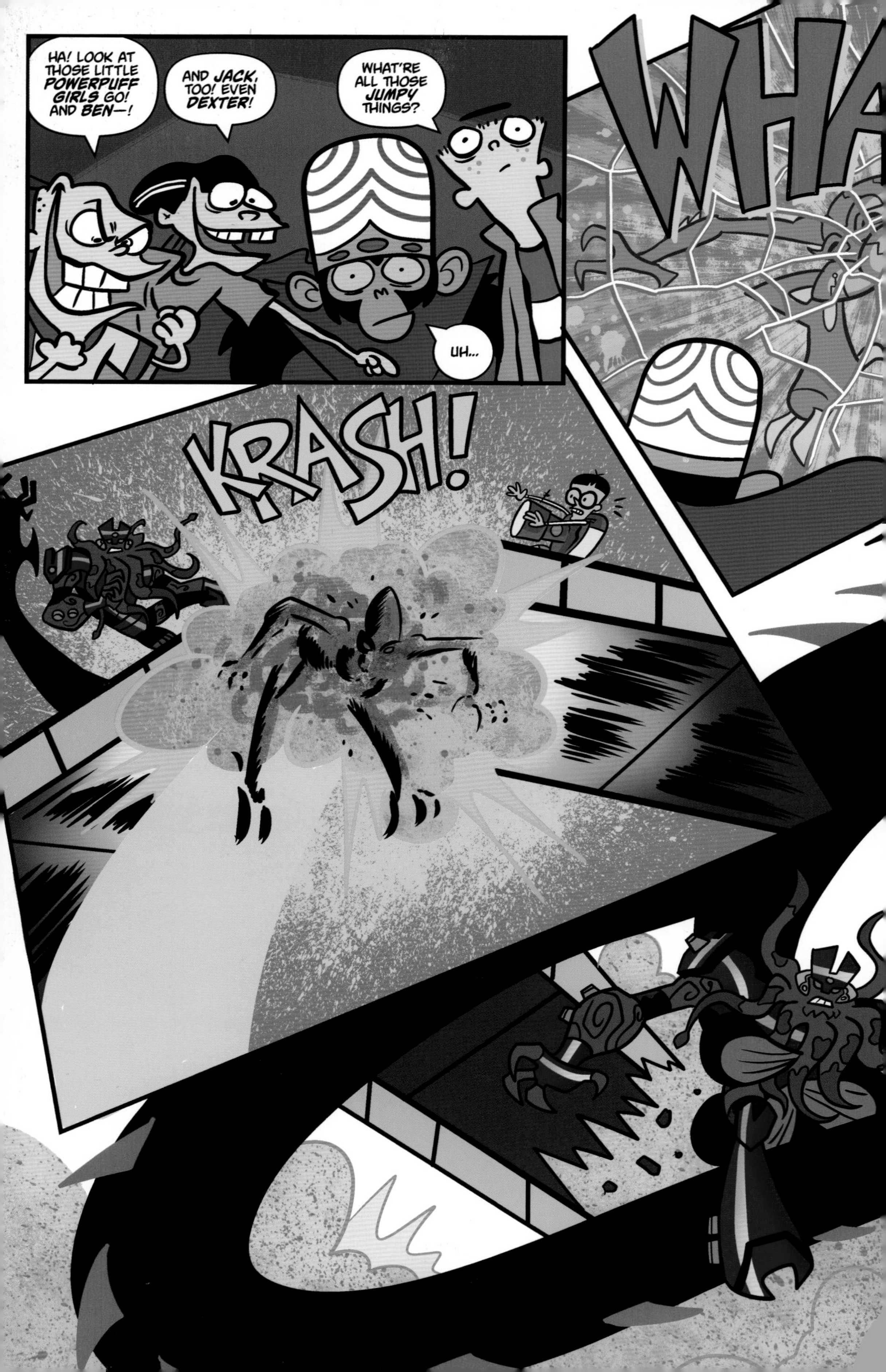

HA! LOOK AT THOSE LITTLE POWERPUFF GIRLS GO! AND BEN—!
AND JACK, TOO! EVEN DEXTER!
WHAT'RE ALL THOSE JUMPY THINGS?
UH...
WHA
KRASH!

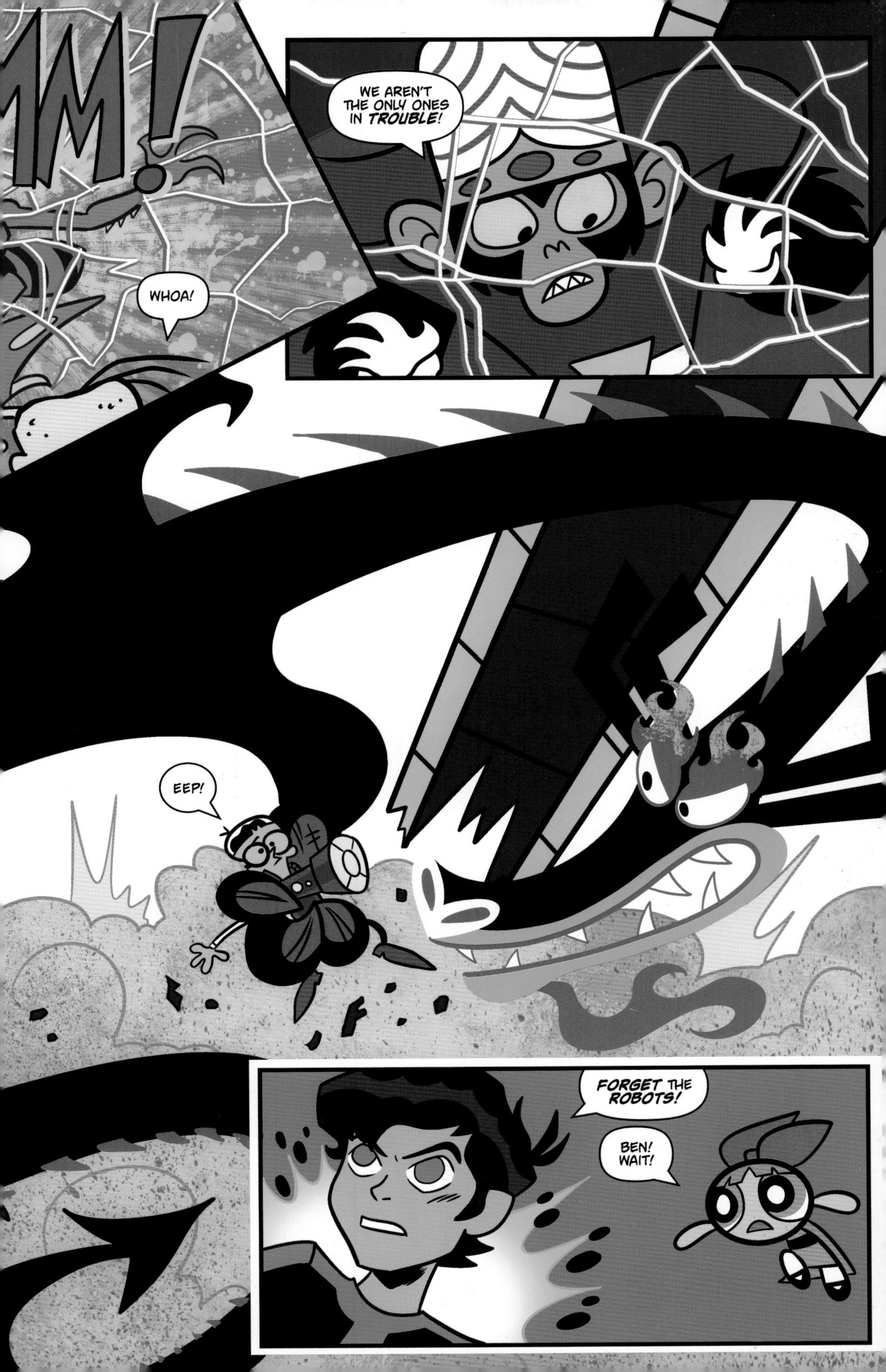

MM!
WE AREN'T THE ONLY ONES IN TROUBLE!
WHOA!
EEP!
FORGET THE ROBOTS!
BEN! WAIT!

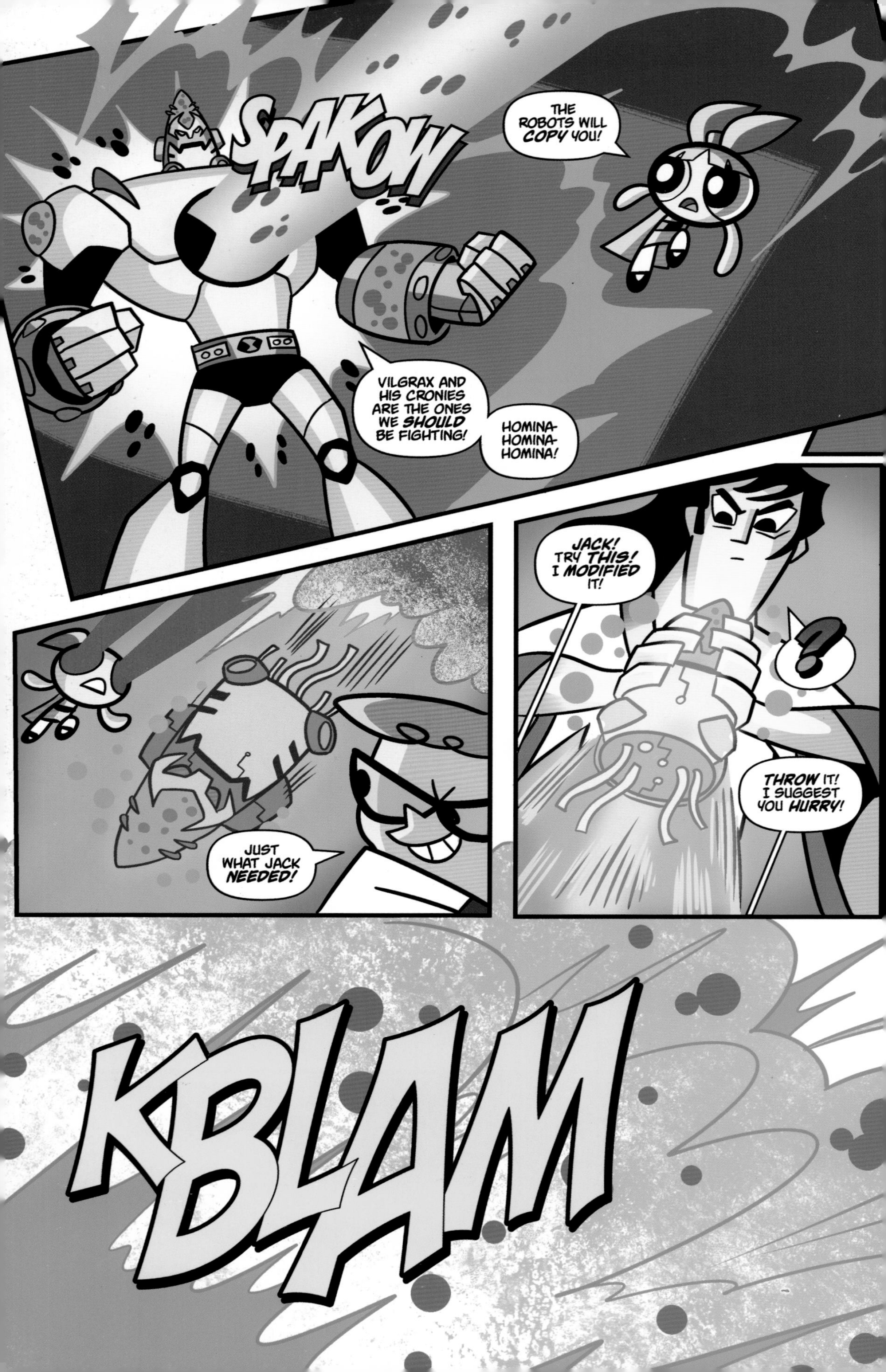
SPAKOW
THE ROBOTS WILL COPY YOU!
VILGRAX AND HIS CRONIES ARE THE ONES WE SHOULD BE FIGHTING!
HOMINA-HOMINA-HOMINA!
JUST WHAT JACK NEEDED!
JACK! TRY THIS! I MODIFIED IT!
!
THROW IT! I SUGGEST YOU HURRY!
KBLAM

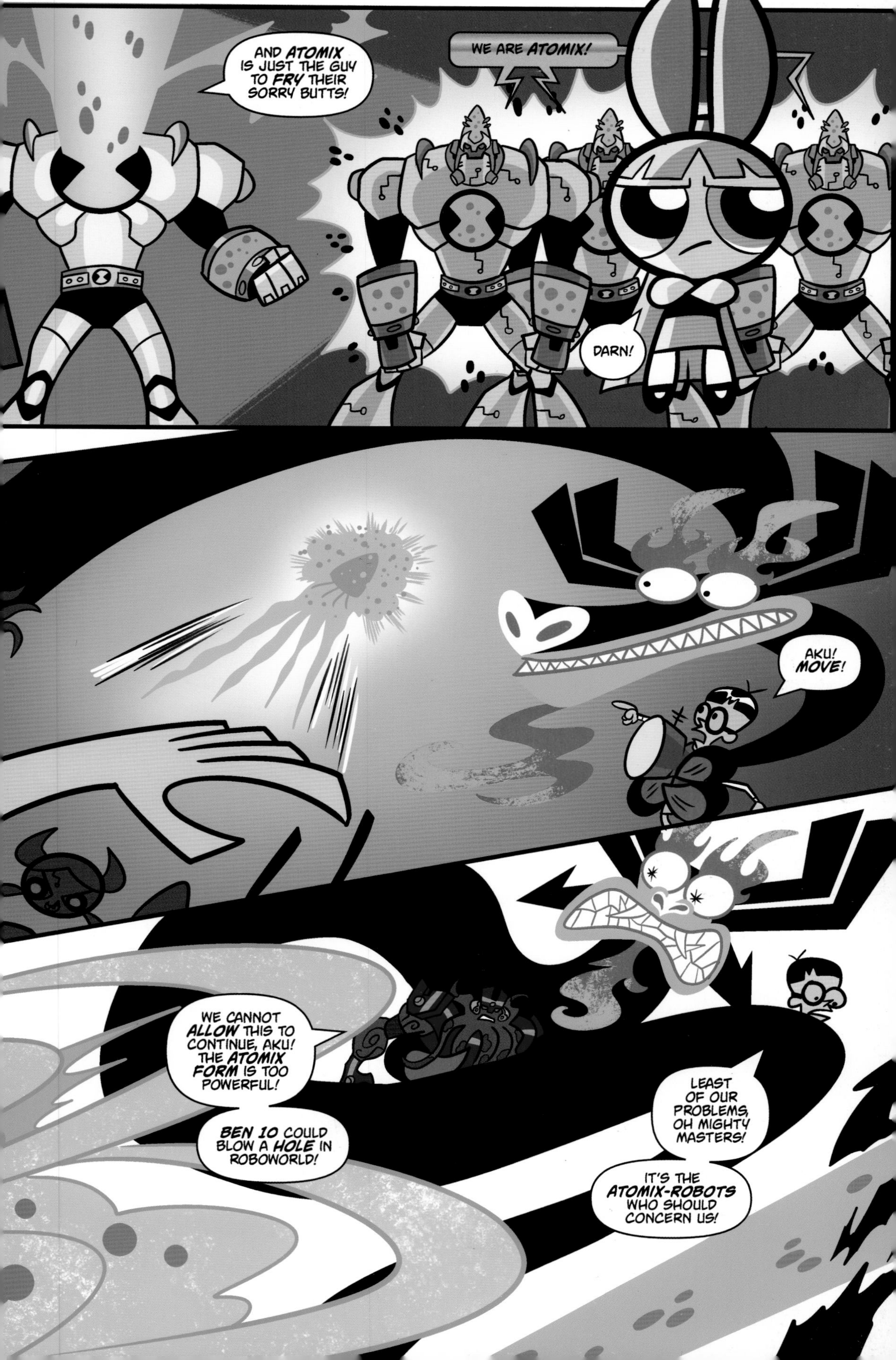
AND ATOMIX IS JUST THE GUY TO FRY THEIR SORRY BUTTS!
WE ARE ATOMIX!
DARN!
AKU! MOVE!
WE CANNOT ALLOW THIS TO CONTINUE, AKU! THE ATOMIX FORM IS TOO POWERFUL!
BEN 10 COULD BLOW A HOLE IN ROBOWORLD!
LEAST OF OUR PROBLEMS, OH MIGHTY MASTERS!
IT'S THE ATOMIX-ROBOTS WHO SHOULD CONCERN US!

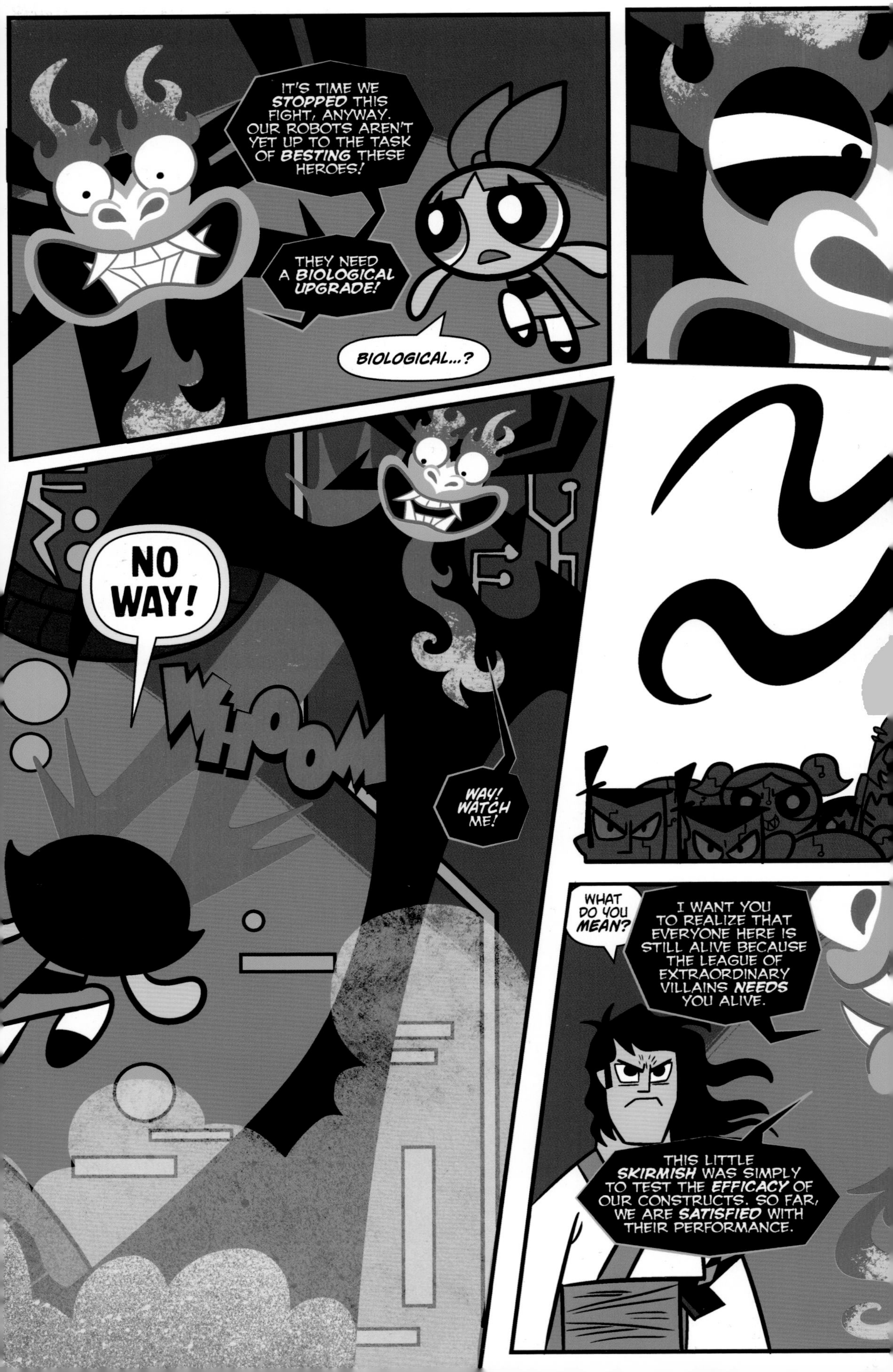
IT'S TIME WE STOPPED THIS FIGHT, ANYWAY. OUR ROBOTS AREN'T YET UP TO THE TASK OF BESTING THESE HEROES!
THEY NEED A BIOLOGICAL UPGRADE!
BIOLOGICAL...?
NO WAY!
WHOOM
WAY! WATCH ME!
WHAT DO YOU MEAN?
I WANT YOU TO REALIZE THAT EVERYONE HERE IS STILL ALIVE BECAUSE THE LEAGUE OF EXTRAORDINARY VILLAINS NEEDS YOU ALIVE.
THIS LITTLE SKIRMISH WAS SIMPLY TO TEST THE EFFICACY OF OUR CONSTRUCTS. SO FAR, WE ARE SATISFIED WITH THEIR PERFORMANCE.

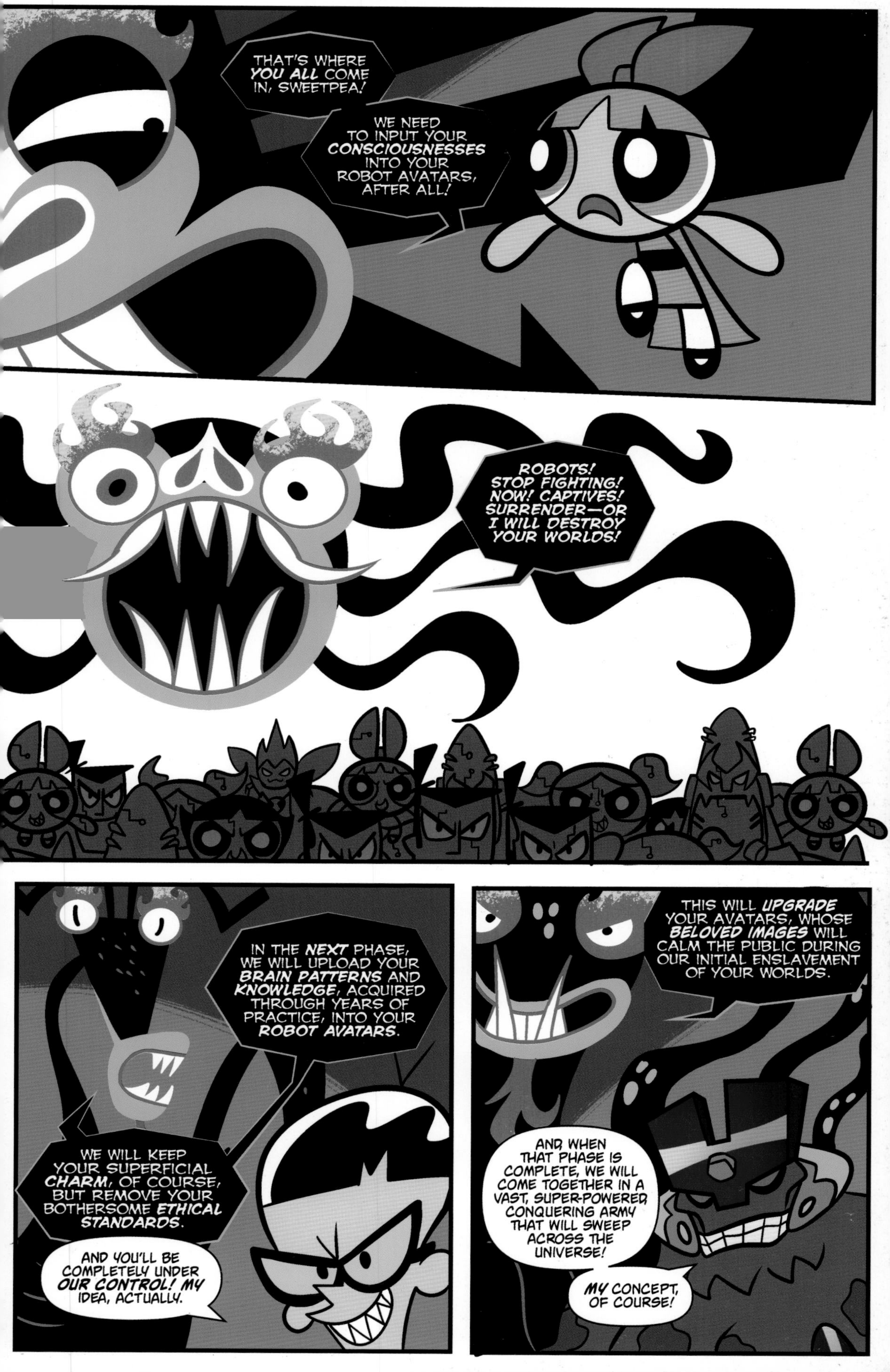
THAT'S WHERE YOU ALL COME IN, SWEETPEA!
WE NEED TO INPUT YOUR CONSCIOUSNESSES INTO YOUR ROBOT AVATARS, AFTER ALL!
ROBOTS! STOP FIGHTING! NOW! CAPTIVES! SURRENDER—OR I WILL DESTROY YOUR WORLDS!
IN THE NEXT PHASE, WE WILL UPLOAD YOUR BRAIN PATTERNS AND KNOWLEDGE, ACQUIRED THROUGH YEARS OF PRACTICE, INTO YOUR ROBOT AVATARS.
WE WILL KEEP YOUR SUPERFICIAL CHARM, OF COURSE, BUT REMOVE YOUR BOTHERSOME ETHICAL STANDARDS.
AND YOU'LL BE COMPLETELY UNDER OUR CONTROL! MY IDEA, ACTUALLY.
THIS WILL UPGRADE YOUR AVATARS, WHOSE BELOVED IMAGES WILL CALM THE PUBLIC DURING OUR INITIAL ENSLAVEMENT OF YOUR WORLDS.
AND, WHEN THAT PHASE IS COMPLETE, WE WILL COME TOGETHER IN A VAST, SUPER-POWERED CONQUERING ARMY THAT WILL SWEEP ACROSS THE UNIVERSE!
MY CONCEPT, OF COURSE!

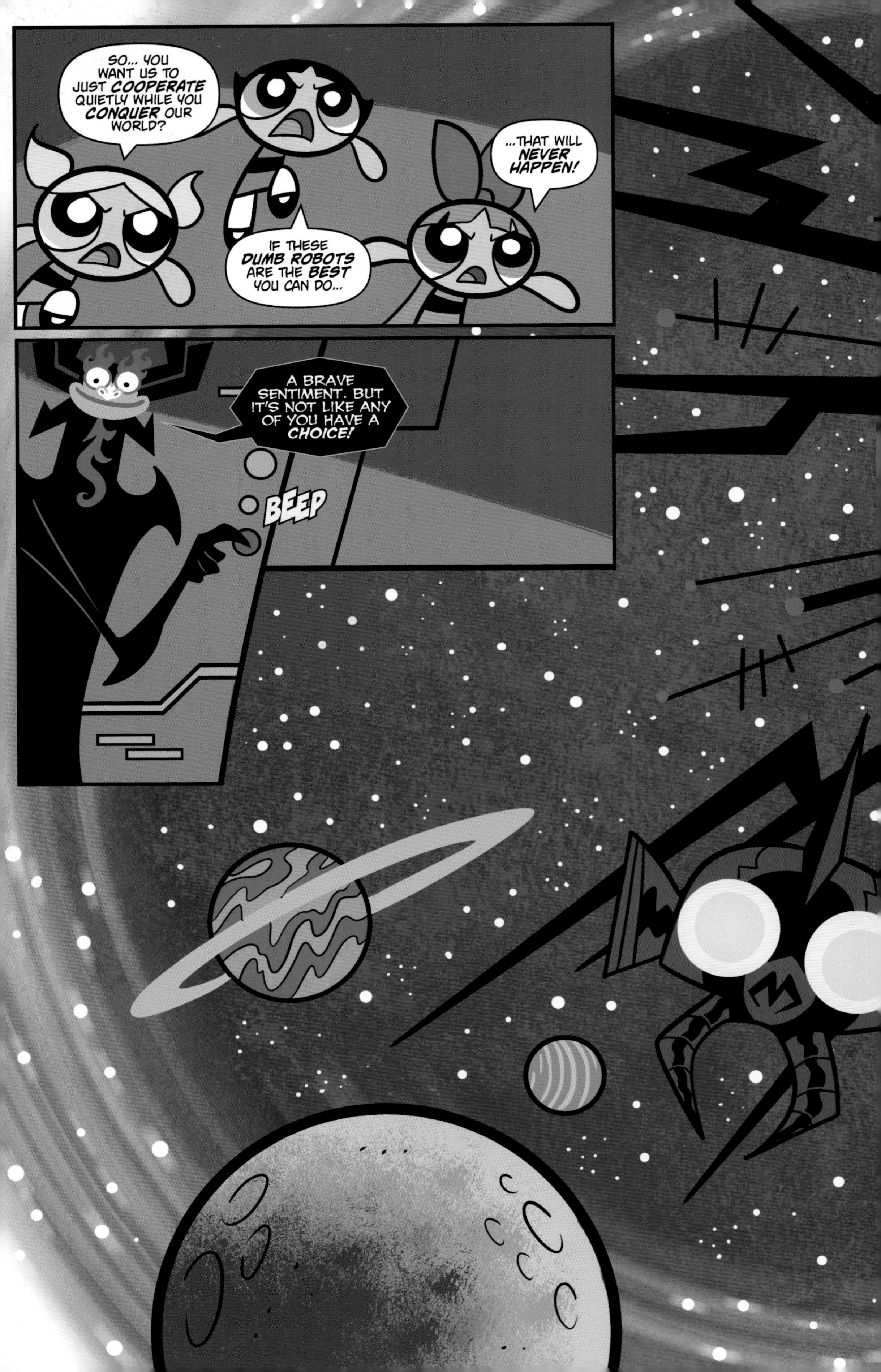

SO... YOU WANT US TO JUST COOPERATE QUIETLY WHILE YOU CONQUER OUR WORLD?
IF THESE DUMB ROBOTS ARE THE BEST YOU CAN DO...
...THAT WILL NEVER HAPPEN!
A BRAVE SENTIMENT. BUT IT'S NOT LIKE ANY OF YOU HAVE A CHOICE!
BEEP

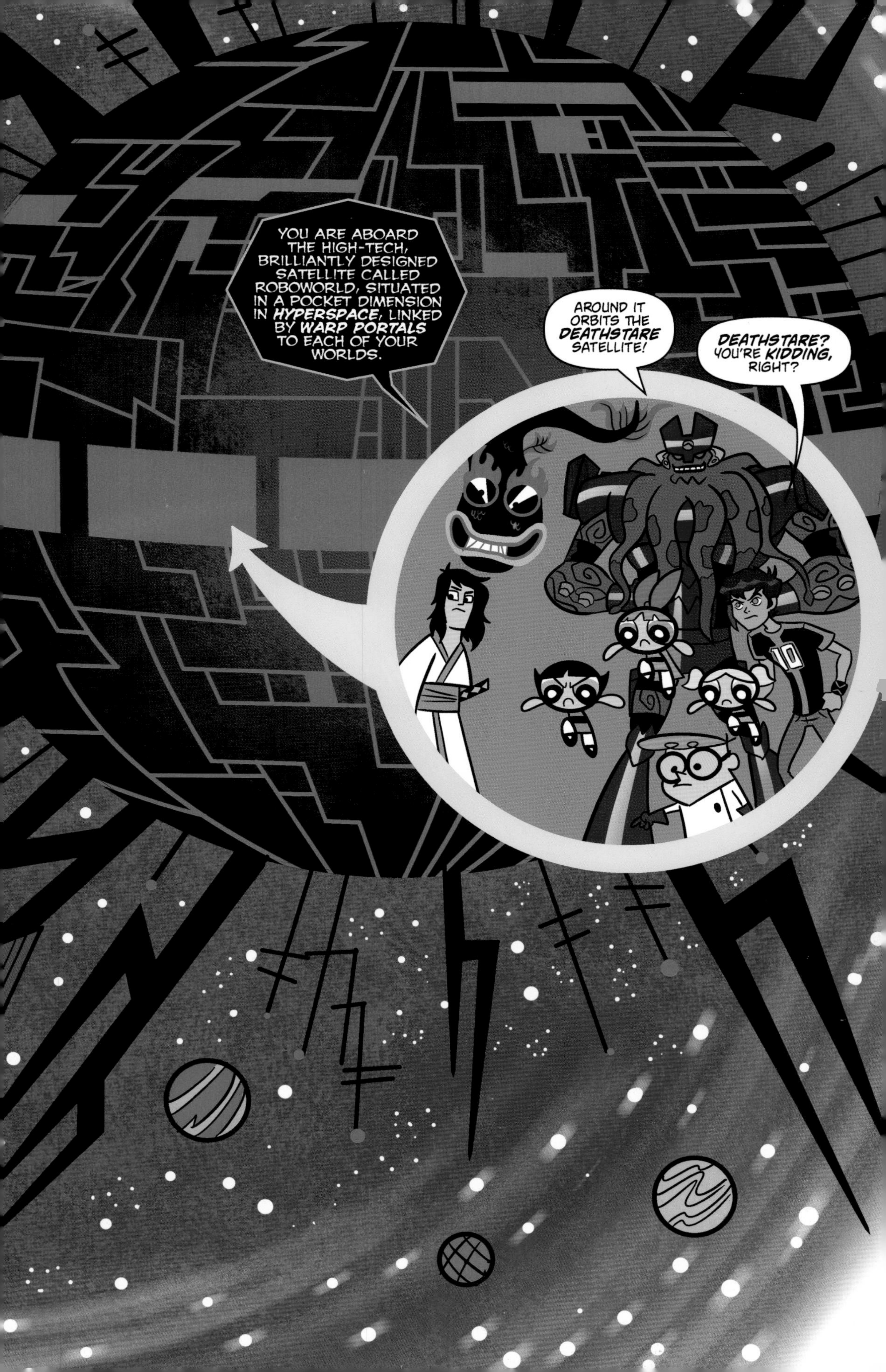
YOU ARE ABOARD THE HIGH-TECH, BRILLIANTLY DESIGNED SATELLITE CALLED ROBOWORLD, SITUATED IN A POCKET DIMENSION IN *HYPERSPACE*, LINKED BY *WARP PORTALS* TO EACH OF YOUR WORLDS.
AROUND IT ORBITS THE *DEATHSTARE* SATELLITE!
DEATHSTARE? YOU'RE *KIDDING*, RIGHT?
10

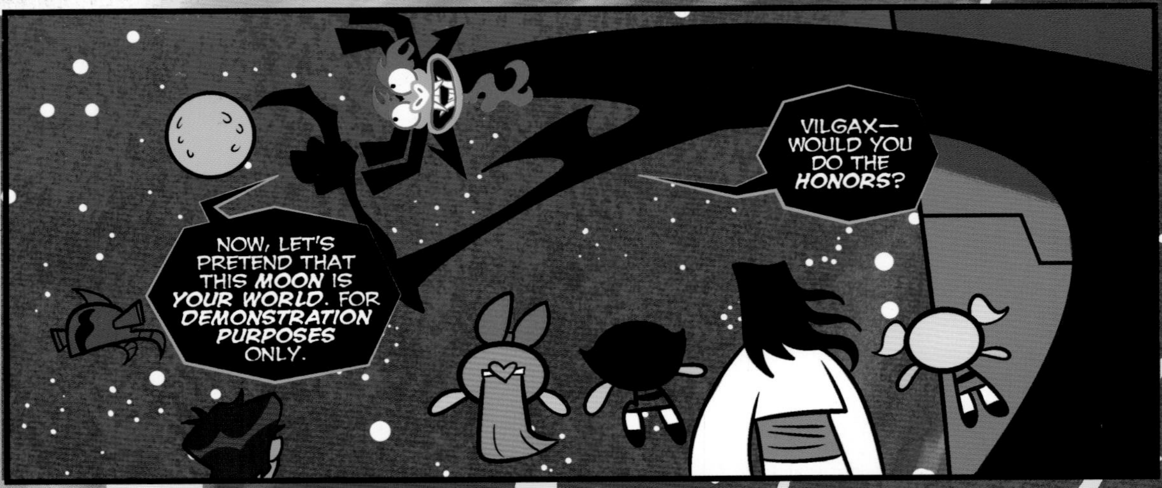

NOW, LET'S PRETEND THAT THIS MOON IS YOUR WORLD. FOR DEMONSTRATION PURPOSES ONLY.
VILGAX— WOULD YOU DO THE HONORS?

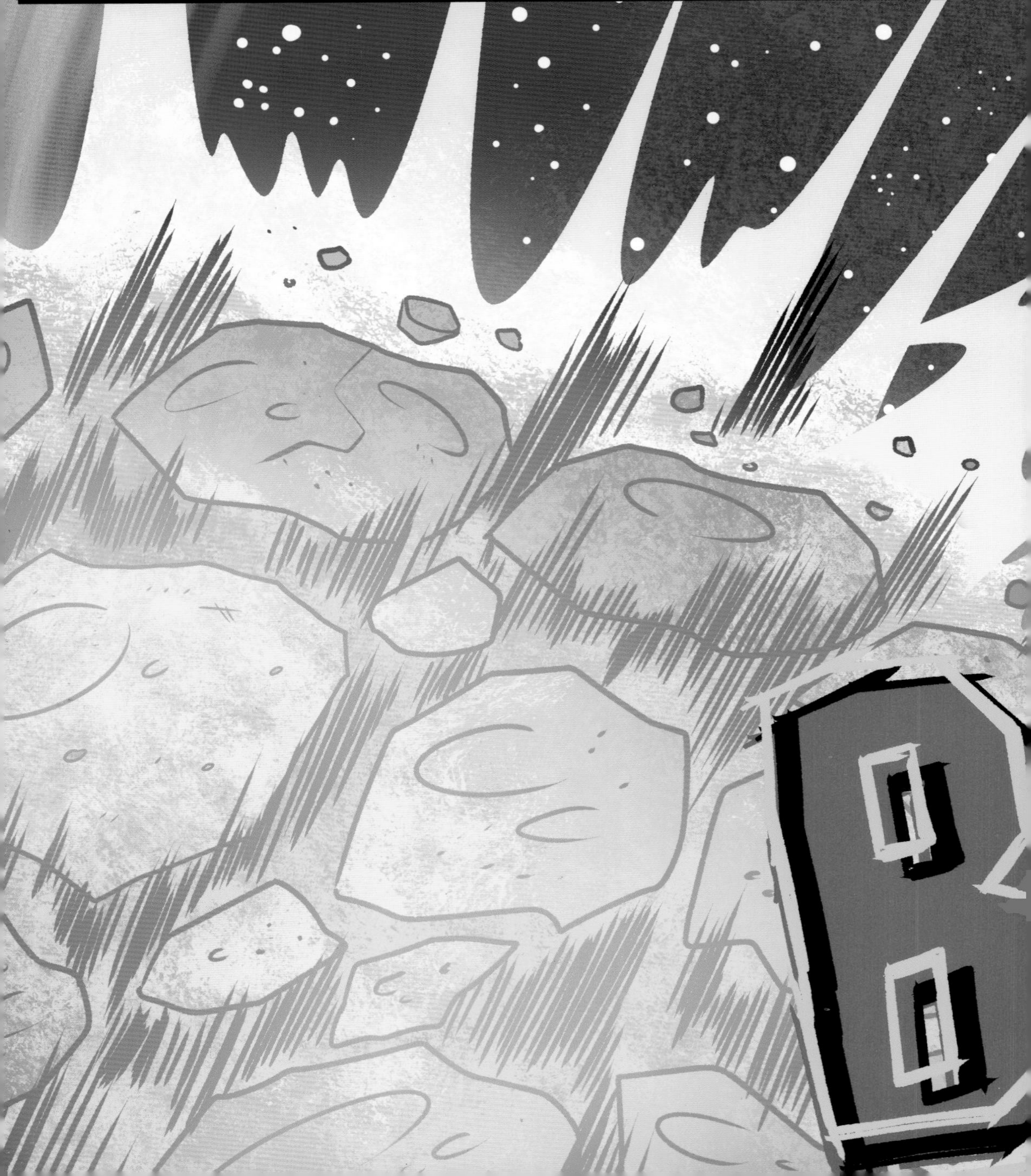

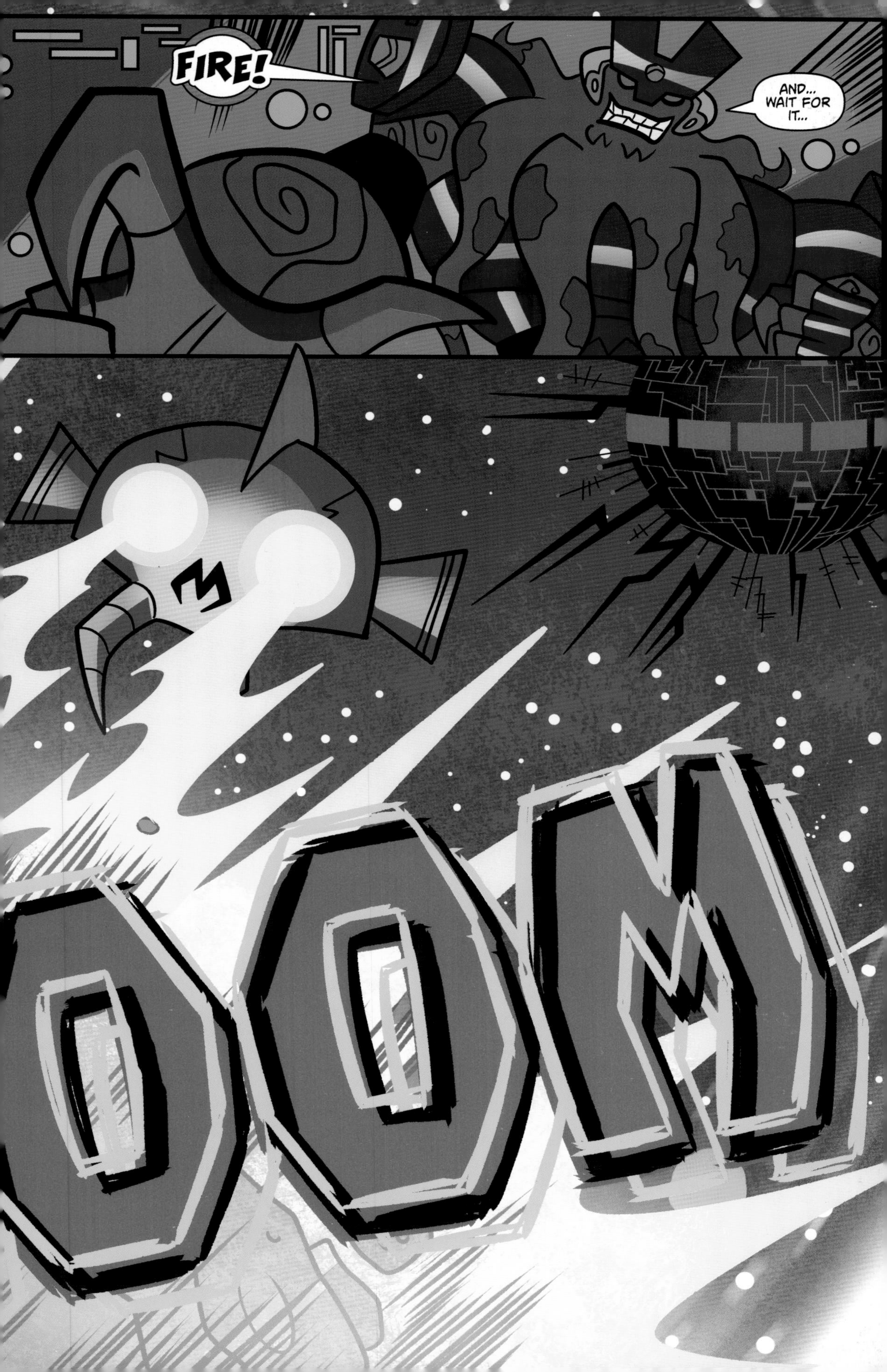
FIRE!
AND... WAIT FOR IT...
OOM

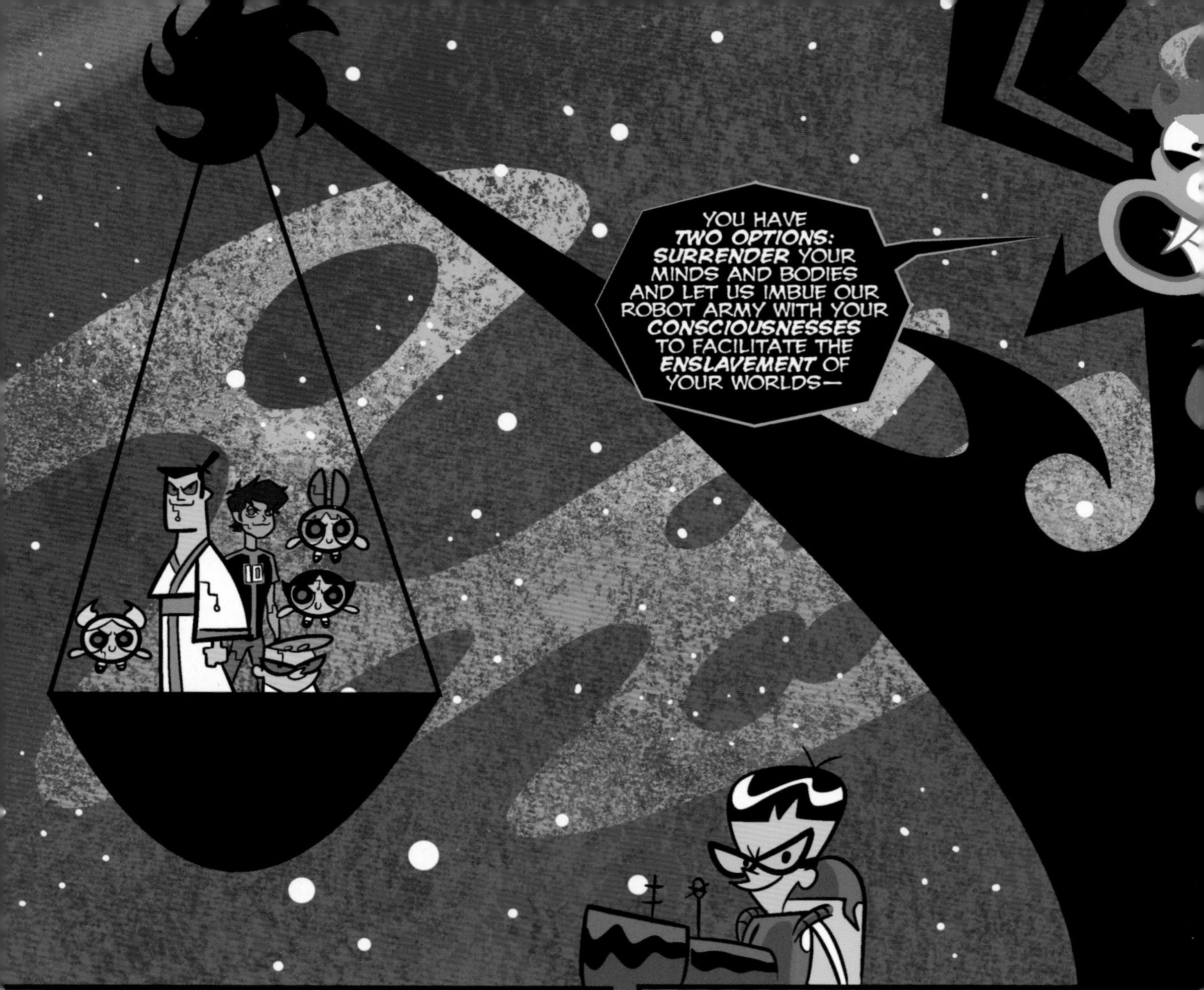
YOU HAVE TWO OPTIONS: SURRENDER YOUR MINDS AND BODIES AND LET US IMBUE OUR ROBOT ARMY WITH YOUR CONSCIOUSNESSES TO FACILITATE THE ENSLAVEMENT OF YOUR WORLDS—

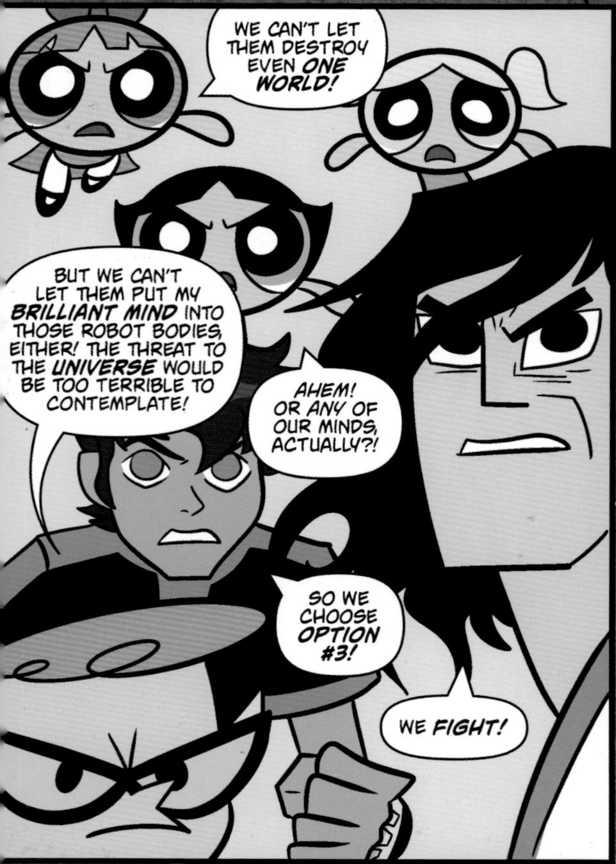
WE CAN'T LET THEM DESTROY EVEN ONE WORLD!
BUT WE CAN'T LET THEM PUT MY BRILLIANT MIND INTO THOSE ROBOT BODIES, EITHER! THE THREAT TO THE UNIVERSE WOULD BE TOO TERRIBLE TO CONTEMPLATE!
AHEM! OR ANY OF OUR MINDS, ACTUALLY?!
SO WE CHOOSE OPTION #3!
WE FIGHT!

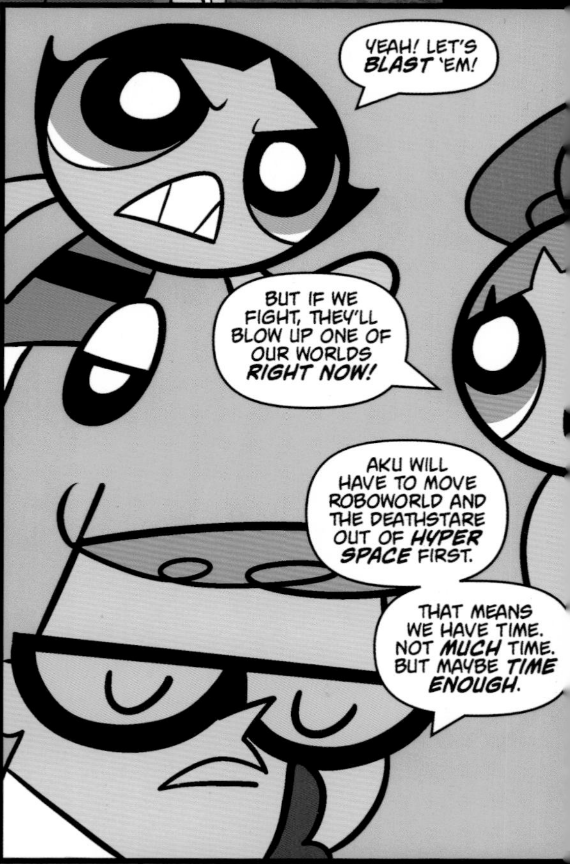
YEAH! LET'S BLAST 'EM!
BUT IF WE FIGHT, THEY'LL BLOW UP ONE OF OUR WORLDS RIGHT NOW!
AKU WILL HAVE TO MOVE ROBOWORLD AND THE DEATHSTARE OUT OF HYPER SPACE FIRST.
THAT MEANS WE HAVE TIME. NOT MUCH TIME. BUT MAYBE TIME ENOUGH.

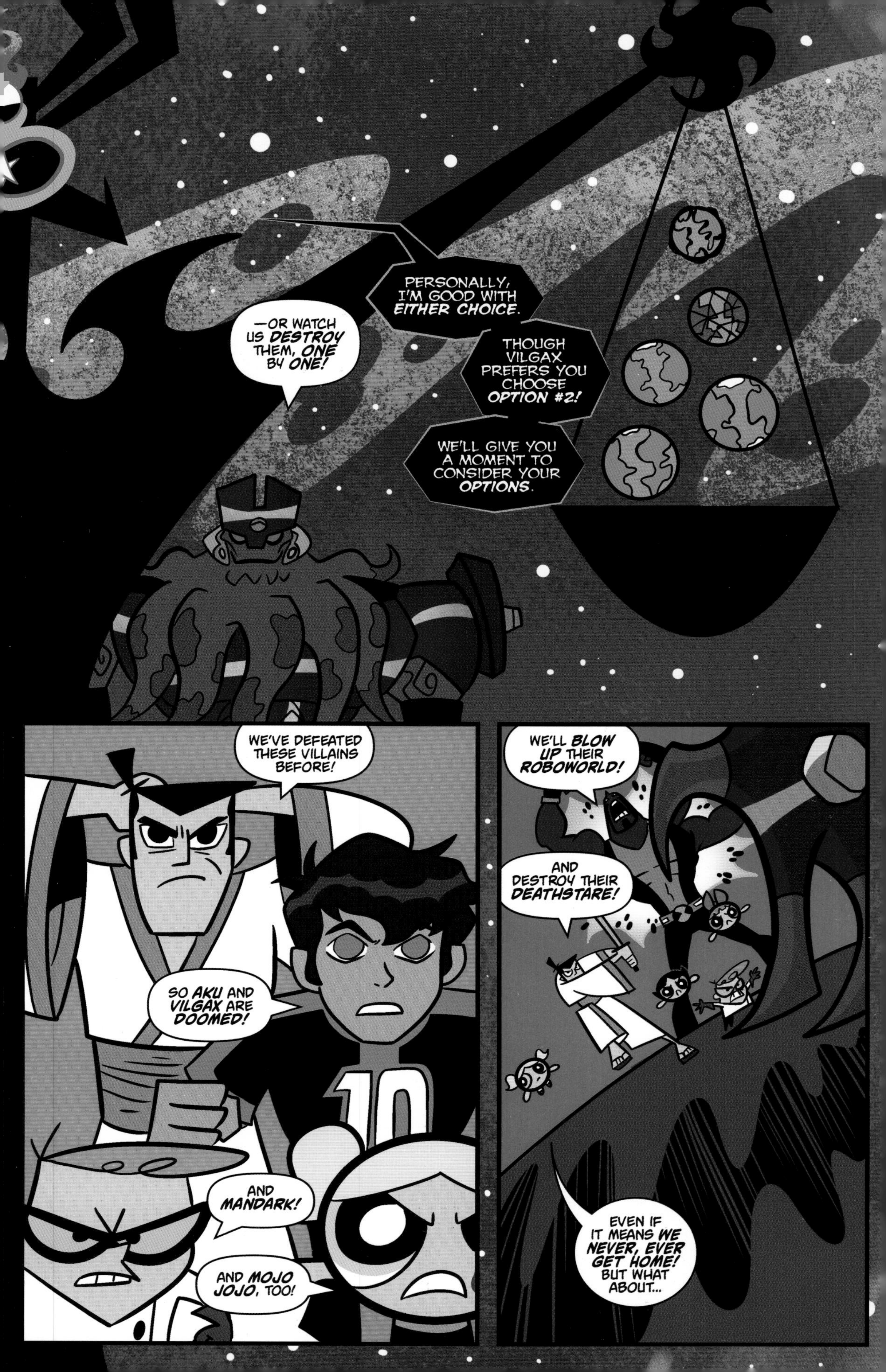
—OR WATCH US DESTROY THEM, ONE BY ONE!
PERSONALLY, I'M GOOD WITH EITHER CHOICE.
THOUGH VILGAX PREFERS YOU CHOOSE OPTION #2!
WE'LL GIVE YOU A MOMENT TO CONSIDER YOUR OPTIONS.
WE'VE DEFEATED THESE VILLAINS BEFORE!
SO AKU AND VILGAX ARE DOOMED!
AND MANDARK!
AND MOJO JOJO, TOO!
WE'LL BLOW UP THEIR ROBOWORLD!
AND DESTROY THEIR DEATHSTARE!
EVEN IF IT MEANS WE NEVER, EVER GET HOME! BUT WHAT ABOUT...

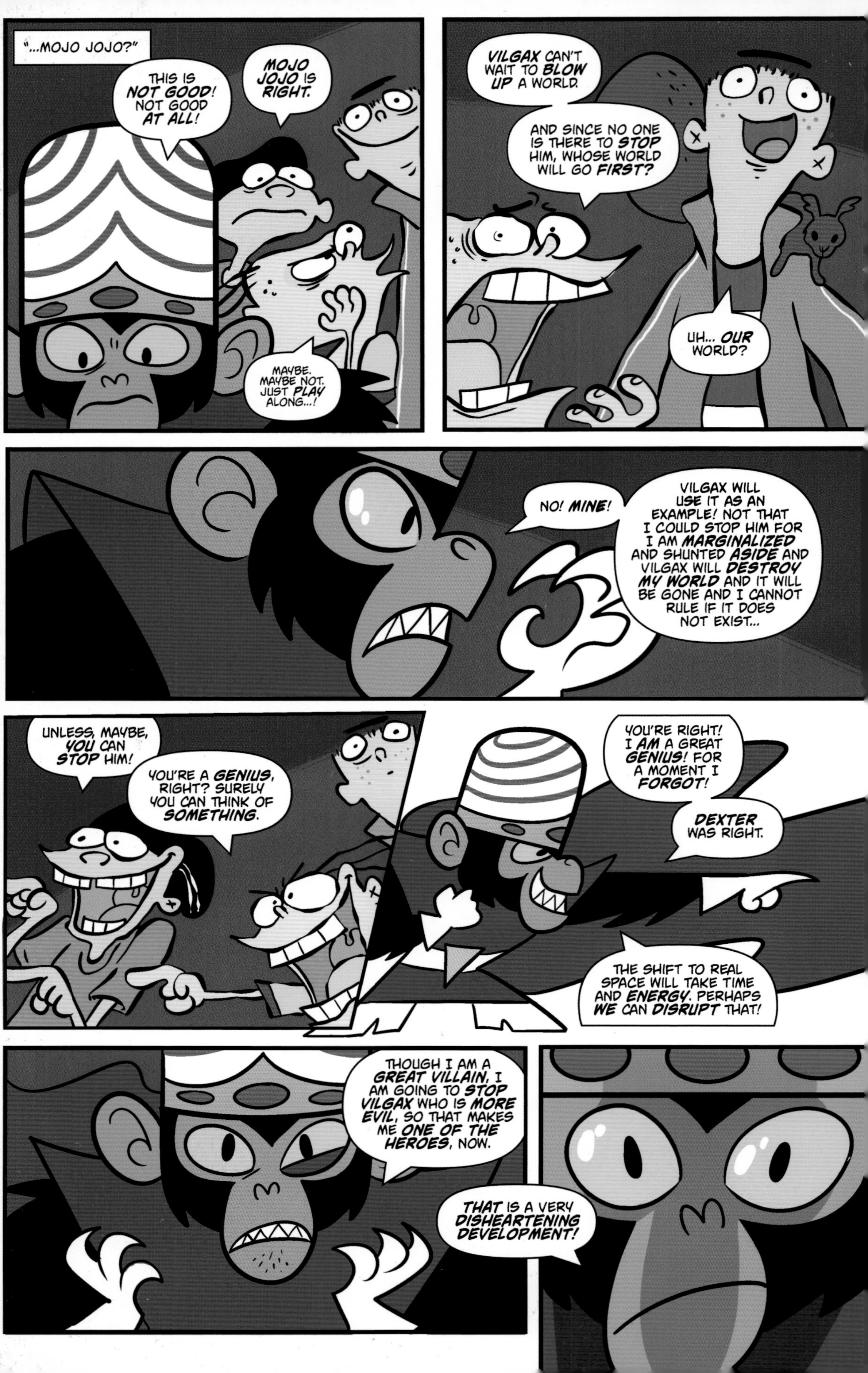
"...MOJO JOJO?"
THIS IS NOT GOOD! NOT GOOD AT ALL!
MOJO JOJO IS RIGHT.
MAYBE. MAYBE NOT. JUST PLAY ALONG...!
VILGAX CAN'T WAIT TO BLOW UP A WORLD.
AND SINCE NO ONE IS THERE TO STOP HIM, WHOSE WORLD WILL GO FIRST?
UH... OUR WORLD?
NO! MINE!
VILGAX WILL USE IT AS AN EXAMPLE! NOT THAT I COULD STOP HIM FOR I AM MARGINALIZED AND SHUNTED ASIDE AND VILGAX WILL DESTROY MY WORLD AND IT WILL BE GONE AND I CANNOT RULE IF IT DOES NOT EXIST...
UNLESS, MAYBE, YOU CAN STOP HIM!
YOU'RE A GENIUS, RIGHT? SURELY YOU CAN THINK OF SOMETHING.
YOU'RE RIGHT! I AM A GREAT GENIUS! FOR A MOMENT I FORGOT!
DEXTER WAS RIGHT.
THE SHIFT TO REAL SPACE WILL TAKE TIME AND ENERGY. PERHAPS WE CAN DISRUPT THAT!
THOUGH I AM A GREAT VILLAIN, I AM GOING TO STOP VILGAX WHO IS MORE EVIL, SO THAT MAKES ME ONE OF THE HEROES, NOW.
THAT IS A VERY DISHEARTENING DEVELOPMENT!

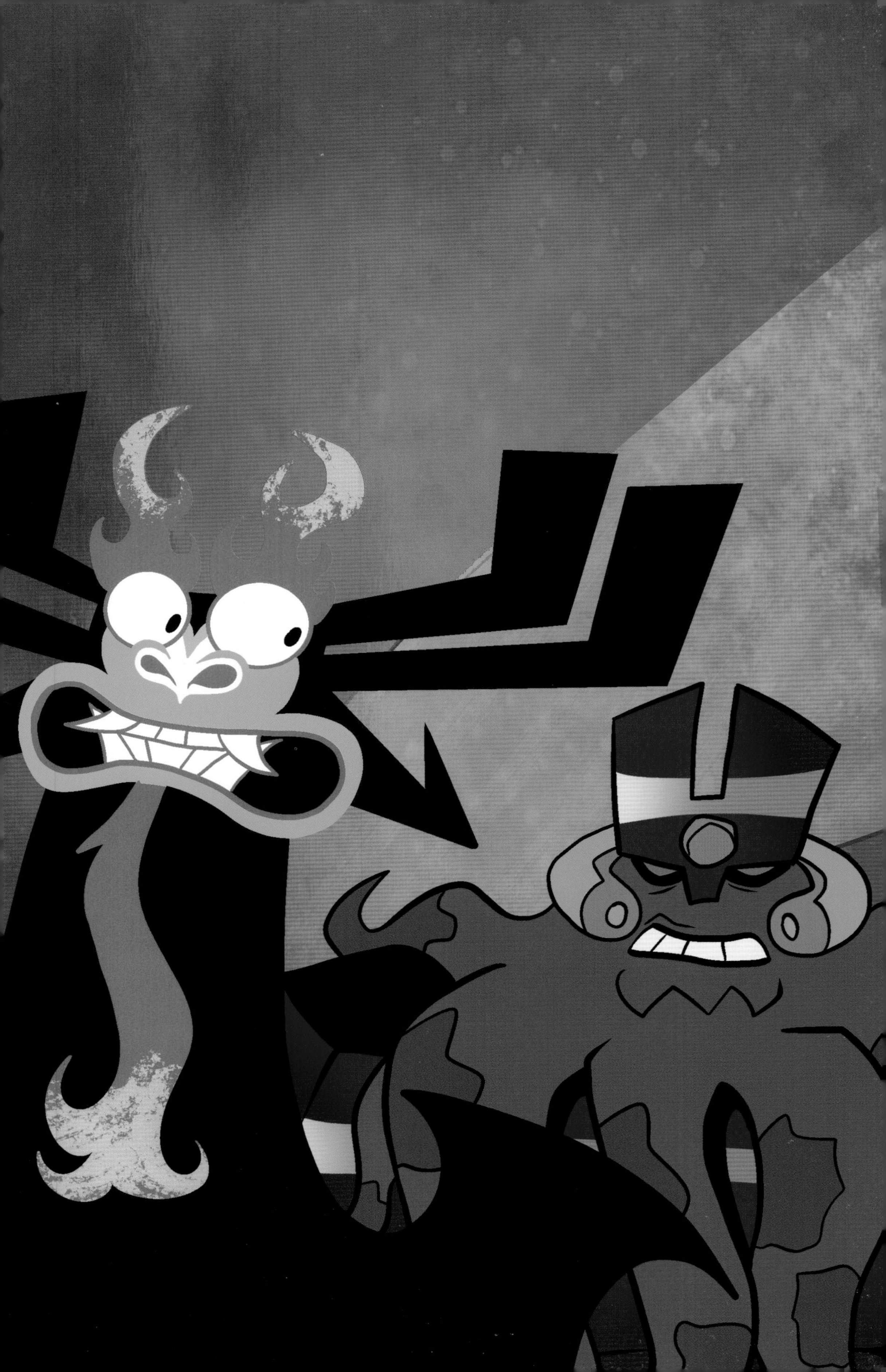

Chapter 5

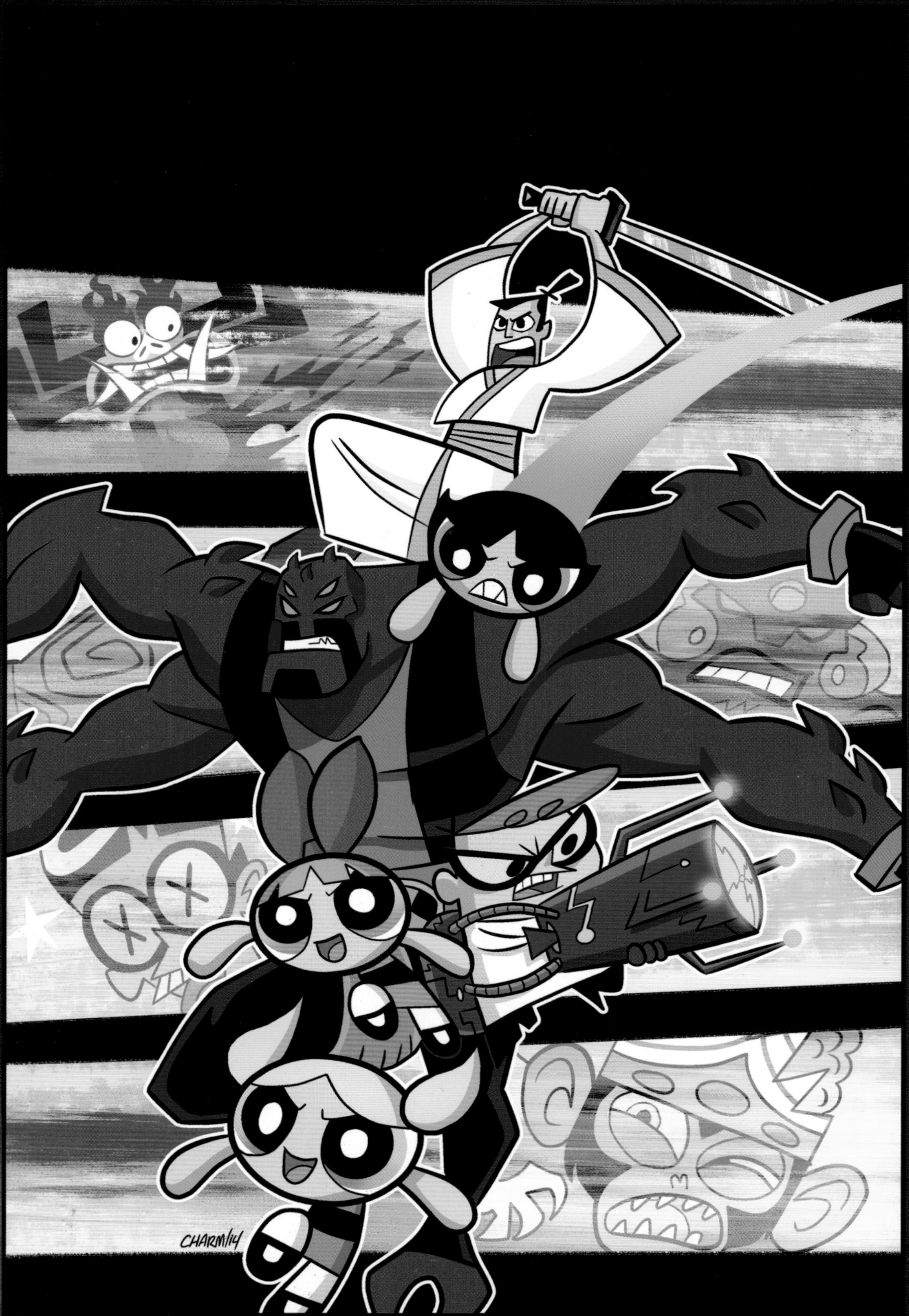
CHARM/14

Cover Art by Derek Charm

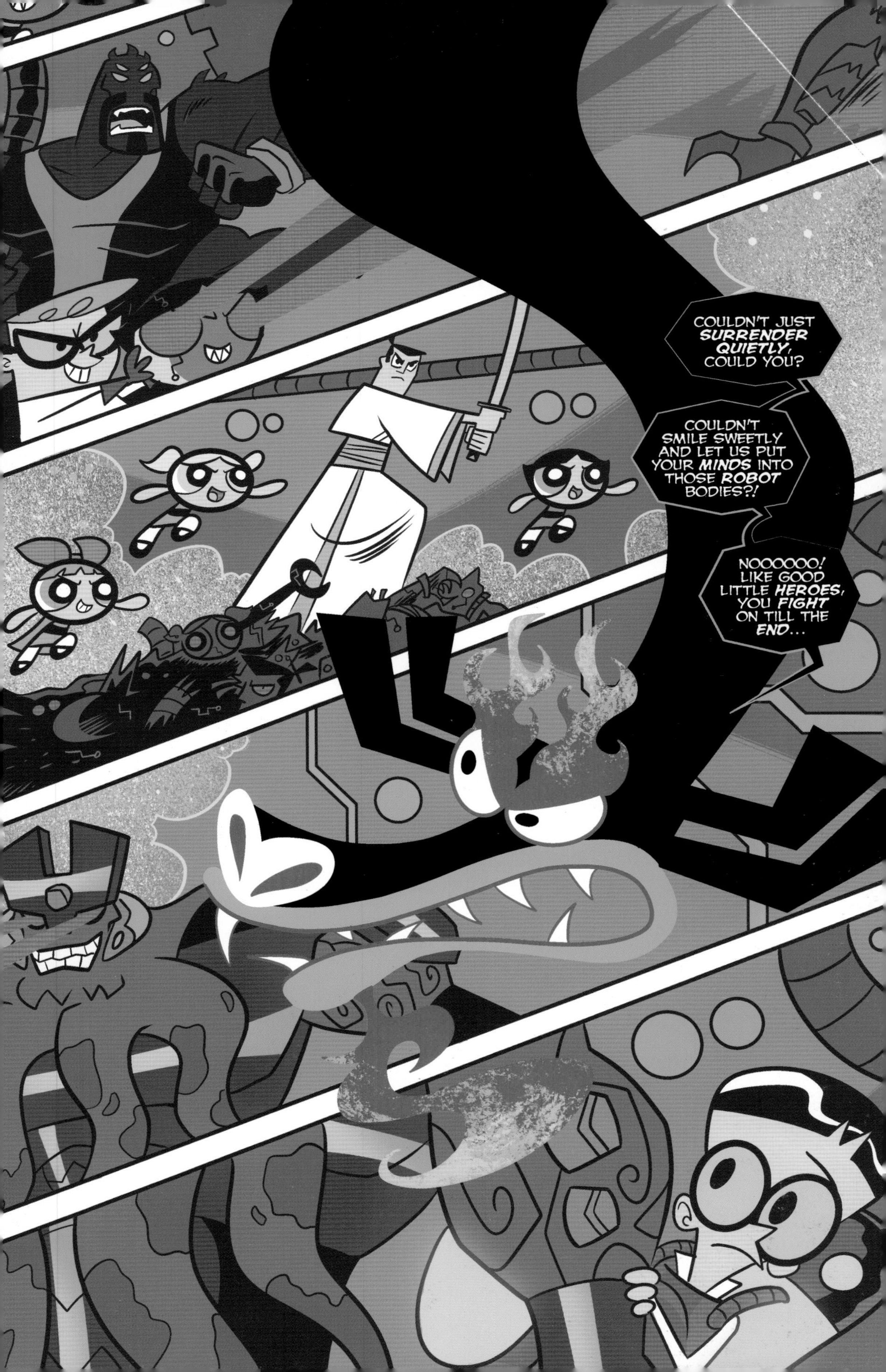
COULDN'T JUST SURRENDER QUIETLY, COULD YOU?
COULDN'T SMILE SWEETLY AND LET US PUT YOUR MINDS INTO THOSE ROBOT BODIES?!
NOOOOOO! LIKE GOOD LITTLE HEROES, YOU FIGHT ON TILL THE END...

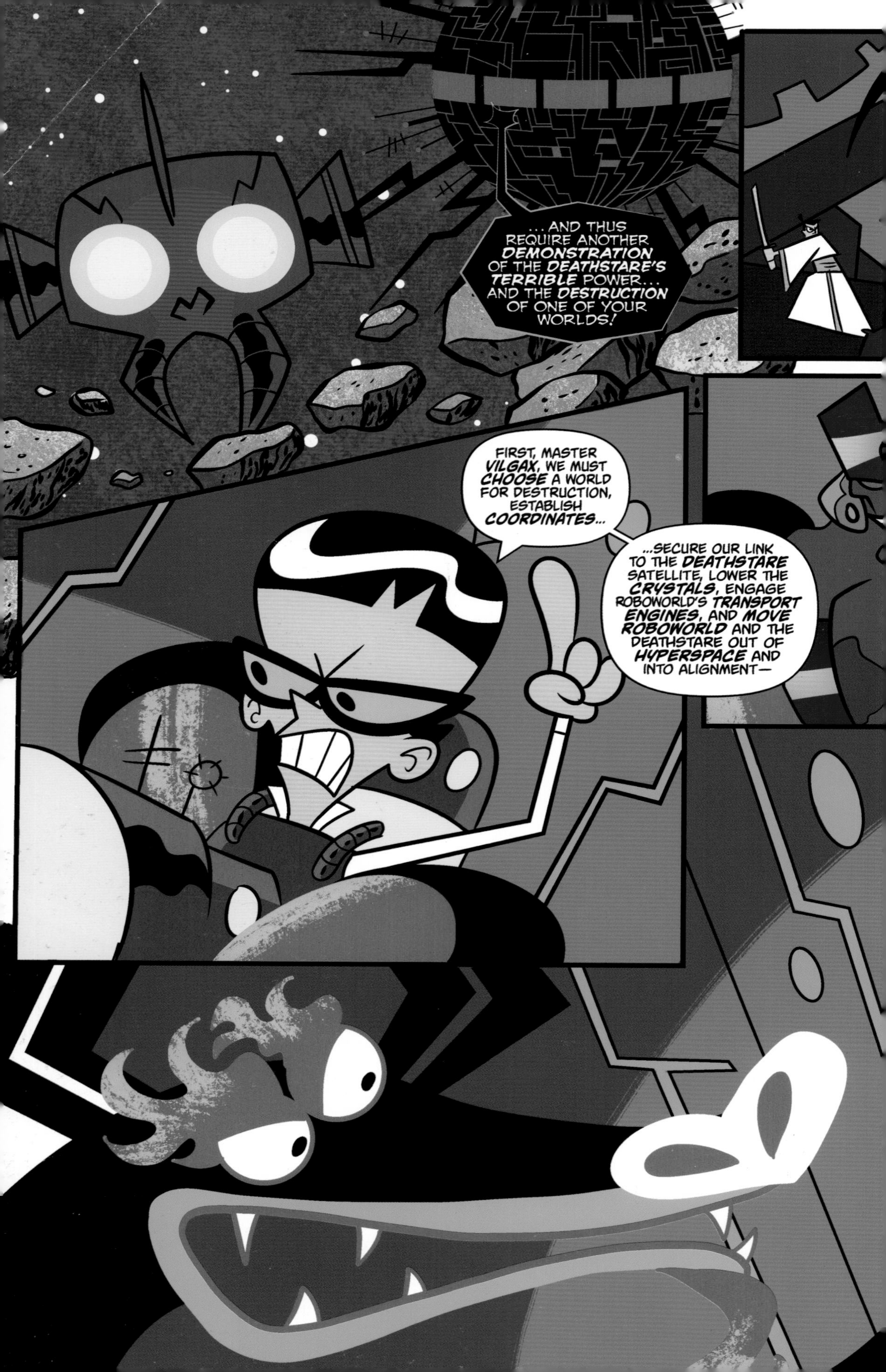
...AND THUS REQUIRE ANOTHER DEMONSTRATION OF THE DEATHSTARE'S TERRIBLE POWER... AND THE DESTRUCTION OF ONE OF YOUR WORLDS!
FIRST, MASTER VILGAX, WE MUST CHOOSE A WORLD FOR DESTRUCTION, ESTABLISH COORDINATES...
...SECURE OUR LINK TO THE DEATHSTARE SATELLITE, LOWER THE CRYSTALS, ENGAGE ROBOWORLD'S TRANSPORT ENGINES, AND MOVE ROBOWORLD AND THE DEATHSTARE OUT OF HYPERSPACE AND INTO ALIGNMENT—

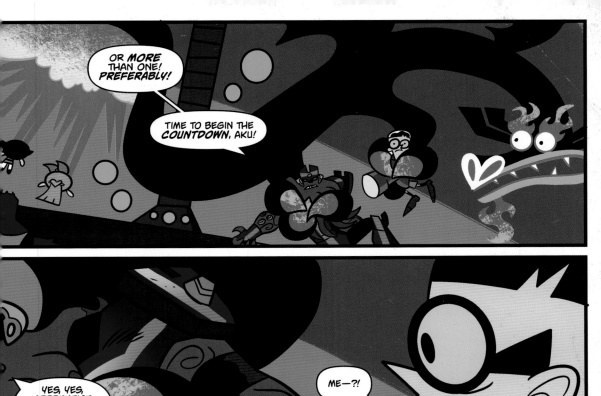

OR *MORE* THAN ONE! PREFERABLY!

TIME TO BEGIN THE *COUNTDOWN*, AKU!

YES, YES, APPRENTICE *MANDARK*. QUITE THE *TO-DO* LIST! BEST YOU *GET STARTED*!

ME—?!

I HAVE *PRESET* THE COORDINATES. YOU HAVE BUT TO ENGAGE THE CRYSTALS AND MOVE ROBOWORLD INTO ORBIT...

...WHILE *VILGAX* AND I KEEP OUR SUBJECTS *TOO DISTRACTED* TO ENGAGE IN FURTHER HEROICS.

ROBOTS, ATTACK!

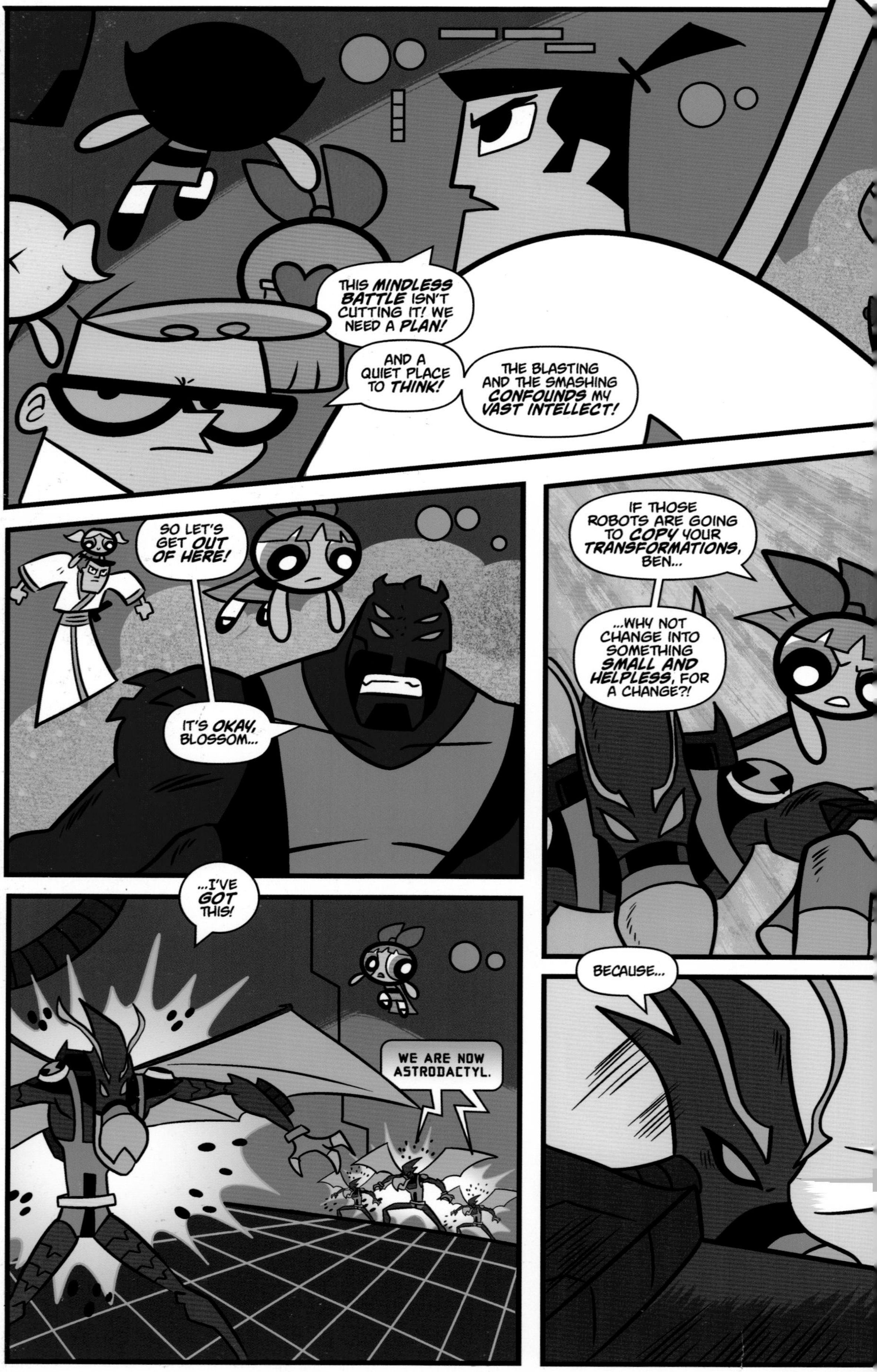
THIS MINDLESS BATTLE ISN'T CUTTING IT! WE NEED A PLAN!
AND A QUIET PLACE TO THINK!
THE BLASTING AND THE SMASHING CONFOUNDS MY VAST INTELLECT!
SO LET'S GET OUT OF HERE!
IT'S OKAY, BLOSSOM...
IF THOSE ROBOTS ARE GOING TO COPY YOUR TRANSFORMATIONS, BEN...
...WHY NOT CHANGE INTO SOMETHING SMALL AND HELPLESS, FOR A CHANGE?!
...I'VE GOT THIS!
WE ARE NOW ASTRODACTYL.
BECAUSE...

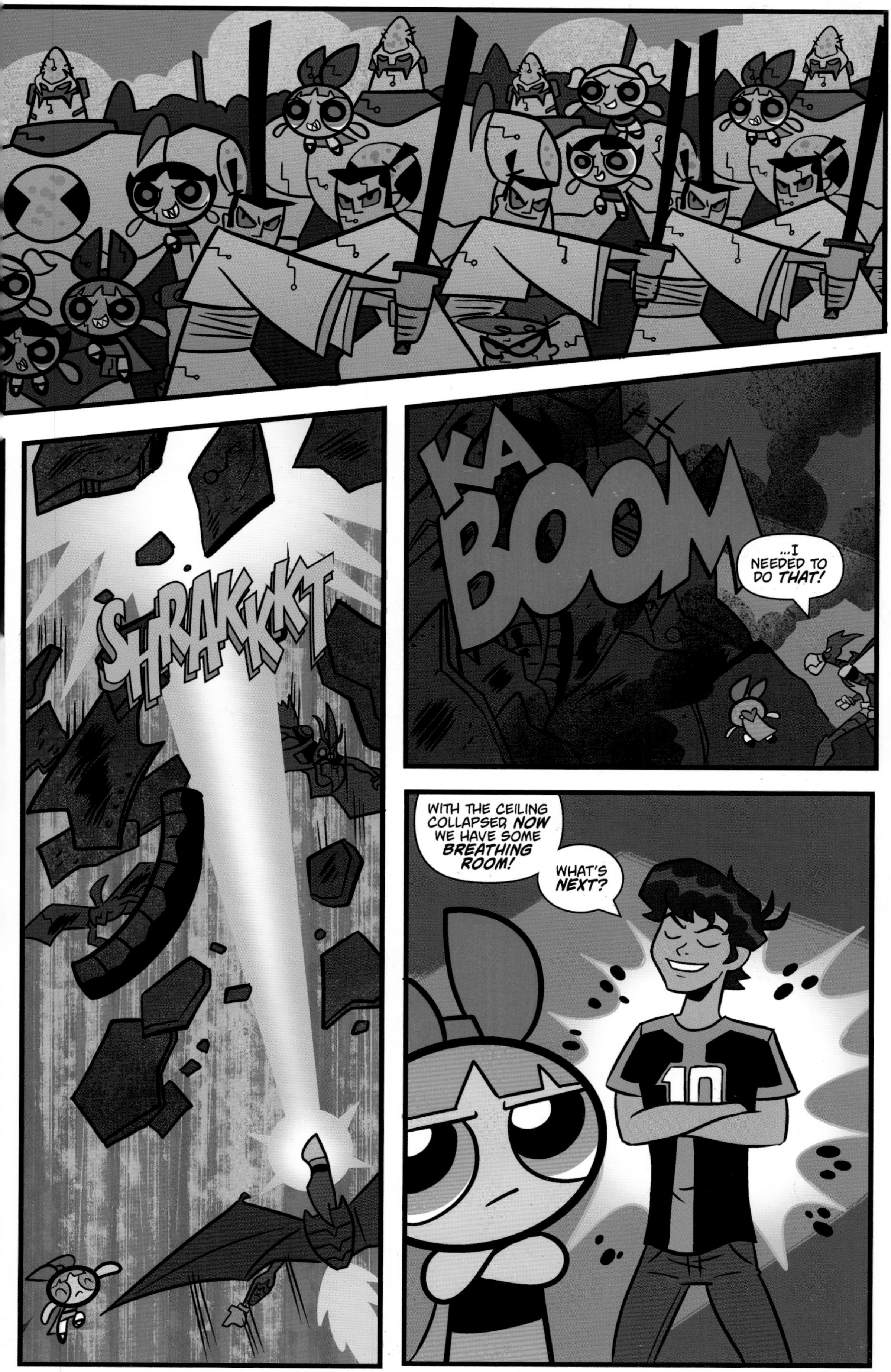
SHRAKKKT
KA BOOM
...I NEEDED TO DO THAT!
WITH THE CEILING COLLAPSED, NOW WE HAVE SOME BREATHING ROOM!
WHAT'S NEXT?

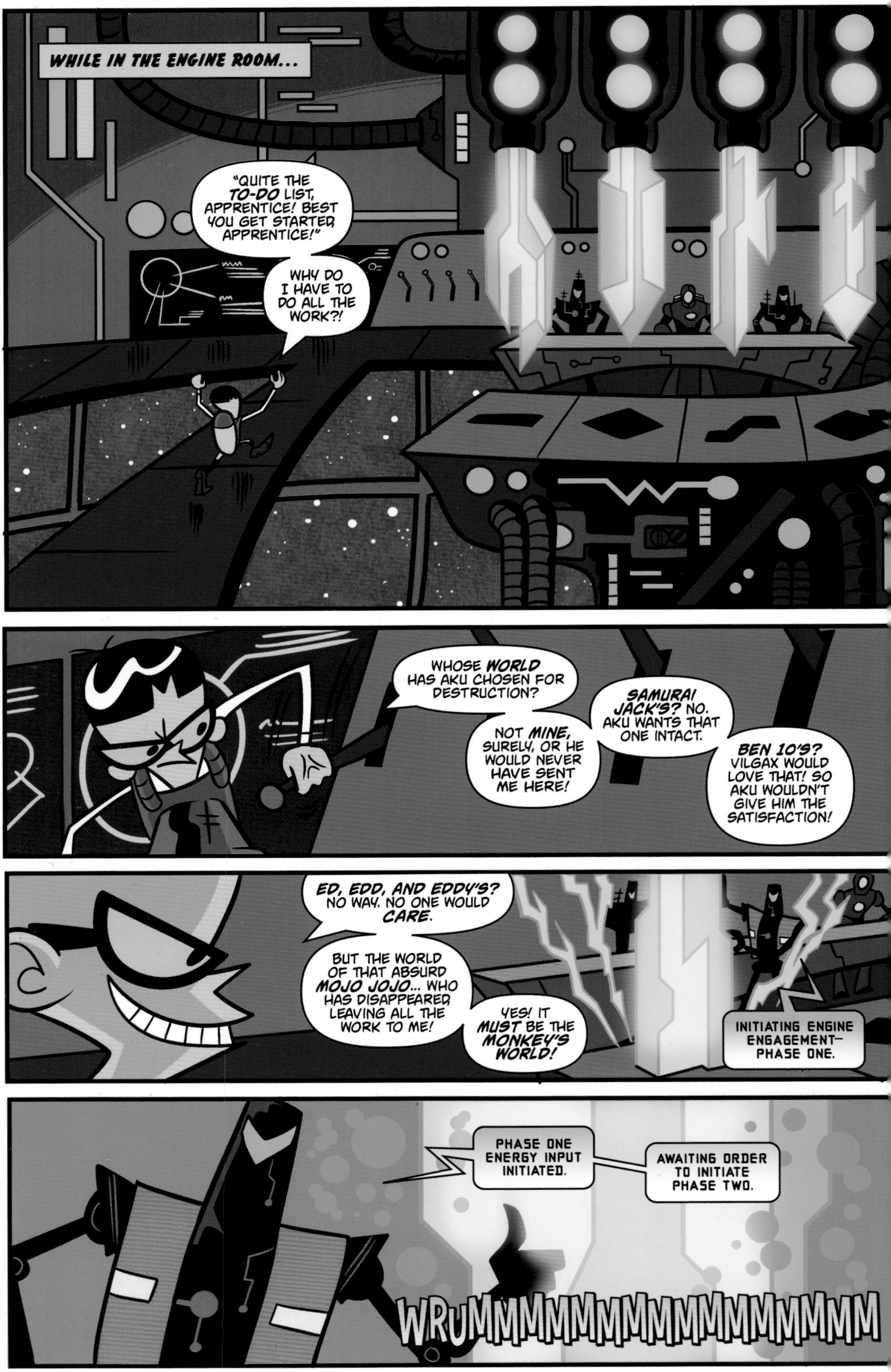
WHILE IN THE ENGINE ROOM...
"QUITE THE TO-DO LIST, APPRENTICE! BEST YOU GET STARTED, APPRENTICE!"
WHY DO I HAVE TO DO ALL THE WORK?!
WHOSE WORLD HAS AKU CHOSEN FOR DESTRUCTION?
NOT MINE, SURELY, OR HE WOULD NEVER HAVE SENT ME HERE!
SAMURAI JACK'S? NO. AKU WANTS THAT ONE INTACT.
BEN 10'S? VILGAX WOULD LOVE THAT! SO AKU WOULDN'T GIVE HIM THE SATISFACTION!
ED, EDD, AND EDDY'S? NO WAY. NO ONE WOULD CARE.
BUT THE WORLD OF THAT ABSURD MOJO JOJO... WHO HAS DISAPPEARED, LEAVING ALL THE WORK TO ME!
YES! IT MUST BE THE MONKEY'S WORLD!
INITIATING ENGINE ENGAGEMENT— PHASE ONE.
PHASE ONE ENERGY INPUT INITIATED.
AWAITING ORDER TO INITIATE PHASE TWO.
WRUMMMMMMMMMMMMMMMMMMM

AND NEARBY...

THEY'RE REALLY GONNA *TOAST* SOMEBODY'S WORLD?

THAT IS SERIOUSLY *MESSED UP,* DUDE.

TOAST IS GOOD.

WURMMMMMMMMMMMMM

WHAT'S *THAT?*

THE TRANSPORT *ENGINES* ARE BEING ENGAGED. IN MERE MOMENTS, ROBOWORLD WILL BE IN POSITION.

AND SET TO *BLOW UP* A WORLD!

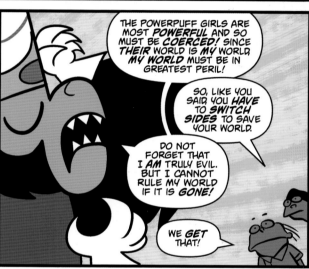

THE POWERPUFF GIRLS ARE MOST *POWERFUL* AND SO MUST BE *COERCED!* SINCE *THEIR* WORLD IS *MY* WORLD, *MY WORLD* MUST BE IN GREATEST PERIL!

SO, LIKE YOU SAID, YOU *HAVE* TO *SWITCH SIDES* TO SAVE YOUR WORLD.

DO NOT FORGET THAT I *AM* TRULY EVIL. BUT I CANNOT RULE MY WORLD IF IT IS *GONE!*

WE *GET* THAT!

WE MUST *DESTROY ROBOWORLD* AND THE *DEATHSTARE!*

WE—?

IF WE DESTROY ROBOWORLD, WON'T *WE* GET DESTROYED *WITH* IT!

MAYBE. PROBABLY. MORE THAN LIKELY. BUT NOT NECESSARILY. FOLLOW ME!

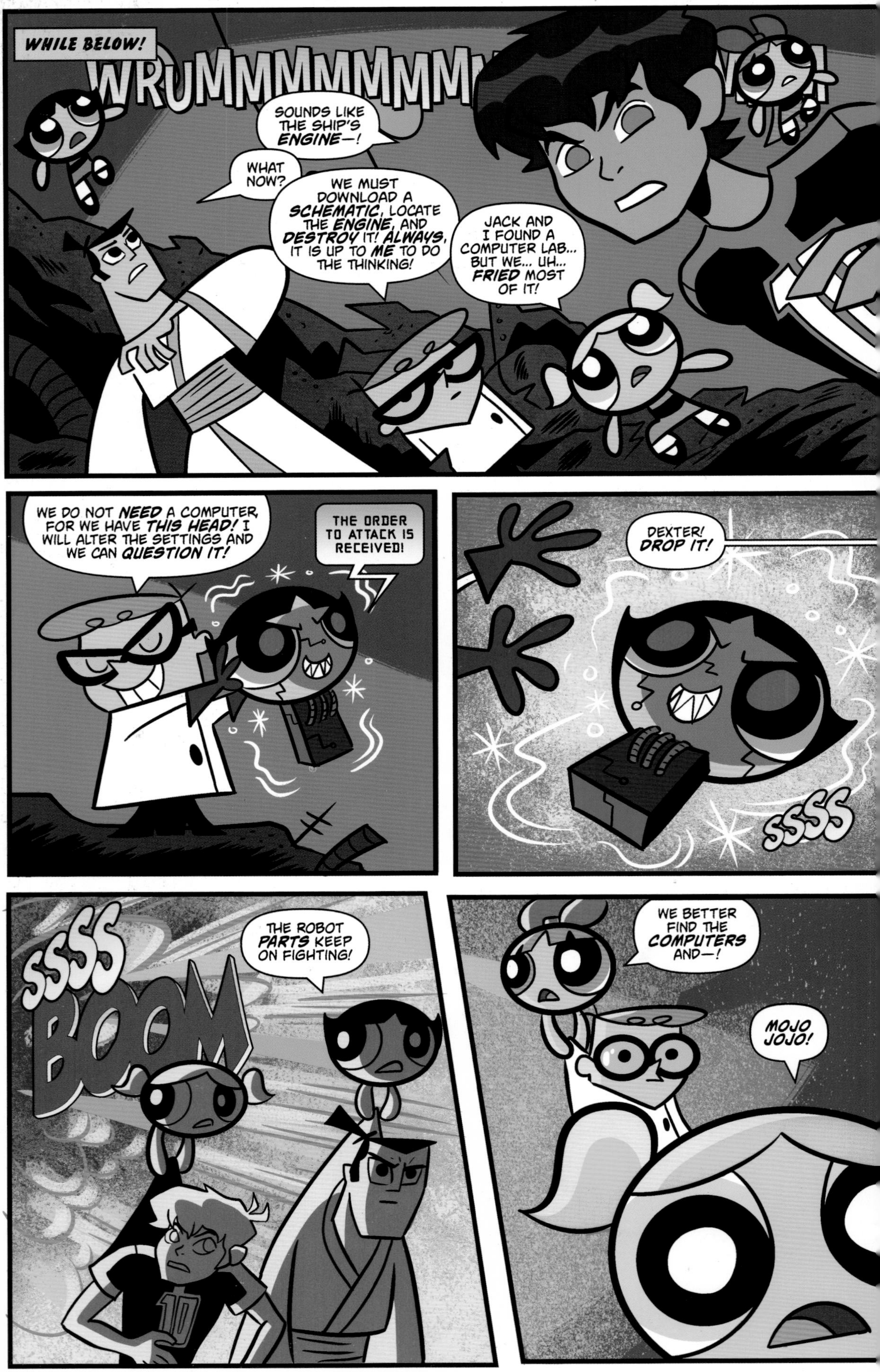

WHILE BELOW!
WRUMMMMMMMMM
SOUNDS LIKE THE SHIP'S ENGINE—!
WHAT NOW?
WE MUST DOWNLOAD A SCHEMATIC, LOCATE THE ENGINE, AND DESTROY IT! ALWAYS, IT IS UP TO ME TO DO THE THINKING!
JACK AND I FOUND A COMPUTER LAB... BUT WE... UH... FRIED MOST OF IT!
WE DO NOT NEED A COMPUTER, FOR WE HAVE THIS HEAD! I WILL ALTER THE SETTINGS AND WE CAN QUESTION IT!
THE ORDER TO ATTACK IS RECEIVED!
DEXTER! DROP IT!
SSSS
SSSS
BOOM
THE ROBOT PARTS KEEP ON FIGHTING!
WE BETTER FIND THE COMPUTERS AND—!
MOJO JOJO!

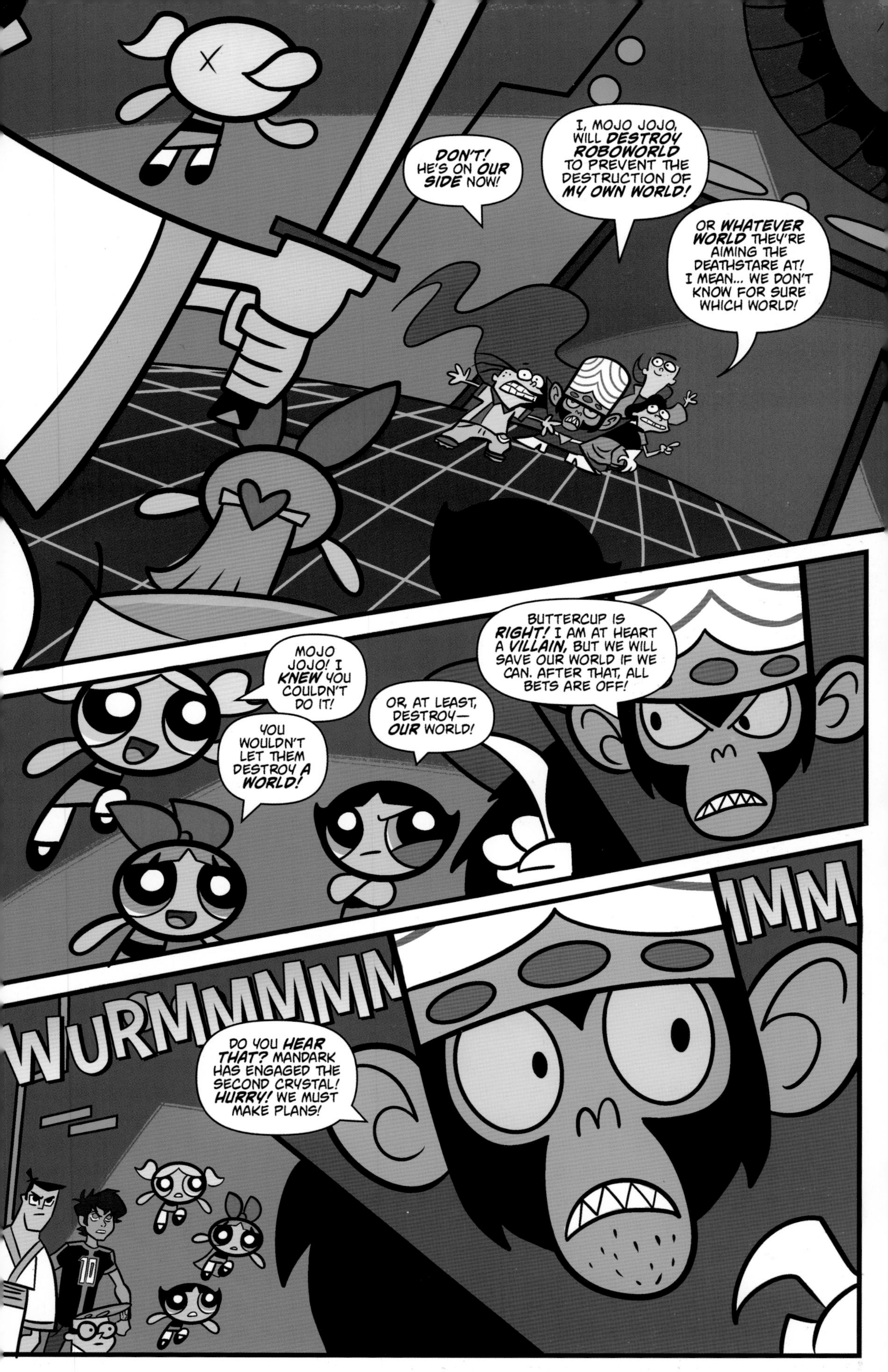
DON'T! HE'S ON OUR SIDE NOW!
I, MOJO JOJO, WILL DESTROY ROBOWORLD TO PREVENT THE DESTRUCTION OF MY OWN WORLD!
OR WHATEVER WORLD THEY'RE AIMING THE DEATHSTARE AT! I MEAN... WE DON'T KNOW FOR SURE WHICH WORLD!
MOJO JOJO! I KNEW YOU COULDN'T DO IT!
YOU WOULDN'T LET THEM DESTROY A WORLD!
OR, AT LEAST, DESTROY— OUR WORLD!
BUTTERCUP IS RIGHT! I AM AT HEART A VILLAIN, BUT WE WILL SAVE OUR WORLD IF WE CAN. AFTER THAT, ALL BETS ARE OFF!
WURMMMMMMMMM
DO YOU HEAR THAT? MANDARK HAS ENGAGED THE SECOND CRYSTAL! HURRY! WE MUST MAKE PLANS!

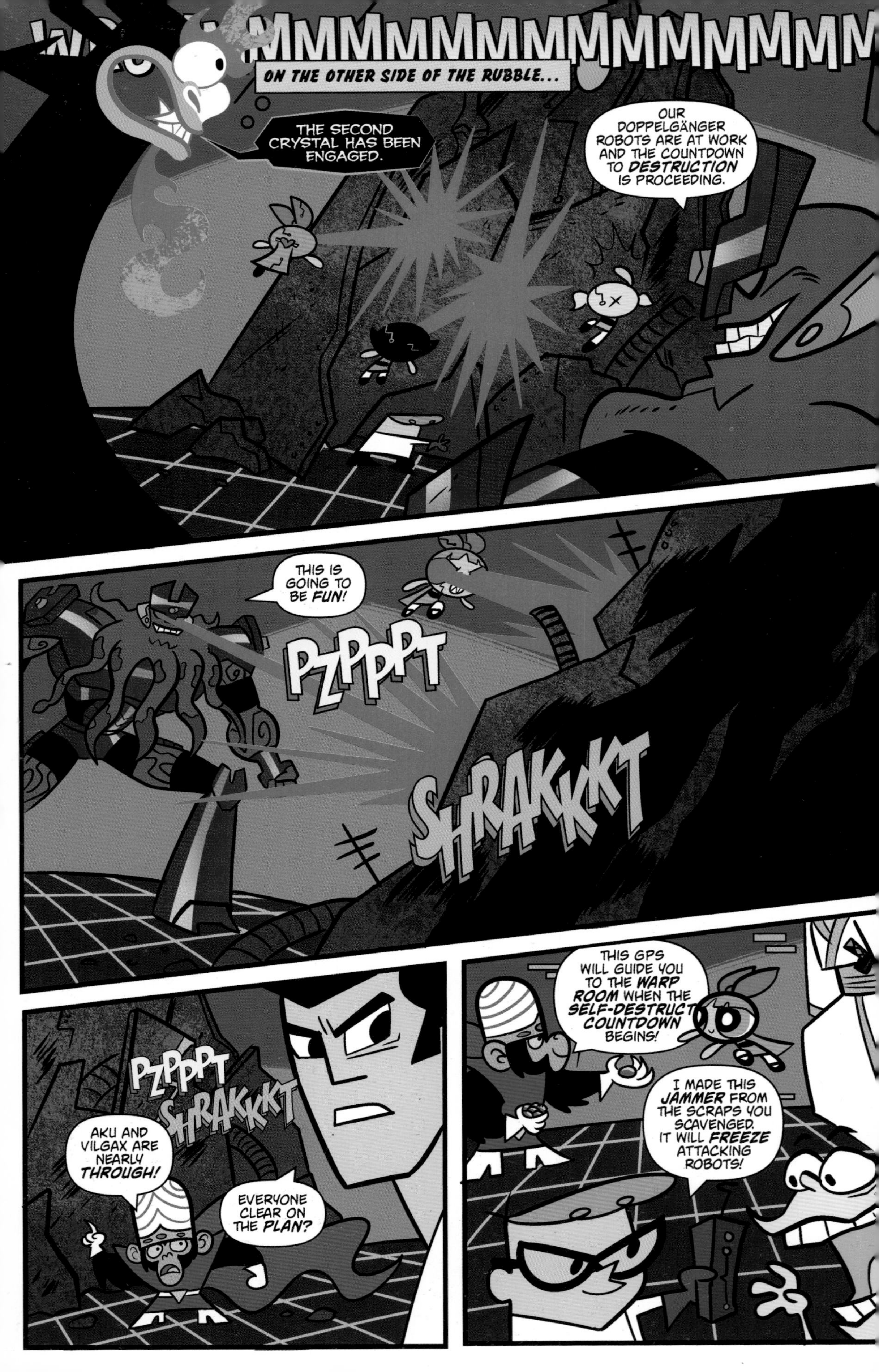

MMMMMMMMMMMMMMMMM
ON THE OTHER SIDE OF THE RUBBLE...
THE SECOND CRYSTAL HAS BEEN ENGAGED.
OUR DOPPELGÄNGER ROBOTS ARE AT WORK AND THE COUNTDOWN TO DESTRUCTION IS PROCEEDING.
THIS IS GOING TO BE FUN!
PZPPPT
SHRAKKKT
PZPPPT
SHRAKKKT
AKU AND VILGAX ARE NEARLY THROUGH!
EVERYONE CLEAR ON THE PLAN?
THIS GPS WILL GUIDE YOU TO THE WARP ROOM WHEN THE SELF-DESTRUCT COUNTDOWN BEGINS!
I MADE THIS JAMMER FROM THE SCRAPS YOU SCAVENGED. IT WILL FREEZE ATTACKING ROBOTS!

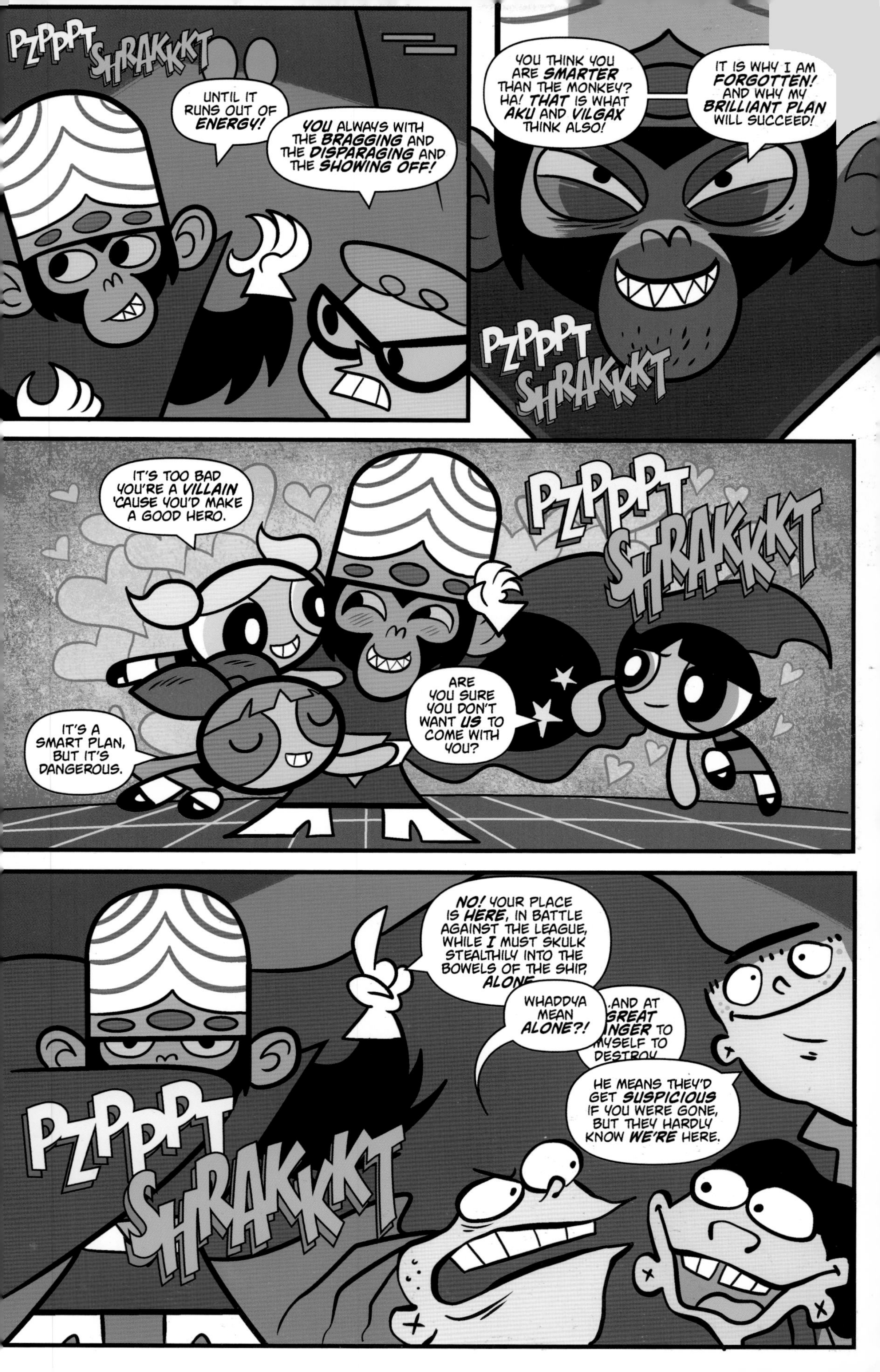
PZPPPT SHRAKKKT
UNTIL IT RUNS OUT OF ENERGY!
YOU ALWAYS WITH THE BRAGGING AND THE DISPARAGING AND THE SHOWING OFF!
YOU THINK YOU ARE SMARTER THAN THE MONKEY? HA! THAT IS WHAT AKU AND VILGAX THINK ALSO!
IT IS WHY I AM FORGOTTEN! AND WHY MY BRILLIANT PLAN WILL SUCCEED!
PZPPPT SHRAKKKT
IT'S TOO BAD YOU'RE A VILLAIN 'CAUSE YOU'D MAKE A GOOD HERO.
PZPPPT SHRAKKKT
ARE YOU SURE YOU DON'T WANT US TO COME WITH YOU?
IT'S A SMART PLAN, BUT IT'S DANGEROUS.
NO! YOUR PLACE IS HERE, IN BATTLE AGAINST THE LEAGUE, WHILE I MUST SKULK STEALTHILY INTO THE BOWELS OF THE SHIP, ALONE
WHADDYA MEAN ALONE?!
.AND AT GREAT NGER TO YSELF TO DESTROY
HE MEANS THEY'D GET SUSPICIOUS IF YOU WERE GONE, BUT THEY HARDLY KNOW WE'RE HERE.
PZPPPT SHRAKKKT

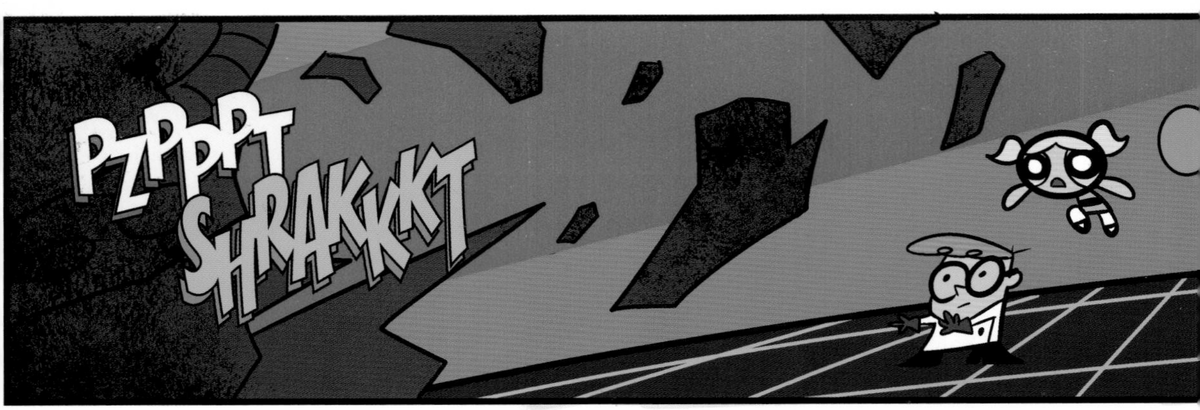
PZPPPT
SHRAKKKT

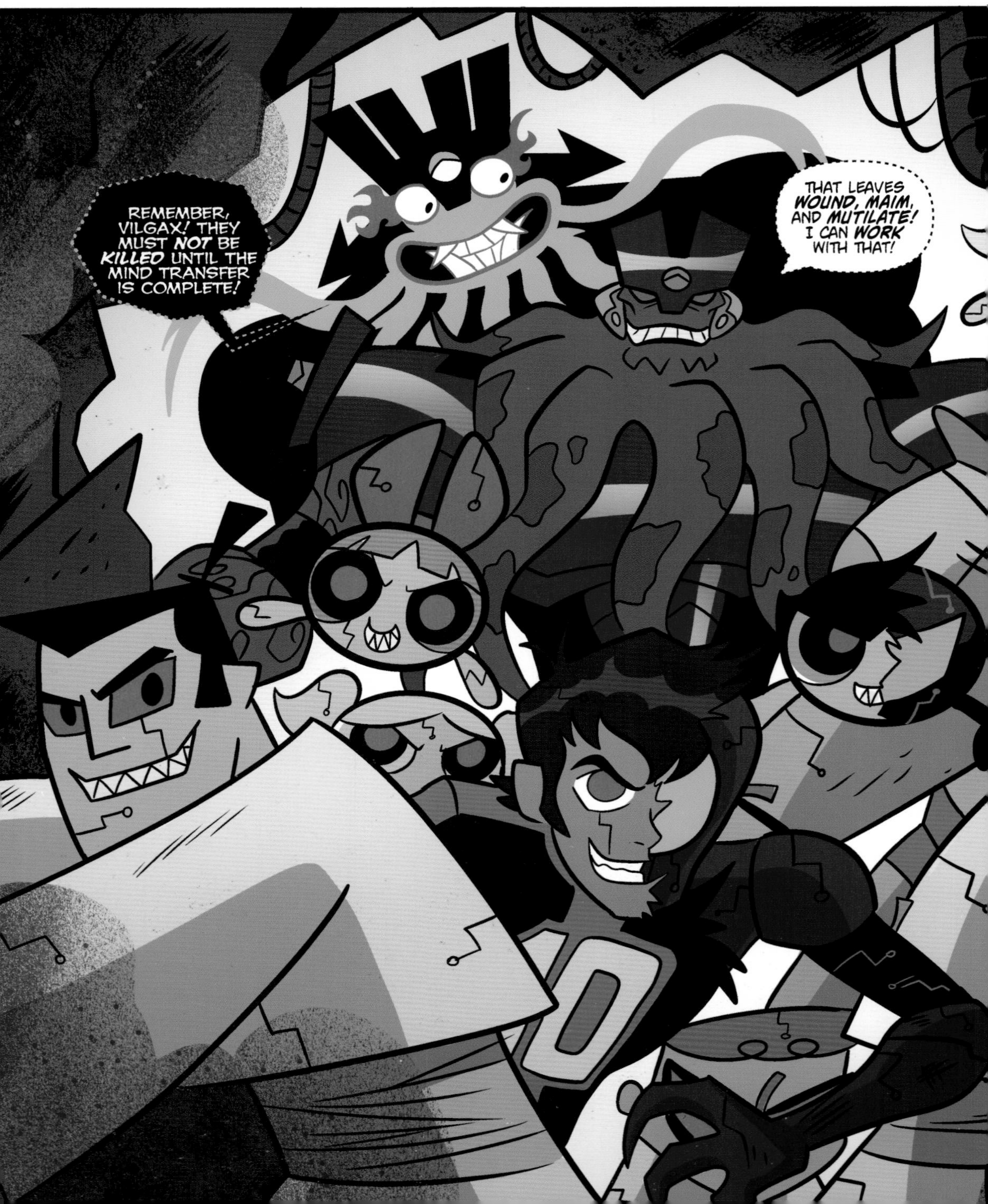
REMEMBER, VILGAX! THEY MUST **NOT** BE **KILLED** UNTIL THE MIND TRANSFER IS COMPLETE!
THAT LEAVES **WOUND, MAIM,** AND **MUTILATE!** I CAN **WORK** WITH THAT!

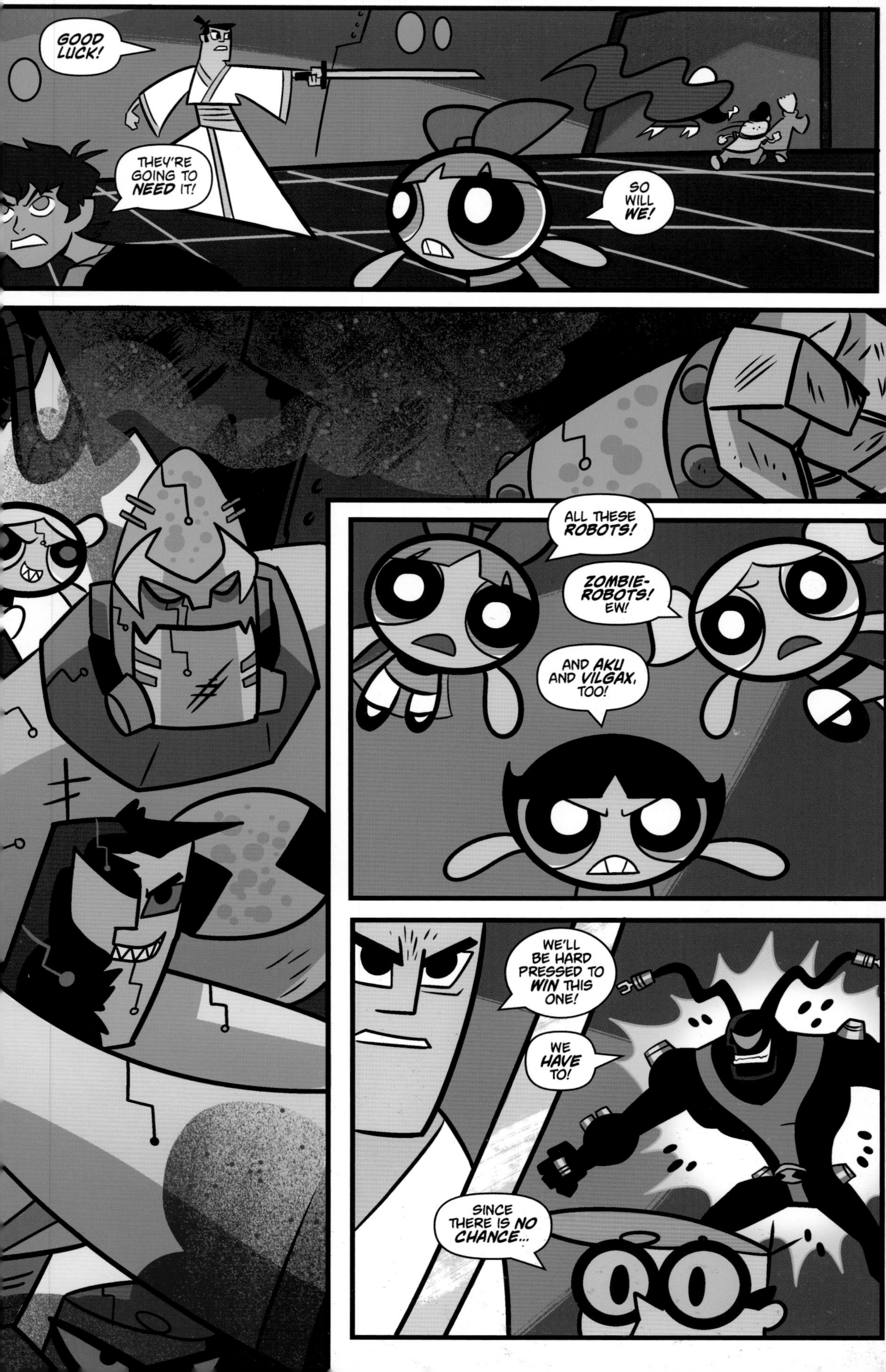
GOOD LUCK!
THEY'RE GOING TO NEED IT!
SO WILL WE!
ALL THESE ROBOTS!
ZOMBIE-ROBOTS! EW!
AND AKU AND VILGAX, TOO!
WE'LL BE HARD PRESSED TO WIN THIS ONE!
WE HAVE TO!
SINCE THERE IS NO CHANCE...

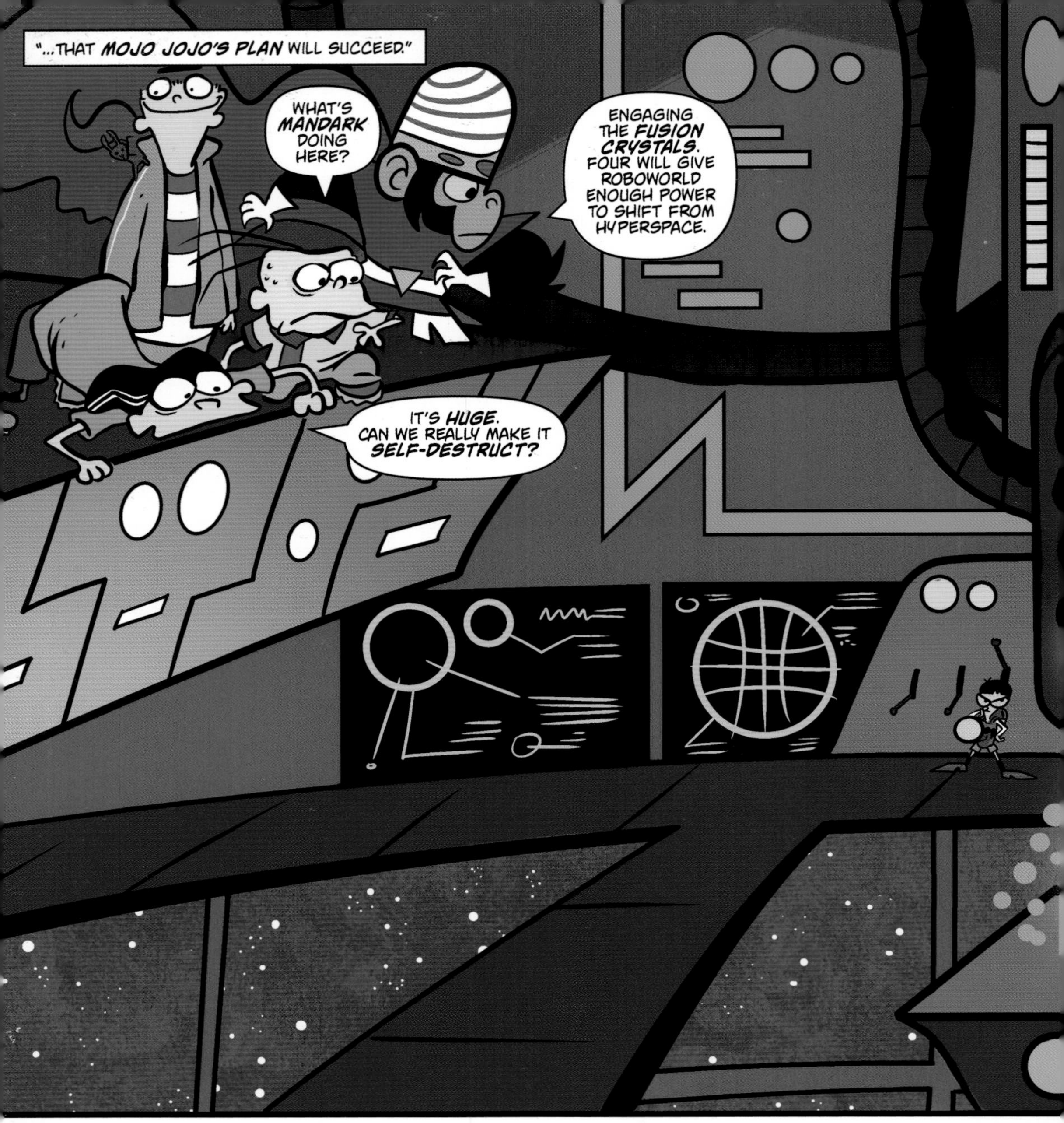
"...THAT MOJO JOJO'S PLAN WILL SUCCEED."
WHAT'S MANDARK DOING HERE?
ENGAGING THE FUSION CRYSTALS. FOUR WILL GIVE ROBOWORLD ENOUGH POWER TO SHIFT FROM HYPERSPACE.
IT'S HUGE. CAN WE REALLY MAKE IT SELF-DESTRUCT?

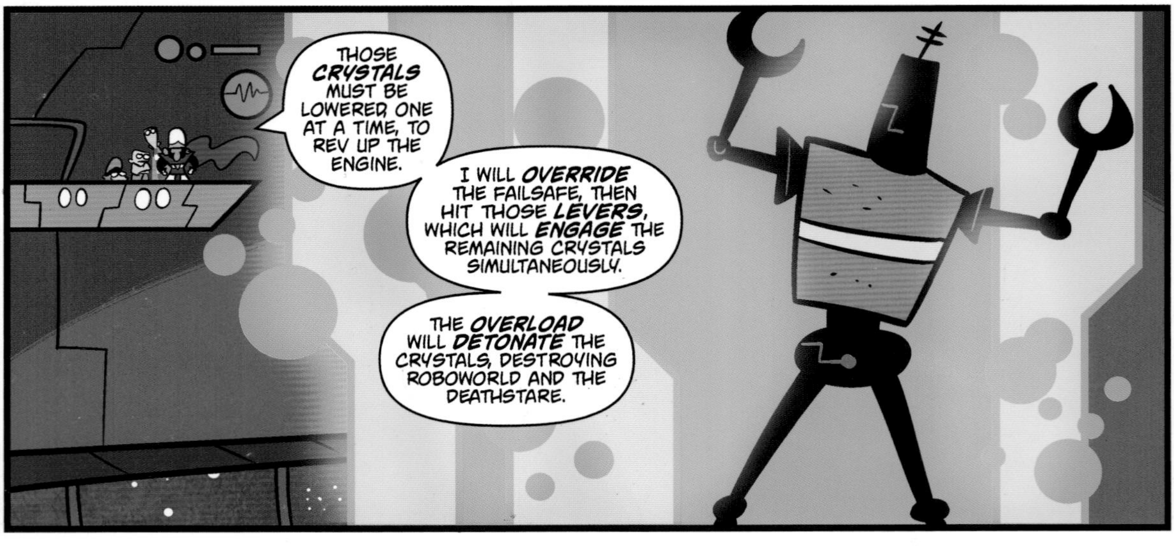
THOSE CRYSTALS MUST BE LOWERED ONE AT A TIME, TO REV UP THE ENGINE.
I WILL OVERRIDE THE FAILSAFE, THEN HIT THOSE LEVERS, WHICH WILL ENGAGE THE REMAINING CRYSTALS SIMULTANEOUSLY.
THE OVERLOAD WILL DETONATE THE CRYSTALS, DESTROYING ROBOWORLD AND THE DEATHSTARE.

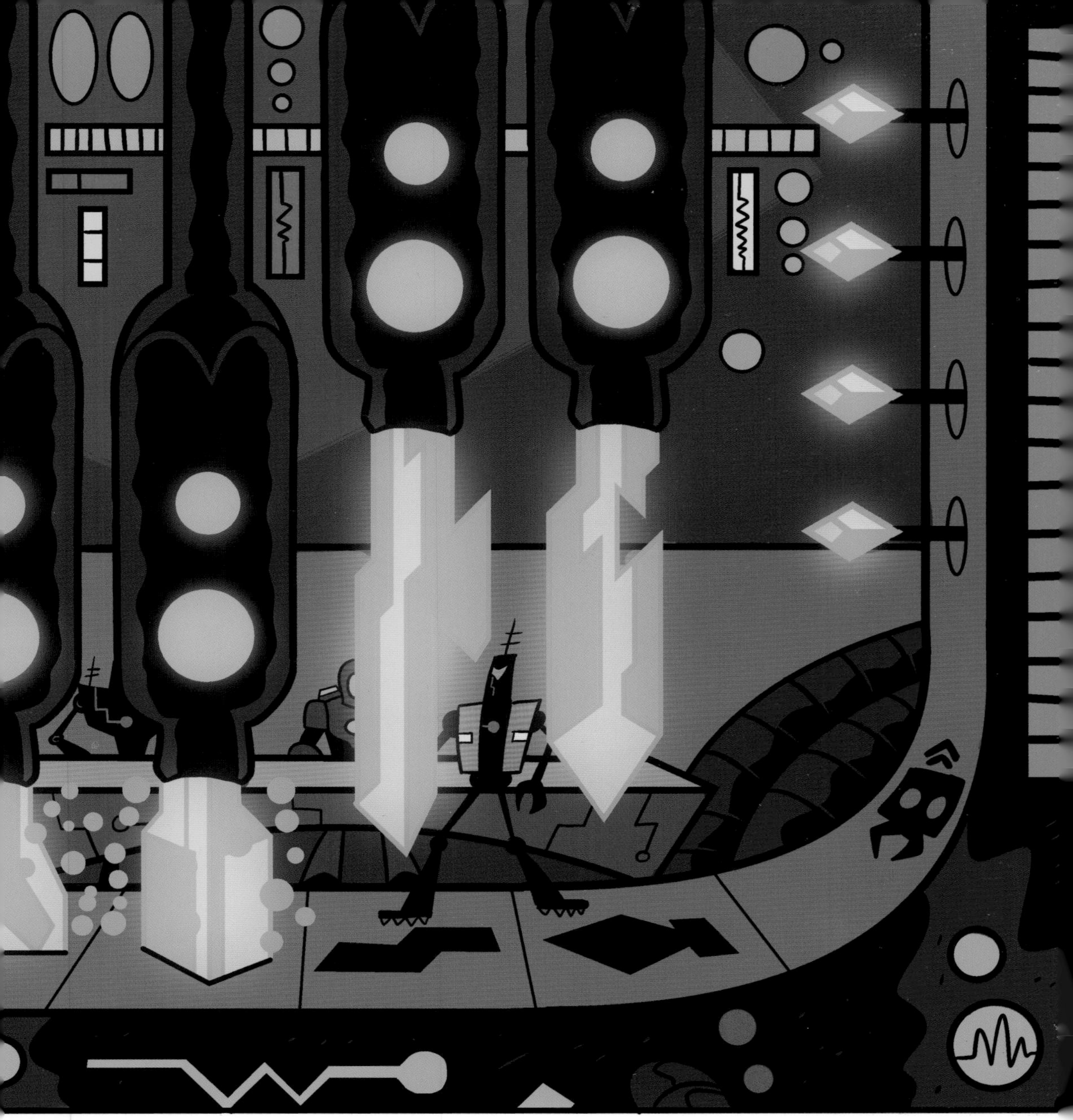

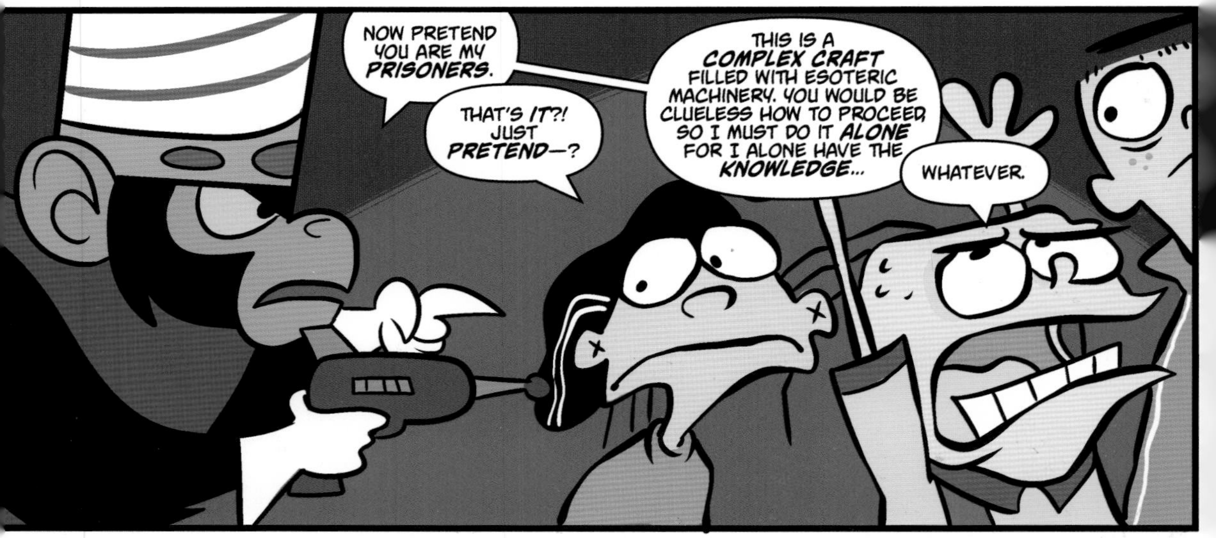

NOW PRETEND YOU ARE MY PRISONERS.
THAT'S IT?! JUST PRETEND—?
THIS IS A COMPLEX CRAFT FILLED WITH ESOTERIC MACHINERY. YOU WOULD BE CLUELESS HOW TO PROCEED, SO I MUST DO IT ALONE FOR I ALONE HAVE THE KNOWLEDGE...
WHATEVER.

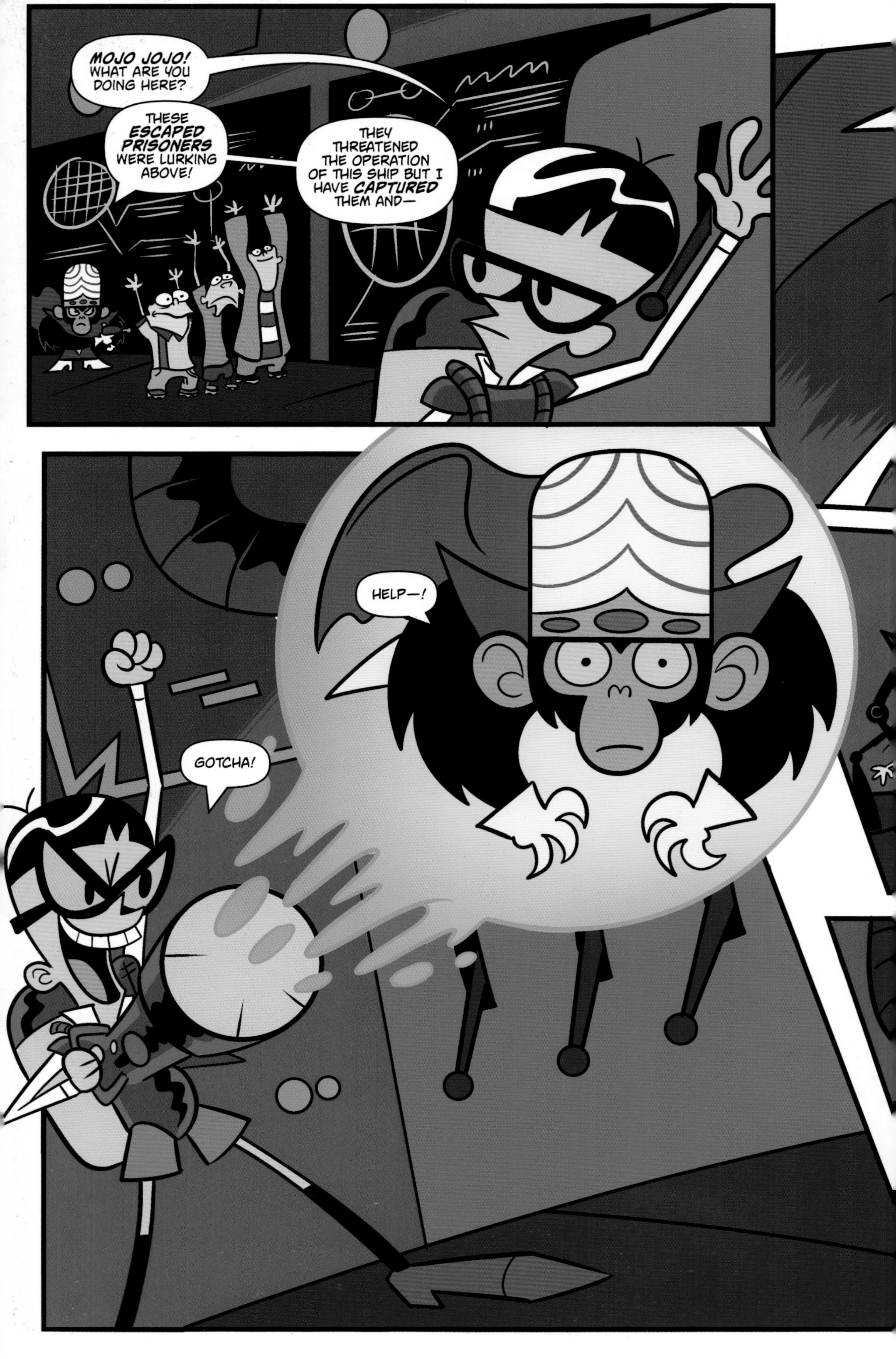
MOJO JOJO! WHAT ARE YOU DOING HERE?
THESE ESCAPED PRISONERS WERE LURKING ABOVE!
THEY THREATENED THE OPERATION OF THIS SHIP BUT I HAVE CAPTURED THEM AND—
HELP—!
GOTCHA!

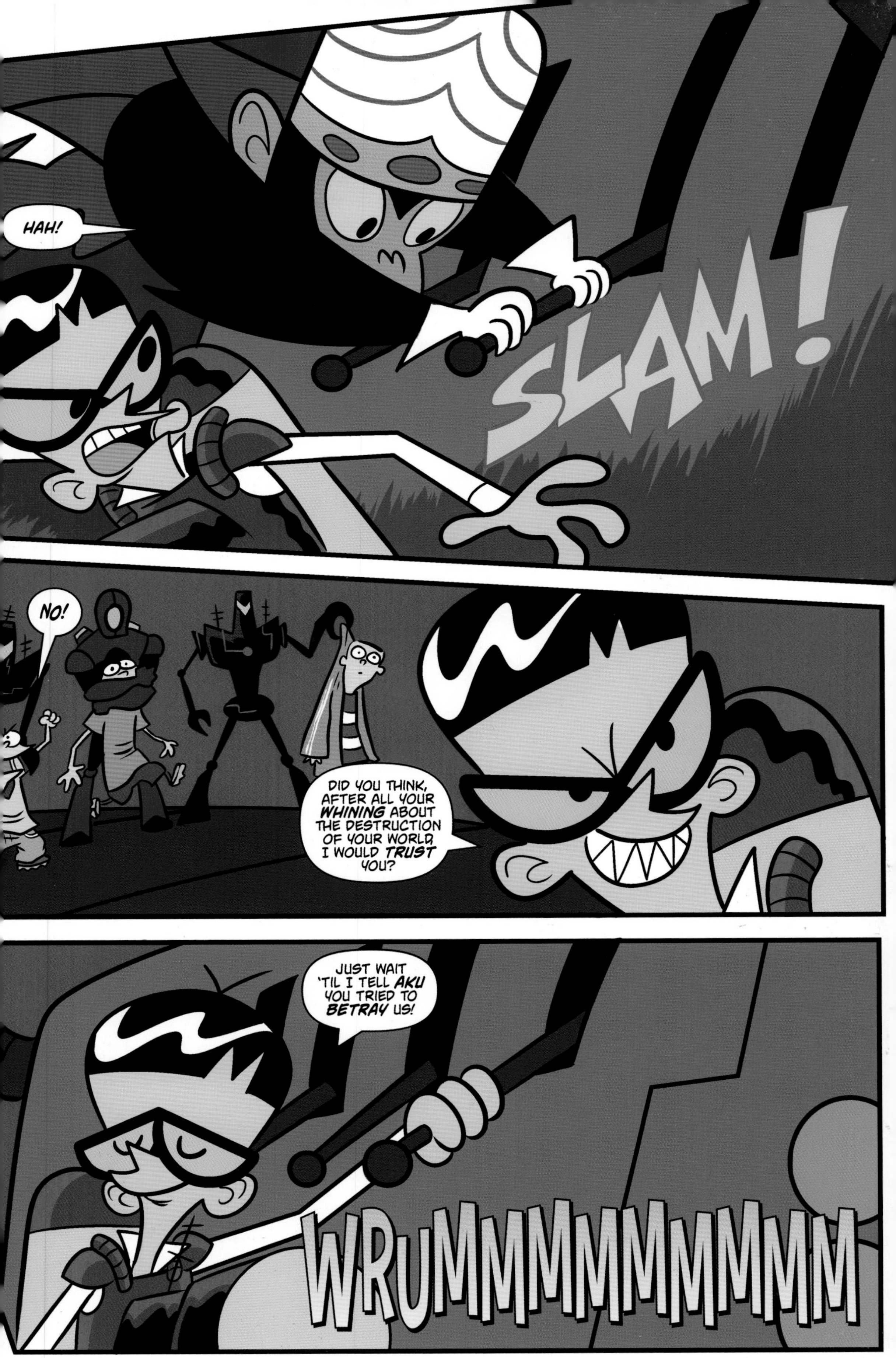
HAH!
SLAM!
NO!
DID YOU THINK, AFTER ALL YOUR WHINING ABOUT THE DESTRUCTION OF YOUR WORLD, I WOULD TRUST YOU?
JUST WAIT 'TIL I TELL AKU YOU TRIED TO BETRAY US!
WRUMMMMMMMMMMM

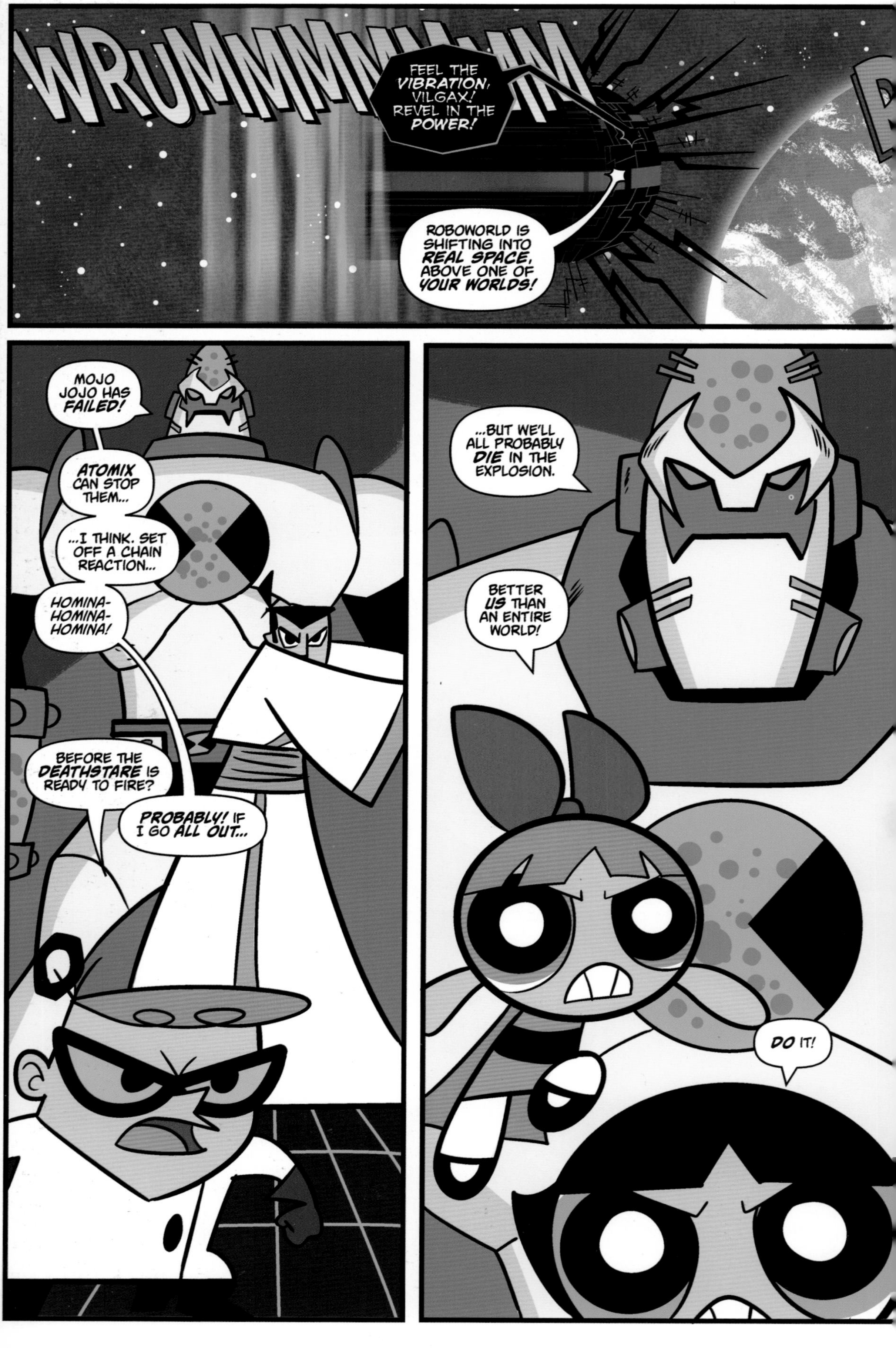

WRUMMMMMMMM
FEEL THE VIBRATION, VILGAX! REVEL IN THE POWER!
ROBOWORLD IS SHIFTING INTO REAL SPACE, ABOVE ONE OF YOUR WORLDS!
MOJO JOJO HAS FAILED!
ATOMIX CAN STOP THEM...
...I THINK. SET OFF A CHAIN REACTION...
HOMINA-HOMINA-HOMINA!
BEFORE THE DEATHSTARE IS READY TO FIRE?
PROBABLY! IF I GO ALL OUT...
...BUT WE'LL ALL PROBABLY DIE IN THE EXPLOSION.
BETTER US THAN AN ENTIRE WORLD!
DO IT!

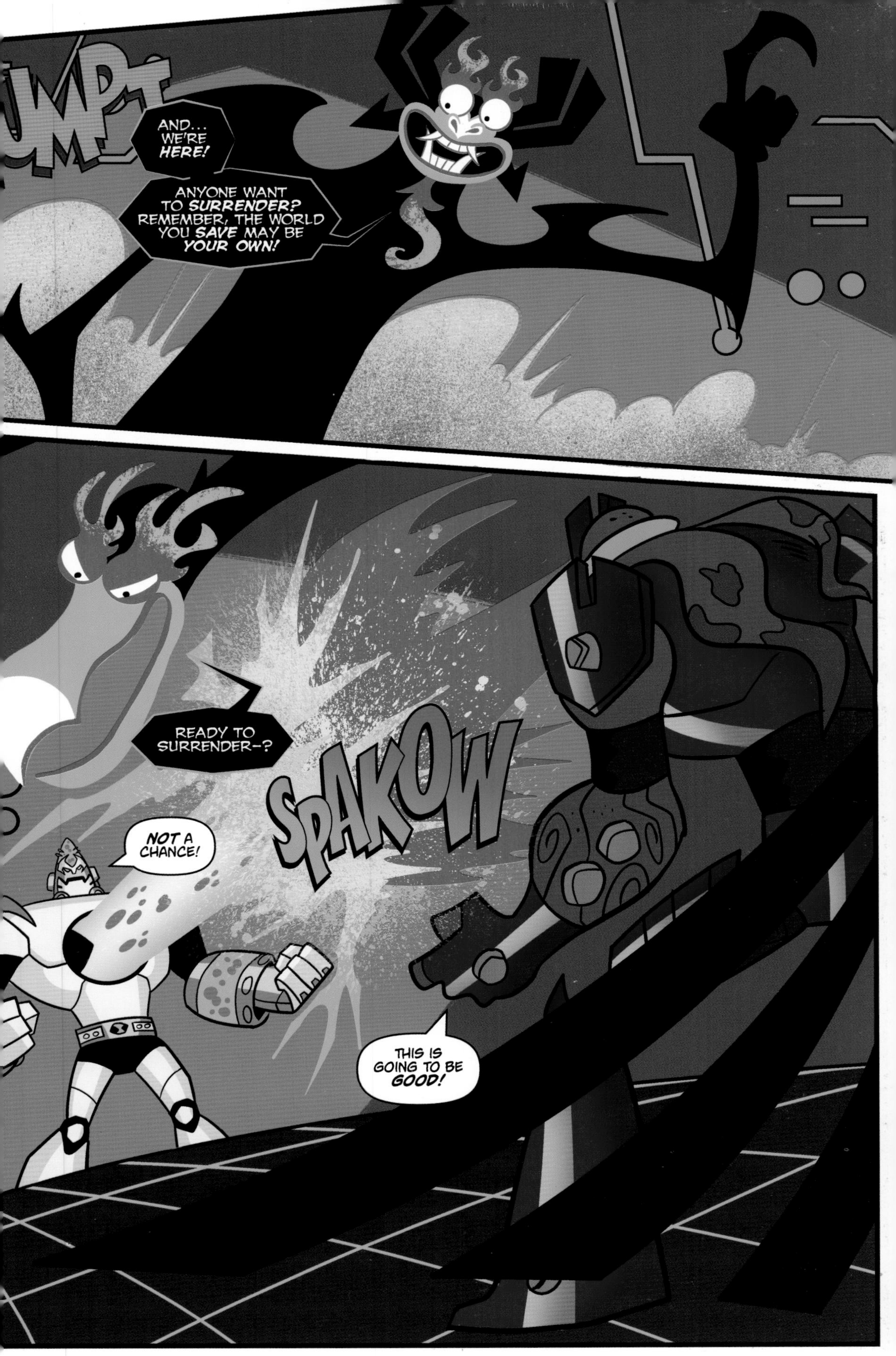

UMPT
AND... WE'RE HERE!
ANYONE WANT TO SURRENDER? REMEMBER, THE WORLD YOU SAVE MAY BE YOUR OWN!
READY TO SURRENDER-?
NOT A CHANCE!
SPAKOW
THIS IS GOING TO BE GOOD!

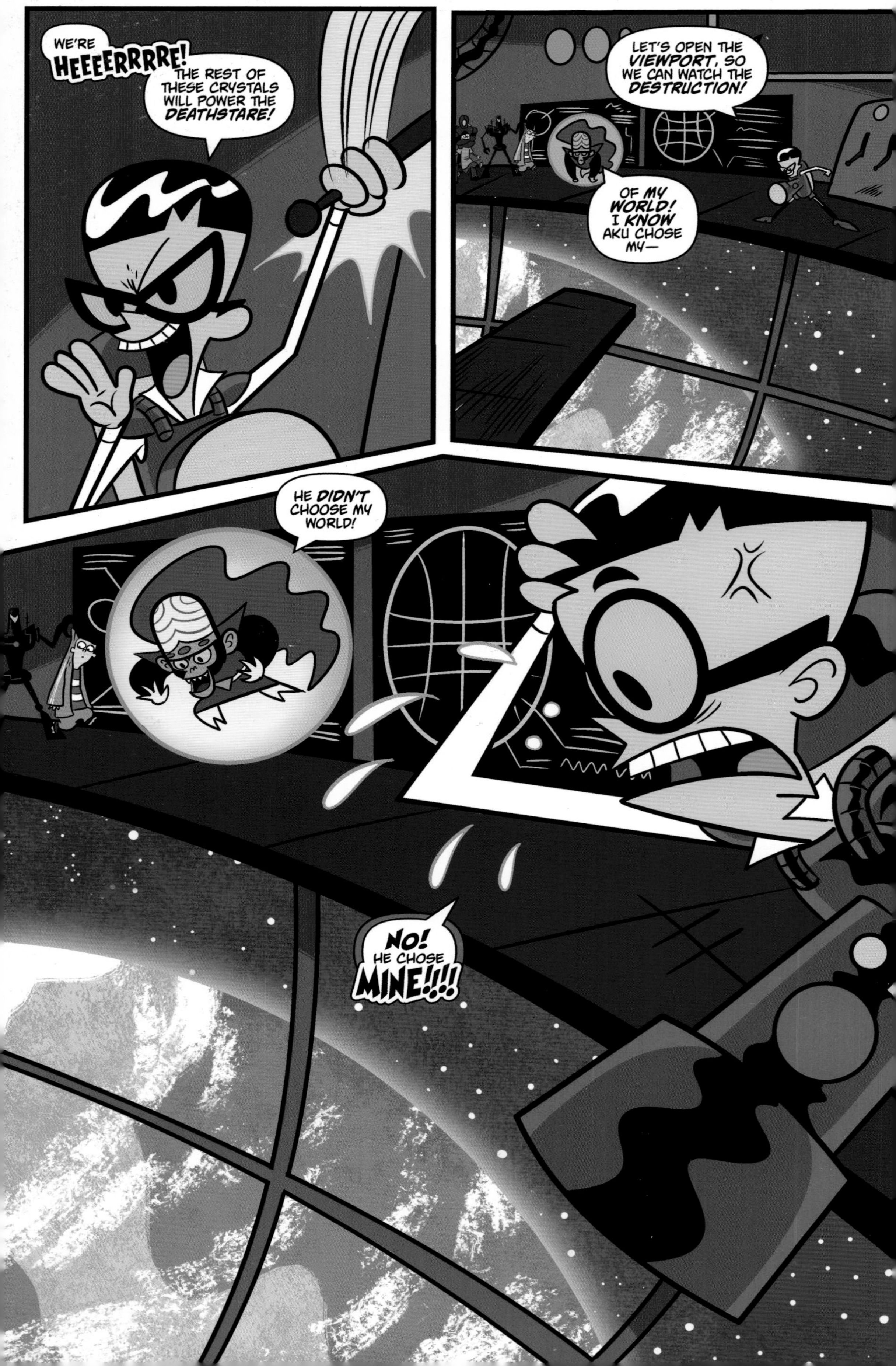
WE'RE HEEEERRRRE!
THE REST OF THESE CRYSTALS WILL POWER THE DEATHSTARE!
LET'S OPEN THE VIEWPORT, SO WE CAN WATCH THE DESTRUCTION!
OF MY WORLD! I KNOW AKU CHOSE MY—
HE DIDN'T CHOOSE MY WORLD!
NO! HE CHOSE MINE!!!!

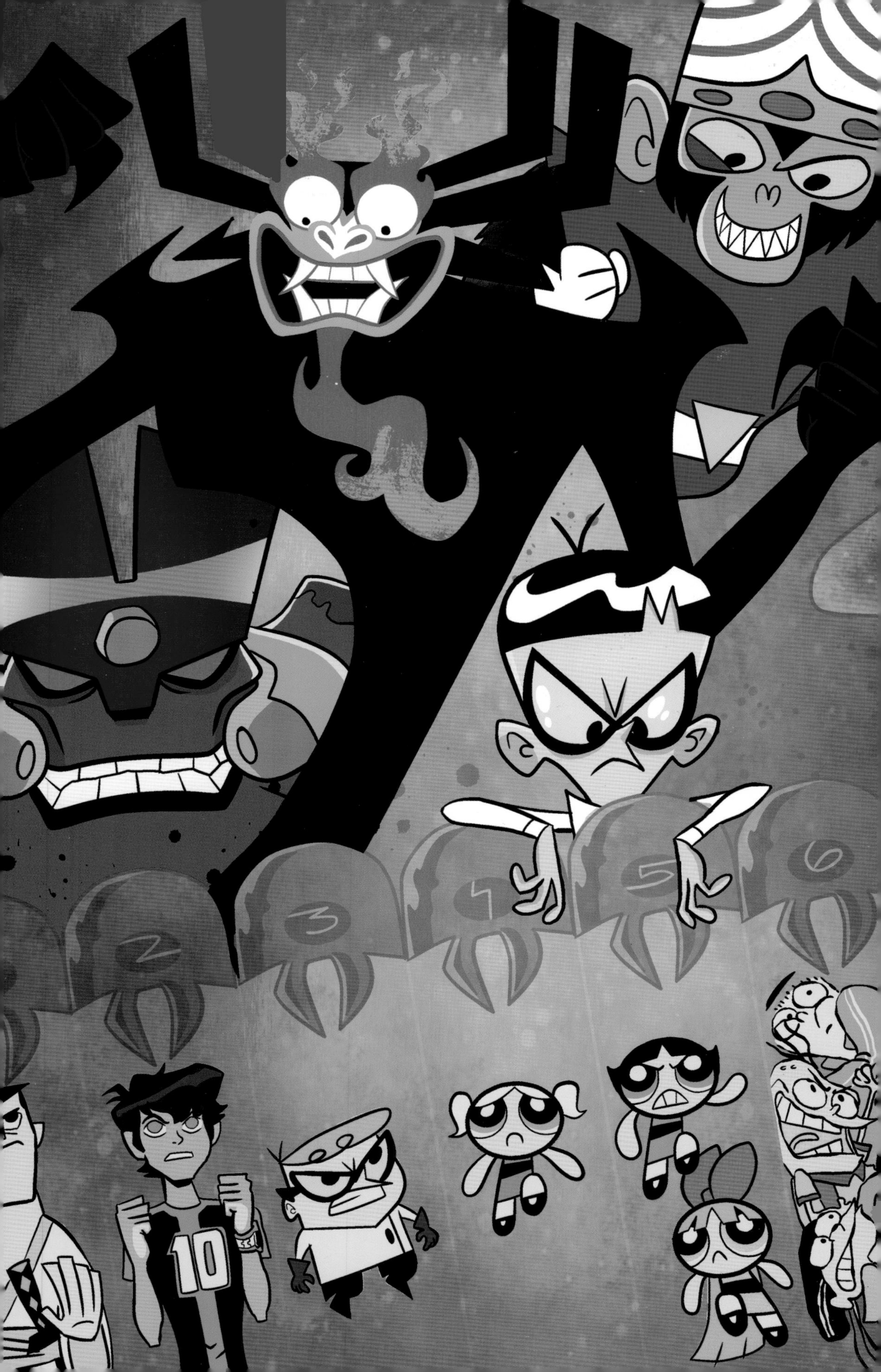

Chapter 6

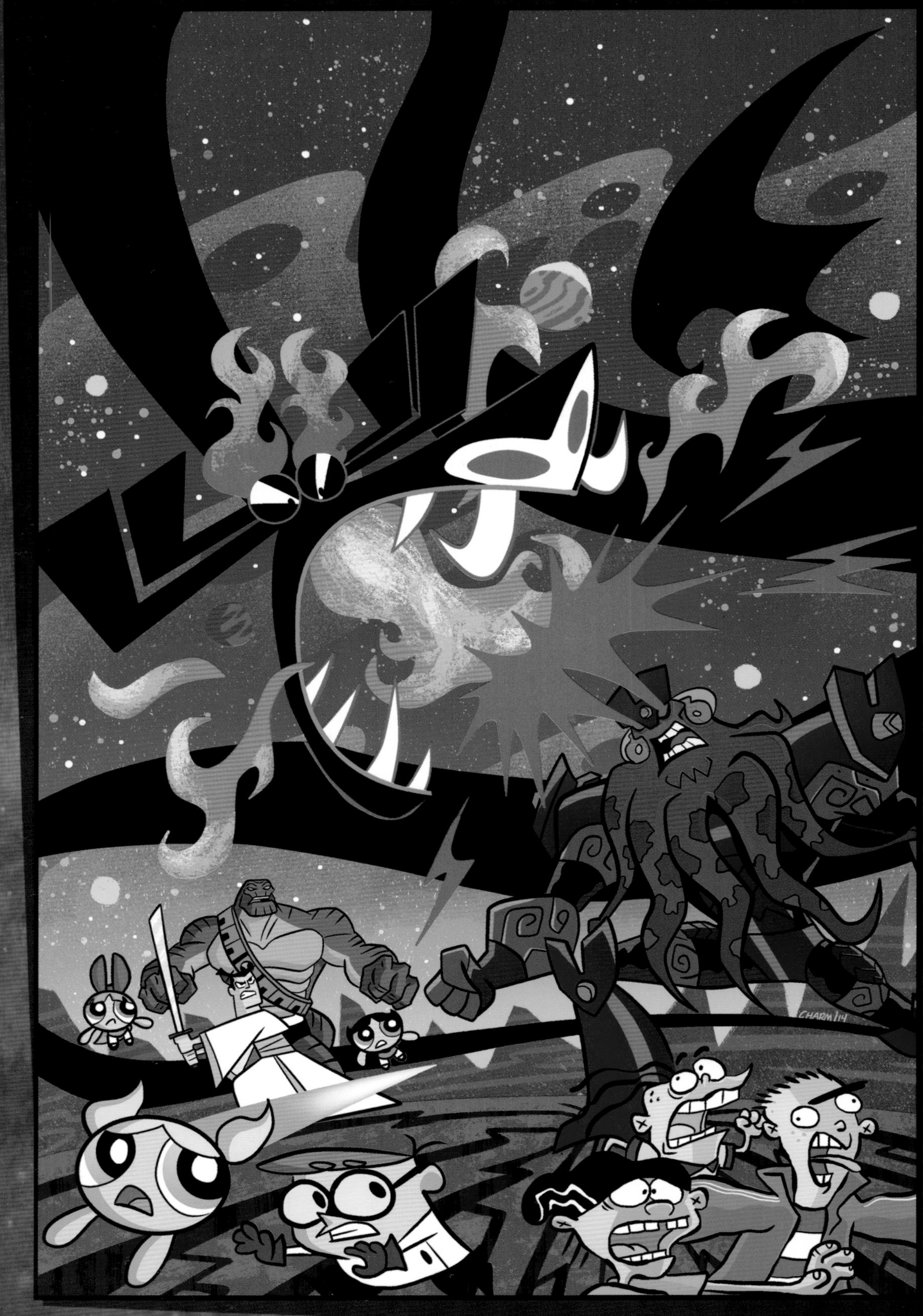
CHARM/14

Cover Art by Derek Charm

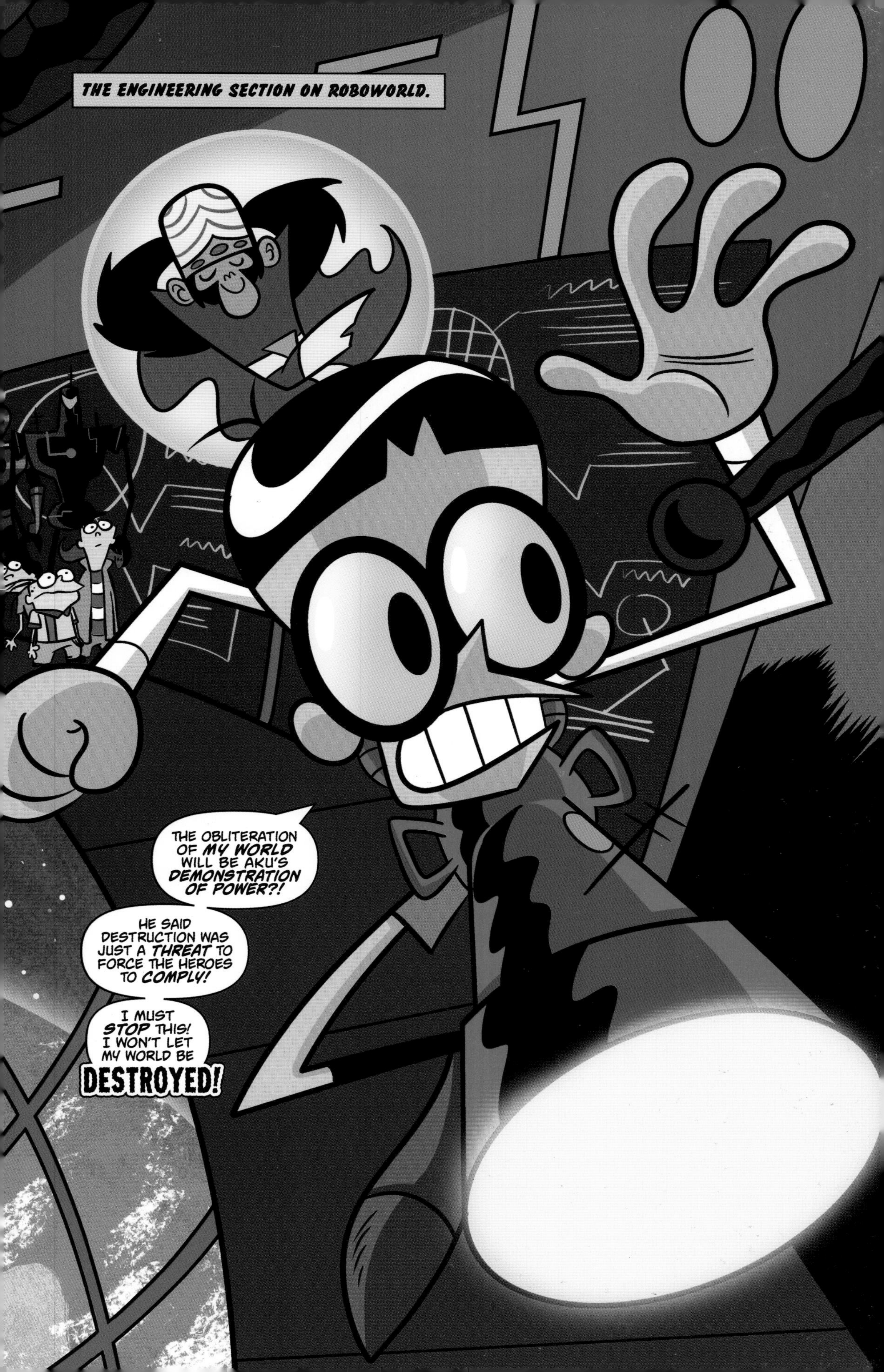
THE ENGINEERING SECTION ON ROBOWORLD.
THE OBLITERATION OF MY WORLD WILL BE AKU'S DEMONSTRATION OF POWER?!
HE SAID DESTRUCTION WAS JUST A THREAT TO FORCE THE HEROES TO COMPLY!
I MUST STOP THIS! I WON'T LET MY WORLD BE DESTROYED!

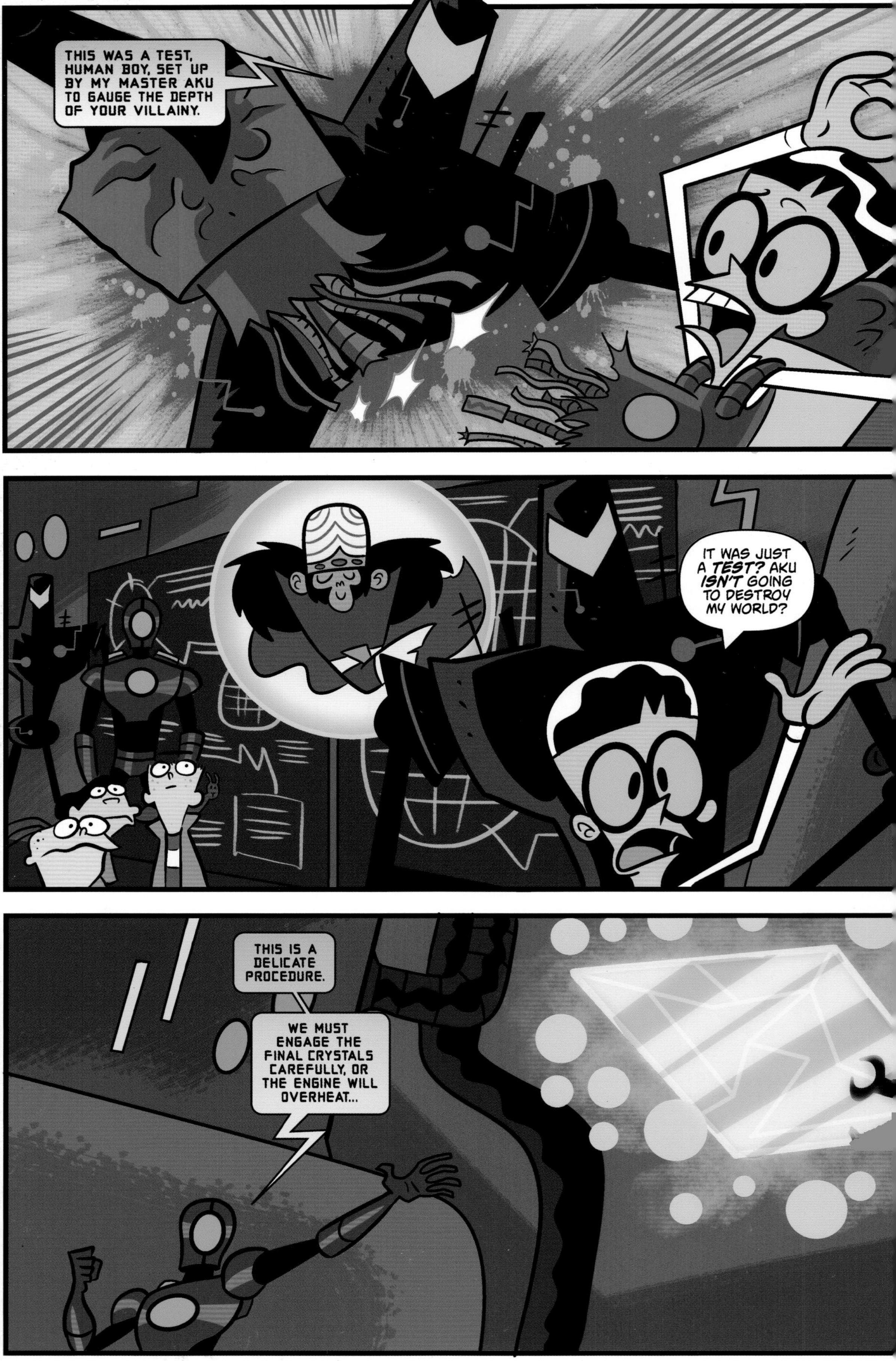
THIS WAS A TEST, HUMAN BOY, SET UP BY MY MASTER AKU TO GAUGE THE DEPTH OF YOUR VILLAINY.
IT WAS JUST A *TEST?* AKU *ISN'T* GOING TO DESTROY MY WORLD?
THIS IS A DELICATE PROCEDURE.
WE MUST ENGAGE THE FINAL CRYSTALS CAREFULLY, OR THE ENGINE WILL OVERHEAT...

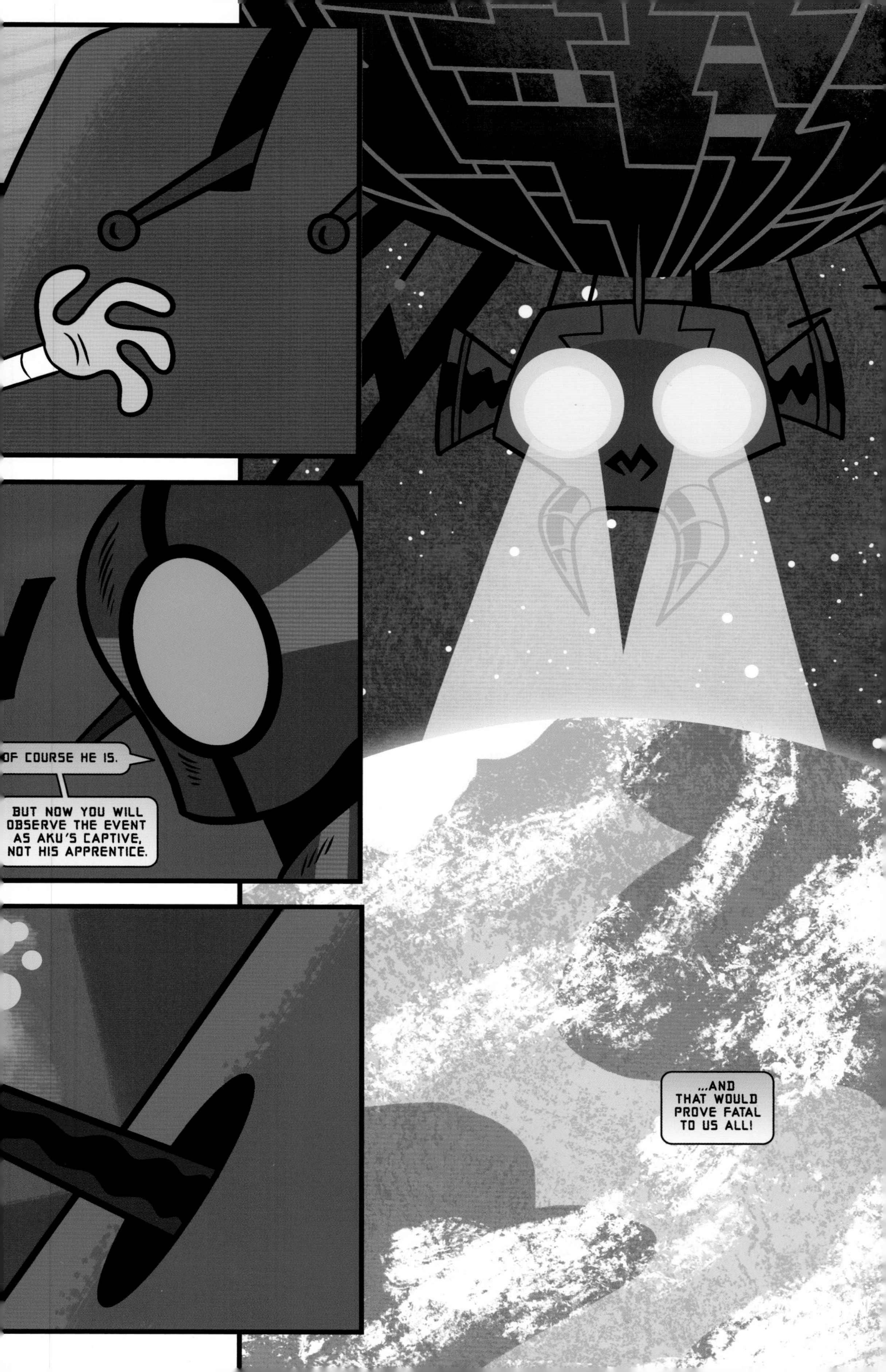
OF COURSE HE IS.
BUT NOW YOU WILL OBSERVE THE EVENT AS AKU'S CAPTIVE, NOT HIS APPRENTICE.
...AND THAT WOULD PROVE FATAL TO US ALL!

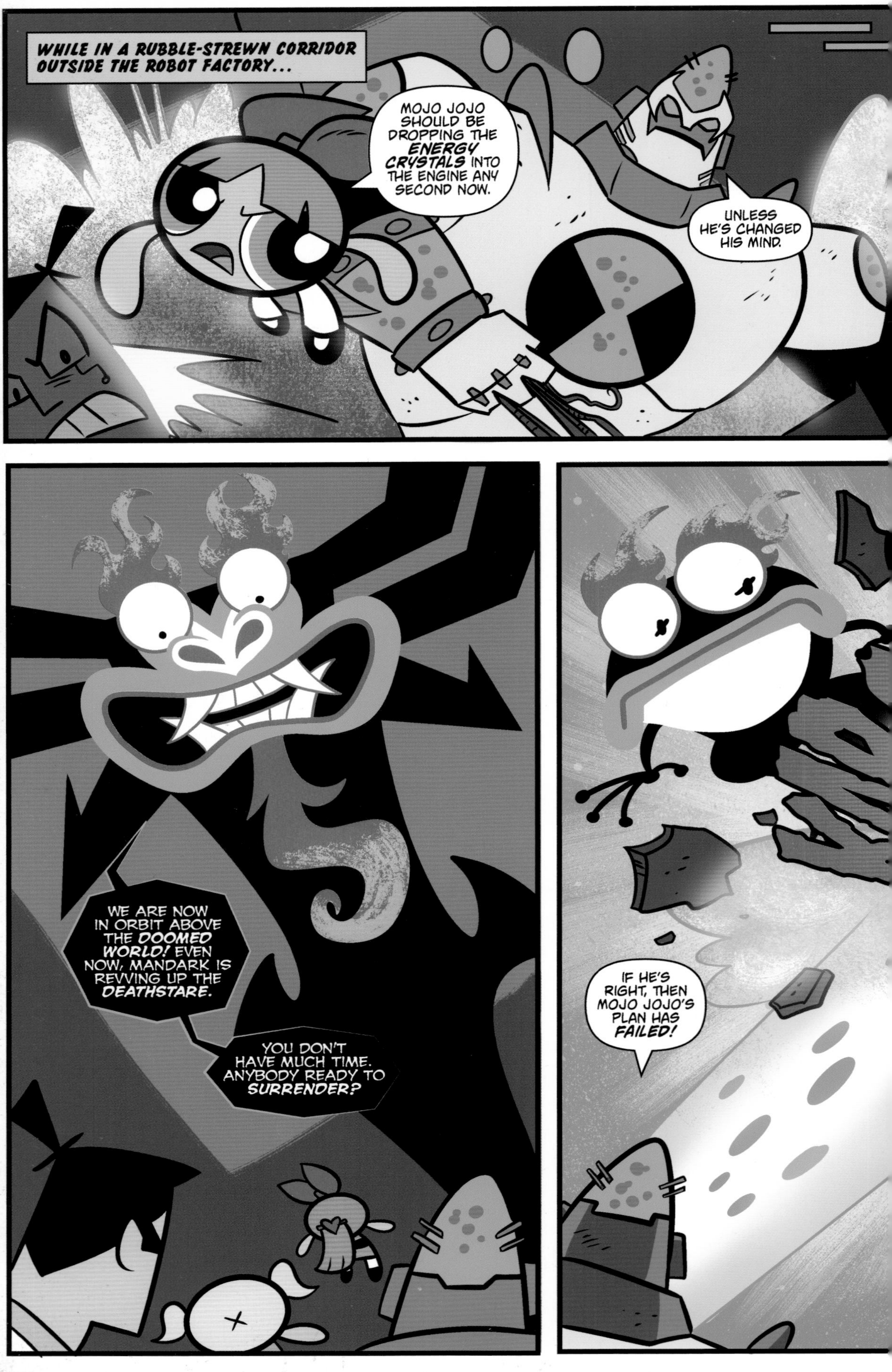
WHILE IN A RUBBLE-STREWN CORRIDOR OUTSIDE THE ROBOT FACTORY...
MOJO JOJO SHOULD BE DROPPING THE ENERGY CRYSTALS INTO THE ENGINE ANY SECOND NOW.
UNLESS HE'S CHANGED HIS MIND.
WE ARE NOW IN ORBIT ABOVE THE DOOMED WORLD! EVEN NOW, MANDARK IS REVVING UP THE DEATHSTARE.
YOU DON'T HAVE MUCH TIME. ANYBODY READY TO SURRENDER?
IF HE'S RIGHT, THEN MOJO JOJO'S PLAN HAS FAILED!

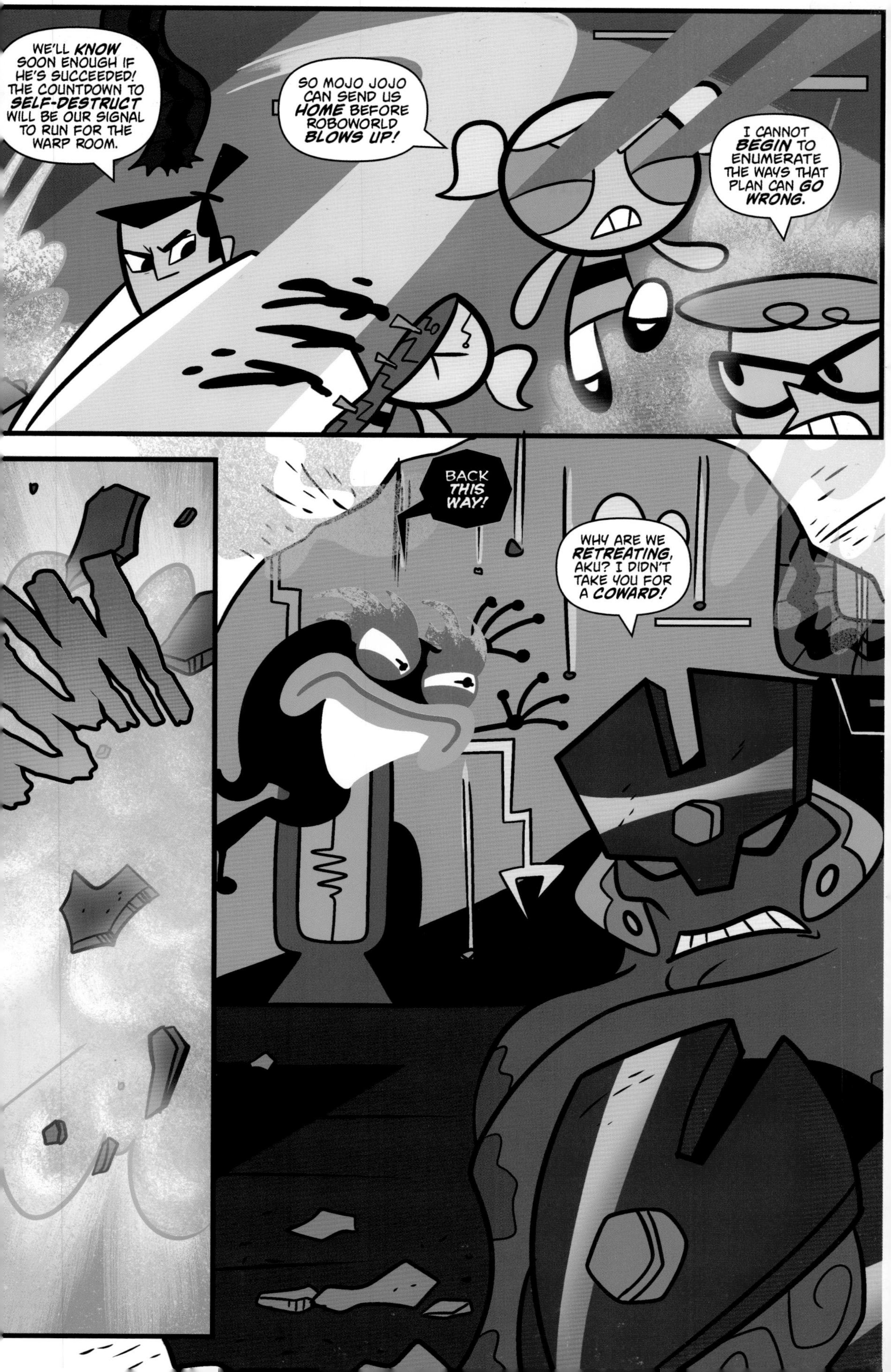
WE'LL KNOW SOON ENOUGH IF HE'S SUCCEEDED! THE COUNTDOWN TO SELF-DESTRUCT WILL BE OUR SIGNAL TO RUN FOR THE WARP ROOM.
SO MOJO JOJO CAN SEND US HOME BEFORE ROBOWORLD BLOWS UP!
I CANNOT BEGIN TO ENUMERATE THE WAYS THAT PLAN CAN GO WRONG.
BACK THIS WAY!
WHY ARE WE RETREATING, AKU? I DIDN'T TAKE YOU FOR A COWARD!

WHEREAS, ALL ALONG, I TOOK YOU FOR A FOOL!
IT IS TIME, VILGAX, FOR OUR HEROES TO SEE WHAT THEIR STUBBORNNESS WILL COST THEM!
THAT'S MY WORLD!
STILL TIME TO CHANGE YOUR MINDS.
FIRST YOUR WORLD, THEN MINE, THEN THE NEXT... UNTIL WE CAVE!
AND THEN, NOBODY ANYWHERE WILL BE SAFE!
SO WE GO TO PLAN B! WE HIT THEM WITH EVERYTHING WE HAVE.
DESTROY THIS SHIP...
...AND US WITH IT!
AND AT LEAST WE KNOW OUR WORLDS WILL BE OKAY!

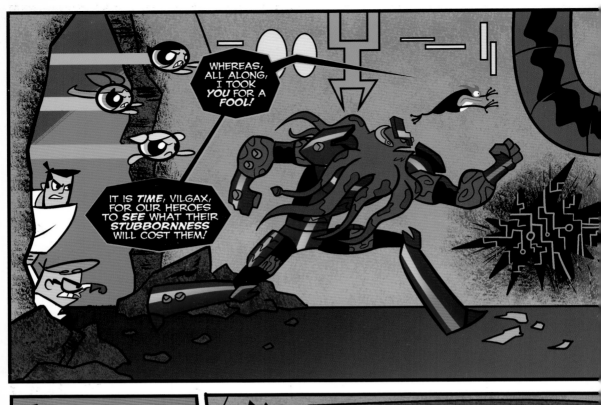

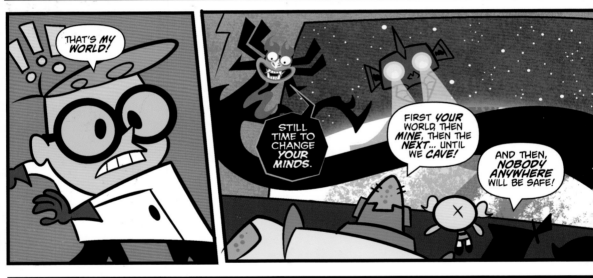

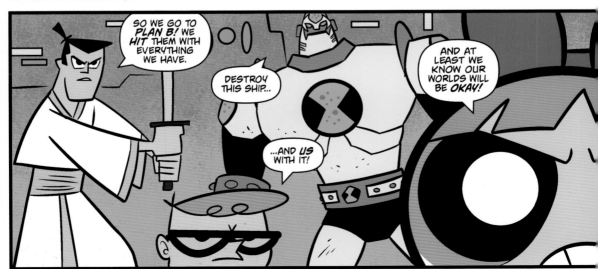

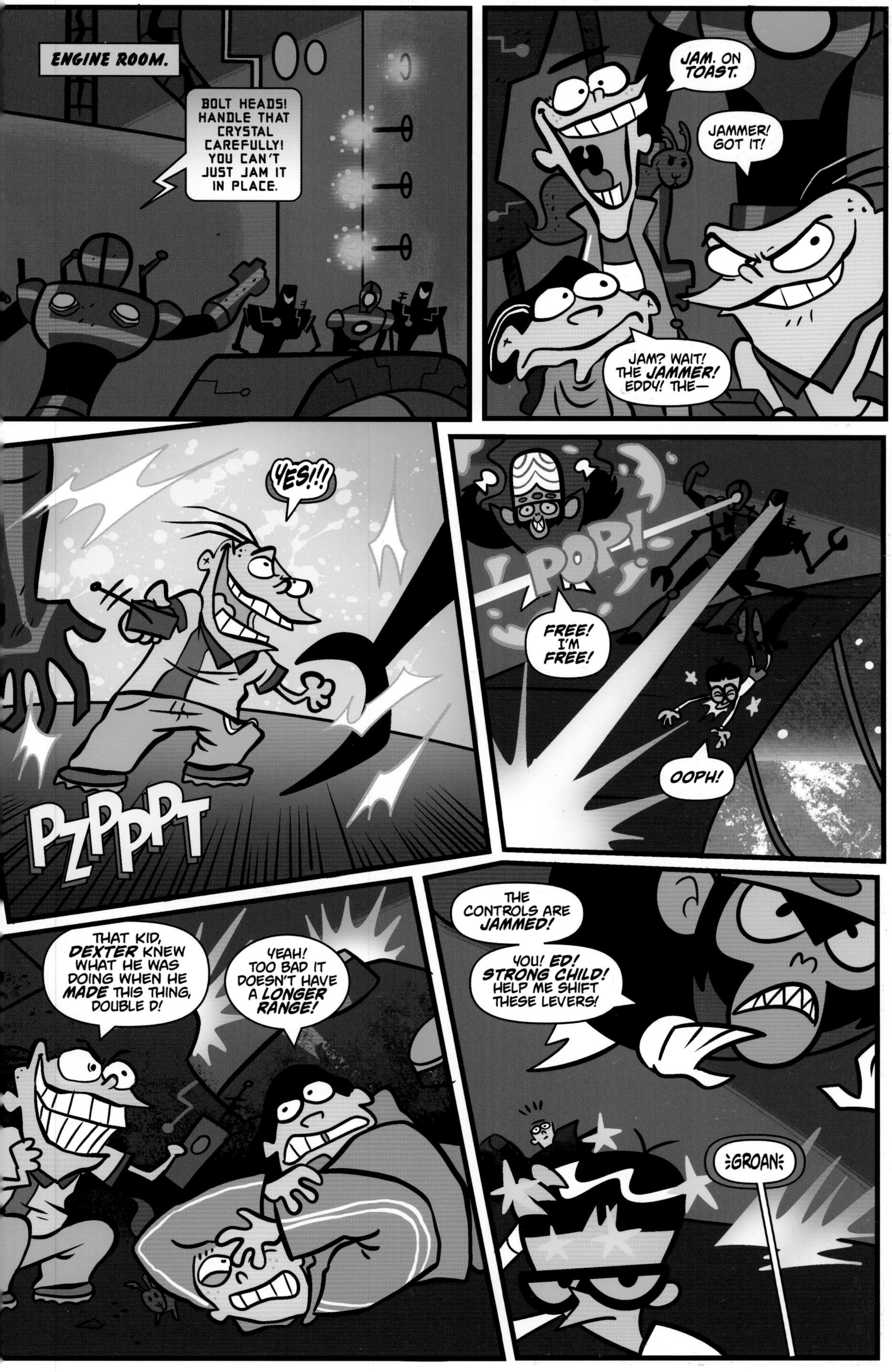
ENGINE ROOM.
BOLT HEADS! HANDLE THAT CRYSTAL CAREFULLY! YOU CAN'T JUST JAM IT IN PLACE.
JAM. ON TOAST.
JAMMER! GOT IT!
JAM? WAIT! THE JAMMER! EDDY! THE—
YES!!!
PZPPPT
POP!
FREE! I'M FREE!
OOPH!
THAT KID, DEXTER KNEW WHAT HE WAS DOING WHEN HE MADE THIS THING, DOUBLE D!
YEAH! TOO BAD IT DOESN'T HAVE A LONGER RANGE!
THE CONTROLS ARE JAMMED!
YOU! ED! STRONG CHILD! HELP ME SHIFT THESE LEVERS!
GROAN

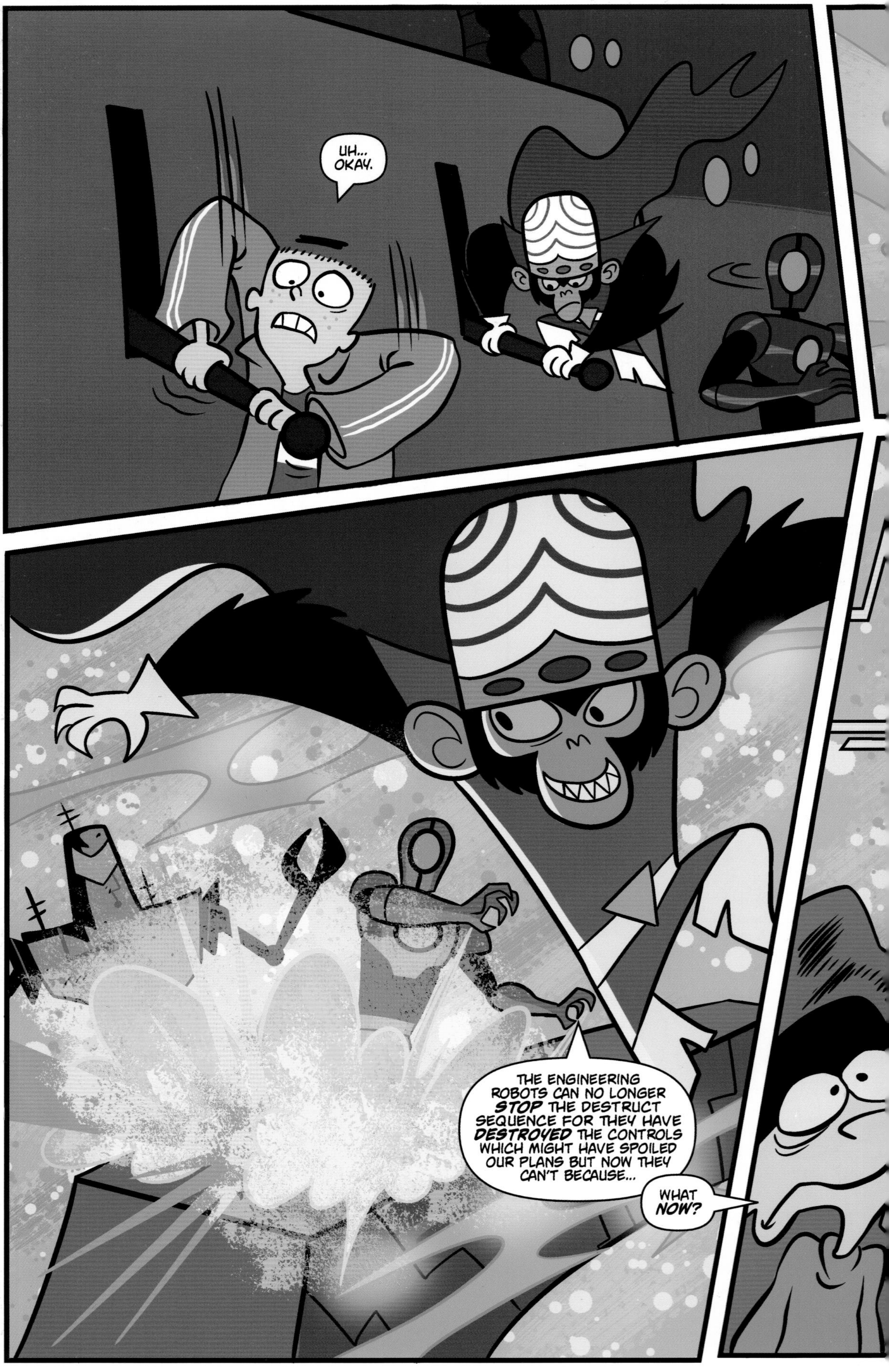
UH... OKAY.
THE ENGINEERING ROBOTS CAN NO LONGER STOP THE DESTRUCT SEQUENCE FOR THEY HAVE DESTROYED THE CONTROLS WHICH MIGHT HAVE SPOILED OUR PLANS BUT NOW THEY CAN'T BECAUSE...
WHAT NOW?

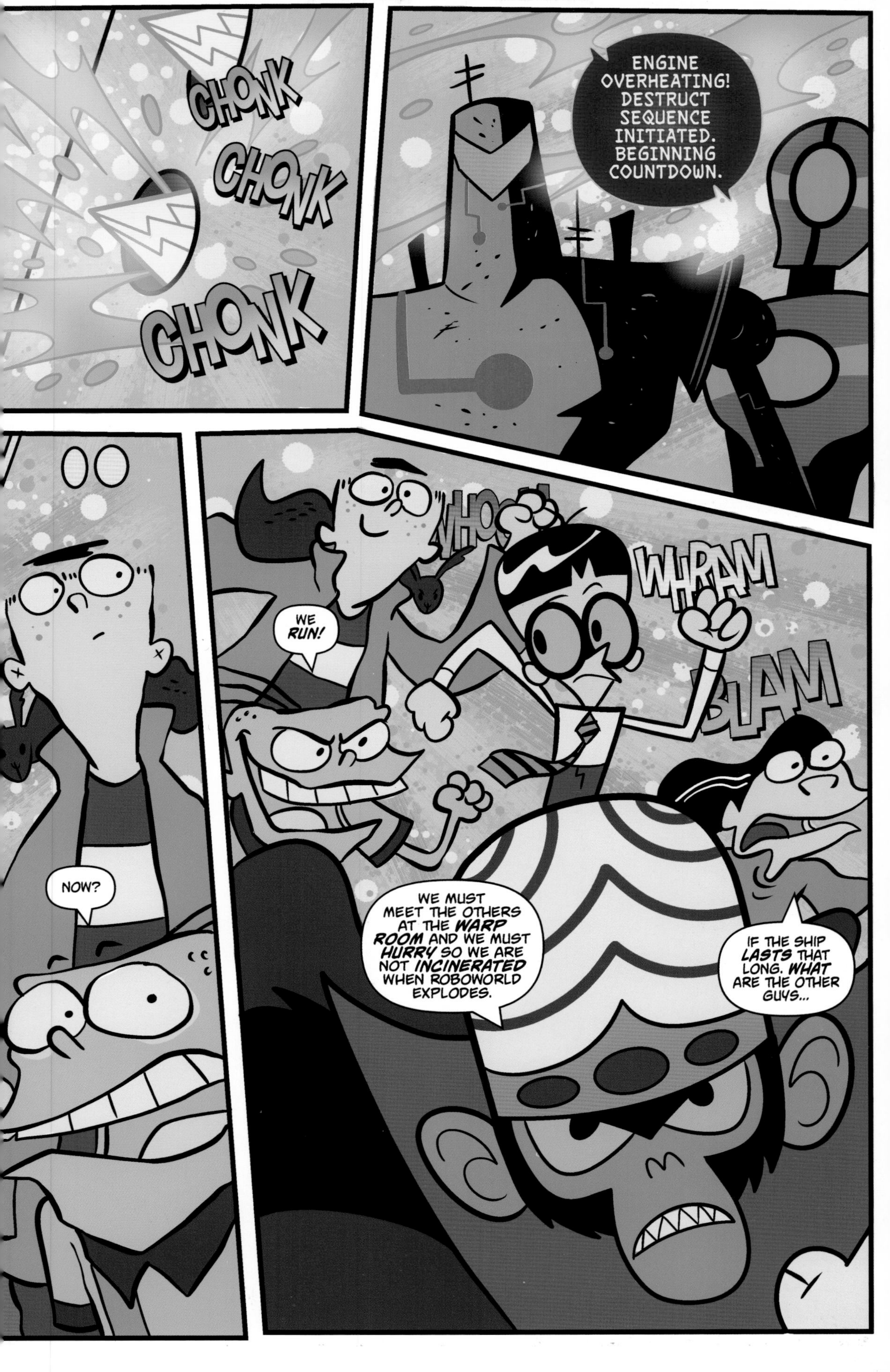
CHONK
CHONK
CHONK
ENGINE OVERHEATING! DESTRUCT SEQUENCE INITIATED. BEGINNING COUNTDOWN.
NOW?
WE RUN!
WHRAM
BLAM
WE MUST MEET THE OTHERS AT THE WARP ROOM AND WE MUST HURRY SO WE ARE NOT INCINERATED WHEN ROBOWORLD EXPLODES.
IF THE SHIP LASTS THAT LONG. WHAT ARE THE OTHER GUYS...

"...DOING UP THERE?!"
ENGINE OVERHEATING! DESTRUCT SEQUENCE INITIATED. BEGINNING COUNTDOWN.
MOJO JOJO DID IT!
HIM AND ED, EDD AND EDDY!
LESS TALK, MORE ACTION! TO THE WARP ROOM! NOW!
HARD AS THAT IS TO BELIEVE!
AND YOU CALLED ME A FOOL! YOU MISCALCULATED EVERY STEP OF THE WAY!
LIKE YOUR MANIA TO USE THE WEAKNESS OF OTHERS-!
AS USUAL, YOU OFFER NOTHING CONSTRUCTIVE. JUST ONE COMPLAINT AFTER ANOTHER!
SURELY EVEN YOU DON'T THINK I'D LEAVE THE FATE OF ROBOWORLD TO CHANCE.
I HOLD IN MY HAND THE MASTER CONTROL THAT WILL SHUT DOWN THE DESTRUCT SEQUENCE-

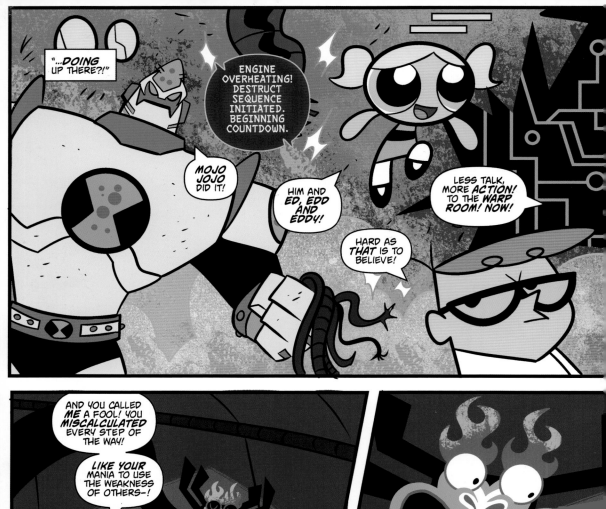

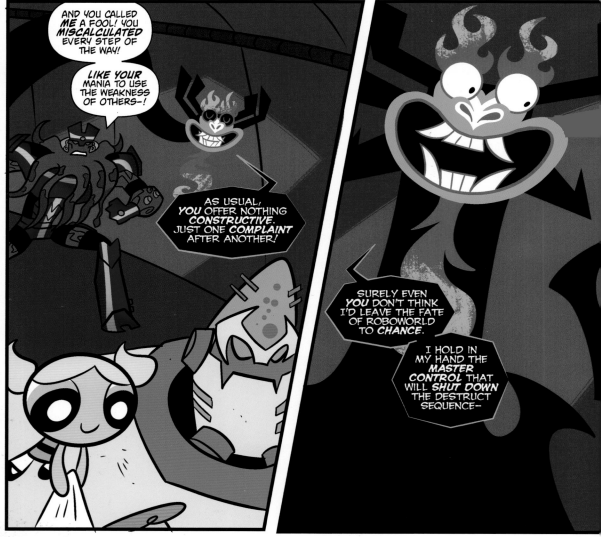

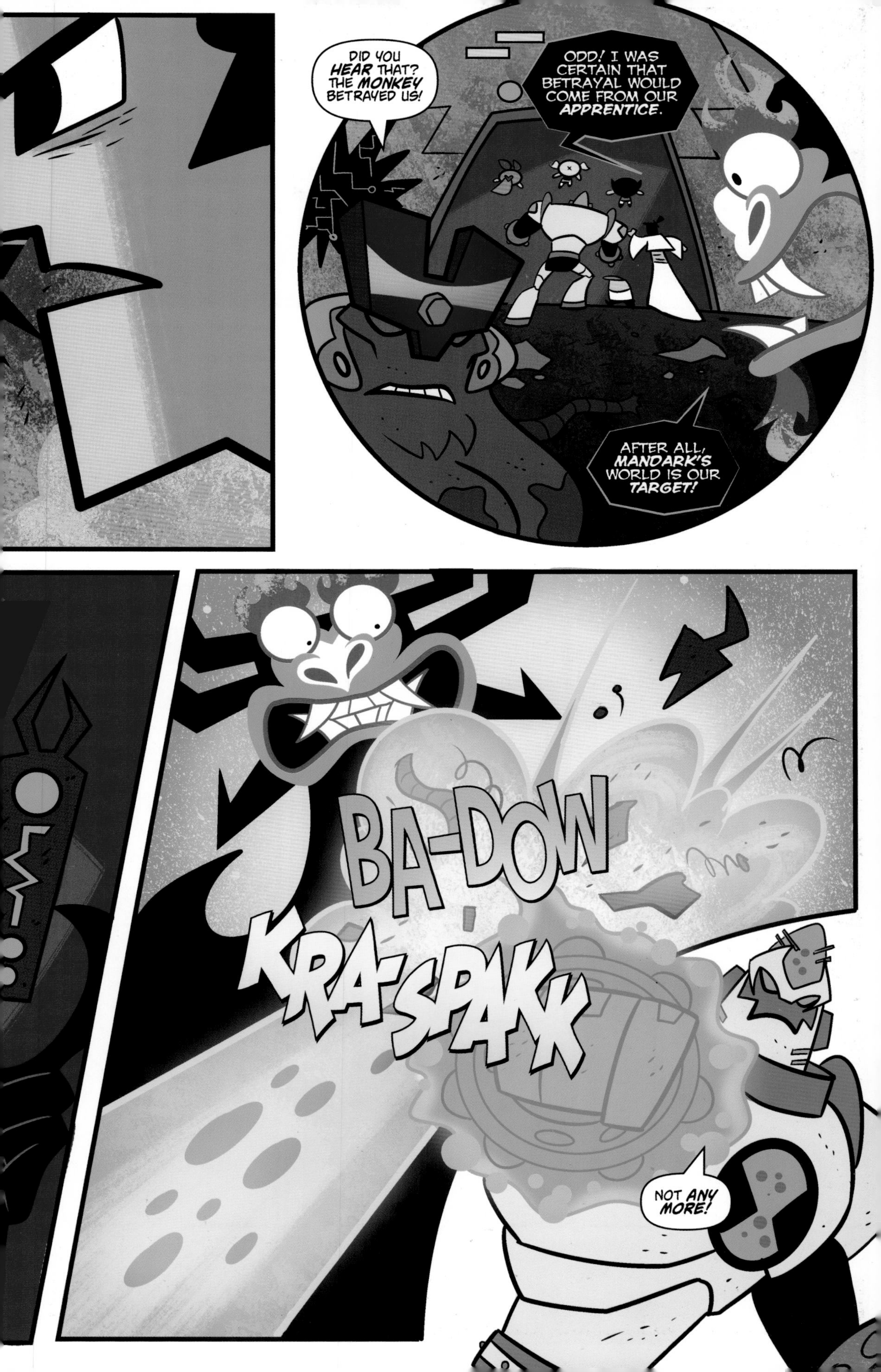
DID YOU HEAR THAT? THE MONKEY BETRAYED US!
ODD! I WAS CERTAIN THAT BETRAYAL WOULD COME FROM OUR APPRENTICE.
AFTER ALL, MANDARK'S WORLD IS OUR TARGET!
BA-DOW
KRA-SPAKK
NOT ANY MORE!

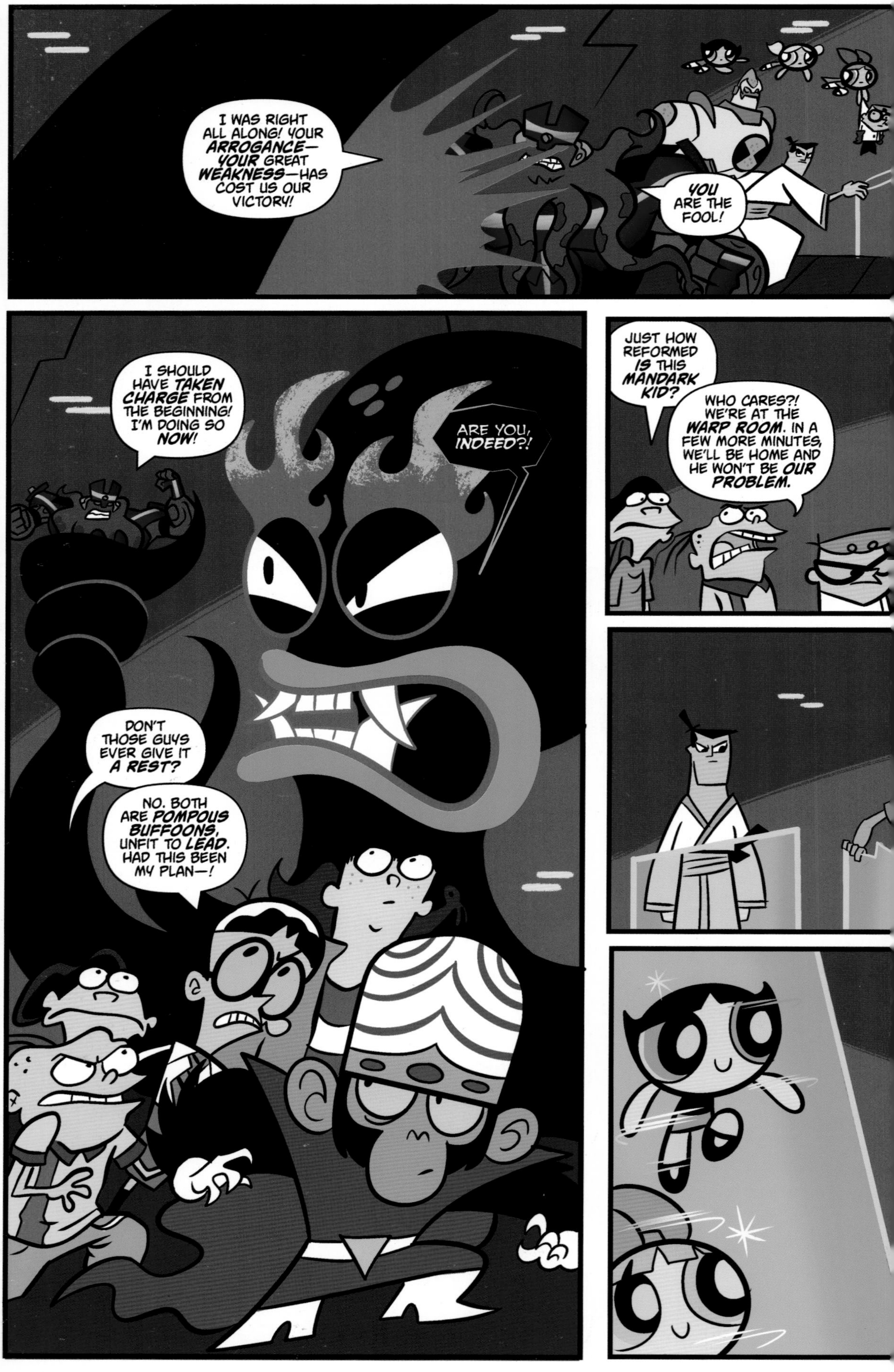
I WAS RIGHT ALL ALONG! YOUR ARROGANCE—YOUR GREAT WEAKNESS—HAS COST US OUR VICTORY!
YOU ARE THE FOOL!
I SHOULD HAVE TAKEN CHARGE FROM THE BEGINNING! I'M DOING SO NOW!
ARE YOU, INDEED?!
DON'T THOSE GUYS EVER GIVE IT A REST?
NO. BOTH ARE POMPOUS BUFFOONS, UNFIT TO LEAD. HAD THIS BEEN MY PLAN—!
JUST HOW REFORMED IS THIS MANDARK KID?
WHO CARES?! WE'RE AT THE WARP ROOM. IN A FEW MORE MINUTES, WE'LL BE HOME AND HE WON'T BE OUR PROBLEM.

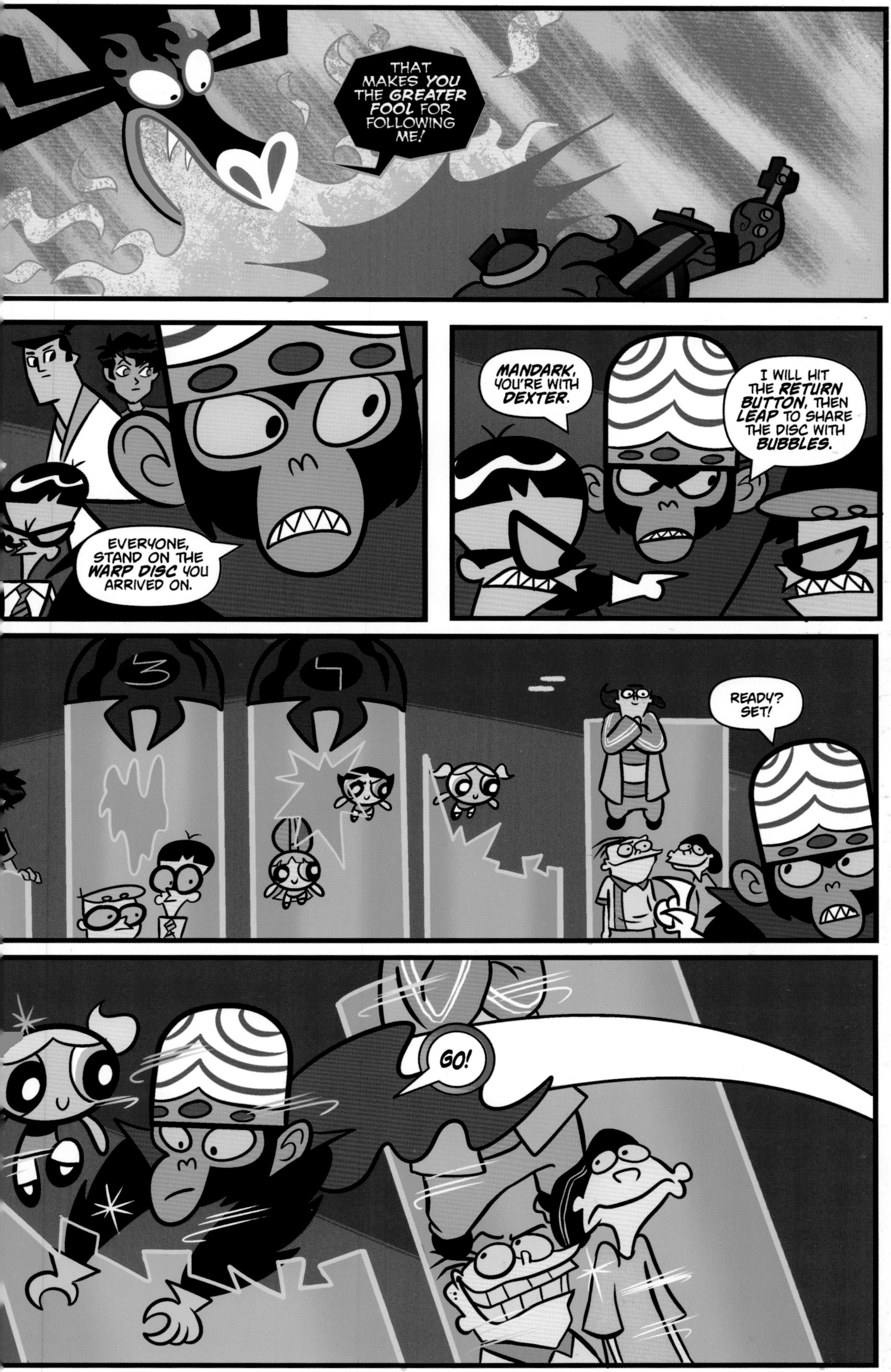
THAT MAKES YOU THE GREATER FOOL FOR FOLLOWING ME!
EVERYONE, STAND ON THE WARP DISC YOU ARRIVED ON.
MANDARK, YOU'RE WITH DEXTER.
I WILL HIT THE RETURN BUTTON, THEN LEAP TO SHARE THE DISC WITH BUBBLES.
READY? SET!
GO!

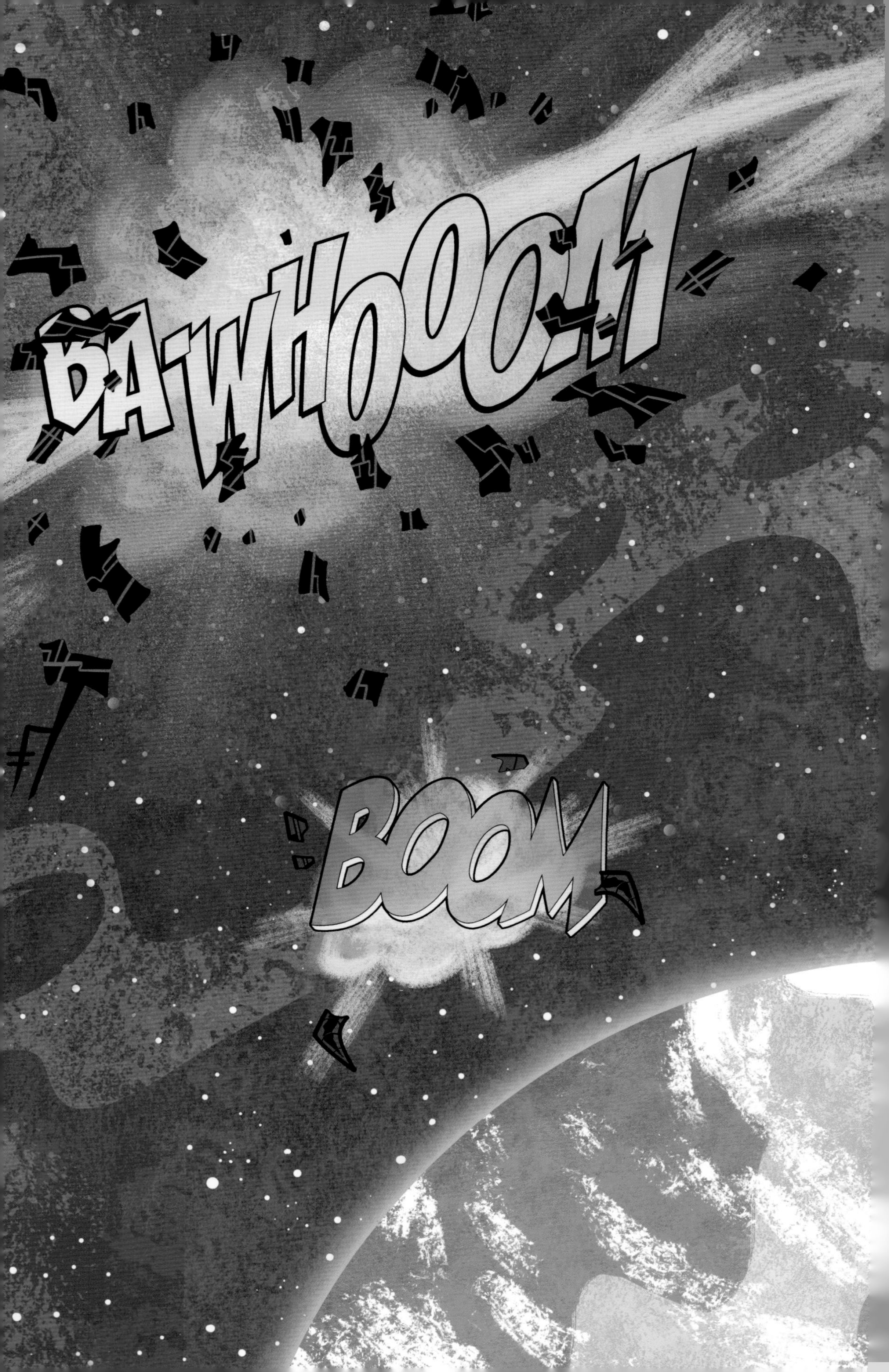
BA-WHOOOM
BOOM

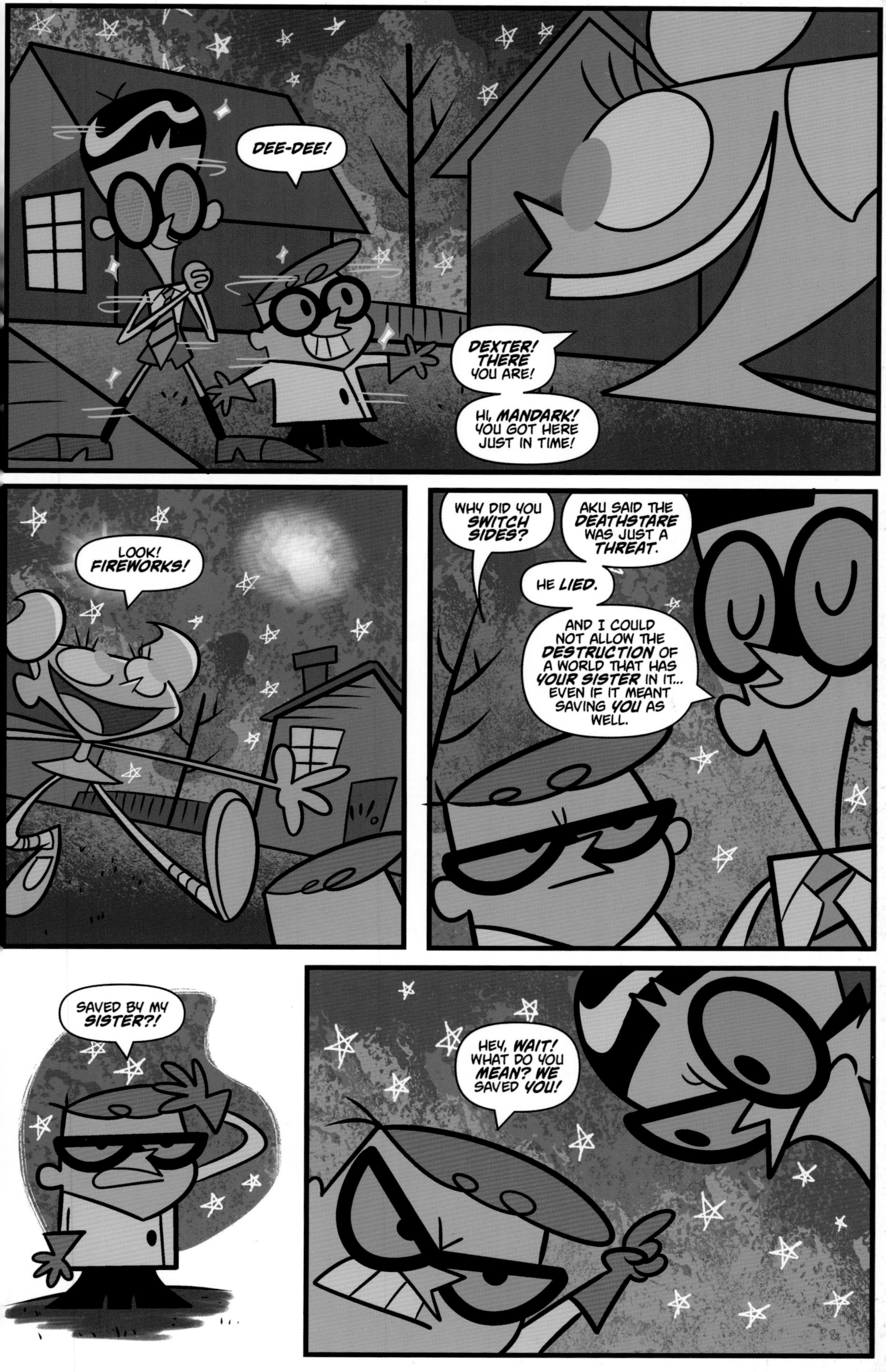
DEE-DEE!
DEXTER! THERE YOU ARE!
HI, MANDARK! YOU GOT HERE JUST IN TIME!
LOOK! FIREWORKS!
WHY DID YOU SWITCH SIDES?
AKU SAID THE DEATHSTARE WAS JUST A THREAT.
HE LIED.
AND I COULD NOT ALLOW THE DESTRUCTION OF A WORLD THAT HAS YOUR SISTER IN IT... EVEN IF IT MEANT SAVING YOU AS WELL.
SAVED BY MY SISTER?!
HEY, WAIT! WHAT DO YOU MEAN? WE SAVED YOU!

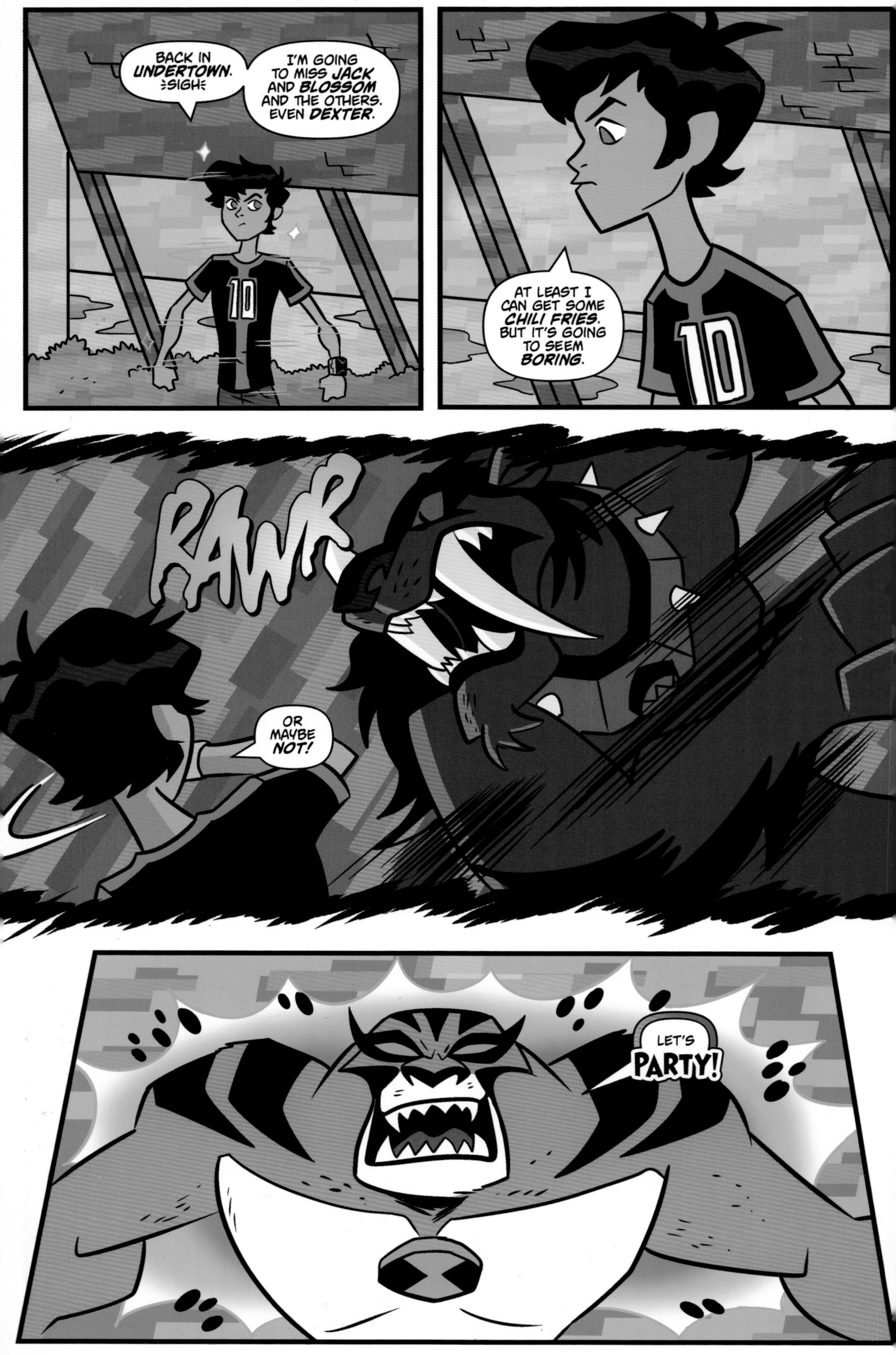
BACK IN UNDERTOWN. ≡SIGH≡
I'M GOING TO MISS JACK AND BLOSSOM AND THE OTHERS. EVEN DEXTER.
AT LEAST I CAN GET SOME CHILI FRIES. BUT IT'S GOING TO SEEM BORING.
RAWR
OR MAYBE NOT!
LET'S PARTY!

IT'S GOOD TO BE *HOME*.

I'M GONNA MISS *MOJO JOJO*.

YEAH! HE WAS A *SMART MONKEY*. WE COULD HAVE GOTTEN *RICH*, PUTTING ON *SHOWS* WITH HIM AS THE MAIN ATTRACTION!

WOULD THAT BE *BEFORE* OR *AFTER* HE TRIED TO *CONQUER* OUR WORLD?

BUT WE GOT A COOL *SQUIRREL!*

YEAH, BUT HE AIN'T NO *TALKIN'* SQUIRREL.

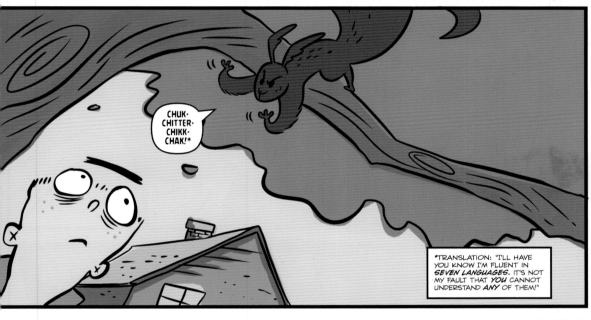

CHUK· CHITTER· CHIKK· CHAK!*

*TRANSLATION: "I'LL HAVE YOU KNOW I'M FLUENT IN *SEVEN LANGUAGES*. IT'S NOT MY FAULT THAT *YOU* CANNOT UNDERSTAND *ANY* OF THEM!"

LET'S HIT THE *JUNKYARD!* I'LL BET THERE ARE *ROBOT PARTS* WE CAN SCAVENGE!

I WANT A *JAWBREAKER!*

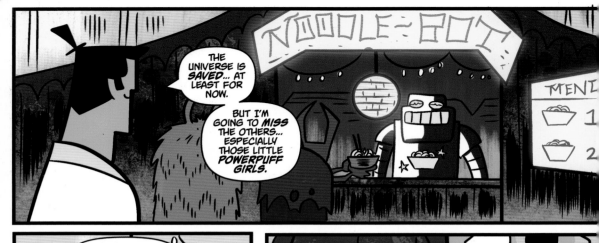

NOODLE-BOT!

THE UNIVERSE IS *SAVED*... AT LEAST FOR NOW.

BUT I'M GOING TO *MISS* THE OTHERS... ESPECIALLY THOSE LITTLE *POWERPUFF GIRLS.*

MEN[U]

INNOCENT *KIDS*— IT'S WHAT THE *FIGHT FOR RIGHT* IS ALL ABOUT.

NOODLES, PLEASE.

SIR! ARE YOU REALLY *SAMURAI JACK?*

THERE'S A *MONSTER!*

PLEASE! COME *SAVE US!*

HOLD THAT ORDER! I'LL BE *BACK!*

THANK YOU, MOJO JOJO!

YOU HELPED US SAVE A *WHOLE WORLD!*

AND MAYBE EVEN THE *ENTIRE UNIVERSE.*

YOU'RE A *HERO!*

NO! I AM *NOT* A HERO!

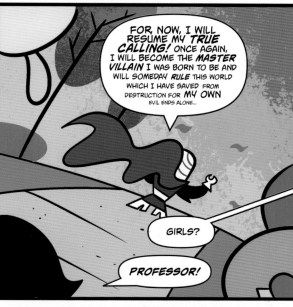

FOR, NOW, I WILL RESUME MY *TRUE CALLING!* ONCE AGAIN, I WILL BECOME THE *MASTER VILLAIN* I WAS BORN TO BE AND WILL SOMEDAY *RULE* THIS WORLD WHICH I HAVE SAVED FROM DESTRUCTION FOR *MY OWN* EVIL ENDS ALONE...

GIRLS?

PROFESSOR!

WHERE HAVE YOU *BEEN?*

AWAY! IN *HYPERSPACE!* WE SAVED THE *UNIVERSE!*

WE'RE GLAD TO BE *HOME* BUT WE MISS OUR *NEW FRIENDS.*

AND MOJO JOJO WAS A *HERO!* WAIT TILL YOU HEAR WHAT *HAPPENED!*

AND SO ONCE AGAIN, THE DAY IS SAVED THANKS TO... THE *POWERPUFF GIRLS* AND BEN AND JACK AND *DEXTER* AND *ED, EDD & EDDY!* AND *MOJO JOJO,* TOO!

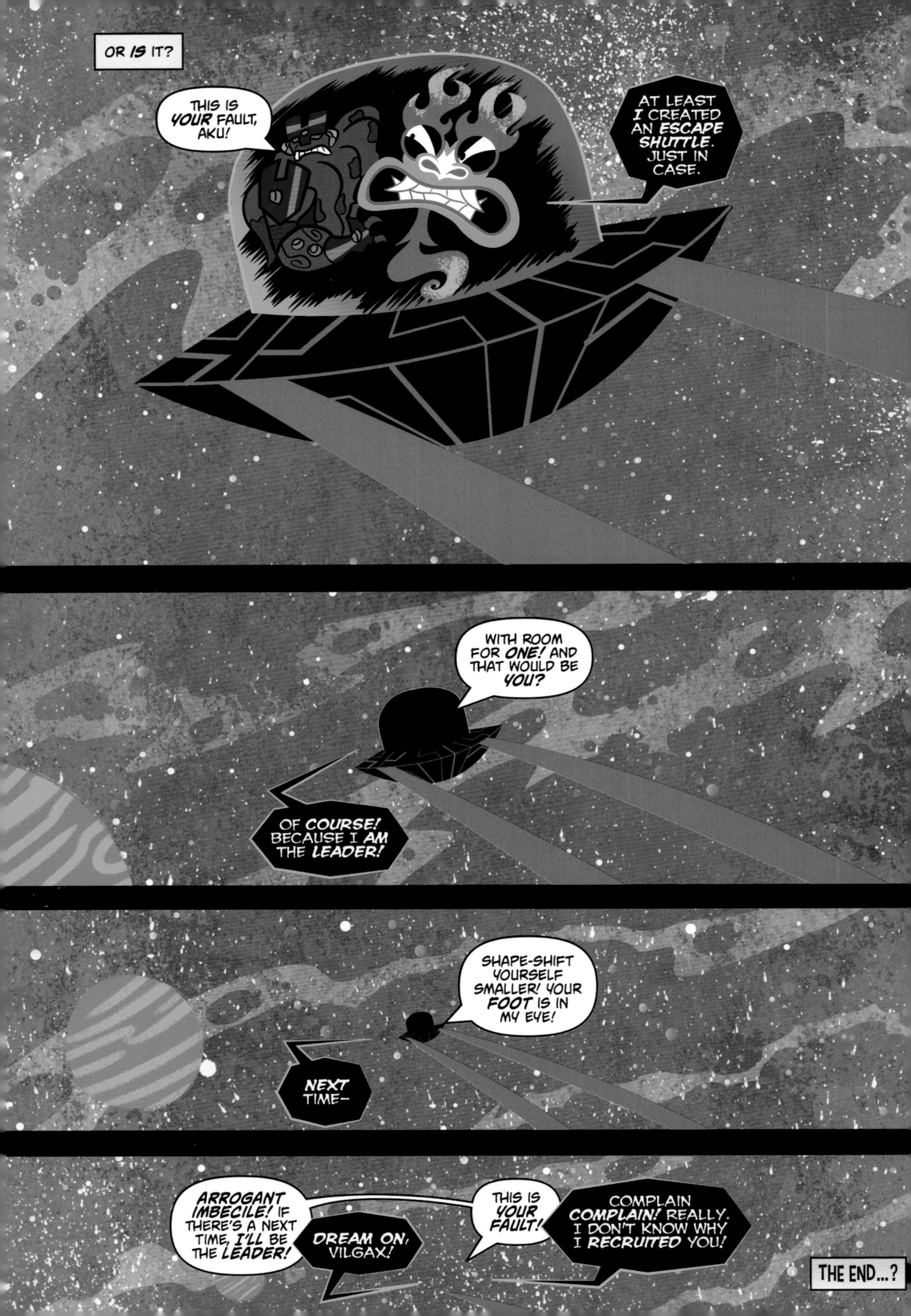
OR IS IT?
THIS IS YOUR FAULT, AKU!
AT LEAST I CREATED AN ESCAPE SHUTTLE. JUST IN CASE.
WITH ROOM FOR ONE! AND THAT WOULD BE YOU?
OF COURSE! BECAUSE I AM THE LEADER!
SHAPE-SHIFT YOURSELF SMALLER! YOUR FOOT IS IN MY EYE!
NEXT TIME–
ARROGANT IMBECILE! IF THERE'S A NEXT TIME, I'LL BE THE LEADER!
DREAM ON, VILGAX!
THIS IS YOUR FAULT!
COMPLAIN COMPLAIN! REALLY. I DON'T KNOW WHY I RECRUITED YOU!
THE END...?

SUPER SECRET CRISIS WAR!

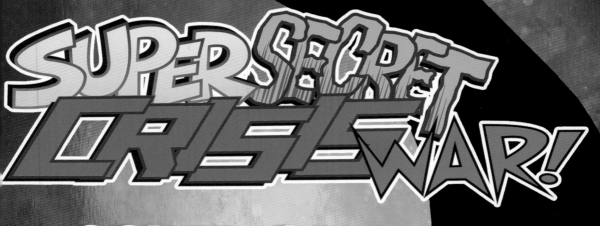

COVER GALLERY

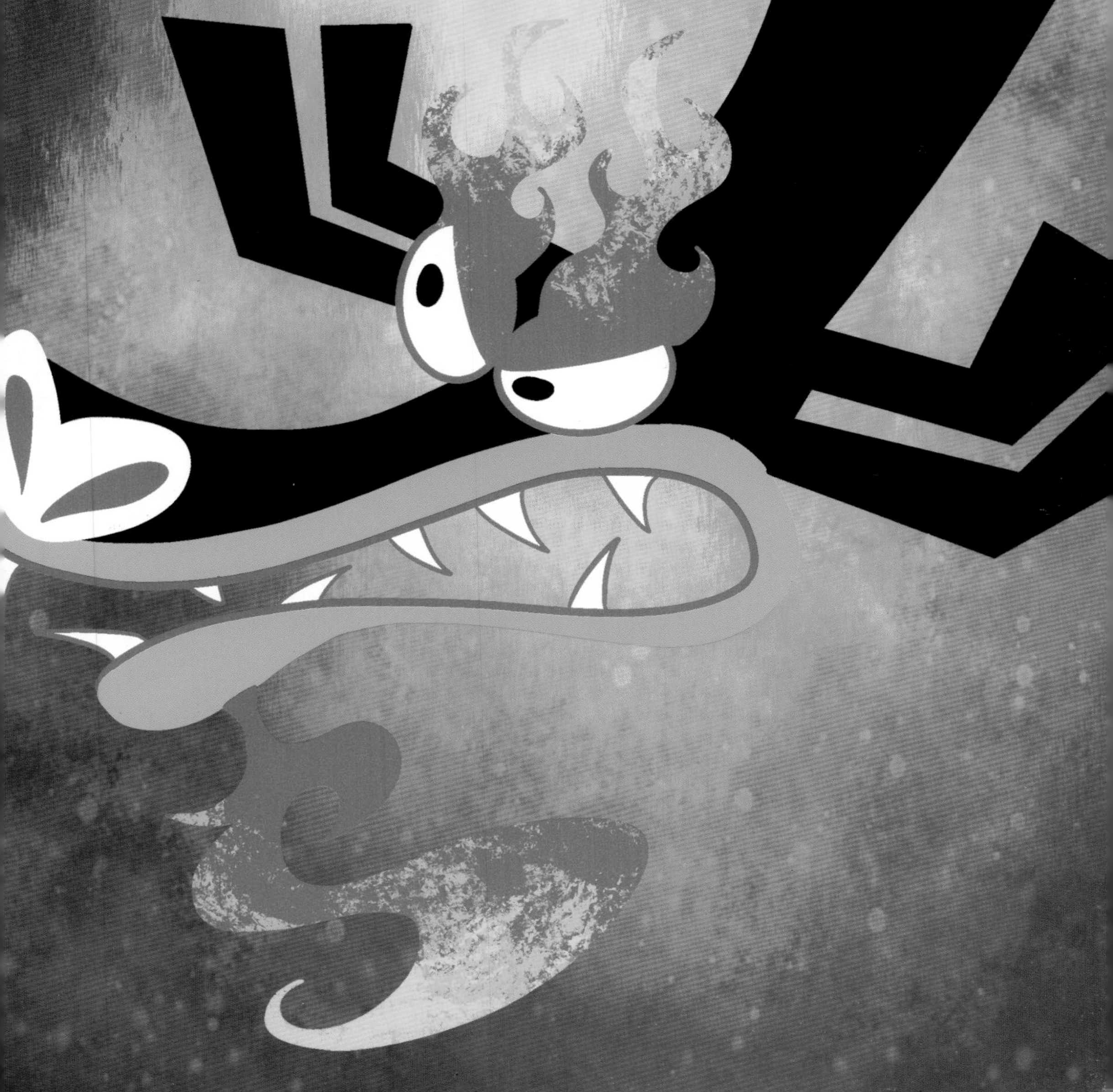

Cover art by Troy Little

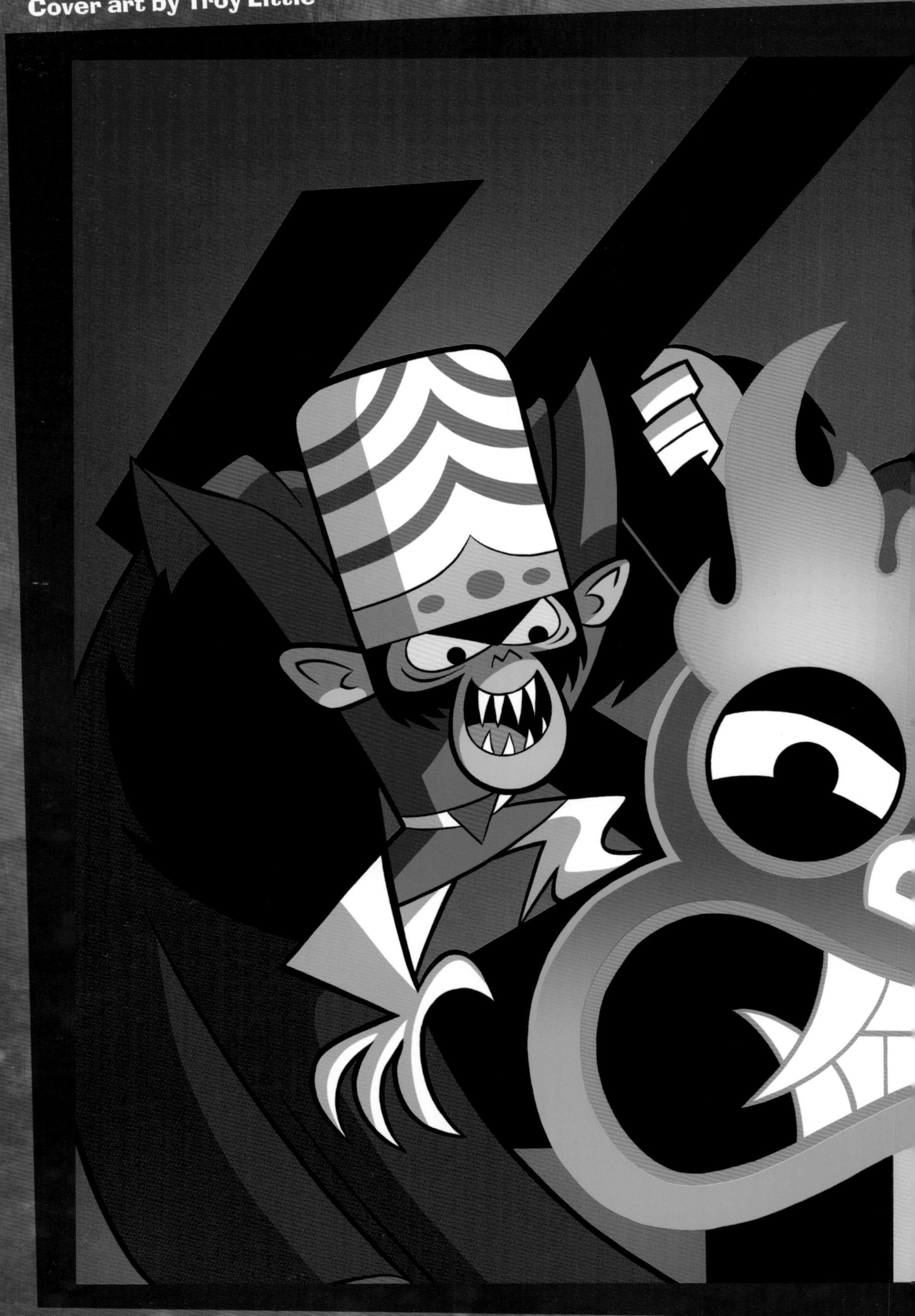

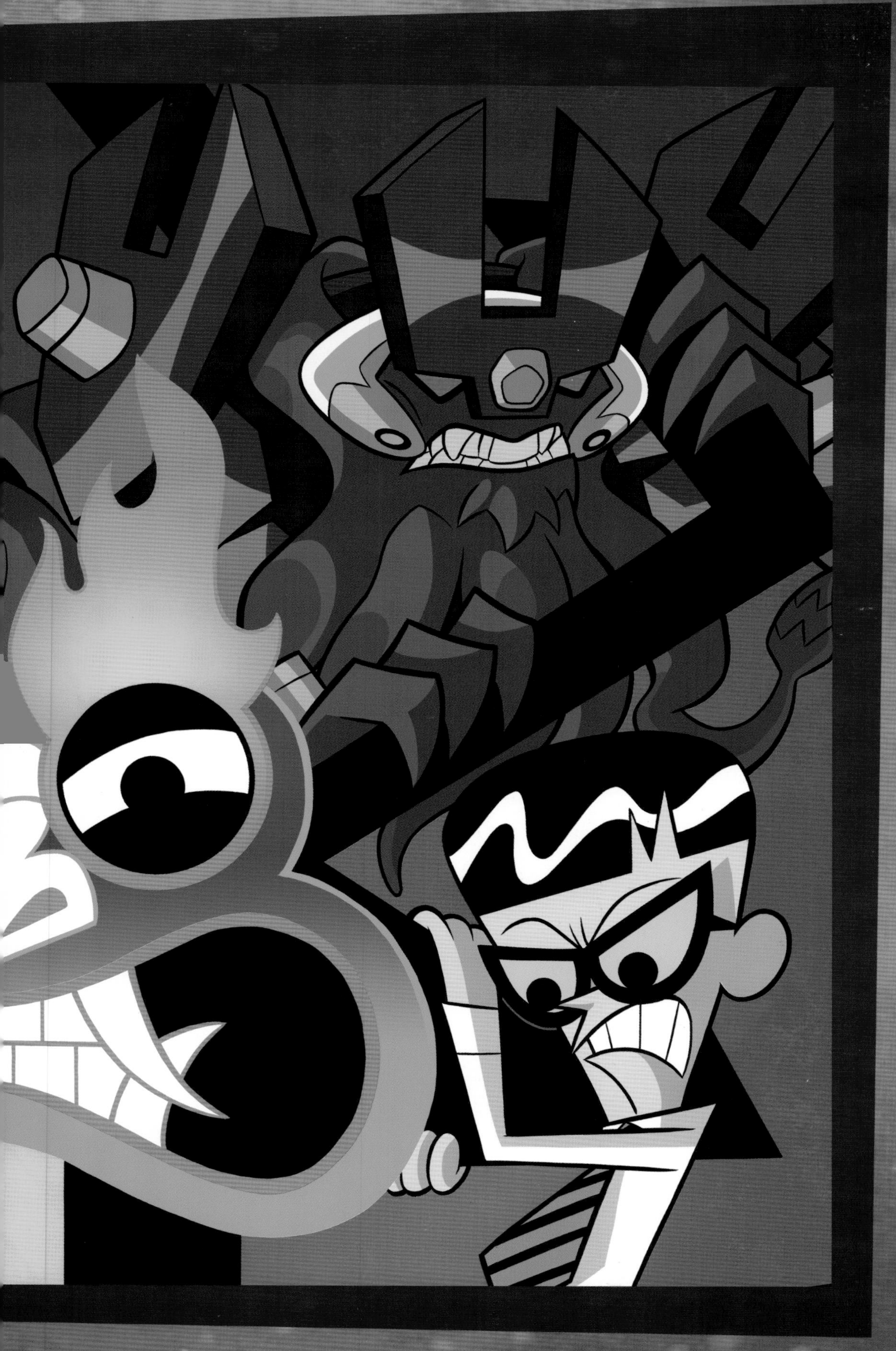

Cover art by Troy Little

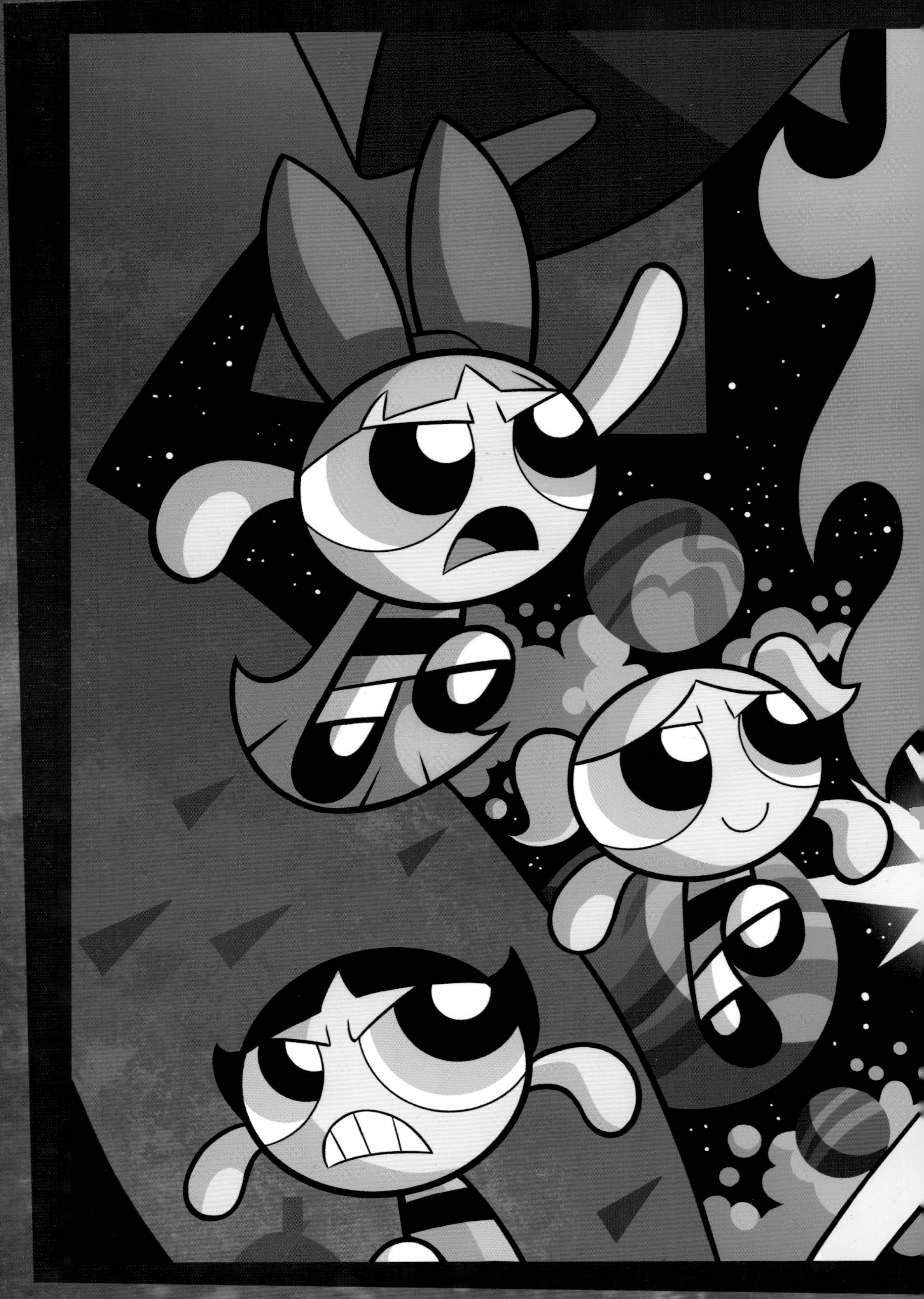

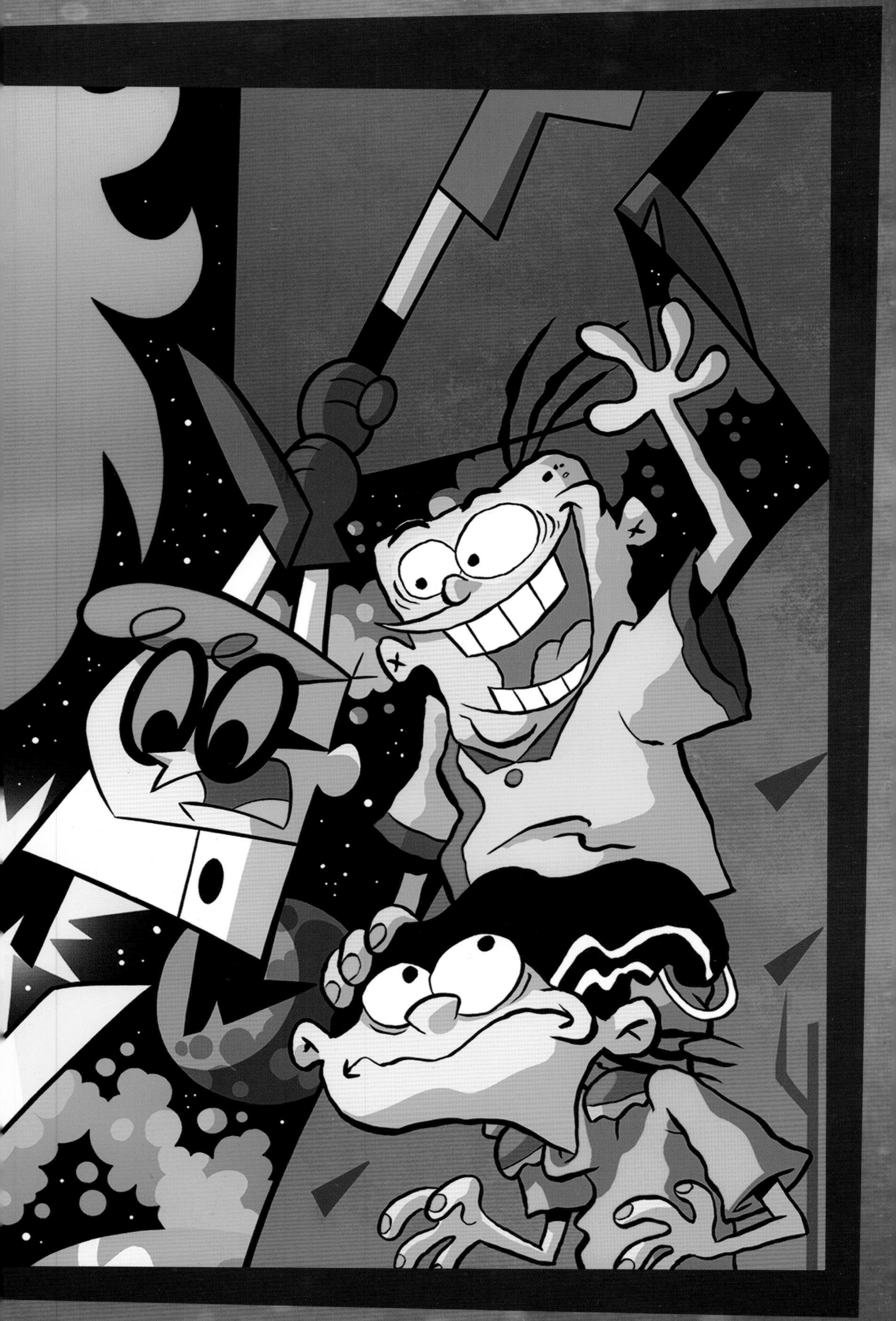

Cover art by Troy Little

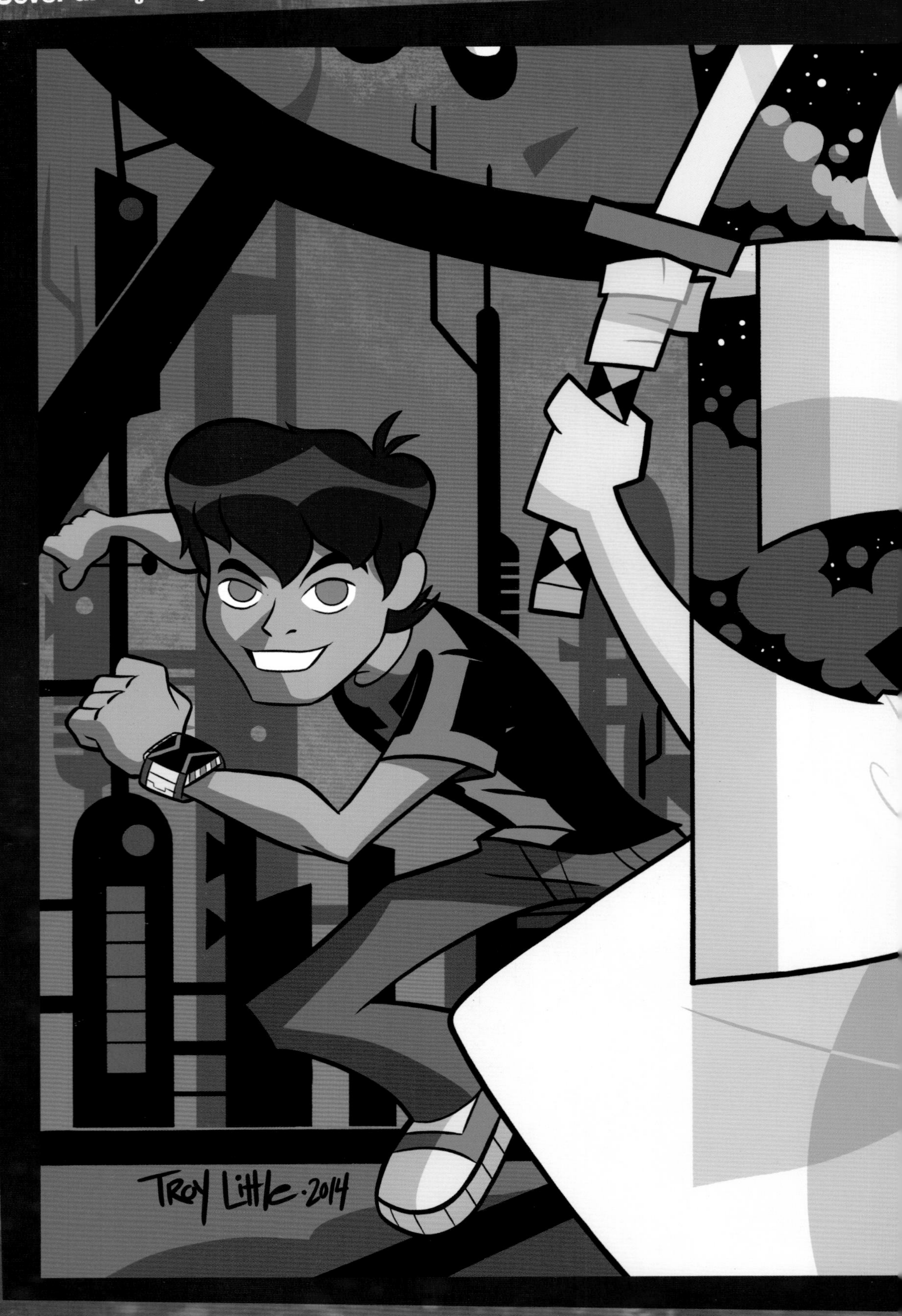
TROY LITTLE · 2014

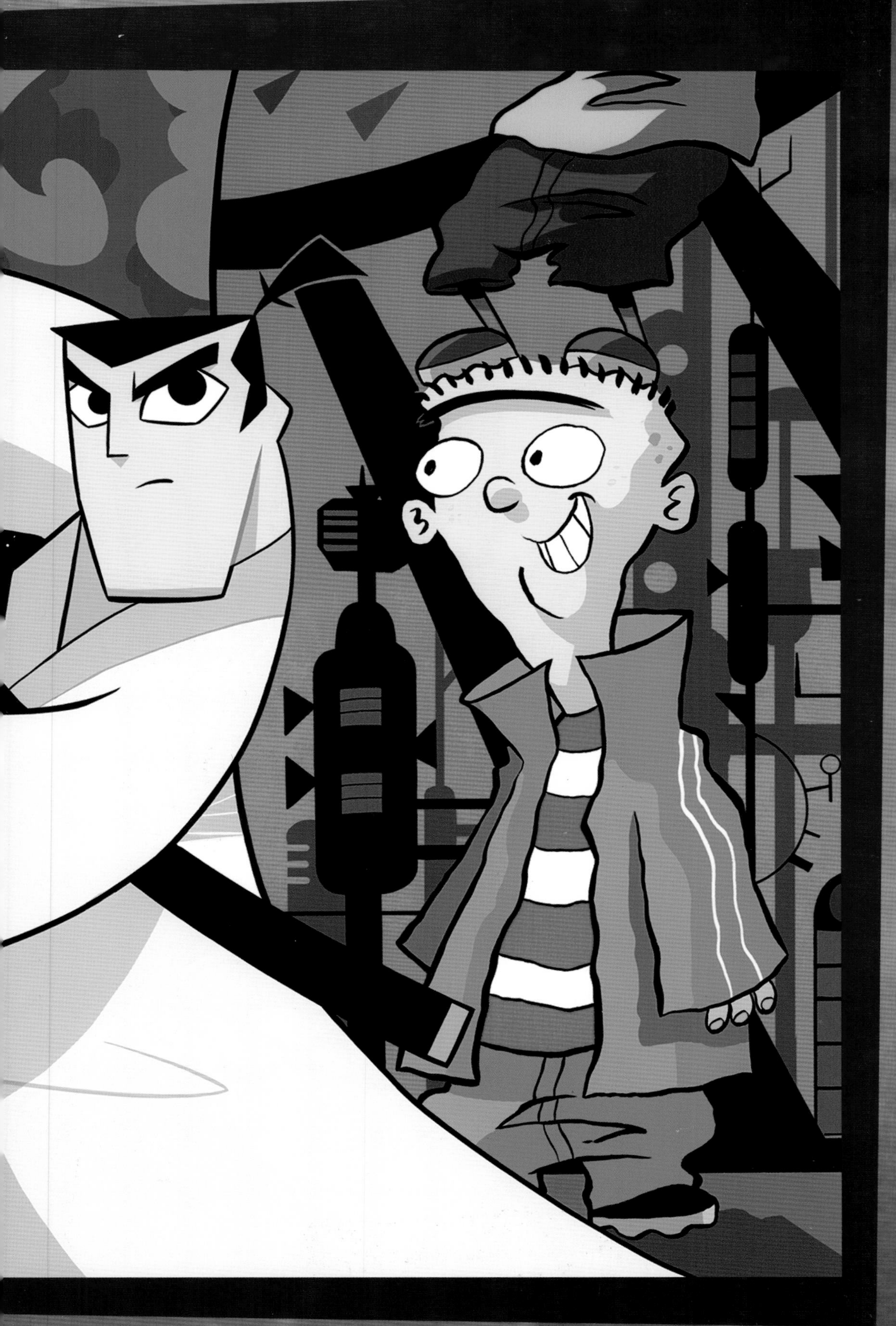

Cover art by Derek Charm

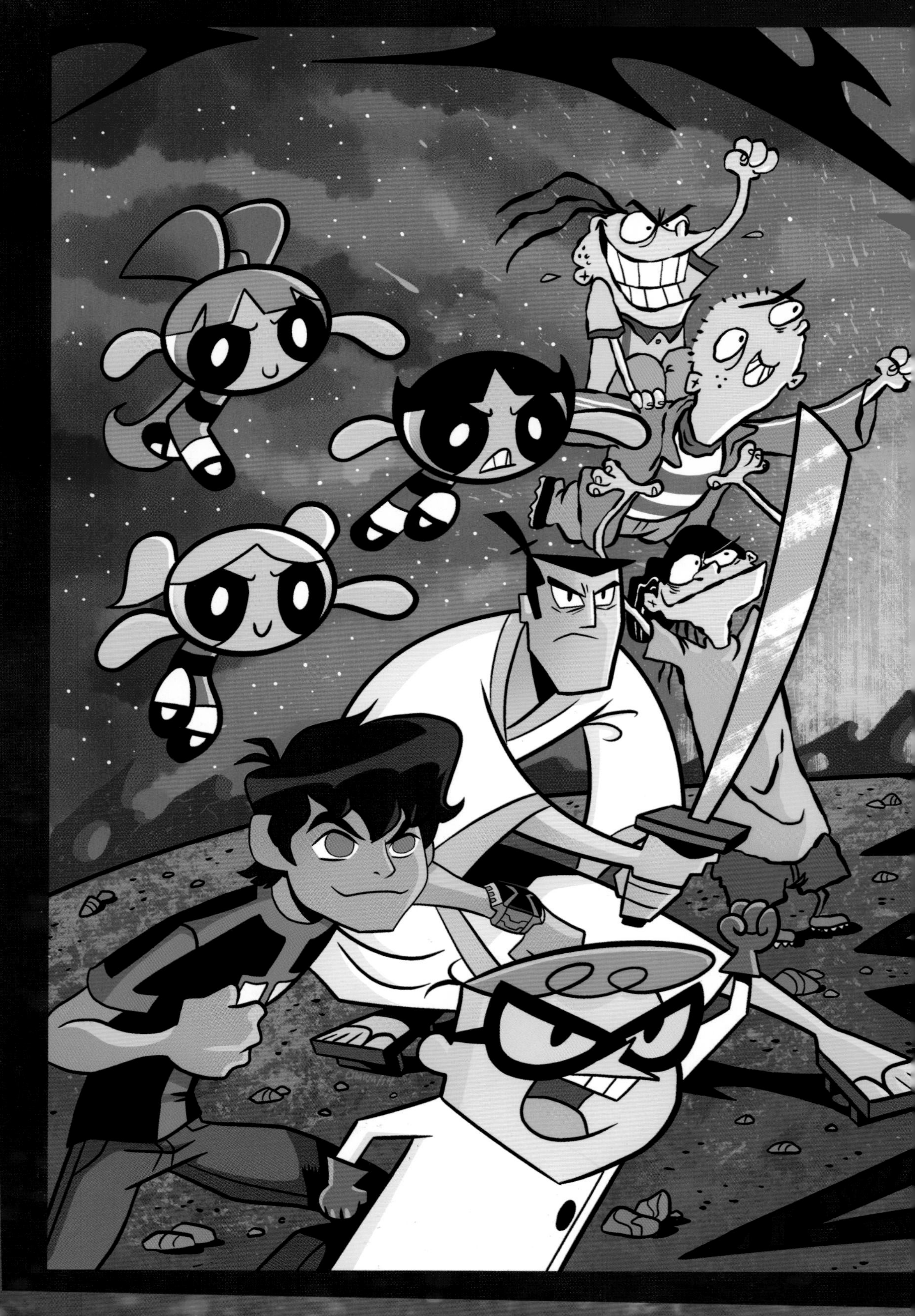

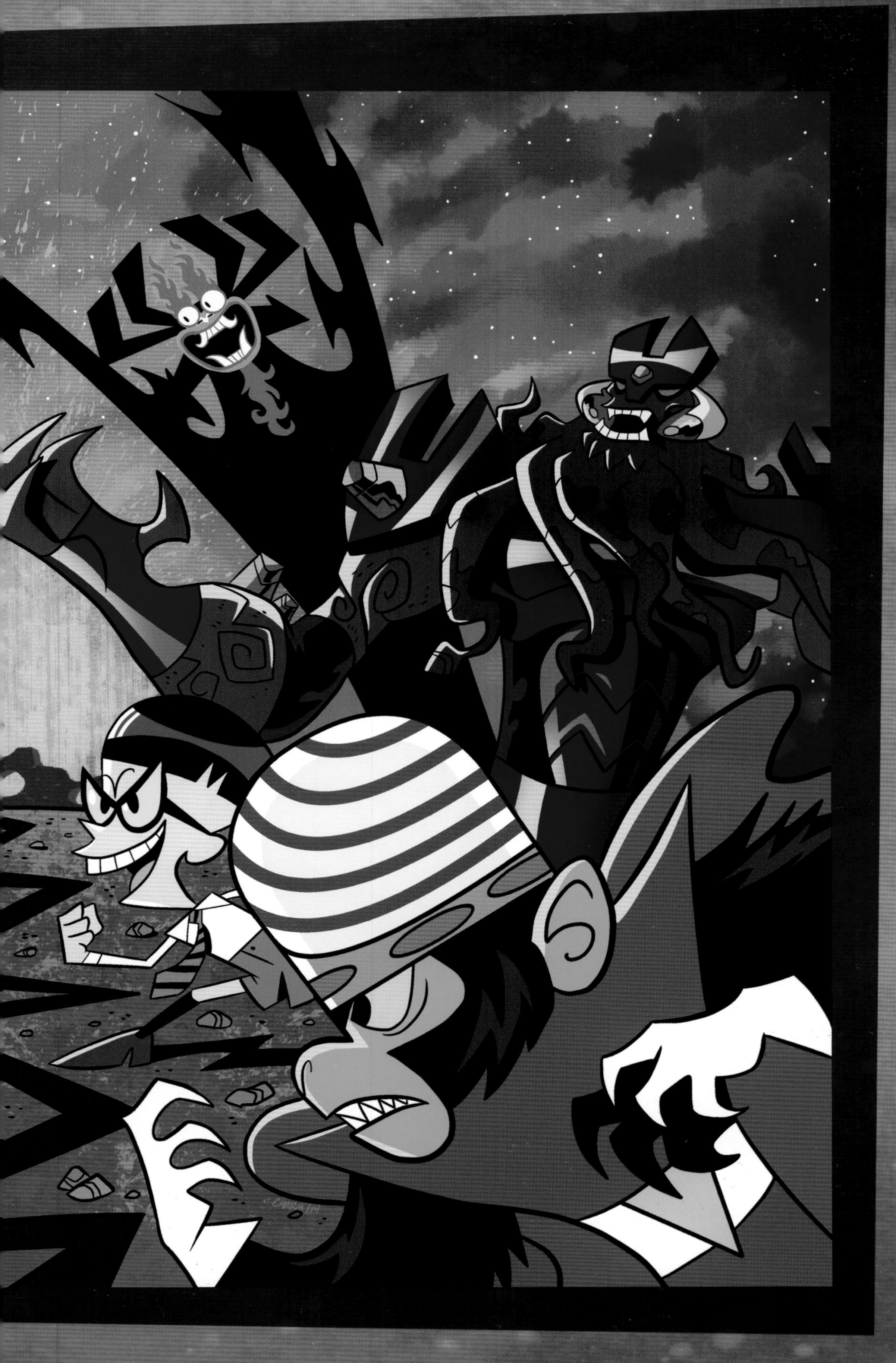

Cover art by Katie Cook

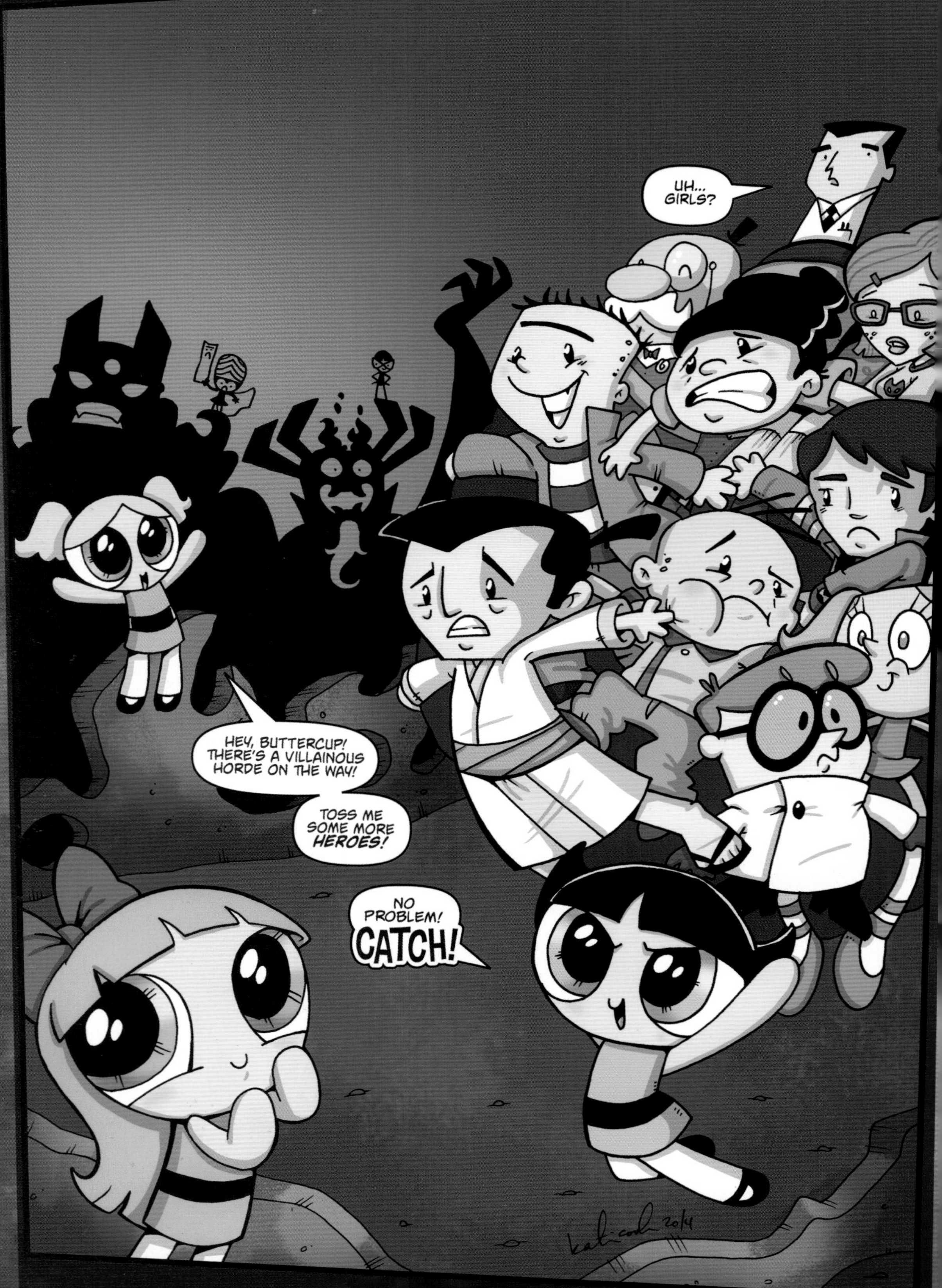
UH... GIRLS?
HEY, BUTTERCUP! THERE'S A VILLAINOUS HORDE ON THE WAY!
TOSS ME SOME MORE HEROES!
NO PROBLEM! CATCH!

Cover art by Andy Suriano

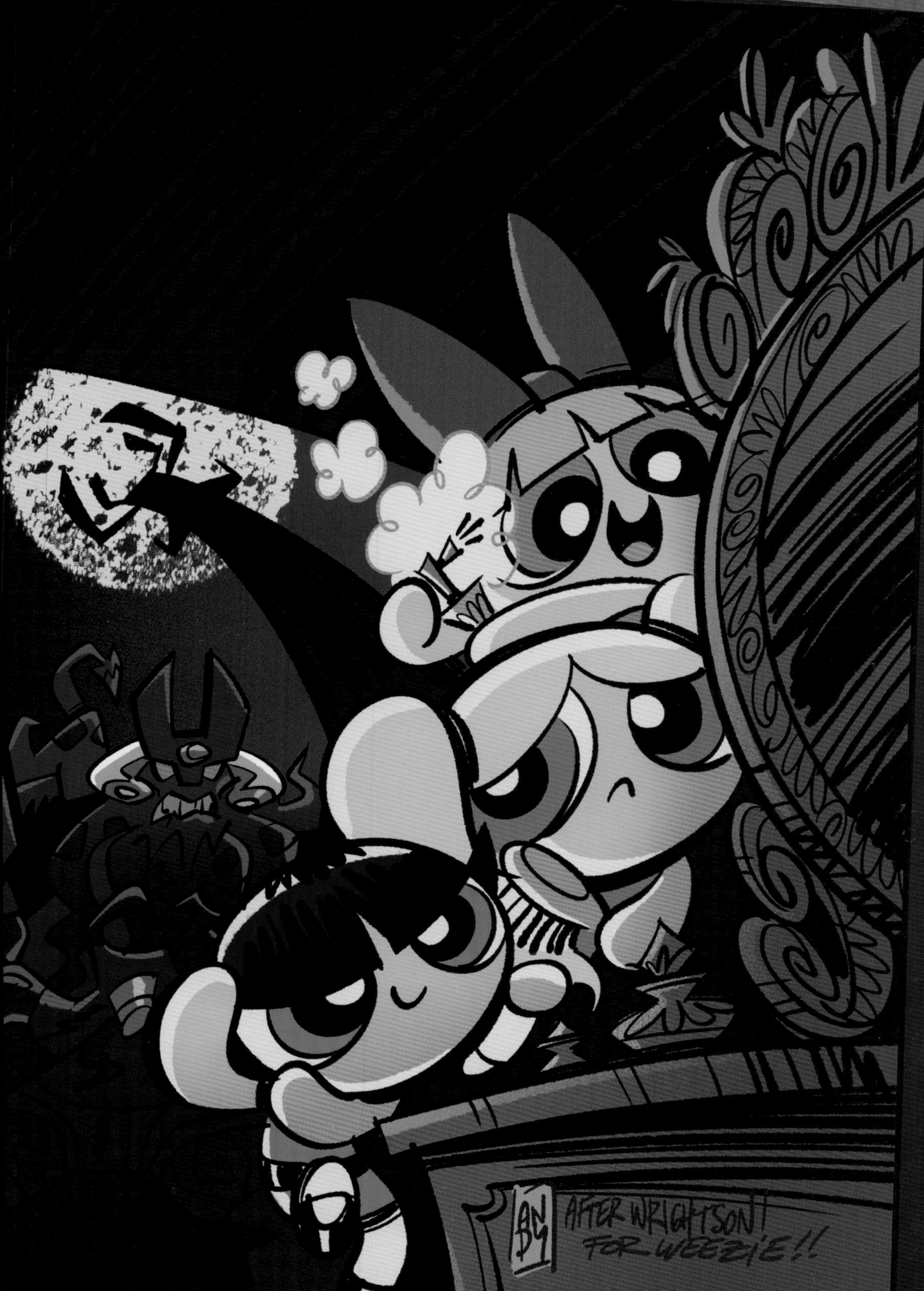

ANDY
AFTER WRIGHTSON!
FOR WEEZIE!!

Cover art by Dan Schoening

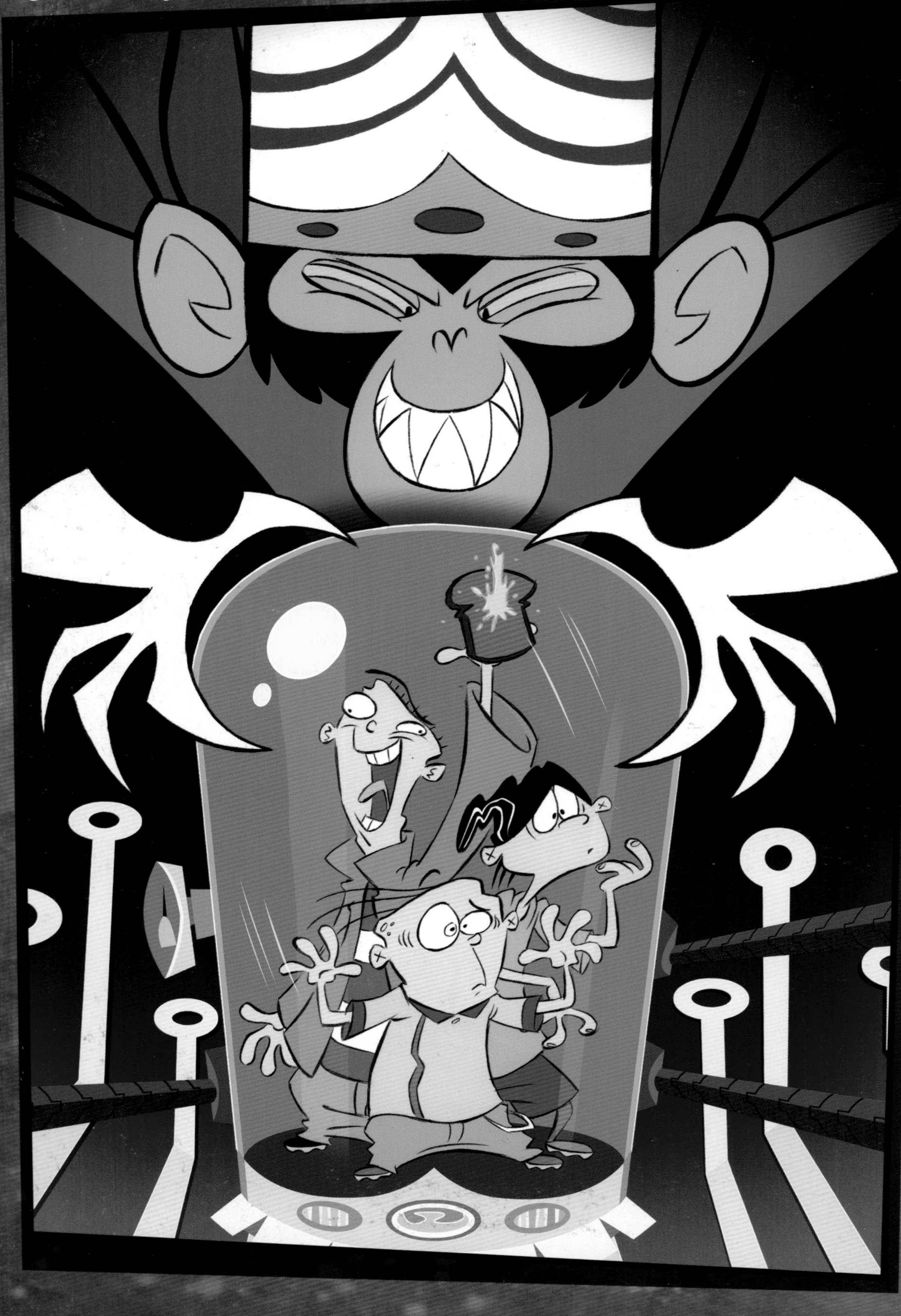

Cover art by Erica Henderson

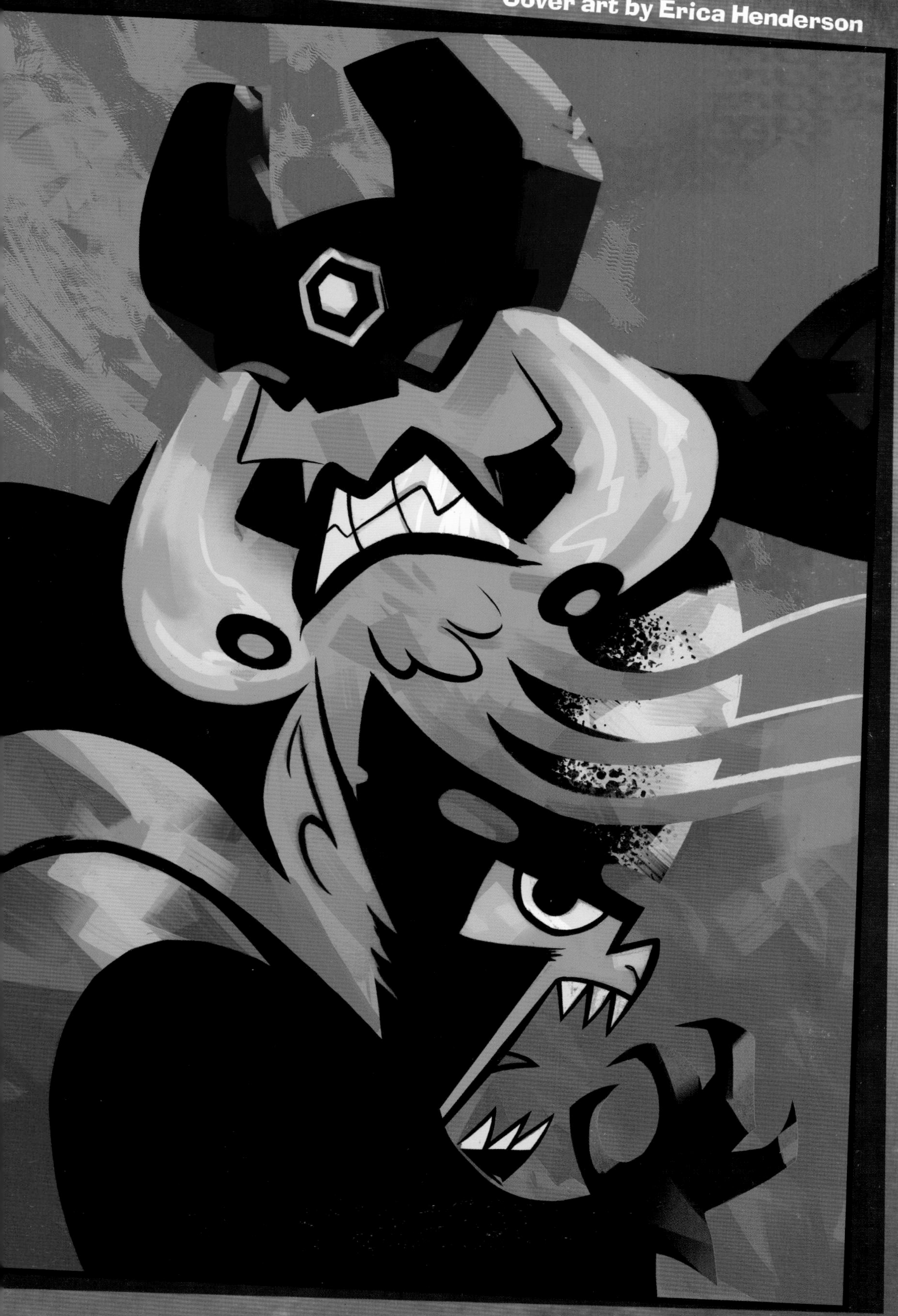

Cover art by Dustin Nguyen

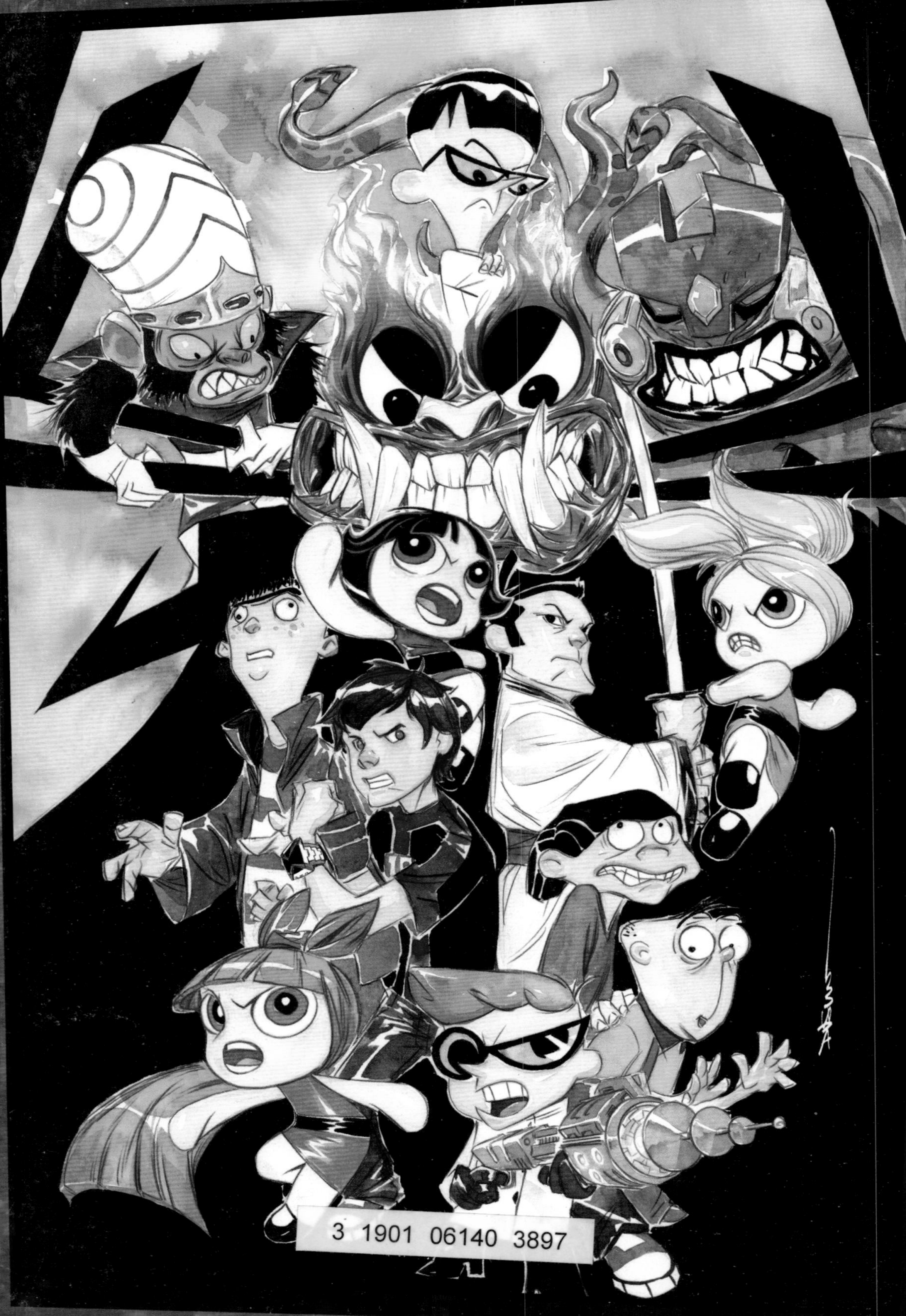